[A]n excellent thriller with plenty of plot twists and turns, interesting characters, and unusual settings.... The pace of the book and the depth of the characters keeps the reader turning pages.... A great book for thriller readers and armchair travelers.

- Manhattan Book Review

A moving love story that isn't at all about the romance. Instead, we are transported to the Middle East and see through the eyes of someone who appreciates the nuances of the local culture.... The suspense is incredible and will keep you turning the pages, no matter how hard you try to stop.

- Joana James, Readers' Choice

Exquisite writing [evoking] a bygone era of travel in an increasingly troubled time, the late 70s.... I traveled in Afghanistan around that time period and found the depiction to be accurate and heart-achingly nostalgic. The interactions with the Afghan and Iranian characters are also alive and compassionate, and Baker has a fine ear for dialogue and dialect....

– Debra Denker, author of *Sisters on the Bridge of Fire: One Woman's Journey in Afghanistan, India and Pakistan*

A great book, especially for those who love travel.

-    San Francisco Book Review

vanished.

A NOVEL

N. V. Baker

Night Watchman Press
NEW MEXICO

For review copies of the novel, please contact Night Watchman Press, at night-watchmanpress@gmail.com.

Cover design: Melissa Williams Design
Cover photographs: Repina Valeriya, Scisetti Alfio, Shutterstock
Book Layout: BookDesignTemplates.com

vanished./ N. V. Baker. - 1st ed.
ISBN 13: 978-0-9979936-1-5

To Peter, my favorite fellow traveler

To travel hopefully is a better thing than to arrive.

ROBERT LOUIS STEVENSON
"El Dorado" (1878)
Virginibus Puerisque & Other Essays

FROM BANGKOK TO ISTANBUL &
KABUL TO TEHRAN

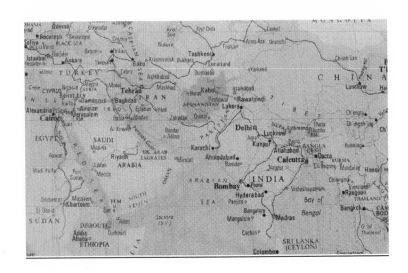

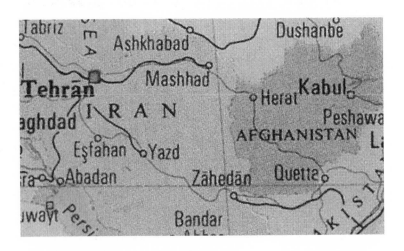

From *The New York Times Atlas of the World* (New York:
Times Books, 1978)

CHAPTER ONE

August 23, 1978
Wednesday

In her shabby room in Kabul, Cassie decided she'd had enough of the doll. The realization was tinged with a little guilt -it had been a gift after all - and some regret, a traveling companion for weeks, since the train from Muzaffarpur, India. But the doll was almost a foot long, with unbending legs, the cheap plastic sort sold at train stations they'd passed, and it demanded too much space in her backpack. The doll violated her careful packing plan of five months before, when she'd left New Orleans with minimal clothes and gear, only what she would need, only what she could carry. She'd even eschewed face blush, if she'd ever need it, instead counting on rose-colored lipstick smudged on her cheeks. She'd violated the plan herself when she picked up a shawl in Bangkok and small feather pillow in Malaysia, but they were essential for sleeping in second and third-class trains.

Eating chunks of sweet watermelon, Cassie sat cross-legged on the room's tattered carpet. It might have been beautiful once, the product of painstaking labor by small-fingered Afghan girls, most likely. She didn't mind sitting on the floor and, in any case, she had no choice. The room in the Jam Hotel boasted no furniture but a low

1

table and a mattress. She studied the round unblinking face of the doll. "We part ways here, Maude," she informed it. "You should be with a little girl."

A girl. Maybe that's how the Hindu mother had seen her in the women's second-class compartment three weeks before, red henna decorating the palms that presented the doll. Cassie was twenty-four but not big. Not like the mother, her substantial girth swathed in a yellow silk sari. Even the small chubby son appeared to weigh more than Cassie did. The gift was an implied trade. The curious mother had rummaged through Cassie's backpack and decided she wanted the two inflatable plastic hangers. Cassie had intended to give her just one, since hangers were scarce in the rooms she could afford. But the mother, delighted, had taken both, and somehow Cassie's harmonica had disappeared as well, probably in the boy's pocket. She couldn't complain; the family had shared their meal with her: spicy cucumbers and a red dusty powder with a bitter taste. Sumac maybe, dried crawfish?

So she had reluctantly acquired Maude, and carted it with her through the rest of India and Pakistan. Now the doll would be left behind to find its own way in Central Asia. Maude, propped upright against the mattress, accepted her fate with stoic silence.

Cassie finished her bites of melon, set the rest aside for Ralph, and stood. Her hands and mouth felt sticky with juice, and she wiped them off on her towel. She marveled again that such succulent fruits could grow in this arid place. They'd long been a hallmark of Afghanistan; Marco Polo had mentioned them seven hundred years ago. They were a godsend, really, since it was Ramadan and restaurants wouldn't open until eight in the evening, a little earlier for non-devout foreigners. Then she and Ralph would have kebabs and naan, only thirteen Afs per plate, about thirty cents.

Getting food, though, was not always easy. Three days before, in Pakistan, they had spotted a beautiful loaf of bread on display in a baker's window, and she'd counted out coins to buy it. But the bread was as dusty and old as this carpet. She had given most of it away, to a stooped woman begging a block away. The loaf disappeared into folds of her dirty black burqa. Cassie was ashamed at the poor quality of the gift, uncomfortably aware of her own affluence.

Ralph would be returning soon. He was a writer, out collecting "life experiences," as he put it. She had met him a year ago at a poetry reading, and almost instantly fallen in love. He was tall and good-looking, brown hair in a ponytail, soulful brown eyes. He wrote stories and poetry, and talked about writers he admired and the sacred trust of the craft. He had seemed so knowledgeable and deep that she'd felt a little intimidated at first, and more than a little pleased, even privileged, that he was interested in her. He treated her as an equal, not a fragile thing on a pedestal, and she liked that. Some of her idealism had faded - doesn't it invariably? But she still thought of him as her great love. How thrilled she was when he had said he'd come along on this journey. An overland trip around the world had long been her dream, her passion, and she had been saving for years. But he had embraced it as his own, borrowing money from his parents to help cover his expenses. He even told their friends it had been his dream too. This was evidence, she thought, that they were soul-mates.

After they'd arrived in Kabul yesterday afternoon, they met a few sleepy-eyed Australian travelers slumped in chairs in the Jam's lounge. They reminded Cassie of the stoned travelers and expats she'd seen in Chiang Mai and Kathmandu, places with easy access to hashish. Hashish must be here as well, she thought as Ralph started up a conversation with one of them. He wasn't Australian, though; a guy from southern California. Then she and Ralph had joined the friendly group, spending much of the evening sharing beer and stories about places they'd seen on their travels.

Last night, Ralph told her he'd decided to take on Danny, the California guy, as a city guide for today. Cassie had been invited along but had demurred. She really needed to find a money exchange and wash her hair. And she hadn't felt that well this morning. Maybe it was the heat that enervated her so. Maybe she was simply hungry. She certainly was thirsty most of the time. She had come to hate the iodine taste of treated water.

An ice-cold shower down the hall had energized her, though. It was the only temperature available, but she didn't mind. She'd developed a system after weeks without hot water. First, she'd wash her face in the sink. Then she'd step into the shower and quickly wash her body, leaving her long sandy-colored hair as dry as possible, a cloak around her shoulders. She'd towel off before bending her head into the weak stream to shampoo. She added a variation this time, putting her dirty jeans on the floor of the shower so that soap, water and her feet could beat out the grime. The jeans were drying now at the end of the bed. Not ideal, but what could she do without a chair or a hanger? At least they'd dry faster here than in humid Thailand.

Hunger a little satiated and hair still damp, Cassie picked up her pocket journal and reread the lines from the previous night's entry:

> *Just sent the 5th roll of film back for processing in the States, mostly photos from India. I think Mom & Dad will like them. Unfortunately, I'm now out of slide film. All I have left is the print film Jack sent. I didn't have luck finding slide film in Pakistan. Will have to check here.*
>
> *We left Peshawar at dawn today. Fresh mango drink and 6 cookies at the border; bread, dates & tea for lunch at a roadside café; kebabs last night after we arrived in Kabul. We're staying at Jam Hotel near Chahrahi Taurabaz Khan, called Chicken Street. Room price is good: $3.50/a double.*
>
> *Took 1½ hours to cross the border into Afghanistan. Khyber Pass is fascinating, edged with ruins. We were held up*

briefly at a security checkpoint. Soldiers everywhere here; situation tense. But as Americans we're ok.

That was as far as she'd gotten before they went to the Jam lounge last night. For today's entry, she settled on her knees in front of the low table and found a prized pen in her bag.

> *Exchange rate: 39 Afs to $1. En route to the bank, I saw several Afghan women in chic western clothes. Talked with one who's a doctor. She told me women who wear traditional robes called burkas (sp?) are mostly from rural villages. I also met a Russian engineer at the bank. (Lots of Soviets here.) He spoke a little English & said he hadn't met an American woman before. Then he asked me out to dinner! I said no thanks of course. But he's right. I haven't met any American women either, or, in fact, many Americans at all. Travelers are mostly British, Australian or French. We're all on the same path between Asia & Europe, like ants.*

Cassie stopped. She couldn't think of anything else to note. The afternoon wasn't that interesting, and paper and ink were scarce. She tended to hoard both when making journal entries and writing letters home, even to her parents.

She'd picked up a letter from them at General Delivery in Lahore a few days before, and her father sounded anxious. Her mother wasn't thrilled at her being so far away, either, but she seemed to understand her daughter's obsession with travel. Cassie needed to let them know she was alive and mostly well. She pulled out a sheet of blue air postal paper, so thin that it was almost translucent.

> *I hope you got my last letter from Srinigar. We stayed a week on the houseboat on Dal Lake. You'll see from the photos*

that are coming. We were able to hire a shikara (a long boat with pillows) to take us around the lake, past once elegant lakeside gardens of Mughal princes and through acres of white lotus blooms.

From Srinigar, I wanted to see Ladakh but monsoon rains make traveling into the Himalayas tough. So we went to Amritsar & Peshawar and yesterday crossed into Afghanistan. We're in Kabul now at a small hotel that caters to young travelers. We're both well, taking vitamins and getting lots of exercise walking. Ralph is busy writing and I'm taking a million photos. I just sent back my fifth roll to the States for developing, which you should get in a few weeks.

She shifted her sore knees; the carpet gave little padding. She added,

I picked up your letter in Lahore. Thanks so much! Next mail pickup is Tehran General Delivery. Your letters mean a lot to me. Mom, I hope your arthritis is better. Dad, have a happy birthday next month! A gift is on its way (mailed from Srinigar). I love & miss you both. Please give my love to Miss Millie too. I'll write again soon.

Cassie signed her name and added a postscript: "Ralph says hi!"

That letter sealed, she brought out another sheet of postal paper. At the top, she wrote, "Hi, Jack." She had smiled when Jack told her about the trouble his name was causing friends in the aftermath of the plane hijackings. She knew it was no joke, with three hijackings last year and another just weeks before they met. Still, he told the story with such an engaging self-deprecating humor. Perhaps that explained how easily they talked that day last April, starting at the check-in counter in the New Orleans airport and ending ten hours later in San Francisco.

It felt a little odd to correspond with someone she barely knew, yet she wrote to him weekly, sometimes more often, and spent intervening days thinking about which experiences she'd recount, what phrases she'd use. There had been two letters from him waiting at Lahore. In one, he'd included a photo of himself with a Labrador puppy. In the other, with lots of padding, was a roll of Kodak print film, 36-exposure. She preferred slides, but the gesture was generous. And timely.

Writing to him was a release; she could be as opinionated and honest as she wanted. More than with her parents, of course, because they worried so much. Even more than with Ralph, because she wanted him to think the best of her. With Jack, honesty was easy. After all, she didn't know when or if she'd ever see him again.

In minute handwriting to fit as much as possible on the page, she wrote:

> *Thanks for writing & sending film - much appreciated! I laughed when I read about your adorable new puppy; Sherlock clearly has excellent taste in shoes. I hope you both are well and that your dissertation is coming along.*
>
> *Sorry to hear the news about your breakup with Helene. I know it must hurt. Maybe it's just temporary, like she says. I'm glad you've got Sherlock.*

Cassie paused. Without Helene, Jack might be interested in her. She instantly put that idea away, a tiny folded note in her brain's back pocket. She loved Ralph. And Jack was in San Francisco, thousands of miles away; an intellectual, doing serious work. In comparison, she was still a kid.

She continued writing.

> *I sent you a postcard from Amritsar. Did you get it? We traveled thru Pakistan for a few days, and now are in Kabul.*

The Khyber Pass is stunning – mountainsides like black glass, crowned with ruins of fortresses and caravanserais.

Something must be going on here. There were lots of tanks & troops near the border. Then, outside Kabul, our bus was pulled over so soldiers could board & check our papers. One aimed a gun at my head as he held out his hand for our passports. I had both in my bag & quickly handed them over. Ralph missed the whole thing. He was reading Frank Herbert's Dune and didn't even look up. Finally an officer arrived & waved the soldier away. He barely glanced at the passports before handing them back and thanking me politely in English. Strange times!

She stopped, suddenly conscious that her palms were damp and her breathing rapid and shallow. She didn't remember being frightened at the time; was this her body's delayed response? A new experience, having a firearm pointed at her head. The episode probably lasted no more than a minute, but it felt much longer in retrospect. As if she had sat all afternoon in that aisle seat with an armed soldier looming over her. She wished now she had looked at him squarely, seen his face, given him human form. But she had kept her eyes averted, her head down, trying to seem insignificant. After the soldier left and then the officer, other soldiers came and grabbed a young Afghan sitting behind her. She watched as they roughly pulled him from his seat. For a second, he caught her eye. She wondered who he was: a criminal, a conspirator, or an ordinary man on an ordinary bus. She wondered what happened to him.

Cassie wished she could talk with Ralph about it, but he hadn't been paying attention. Instead, with his long frame hunched up next to the window, he had kept reading. She was glad he wasn't overly protective, that he saw her as capable and independent, but she could have used his support. She almost wrote that in her letter to Jack, but it felt like a betrayal. And, after all, what could Ralph have done?

At that moment, Ralph walked in and Cassie hastily slid her parents' letter on top. He wasn't the jealous type, he'd made that plain early in their relationship. Even so, she didn't want him to see the letter; he already made enough disparaging comments about Jack. Ralph would crook his fingers in invisible quotation marks and call Jack her "pen pal professor." He meant it sarcastically; Jack was still in graduate school, and Ralph didn't hold graduate studies in high regard. The important thing, he told her repeatedly, is to live life.

Ralph was in an exuberant mood. "Great news! Come on," he almost shouted. "We're meeting Danny and his friend."

Cassie stood, ran her fingers through her drying hair, then slipped on flip flops. She grabbed her travel bag, and stuffed the journal, pen and letters inside next to the camera.

"For kebabs?" she asked hopefully. "I'm starving. Aren't you? And there's still some watermelon left …."

"No, thanks. I got something to eat while we were out." He strode from the room, clearly excited by something. "Wait until you hear," he said over his shoulder.

She trailed after him to the Jam's seedy lounge area. A makeshift bar was set up along a side wall, with a crudely lettered sign in English offering beer, hot tea, Coke and Limea. Nothing was refrigerated or iced. Perhaps at more expensive hotels, but the Jam's amenities were simple; drinks here were chilled slightly in a tub of lukewarm water. Cassie noticed that the room smelled pungent and sweet, almost cloying. She suspected it was incense to mask the reek of some of the unbathed clientele.

Ralph approached two men seated at a corner table. One was mellow Danny, Ralph's guide for the day. He was tall and well-muscled with a tan weathered look that fit well in the rustic surroundings. In contrast to other travelers, his hair was very short, little more than fuzz. He had explained the day before that he'd shaved his head when he had briefly lived at an ashram in northern India. Now he wore the wool felt cap ubiquitous in Kabul.

Cassie hadn't seen the other man before.

"Hey, Danny, you remember Cassie, my girlfriend," Ralph said. Danny nodded and grinned at her. Then Ralph turned toward the unknown man and added, "This is Martin, Danny's friend."

"Marton," the man corrected. "With an O." He nodded briefly in her direction.

He hadn't been there yesterday, laid low by a bout of diarrhea, Danny reported. Marton, dropping his head shyly, flushed with color. Their table was littered with brown beer bottles and a solitary bottle of Limea, still half full in front of Marton.

"Been here awhile?" she asked Ralph with a tight smile that belied her irritation. Beer wasn't cheap.

"Here's the great news," he said. "Marton has a VW van and he's driving to see friends in Geneva. He's invited us along. We just help with gas. No more buses, babe! Isn't that great? Later, he plans to sell it for only three hundred bucks. We could buy it and keep traveling around Europe. We can camp in it, Marton says. There's a bed and everything. Think of the money we'll save on hotel bills."

"Runs all right," Marton explained. "Tires are pretty new. A 1968 Volkswagen, a good year." He lit a cigarette.

Ralph nodded at Cassie eagerly. A good year.

Cassie studied Marton as he spoke. He was shorter than Ralph and less muscled than Danny, a thin pale man with quick movements. His eyes were half hidden by his long black hair, and he looked down a lot, especially avoiding eye contact with her. There was something about his mannerisms that spoke of uncertainty, caution. She couldn't read him very well. She couldn't place his accent.

"Maybe so," she said hesitantly. She caught Ralph's frown in the corner of her eye, and amended her response. "Well, actually, that does sound like a good plan. Getting a ride. We'll have to think about buying it though." Ralph relaxed and nodded.

Marton said, "Of course."

Cassie added, "We're going to Bamiyan tomorrow to see the Buddha statues, but we'll be back in a few days."

Now Marton was slowly shaking his head and Ralph quickly interjected, "That won't work, babe. First, it's a seven-hour bus ride to Bamiyan, and we don't know when we'll get back here. Buses don't run every day, you know. And second, they need to leave tomorrow," His gesture encompassed both men. To her quizzical look, he added, "Danny's coming as far as Herat."

"But we've just arrived in Kabul." Cassie tried to keep the whine out of her voice.

"Well, you ask me, there's not a lot to see here. And we can always come back someday." Ralph helped himself to one of Marton's cigarettes. Cassie saw a tiny flicker of Marton's eyelids; irritation?

"You'll like Herat," Danny jumped in. "You like history, don't you? There's lots of history there; it was part of the old Silk Road. Alexander the Great was there. Genghis Khan and Tamerlane. A really cool mosque. Hey, and Persian poets," he turned, appealing to Ralph.

Ralph nodded enthusiastically. "I could get into Persian poets."

That quickly, the decision seemed to be made. Danny bought more beer as they worked out the details of splitting gas costs and sharing driving. On Danny's urging, Marton produced a road map of Afghanistan. Ralph and Danny pored over it, animated and excited. Even the guarded Marton seemed pleased.

Cassie wished she felt the same.

CHAPTER TWO

March 10, 2007

Saturday

Jack Hunter took a sip of coffee. It was lukewarm. Too long in the stainless steel urn that commanded the center of the conference hotel's table. Beneath the urn, a coffee-stained white table cloth; around it, white cups and saucers arrayed, ready and waiting for the next drowsy professor to emerge from an overlong panel presentation. Jack had slipped out a little early. Shifting the weight of the worn leather satchel on his shoulder, he carefully carried his cup to a vacant standing table nearby.

Conference sessions were tiring. The sparsely scattered audience in overly air-conditioned meeting rooms; the publishers' hall where folding tables were piled with books that almost no one would ever read, including his own. The panels themselves could be lively and engaging, but too often were not. Some presenters were simply poor speakers; others were focused on such minutiae that their arguments made little sense to the uninitiated. But he couldn't fault his fellow academics. They were like him, coming here because it was expected. Conference participation and networking were part of the game.

Jack didn't really need to play that game anymore. A full professor, he had already made a contribution to the field: two scholarly books, several book chapters, and numerous peer-reviewed articles in top journals. He successfully mentored younger faculty and graduate students, taught popular and rigorous courses, organized conference panels, and engaged in public education, including commenting on American foreign policy and international crises in local news media. Recently, though, he found himself losing interest. Only six years from retirement, he could afford to relax. Yet he didn't.

He stretched and rolled his tight shoulders. He'd been sitting too long. Maybe he could break away from the conference routine and find the hotel gym. Or take a walk along the Las Vegas strip. It was March and the temperature was pleasant. But he felt obligated to attend sessions. A junior colleague was presenting at the next one; her paper focused on immigration policy, not his area of interest. But still.

His wife Helene said once she admired his sense of responsibility, his dependability. Not the most romantic character trait. He always did his duty, he thought drolly. He might have had a decent career in the military if he hadn't come of age during the Vietnam War. As it was, his younger self had worried about his draft lottery number. Luck alone had granted him a high enough number to keep him out of Vietnam and the Cambodian campaign.

Cambodia had played a different role in his life. Like others on campus, he had been furious when news broke that Richard Nixon had ordered the covert bombing of Vietnam's neutral neighbor and then sent in U.S. troops. By 1972, Jack was making speeches on the campus quad and marching with fellow students against Nixon's "illegal invasion." The Cambodian incursion triggered his interest in foreign policy and the presidency, which eventually led to a doctorate and his career. At the campus protests, he also had met Helene, a freshman biology major. She was only 17 at the time, super bright, intense, and gorgeous. How could he not fall head over heels?

His life path: all because of Richard Nixon. Jack set down the coffee cup. The irony of the realization unsettled him.

He looked around. The fifteen-minute break between sessions was bringing scores of attendees pouring into the lounge. Jack played a game with himself, pretending to study them as an exotic tribe, observing their dress and mannerisms, identifying their clan groupings and social hierarchy.

Most of the men and women wore gray or navy or black suits, and carted the canvas conference tote bag proclaiming 2007 in bold print. Their name tags and affiliations hung around their necks on lanyards, a pedestrian intrusion on polished veneers. And it was a veneer for many; this time in the afternoon, hair was mussed, neckties askew. On several men, Jack noted shirt tails pulling free.

The crowd surged and circulated between the tables. Younger conference attendees glanced at name tags, searching for someone notable in the field, to proffer their business cards and, if lucky, get an inside track on a job. The older ones scanned the crowd for colleagues. The low rumble of a hundred polite conversations was occasionally punctured by a loud laugh or exclamation.

"Jack!" he heard someone call. His head jolted around. He was part of the tribe as well, not a cultural anthropologist. He searched in the direction of the voice.

A middle-aged man with an excellent haircut and well-tailored suit was making his way toward him, big grin and outstretched hand. He gripped Jack's hand tightly. "Say, old man, I was hoping I'd run into you!" His polish was authentic; the man exuded inside-the-Beltway élan.

Jack smiled. "Frank, how are you? I'm a little surprised to see you here. How will the White House manage without you?"

"Very funny, Jack. The White House gets along without me just fine. Well, almost fine."

Frank Constant had been his graduate assistant – what – twenty years ago? With his master's degree in hand, he had moved on to a prestigious Ph.D. program. No sooner had he completed the degree than the first Bush administration had plucked him up. Since then, he'd bounced happily between conservative think tanks, FOX news commentary, and the occasional classroom at an elite school. Now he was high up in the second Bush White House, an unusual but coveted career trajectory for a political scientist.

Frank added, "Sorry I missed your panel. I did read your abstract. Interesting argument. Still coddling terrorists, I see." He gave a good-natured and confident chuckle.

"And how's that police state going?" Jack smiled in return, deftly hiding his annoyance with his former student's politics. "Too bad about the Constitution getting in your way.'"

Frank shook his head in mock dismay and glanced at his watch. "Would love to stay and chat, but I've got to go. Late lunch with my publisher." He grinned with genuine glee, "Third edition."

"Congratulations," Jack said stiffly. He had read Frank's book and admired the facile writing and clean organization. But it was based on such loose scholarship that its commercial success – much less his former student's academic standards - troubled him. Yet Jack was sincere when he added, "I'm sorry we won't have a chance to talk." He still felt an unlikely paternal kinship with Frank. And he admitted an ulterior motive to himself; perhaps he'd be able to talk some sense into Frank's head and, by extension, the Oval Office. Or at least hear some interesting political stories he could share with his presidency students on Tuesday.

Frank grinned. "Well then, how about dinner later?"

Jack was surprised at the invitation, and that Frank wasn't networking with influential pundits in town. He felt both flattered, and annoyed at himself for feeling flattered. Yet he didn't like dining alone, and most of his conference colleagues had left soon after the morning's panel. Dinner and a friendly argument might be invigorating. "That'll work," he said, nodding.

"Terrific. Let's meet in the lobby at eight." Frank handed Jack a beautifully embossed business card, and then he was gone.

THE AFTERNOON WENT as expected. Jack learned a few things about immigration policy he didn't know and provided useful feedback to his young colleague before she headed out for drinks with old friends from graduate school.

Now it was eight. He wasn't used to eating late; Helene liked to have dinner by six so she could return to the lab if she needed to. But at conferences, regular schedules tended to go out the window.

The restaurant was Japanese, the atmosphere elegant. As they were escorted to their table, Jack felt underdressed in his khakis and polo shirt. Frank, still in his suit, had evidently been drinking earlier in the evening, and his ebullient mood started to elevate Jack's.

They ordered drinks and Frank turned to his former professor. "So, tell me Jack, why are you still at State?"

Jack was startled. "What do you mean?" Then he got it; Frank had recently been forwarding emails with job announcements at prestigious universities.

"You're a terrific professor. You do good research – not that I agree with your conclusions, of course. You could go lots of places. Why stay there? Low pay. Heavy teaching load. No research support to speak of."

"I thought Republicans loved the Heartland," Jack pointed out. "And you seem to have gotten a good enough education."

"I'm exceptional," Frank flashed a quick grin. "And I love State, don't get me wrong. It's my home. But," he paused for effect, "it's a backwater."

"I disagree. I've got great colleagues and interesting research opportunities. And some really outstanding students. I don't want to leave."

"You never want to be in the center of things? Washington or New York? Making policy, not just writing about it. You'd have a bigger microphone."

"For my leftist socialist ideas?" Jack joked.

Frank chuckled. "Point well taken. Stay the hell outa my town!" He sipped his drink.

A long minute passed as Frank studied the menu and Jack studied him. Even as a student, he had never been unsure of himself, never modest in his claims. There were times when Jack admired Frank's ambition and ability to promote himself. Jack had none of that. Now he mused aloud, "I never aspired to be an academic superstar, Frank. I love teaching; that's who I am." He looked directly at his companion, "Seriously. A life well lived and no regrets."

The waiter took their orders and the menus. Frank carefully lined up his silverware. "Sounds like a headstone, Jack. I'm not sure it's true, 'no regrets' and all, but I get the picture. It's safe and comfortable in your niche." Loud laughs at the next table briefly interrupted their conversation. When the decorous ambience resumed, Frank did as well, "Even so, there's Helene to consider. She could have greater ambitions."

A tension seized Jack's spine. Helene's career was not a subject he intended to discuss with Frank. He didn't check the defensive irritation in his voice. "She's got a million dollar grant doing research on infectious disease. A state-of-the-art lab. A post-doc working with her. *Where* she happens to do the research doesn't concern her. Or me, as long as she's happy."

"Of course, of course," he held up a hand. "No offense intended. She's one amazing woman, that's all I meant. She could be head of the CDC or something, maybe doing health policy in the White

House." He paused. "Okay, knowing her, a *Democratic* White House." He added playfully, "Should – God forbid - such a thing ever happen again."

"You don't know Helene. She hates politics; she loathes administrative work. Even completing grant reports is a chore she tries to delegate. Our backwater suits her fine."

Frank said nothing for a few moments, then nodded. "I'm sure it does. Sorry I brought it up."

The meal arrived, and their discussion veered back to less charged topics of war and peace, terrorism threats and civil liberties - issues they knew well and were comfortable debating. They lingered over a last glass of wine.

Then, discretely slipping a credit card into the restaurant's padded leather portfolio, Frank smiled, "My treat. Please." He stretched his arms. "Let's get out of here. It's Saturday night and we're in Vegas, for Christ's sake. Let's check out the town."

"I can't. I have an early flight."

"C'mon, Jack. Schedule a fucking wake-up call. I bet you're already packed."

It was true; Jack was. But he wasn't sure he wanted to expend the effort. He looked forward to returning to his quiet room, reading one of the academic books he'd picked up. "I don't know, Frank. I'm not as young as you are." They were walking toward the restaurant's front door.

Frank laughed. "Age has nothing to do with it. I may be conservative in politics, but you're the real diehard conservative. Loosen up, Jack. Don't be so dull. How does Helene put up with you?"

The remark stung. Jack couldn't think of a retort. Was he dull? He blinked. "Maybe I can come for a little while."

"That's the spirit!" Frank slapped his shoulder. Then he pointed in the direction of the restrooms. "Back in a flash," he said.

Alone for the moment, Jack stood awkwardly, inadvertently blocking the restaurant door. While irked with himself for agreeing, Jack had to concede Frank's point; he recognized a growing stodginess in himself, and he didn't like it. He used to be adventurous. What happened to the student radical?

He pulled out his cell phone and called home.

"Hello?" Helene's cautious phone voice with the subtext, who the hell is calling at this hour?

"Hi, sweetheart," Jack said with a cheerfulness he didn't feel.

"Jack. What's wrong?"

"Nothing's wrong. I just thought I'd call. The conference went fine. I'm leaving early in the morning."

"Yes, I know." Another pause. Helene wasn't big on small talk.

"You'll never guess who I've just had dinner with. Frank Constant. Remember him?"

A pause. "The Nazi?"

"He's not a Nazi." Jack's tone was more aggressive than he intended, but he was impatient when otherwise intelligent people conflated conservative thought with Nazi ideology. In his view, it made Nazism too mainstream, too ordinary. Helene knew that; they'd had this conversation before. Already he was regretting the phone call. He should have guessed; she had never liked Frank.

He could almost see the shrug when she said, "Whatever. Off to bed now?"

"Actually, we're heading out for a little while to explore the city."

This was unexpected. "But you hate casinos and you disapprove of gambling."

Her comment made him sound like a Puritan. "I don't disapprove of gambling. Why do you think I disapprove?"

"There's that whole thing about exploiting people's weaknesses? And you have an early flight."

"Yes, I know. I'll get a wake-up call."

"Don't miss your flight."

"I won't. Well, I miss you. I look forward to being home tomorrow."

"Okay," she said. "Goodnight."

She rang off just as Frank returned.

In fact, Jack admitted to himself, casinos did depress him. Las Vegas depressed him. Maybe he was just depressed in general. He thought, this is not a good idea. He went along anyway.

THE CASINO WAS too bright, too loud, too claustrophobic, too hypnotic. After an hour watching Frank gamble and make derisive comments about the House, Jack decided to leave. He wished Frank good night and safe travels and, still full from dinner, opted to walk back to the hotel.

Jack stepped off a curb and crossed the busy thoroughfare, glancing at the traffic. His fellow pedestrians were lively and drunk, the city's neon lights garish. The night was just starting for much of Las Vegas but oddly he felt that everything was about to end. The future felt doubtful, even bleak. This was a mood that he used to call existential angst when he was a college senior. Who was he? What was the purpose of life, of his life in particular?

As he stepped back on the curb, he reassured himself: his work had had an impact; he had touched lives. Yet an undeniable sense of uncertainty needled him. Had he taken the right path? Arriving at his hotel, he realized with a jolt where the feeling had come from. The letters from Cassie.

In February, everyone in the Department had received an order from the college dean to pack up their offices by the end of June; they had to move to another building over the summer. The edict shocked him. In the twenty-four years that he had occupied the same office,

Jack had never even cleaned out his filing cabinet, never winnowed unwanted books from his shelves. So late last month on slow afternoons, he started the culling and packing process: sorting, shredding, tossing and boxing everything he had amassed at the university. He had discovered and discarded first drafts of manuscripts, old correspondence, photocopies of journal articles, and a dozen versions of lecture notes from semesters past. Dispirited, he realized that much of what he'd valued and saved was just trash.

The week before the conference, cleaning out a bottom drawer in a file cabinet, he found a heavily taped cardboard box labeled "MA Thesis Notes" in red marker. The label, he knew, was false; the actual contents he had never forgotten, even after a quarter of a century. His hands automatically raised the box from the drawer; found scissors to slice through the tape; and lifted out a stained and stuffed manila envelope, the only item inside.

He thought back to San Francisco, a year after they were married, when Helene had found the fat manila envelope as they were packing up to move. She'd been adamant that he throw the letters away, and had even watched when he dropped the manila envelope into the garbage bin outside. He complied; she was heavily pregnant with their daughter and he didn't want to upset her. But that night he couldn't sleep. He couldn't let those letters end up in a landfill. So after Helene was asleep and before the garbage truck arrived, he donned robe and slippers and retrieved the letters. In the garage, he boxed them up, gave them a new identity, and stacked the box with the others bound for his new campus office.

On that cold morning last week, he finally held the manila envelope again. Against his will, he opened it and pulled out one of the many flimsy blue airmail envelopes.

We've arrived in Kathmandu! I just returned from a twi-light stroll down its narrow streets, past pocket-sized shops sell-

ing amazing things – gemstones, the Gurhka daggers called kukris (sp?), fragrant herbs, Tibetan prayer wheels, sarongs. Above the shops, suspended from overhead balconies, are richly patterned wool rugs. And so many children dashing pell-mell down the streets! They should wear bells like the passing bicycles and rickshaws. One small boy stopped to sing Alouette for me. I considered buying food from a sidewalk stand; it smelled so tempting. But I'm trying to be careful - hepatitis is said to be rampant here. Yet I'm totally charmed. The decaying red brick temples with weeds growing out of their tiled roofs, the winding dark passages that are so mysterious and inviting, and the people, of course. I love it here. You would too.

The letter continued, but Jack had to put it down. It hurt him to read it. He remembered his first thoughts when he'd received the letter – that he'd leave for Kathmandu tomorrow! Then, a few minutes later, soberly assessing his current commitments, he promised himself that he would go sometime, that he would see the world. But he never did. In fact, there was so much he had never done.

At that instant, a searing regret surged over and through him, soaking into his skin and staying with him even now, in the dry night air of Las Vegas, of all places.

He was being melodramatic. He didn't regret his life, not at all. He had a smart and beautiful wife. They had two wonderful grown children, a lovely house, and lots of plans for the future when they would retire and have time to do all that he and Helene had dreamed of. He admonished himself: he would not look at those old letters again. They just upset him. He'd toss them when he got back to his office on Monday.

EARLY THE NEXT morning, Jack maneuvered the heavy suitcase awkwardly down the plane's aisle, in slow step with a hundred others in economy class. He grunted as he lifted it into the overhead compartment. He was heading home, and once again carting too many books. Why did he do this, picking up more books whenever he went to an academic conference? In the old days, it didn't matter; he would have checked a bag as heavy as this. Now baggage fees dissuaded him. He could afford them, of course, but he objected to paying them on principle. So, on principle, he'd probably throw his back out. Helene would love that. He'd never hear the end of it.

That was unfair, he thought. Helene cared for him. If she scolded him, it was because he was taking risks that he shouldn't be taking at his age. He had to learn to slow down, take things easier.

Not that she was slowing down any. A major NHS grant had come through and she was spending more time than ever in the lab. Sure, he missed seeing her, but how could he complain? It was such an important project and a major feather in her cap, he thought proudly. His wife, the brilliant scientist. And still attractive in her early fifties.

The man in the aisle seat shifted so Jack could get past to the window. As he strapped on his seat belt, he thought again about his heavy carry-on. A sudden memory jarred him, sharp and unexpected. The comment that girl Cassie had made about her heavy backpack all those years ago.

Like today, he had been going home from an academic conference. It was toward the end of his third year of doctoral studies. He was standing behind her in line to check into a flight home to San Francisco, and his first impression had been unfavorable; she was some hippie flower child – peasant blouse and jeans, long hair, wire frame glasses, with a backpack larger than she was - probably on her way to Haight-Ashbury. She had squatted in front of him, fooling with the straps on the bag, tightening and tucking them out of the way.

Then she stood and saw something behind him. Barely glancing at him, she had asked, "Can you watch my bag for a minute? Thanks," and she had trotted off without waiting for his reply.

He was amazed at how much he still could remember. The memory was so vivid.

His eyes had tracked her. She had rushed to a middle-aged couple standing just beyond the check-in line. The girl had asked them frantically if something was wrong. The woman, dressed in a pale blue pantsuit, said that nothing was wrong, but her father didn't think it was right to just drop her off at the curb. Then the man spoke, "You'll be gone for so long, honey lamb." That phrase stuck in Jack's memory, as well as the forlorn expression on the father's face. The girl had hugged him tightly, then her mother. "I'll be all right, Daddy," she had assured him. Turning to them both, she had added, "I'll be with Becky about a week and then Ralph will come. Once we figure out our trip from there, I'll send you an itinerary. And I'll write every week, I promise." They said a few more endearments and then the girl had returned to the line. The father showed every intention of remaining in place, but the mother had gently pulled him away, guiding him to the terminal's exit. They waved as they departed, and the girl waved back.

The girl seemed sad when she finally looked at Jack and said thanks again. "No problem," he had replied. Jack had felt sheepish he had been critical and judgmental. She was going far away for a long time.

Even so, he had considered her naïve to leave her bag with a stranger in the airport. He suspected that everything she owned was in that backpack. A little later, when they found themselves sitting together in the departure lounge, he had lightly chided her about it. "How did you know you could trust me? What if I had stolen your bag?" She had looked at him earnestly for a half a heartbeat and replied, "How did you know there wasn't a dead body in it?"

He had barked out a surprised laugh.

That was the start of the longest single conversation in his life. And possibly the best one as well. Recalling it now, twenty-nine years later, he didn't laugh. He slumped back in the airplane seat. Usually, he was good humored. He didn't dwell on negative things or pick at emotional scabs. Yet here he was staring out at the tarmac, grieving for what had been lost three decades ago. Grieving for what had never even been.

Jack promised himself to get rid of those damn letters.

CHAPTER THREE

August 24, 1978

Thursday

C assie woke with a vague awareness of Ralph sitting up in bed. It was very early, still dark. Groggy from the late-night discussion, she propped up next to him as her eyes adjusted. He seemed engrossed in thought, so she said nothing. He was probably working on ideas for his novel. He had hardly written in the past few weeks, and she did not want to interrupt deep thoughts.

He must have sensed she was awake. "I'm thinking of changing the way my name is pronounced. Danny says the British pronunciation sounds like Raaf."

She turned away from him, disappointed. "You mean like strafe or chafe?"

"Sounds more authorial, don't you think? Like a serious writer. The American pronunciation is so ..."

She knew what he was trying to say. "*Honeymooners?*"

"Yes! Low brow. So you agree?"

"No. If you're British, fine. If you're not, it sounds pretentious."

His body shifted away from her.

"Sweetheart, Ralph's a fine name, a brilliant name. Ralph Waldo Emerson. Ralph Nader. Ralph Lauren…, Ralph Kramden."

The last name made him chuckle. "You're right." He kissed her lightly and stood to dress. Even in the dark, she knew his travel uniform: jeans, black tee-shirt, sweat shirt.

A knock reverberated on the hotel room's flimsy door. It startled them both. "Wait," Cassie ordered as she rose to grab her own jeans, but Ralph didn't hear her and opened it. Cassie dove back under the covers.

The silhouette of Marton stood in the doorway, a gray hump of backpack hanging from a shoulder. The hall light poured into the room. He glanced at Cassie in the bed, a blanket pulled to her bare shoulders, then looked back at Ralph, raised an eyebrow.

"Ready?"

Ralph nodded vigorously as if afraid of being misunderstood or left behind, and gestured toward the dark shadows of their own packs propped in the corner. The abandoned doll was in the opposite corner, watching.

"Absolutely. We're just getting dressed."

At this, Marton's eyes turned back toward Cassie in bed.

His appraisal unsettled her a little. "Well, when you leave," Cassie announced. She held his gaze.

Marton shrugged, nodded curtly to Ralph and left.

Within five minutes, she and Ralph were drinking tea in the lounge area, at a table with uneven legs. The tea was tepid, left over in a thermos on the bar's counter from the night before. Their backpacks leaned against the wall, readier than Cassie was to embark for Herat. They were alone in the lounge, which was quiet this early. Then Danny stumbled through the door, blinking hard. "I feel like shit," he announced. Once he had poured out a cup of brown liquid, he carried it gingerly to their table. His body collapsed onto a chair, but it had no back, and he had to catch himself quickly to keep from falling off. "Shit," he said, spilling some tea on his leg.

Once balanced on the seat, Danny cradled the chipped cup of tea against one cheek, an amulet against the cruelty of morning. "Why the fuck do we have to get up so fucking early?"

Cassie had not yet looked at her watch; she stole a glance. It was ten to five. Neither she nor Ralph replied. It was a fair question.

Marton's low voice cut in. "Because it's a thousand *fucking* kilometers to Herat. Nothing in-between." He seemed to appear from nowhere and sat at the next table, putting down his keys and a pair of sunglasses. "It's your choice. The van leaves at five." As if it had a mind of its own, not his fault. His tea was hot; steam rose from the cup. Cassie realized that he must have roused one of the kitchen staff, something they had not thought to do.

"Hey, man," Danny pulled himself together, sat a little straighter. "I'm ready anytime."

Marton was wrong. Cassie didn't want to say it, but she did anyway. "According to the map you showed us, there's a village on the way, Chagcharan, I think. We could spend the night there."

He turned slowly to look at her. "A village that's never seen a western woman. You really want to stop there?" The comment implied danger, specific to her but broad enough to expose and endanger them all.

"Or we go south through Kandahar. It's a better road," she insisted. "I'm just saying we have options." All of the men's eyes now were on her. Ralph's hand, she could see, had tightened into a ball. He didn't like confrontation.

Without pause, Marton stated the immutable fact, "I don't want to go through Kandahar."

Marton, she realized, was used to getting his way. She had misread him yesterday; he wasn't uncertain in the least. Cassie considered it. She didn't want to leave for Herat now. Nor did she particularly want his or Danny's company. Marton, in particular, was making her uneasy. But Ralph seemed so eager to go. Perhaps he needed male companionship. They had traveled a long time, just the two of them. And they were already up and packed. She gave a conciliatory shrug. "Fine. I'm ready to go whenever." She reached over and squeezed Ralph's hand; she could feel it relax.

Five minutes later, they were hauling their packs out to a dusty navy-blue van parked beneath a pale streetlight. Marton was already behind the wheel and Danny clambered into the front passenger seat. As Ralph climbed behind Cassie into the van's back, he wrinkled his nose. "What's that stink?"

By way of explanation, Marton said indifferently, "I bought it from some hippie organic farmers outside Geneva. They carried all sorts of crap in here."

"Literally!" Ralph scowled.

Cassie detected the odor as well. She couldn't quite place it but it reminded her of bayou decay. She'd smelled worse. After fifteen minutes, she no longer even noticed it. By then, Marton had pulled the van onto the direct road west to Herat. The pavement was rough. The map had labeled this a minor road.

Time passed. From her perch in the back of the van, Cassie couldn't see much but she could tell the sky was starting to lighten. She craned toward a window and pulled back its flowered curtain. They were climbing. That made sense; this route cut through the Hindu Kush, and it was closed entirely during winter months. But it was clear today, vast treeless vistas stretching to the horizon. Cassie thought this must be like sailing on the ocean. Ralph smiled over at her, contented. They drove on.

But one hundred kilometers out of Kabul, the van veered dangerously. Marton wrestled it to the side of the paved road, cut the engine and got out. Through the curtained window, Cassie saw him squat in the dirt next to the left front tire. She couldn't see what he was inspecting, but she heard him yell something at Danny about ball bearings. The van was crippled. She swept her eyes over the landscape. Nothing was in sight, no village, no huts, no military outpost. Camels grazed on a far hill, scattered like toys on the landscape. No point in just sitting, she thought, and disembarked with the others, joining Marton on the gravel verge. They studied the road for any sign of traffic. None came.

After an hour, a turbaned shepherd wandered over and stood gazing at the four of them crouched in the van's shadow. Their presence seemed to entertain him. The morning was becoming hot. Their only water was in a few canteens in the van; Marton murmured that they should conserve it for now. In the distance, the spine of the mountains appeared vague and pale, like a sepia-toned watercolor. Cassie thought of her old neighbor who painted. A Mercedes sped by, oblivious to their shouts and waves.

After two hours, a decrepit green diesel truck with five Afghan men in the open back stopped on its way to the capital. Via sign language, the driver bargained to haul the van back to Kabul for 2,000 Afs. Marton stared into the distance, as if willing a better option to appear. Having little choice, he finally agreed and handed over half the money with a scowl.

The driver motioned for them to load the van on the back of the truck, so Ralph, Danny, Marton and the five Afghans pushed the van a little further off the road and up a small hill. The driver slowly backed the truck toward it, down into a ditch to bring its back somewhat level with the van. Cassie had tried to join the effort but was jostled out of the way by one of the younger Afghans. The sun rose in full force. Without shade, she squatted on the hillside and watched. Her thirst was extreme. She knew it would be worse for the men pushing the van. She could hear a crunching noise as the bottom of the truck scraped along the rocks. Hot and bored and powerless, Cassie brought out her camera and took a few photos of the landscape, the truck, the men. If they survived, it would make a good story someday.

Time passed slowly as the van was coached onto the truck. When it was done, Cassie, Ralph, Danny and Marton allowed themselves to drink the treated water in their canteens. Ralph looked especially hammered by the heat. When he finished his own water, Cassie shared her canteen with him.

The men climbed into the back, wedging themselves into the narrow space between the van and the truck bed's sides. Still on the road, Cassie was searching for hand holds to hoist herself up when Marton's hand reached down for her. She felt irked at him. This horrible morning was his fault. He should have checked the van; he shouldn't have taken the minor road. She considered ignoring the offer of help, but was too short to easily pull herself up. She grabbed his arm. Another surprise: as slender as he was, his arm was strong and he lifted her easily. Then the driver reclaimed the cab.

They waited. Several clicks but the truck's engine did not turn over. Minutes passed before they accepted the fact that the truck was dead, stuck in the ditch.

They were in the middle of nowhere. Help was not on its way.

Reluctantly, everyone got off the back of the truck. Marton, Danny and Ralph joined the driver under the hood; the others stood around and watched. Cassie circled the truck with her camera. That was when she noticed that the shepherd was still there. He was dogging her footsteps, smiling and singing softly. She moved closer to Ralph and the front of the truck.

The men muttered that the starter was broken. She heard Marton state that they should push-start the engine. No one questioned him. He told the driver, "Second gear." When he gestured what the driver needed to do, the driver nodded. He seemed to know already; this had happened before.

Everyone except the driver – even Cassie and the shepherd – got behind the truck to shove it out of the ditch. The temperature by now was well above one hundred and sweat poured between her shoulder blades and down her forehead, into her eyes. After an hour, the truck regained the pavement. It was already close to the top of a steep rise in the road. More hard pushing brought the truck to the summit. From that point, the driver got the lumbering vehicle coasting downhill and popped the clutch. The engine engaged. Everyone let out a weak cheer as they rushed down the road toward it. While the engine idled, all but the shepherd ran to the back and climbed aboard. This time, Ralph helped Cassie.

They hung on tightly as the driver brought them back to Kabul. When they reached the outskirts of town, Marton leaned toward Cassie and, in a low voice that managed to carry despite the hot wind, said, "Take care of that." He gestured toward the back of her wrist. She looked down and noticed for the first time a half inch gash; clotting blood made it seem even larger. She was glad she'd gotten a tetanus shot before leaving Louisiana.

The truck finally rolled into an auto shop not far from Chicken Street. Two of the Afghan passengers slipped away but the driver and remaining men helped the mechanic and his workers laboriously off-load the van using stacks of brick under each tire. Cassie watched, impressed at the ingenuity.

Finally, in the late afternoon, Cassie, Ralph and Danny trudged back to the Jam Hotel with packs on their backs. Marton stayed behind. On the way, without a word, they walked as one into a tiny shop and bought bottles of Fanta Orange from a tub filled with water. Standing just outside the shop, they poured the lukewarm liquid down their dry throats. Cloying, but less so than lukewarm Coke, their only other option in the shop. They left the glass bottles on the counter.

Cassie and Ralph's room at the Jam was still available; they counted out 270 Afs for two more nights. The bed was made, and two clean worn towels lay folded on the low table. Cassie noted briefly, wistfully, that Maude was gone. Happy trails, she thought. Then, dropping her heavy pack, she grabbed one towel and headed to the shower to cool off.

Later, she and Ralph met Danny in the now crowded lounge. They shared a dried wedge of naan that Danny had forgotten about in his pack. Cassie ate little; she was too tired.

"Shitty day," Danny commented. They all nodded.

"Just curious. How did you meet Marton in the first place?" Cassie asked. She had been wondering about him all day.

Danny scratched his ear and squinted in thought. "On a houseboat on Dal Lake. Hey!" he brightened, "Ralph said you were there too. That's cool! Anyway, I was recovering from Delhi." He looked at Ralph. "Delhi's intense, man. So many people, you can't breathe. That was after I left the ashram I told you about, in Rishikesh. You know the Beatles were there? Well, not at the same time I was. I had to leave there in a hurry. The ashram, not Delhi. This girl and I made it in the temple. I mean, she was really hot. From San Diego, what a co-incidence, right? Another Californian? Well, they frown on that kind of thing, fucking in the temple." He seemed momentarily embarrassed at his language in front of Cassie and quickly looked her way, "Sorry about that. Well, anyway, I went to Delhi and then Srinigar, and I'm on this cheapo houseboat and a small boat pulls up with this guy on his way to Europe. He introduces himself, very formal. It was like, 'Dr. Livingstone, I presume.' We hit it off, talked all night."

Cassie followed; she realized she was getting used to Danny's stream-of-consciousness colloquies.

Now Ralph too was curious. He finished his crust of bread, took a swig of beer. "Talk about what?"

"Everything, man."

Ralph shot Cassie a look. She took it to mean that he thought what she did, that Danny did all the talking that first night. Marton, they suspected, had said little.

"Where's he from? What's his name?" Cassie followed up. If they were going to travel with him, they needed to have some details. Today wasn't reassuring.

Shrugging, Danny seemed unconcerned with that sort of information. "He's Canadian; I saw his passport. He told me his last name but I forgot. It's something weird like Zorro."

From his accent, Cassie knew Marton wasn't Canadian. "A mystery man," she mumbled to herself but the others heard and nodded.

Danny liked the phrase and echoed, "A real mystery man."

BY EIGHT, BACK in the room, Ralph was dead asleep despite the glare of the overhead bulb. Cassie sat on the rug and observed him. His mouth was open and his hair a tangled mess. He still wore his black tee shirt but had stripped to boxer shorts. Ralph looked so sweet in sleep, just a boy. The grime still on his face added to the impression of youth.

Cassie looked down at the pale blue stationery in her hand. She didn't have the energy to finish the letter to Jack tonight. Today was a good story, but it would have to be told another day.

A soft knock on the insubstantial door roused her. She rose and quickly opened it before a second knock could awaken Ralph. Marton stood there. She hadn't seen him since the mechanic's shop.

"Come with me," he whispered.

Curious, Cassie followed, quietly closing the door behind her. They walked down another corridor to Marton's room. She had not been here before. Unlike the room she shared with Ralph, this one was large and well furnished. The mattress rested on a bed frame; the carpet was less worn, in fact was beautiful; a chair upholstered in red patterned wool sat near the window. Another chair, hardback, stood next to the table where Marton's backpack was propped. A lamp was on the table, emitting a soft light. The impression was slightly exotic but comfortable.

"Your wrist," he said. She pushed up her sleeve. She had cleaned the wound with soap and water but it still looked ugly. He fumbled a moment in a side pocket of his backpack and brought out a compact first aid kit. Instead of handing her the tube of antiseptic cream, he took her wrist and gently daubed it on himself. Cassie now noticed that his eyes were pale blue, like a desert noon sky. When he moved her slightly to be closer to the lamp light, she saw a half inch scar along his hairline. He was frowning in concentration as he wrapped a bandage to shield the wound from her bloodied cuff.

"You didn't need to help push the truck, you know." He put the medical kit away.

She rebuttoned her cuff. "Yes, I did. I was as stuck as you were out there. I had to help. I hate feeling useless."

He nodded. "I understand." He paused several seconds before adding, "Let's get something to eat."

The invitation was unexpected. She blinked. "Why not? I'll just drop by the room for my passport and cash."

"You won't need them. I'll pay."

"Okay, thanks. But I still should leave a note for Ralph."

Marton had been heading for the door. He paused and looked back at her. Cassie picked up cues quickly, what people liked and didn't like. Reading Marton's mild disapproval, she reconsidered. She really didn't need to let Ralph know. He was deep asleep and she didn't want to wake him. He would never miss her. And she was suddenly aware of her own insistent hunger.

They left the Jam. In the night, the narrow road leading from the hotel to Chicken Street, ordinarily deserted, was transformed. Ramadan fasting was over for the day, and the tea shop cross from the Jam was open and full of customers. More people passed them on their way to other shops and cafés. Cassie was astonished. She had not been out of the hotel after dark; she had never envisioned this.

Chicken Street itself was vibrant with life. Lights in every shop blazed. Shopkeepers who squatted desultorily in their doorways all day now stood alert, chatting with people as they passed and escorting potential buyers into the inviting warrens deep inside. The air itself seemed to buzz.

Outside the café that sold grilled lamb kebabs and vegetable korma, a line of people waited. They were young men in tailored and starched white shirts and tight black slacks; older men in long tunics, wool vests and baggy trousers, heads wrapped in turbans; and women of indeterminate age in shapeless grey and black burqas, some clutching the hands of small children. These were the people who lived here; this was their city. With a start, Cassie realized how odd and alien she was, an intruder in their world.

She and Marton stood patiently, not speaking, as the line inched forward. Marton brought out bills to procure six spears of hot meat nestled on two snowshoe-shaped pieces of naan. He handed the kebabs to her, so that he could carry a pot of hot tea and cups. Finding a table was impossible but his quick eye spotted two solitary chairs opening up along the back wall. He motioned with his chin.

Using the flat bread as a plate in her lap, Cassie was able to eat without spilling grease on the recently washed jeans. Marton had even less difficulty, as if he had been trained to eat on the run.

Almost instantly, Cassie felt better. Without a napkin, she sucked at her fingers to clean them. "I owe you my first-born," she joked. "Really, that may have been the best meal I ever had."

"Five star," Marton replied deadpan. It wasn't a quip but it was close.

Cassie put her empty tea cup down at her feet, wooden skewers sticking out. "You didn't get angry today," she observed. "I admit that surprises me. You were in such a hurry to leave, and yet here we are, back in Kabul."

"I'm irritated, of course." Marton's eyes swept over the café's clientele. "But angry? Anger is like a rabid tiger. You can't trust it, you can't control it." He turned back to her. "Better to keep it caged, don't you think?"

"I understand." She thought she did. She chewed her bottom lip. "Do you mind if I ask you a question? Who you are, what you do?"

He stared thoughtfully down at his hands. "I'm a man who gets things done." It was a statement of fact, not braggadocio.

"Clearly. But does this man have a name? A hometown? Danny calls you Zorro. Did you know that?"

Looking up at her, blue eyes startling in the café's bright light, he smiled slightly. "We'll trade. I'll answer your two personal questions if you answer two of mine."

Cassie didn't even hesitate. What could he possibly ask of her? She was an open book. She nodded.

"My name is Marton Zámbó. I'm Canadian," She started to inter-ject but he held up his hand. "I was born in Czechoslovakia, in the southern part, and emigrated when I was seventeen."

"Prague Spring, 1968." It was the only thing Cassie knew about Czechoslovakia: its brief period of liberalization that ended with the invasion of Soviet troops almost exactly a decade before. She recalled televised images of tanks rolling down streets, reports of people flee-ing to the West. Marton must have been among them. Perhaps that explained his scar, she thought.

Marton gave a somber nod, but before she could ask more, he continued, "I worked for a while in Canada and then I came here. Now I want to know about you, about why you're doing this. A wom-an traveling to such strange places?"

Jack had asked her a similar question and her answer was ready. "I always wanted to see the world. To travel overland, not by plane. I guess I believed my daydreams." Her tone was ironic, but it was true. She thought back to muggy summer afternoons staring at the gorgeous glossy photographs in *National Geographic*, tracing routes on richly detailed maps. Only much later did she become interested in the articles. It was the images that fascinated her, and the names of places: Madagascar, Samarkand, Kathmandu. With Jack, she had said more. With Marton, she felt too embarrassed to elaborate, to say out loud that the fantasies of youth had brought her here.

"So," he said at last, "You've seen a lot of the world. Disappointed?"

She considered the poverty she'd encountered, the sickness. They weren't in the glossy photographs. "Well, it isn't quite as I imagined it."

"Most westerners come here for drugs. No drugs for you?"

Cassie made a distasteful face.

Marton continued, "The boys did. Danny and Ralph."

"Not Ralph. He came to write. He came to be with me." Cassie's tone was flat and final.

Marton finished his tea and carefully placed his cup on the floor next to hers. "Of course he did. I have another personal question. Why do you dress like that?"

"Like what?" she asked, looking down at her striped cotton shirt and jeans.

Gesturing at her face and body, he searched for a suitable description. "Plain, drab. Eyeglasses, hair in a bun, baggy clothes."

"Plain, drab!?" She thought she looked pretty good. Frankly, the remark offended her, triggered an impulse to leave. But the evening crowd was thick between her and door. She glared at him. "Okay, because, first, I need glasses to see. Second, it's too damn hot to wear my hair down. Three, as for clothes, this is what I've got. Practical and modest for traveling in conservative places. What should I be wearing, a burqa?"

"You're a pretty woman. You should dress like one."

"Yeah, right." She recognized BS when she heard it. A sudden realization occurred to her: "Are you hitting on me?"

"Don't be absurd. Permit me another personal question."

Absurd? That sounded like another insult. "Nope. Sorry, you used up your personal questions."

He asked it anyway. "This Ralph. What do you see in him?"

The insolence of his question provoked her into answering. "I love him, as a matter of fact. As if it's any of your business."

"Yes, of course," he waved his hand dismissively, "But why?"

This time, she was too irate and confused to find the right words. She stood. "It's time I got back." She edged between two chairs and looked over her shoulder at him. "I'll pay you back tomorrow for the dinner," she said and made her way alone out of the café and back to the Jam Hotel.

The overhead light was still on when Cassie returned to the room. Ralph hadn't budged. She collapsed on the rug and stared a long while at his sleeping form. The short walk back had prompted some reflection. Did she know Ralph after all? Was their Great Love also a youthful fantasy? She thought back over the previous day, over the previous weeks.

She was too troubled to sleep; perhaps writing to Jack would calm her down. She picked up the stationery and a pen. Below the earlier entry, she added the day's date.

We headed to Herat this a.m. with 2 guys we met here, but their van broke down on the way & we all had to hitch a ride (with the van) back to where we started. That involved getting someone to stop (an ancient diesel truck), loading the van on its back (without a ramp), push-starting the diesel truck (after it died too) & then off-loading the van (again without a ramp). Hours & hours & hours later, we're back at the Jam hotel. One of the guys seems okay, Danny Mack from California. Ralph likes him. The van's owner is a Canadian who escaped from Czechoslovakia named Marton Zambo. He's kind of an asshole. So we may take a bus to Herat instead of waiting for the van to be fixed. Haven't decided.

Meanwhile, I'm glad we're back - a chance to explore Kabul. The city really comes to life once fasting ends for the day. We walked through Chicken Street tonight - mysterious & strange, like a Peter Lorre/ Sydney Greenstreet movie.

At this pace, we should reach Istanbul in mid-Sept. & stay a few weeks. You told me you always wanted to go there. Now's your chance! I know you have the dog & the dissertation, but if you can, please come. I'd love to see you. I'll send a date & place to meet in my next letter, just in case.

Meanwhile, it's hot! Send ice cream!

Love, Cassie

She reread the letter, at the last minute underlining *please come*. She was surprised at how cheered she felt at the faint prospect of seeing Jack Hunter again.

CHAPTER FOUR

March 12, 2007

Monday

Jack woke early and went for a run through the neighborhood. Over the weekend, he'd spent too much time sitting – at the conference, on the long flight home – and now he needed to shake out his joints and get his heart pounding. He sensed endorphins pulsing through his veins, the best kind of drug. They made up for the dull ache in his knees. They shook cobwebs from his head, too. That's how he thought of it, the sticky moodiness that had wrapped itself around his neural pathways recently.

Last night with Helene had definitely helped. She had seemed glad to see him. She had even made lasagna, his favorite dish, and opened a bottle of Chianti Classico. They talked a lot, mostly about her progress in the lab. After cleaning up the kitchen, they went upstairs hand in hand; they made love.

It wasn't the rousing tumble of their youth, but lovemaking was still glorious, perhaps more so now that they had been together so long. He knew her body so intimately it felt like his own. She was part of him.

Part of him. He hadn't always felt this way. Helene was reserved by nature, even aloof. But he knew it rose from deep insecurity. Her parents, he thought now, were cruel, demanding perfection from her even when she was just a child. As an adult, she replicated the pattern, demanding perfection in the world around her. That made life difficult sometimes, especially for their children. Most especially for their daughter, Sandy. Home life was less tense now that the kids were grown and gone.

Jack himself had long since figured out a way to live peaceably with the lioness. It came out of an admission she once made, that she never felt good enough. She had made that rare confession during their one session of marriage counseling together, eight years earlier. She hadn't returned but he had gone another time or two. No matter; their relationship improved after that. His eyes had opened to her fear, her vulnerability. He learned to be supportive but set boundaries; to concede most of the time, but hold firm on important matters. Now he felt protective of her. Helene, after all, could be her own worst enemy.

This morning, by the time he returned from the run, she had gone. She'd be at the lab all day. He regretted missing her; he had intended to ask her out to lunch. Especially after last night, he realized they needed to spend more time together.

He had an idea. Later today, he'd pick up sandwiches at their favorite deli and surprise her with lunch at the lab. She was busy, he knew, but she had to eat sometime. Even seeing her briefly would be something; they could make plans for a date later in the week. They hadn't gone out on a real date in years.

Showered and dressed, Jack headed to the office. He had made the drive so many times from this house that he did it without thinking. He parked in almost the same spot every day, walked through the same door into the building, up the same stairwell. As usual, he waved at colleagues he saw through their open office doors. In the main department office, he emptied his stuffed mailbox. So much collected there in just the few days of his absence. Estella, the administrative assistant, was on the phone but she grinned when she saw him and waved.

This was a great life, he realized as he opened his office door. Even the partly filled boxes on the floor didn't discourage him this morning. He could return to the task of packing up later. Now he had to finish grading the essays submitted by his presidency students last week. He had carted the essays with him to Las Vegas but had only gotten halfway through. Too much else to think about and do. Today he had no excuses. He had promised he would return the papers tomorrow, and he was serious about meeting that promise. Furthermore, tomorrow was the last day to withdraw from classes, and a few students could use an extra indication of how they were doing academically before deciding to stay. It wasn't an easy course, he knew, but he hoped they would stick with it. He could work with them individually if they needed.

Jack closed his office door to avoid interruptions and settled down to grade. Three hours later, he was finished. His hand felt cramped from clutching his pen (he always graded with pen in hand; green ink, not red. Red was too discouraging). He usually made a lot of comments, provided a lot of feedback. He hoped his students would read them.

He finished entering the grades in his course book just as a knock came on his office door. The door wasn't locked; Ben stuck his head into the room.

"Welcome back! Want to grab a bite to eat?"

Lunchtime already? Jack checked his watch. Not quite. He smiled at his friend and longtime colleague, one of his favorite people in the world. "I'd love to but I'll be dining with a beautiful woman today," he announced theatrically.

"And where might this romantic rendezvous occur?" Ben grinned.

Jack laughed. "The most exclusive venue in town: Helene's lab. Sandwiches from the Good Belly Deli."

"She's a lucky woman," his friend said. "Mind if I tag along to the deli? I'll get something too."

"Excellent idea. We can catch up," he responded, grabbing a light jacket.

Jack drove the short distance. He would have walked – the two of them had made this walk many times over the years – but Ben had recently had knee surgery. On the way, his friend regaled him with stories about the Faculty Senate meeting, the dean's most recent vendetta, and a proposal being floated to raise tuition. Jack grimaced, then he recounted their young colleague's successful panel, updates on friends at other campuses, and the dinner with Frank. Ben was especially interested in Frank's work at the White House. He supervised undergraduate internships and thought Frank might provide entrée for their students.

As he parked at the deli, Jack wondered if he should divulge his crisis of faith at the conference, as he was coming to think of it. But thankfully the crisis was over.

Fifteen minutes later, he dropped off Ben and parked at the biology building. Helene's lab was on the third floor, and Jack took the stairs. Walking down the impersonal hallway, he noticed that office doors were closed and no students were about. He presumed most people were at lunch.

Deli bag in hand, he approached the door to Helene's lab and saw with relief that it was slightly ajar, indicating that she was still there. He grinned at the thought of surprising her with a Reuben on rye. A movement inside the lab caught his eye and he paused.

At first, he didn't understand what he was seeing. There was Helene, her back to door, bent over a microscope, and there was the post doc fellow, Brad something, next to her, his hand caressing her bottom. As Jack watched, his wife swatted Brad's hand away. She hadn't shouted in indignation. She hadn't seemed shocked at all. She hadn't even looked up from the microscope. The caress was so familiar that Jack understood in a moment that far more intimate encounters had occurred between them. He felt nauseated.

The bag fell to the floor. He turned and quickly retraced his steps down the corridor. His legs were so unsteady that he thought he might not make it down the stairs. His hand shook as he unlocked the car. Only when he found himself inside did anger crash over him.

"God damn fucking son of a bitch!" he screamed and punched the steering wheel. He slumped over it, heart pounding, eyes squeezed shut, overcome with shock and fury. Already, his brain was trying to reconcile what he had seen with his image of Helene and their marriage. Surely he had misunderstood the gesture. She was so absorbed in her work that she didn't notice Brad's touch. Brad had only brushed against her, nothing sexual at all. But Jack knew these were wishful lies. He considered storming up the stairs and into her lab, smashing his fist into the postdoc's face.

And then the awful wave of outrage receded, leaving him exhausted and stranded. He sat staring at the wheel several minutes more before he finally started the car engine and slowly drove home.

He unlocked the back door and blinked at the homey kitchen, the most ordinary room in the house. The scene looked alien, full of treachery. When he noticed the lasagna pan still on the dish drying rack, he felt the rage return in force, mingled with fear that last night's dinner and sex had been part of the deception.

Suddenly, he couldn't stand being there and rushed for the stairs, taking two at a time to his second-floor office. When he slammed the door shut, he could finally breathe again; this was his space, his lair.

His office was tucked into an alcove, with the roof line sharply angling down toward the edges of the room. A comfortably stuffed reading chair was placed in a low corner near the room's single window. Bookshelves filled the rest of the wall space, ingeniously constructed to fit the angled walls. Dominating the center of the room was an ancient oak table, deeply scarred, which he used as a desk.

Jack fell heavily into the stuffed chair. He knew he had to think about this, but his brain felt dazed and useless. He dropped his face into his hands. A minute; he'd give himself a minute to recover. Then he would think about what to do next.

More than a minute passed. It was almost four when a sound downstairs roused him from his torpor. He emerged from the fog still furious and hurting but with a clearer mind. He knew he had to face Helene. She'd be angry and defensive at first; that was her way. She might blame him for being inattentive; she might assert she was seduced by a younger man. Eventually, though, she'd be contrite and affirm her love for him. Eventually, she'd ask to be forgiven.

"HOW WAS YOUR day," Helene said, dropping a plastic bag of groceries on the kitchen table. The question lacked a question mark; it sounded perfunctory to Jack's ears, a meaningless courtesy. He didn't answer. He passed her and retrieved a bottle of Laphroaig from the cabinet, an expensive scotch reserved for special occasions. He poured a finger of liquor into a water glass, and sat at the table.

She glanced at him. "Drinking already?" she asked, turning to the refrigerator, putting away cucumbers, tomatoes, zucchini. Her mouth set tightly; she didn't approve of drinking before dark. She turned from the refrigerator and saw his expression.

"What?" Her voice was peeved, conveying the sense that his day had surely not been as taxing as hers.

Seething, Jack looked directly at her. "I know about you and Brad." He let the sentence hang there for a minute. He swallowed a mouthful of the golden liquor.

Yanking out another chair, Helene sat across from him and frowned. "You think you know, Jack."

He swallowed more scotch. The smoky burn hurt his throat; pain felt empowering. He didn't reply.

"Who told you that? I think I can guess who'd have a motive to lie." She crossed her arms over her chest, a classic Helene posture.

He gaped at her, amazed at her deceit. "I saw it. I saw it," he repeated. "Brad groped your ass yet miraculously is still alive. Explain that to me." Jack knew an unwelcome grab would be grounds for homicide in his wife's eyes.

"Oh, please. You're imagining things. The lab's small and he just brushed against me."

Jack didn't have the energy to argue. Helene was adept at turning the tables. He shook his head and took another drink to harden his resolve. He needed to know if this was a new affair. "How many times?" he asked.

"What do you mean?" she replied aggressively.

His tone matching hers, he answered curtly, "Sex, Helene. That's what I mean. Sex."

She snapped back, "You want to know about sex, Jack? You want to know how many men I've screwed? Is that what you're asking?"

She probably intended to sound indignant, profoundly wronged by his question. But her response alarmed him. In a low growl, he asked, "There were others?"

Her eyes widened but this time she didn't reply. He understood instantly.

"There were others," he stated. The ground was shifting again beneath him. His face must have shown that.

His wife stood and rapidly moved to the counter. Her movements were quick and jagged, a marionette with tangled strings. In sudden fury, she turned on him. "You have some nerve, playing the aggrieved husband! You started this whole fucking mess!"

Her outrage shocked him, stoked his own. He had to wait before speaking to get his voice under control. Slowly, firmly, he replied, "I never cheated on you in all of the years of our marriage. Never."

"Our entire marriage is based on a lie. You only married me because your precious love abandoned you. I was the concession prize, Jack. Me." Seeing his puzzled expression, she added, "I know about you and that girl. You were going to leave me, school, everything for her." She sat again and grabbed his glass of scotch; emptied it. Her expression was savage. He had never seen her like this and it frightened him.

"What the hell do you mean?" Helene couldn't be serious.

Breathing heavily, she said nothing. She seemed in no hurry to explain.

Finally, he said, "Do you mean Cassie? Almost thirty years ago? Before we were married? Before we were even engaged?!"

"You would have run away if I hadn't stopped you," she asserted. "Even then, you only married me out of…"

He interrupted, trying to sound logical. "We wrote letters, that's all. A handful of letters. There was never anything between us. I loved you." Why was he defending himself? She was the duplicitous one. He had to ask, "And why didn't you bring this up eight years ago in therapy, if it's been bothering you so goddamn much?"

"Because you and the therapist ganged up on me." She could sound so matter-of-fact.

"Nobody ganged up on you. I can't believe this, Helene. You sleep around and it's my fault?! Because thirty years ago I sent a few letters to a friend I haven't seen since? This is crazy, even for you."

She ignored the jab, instead spitting out, "I was a kid. I trusted you. You said I was special, a treasure. That's what you called me. You were my knight in shining armor. Ha!" She leaned forward in her chair and Jack, instinctively, pulled back. "And just like that you would ruin my life. I had to stop you and I did. And then I thought, okay, water under the bridge, we'll get married. Yet years later, here you are, still pining for her."

"That's bull…," Jack started to answer.

"Last Thursday, Estelle let me into your office to pick up that book on academic freedom you told me about. Guess what I found on the shelf? The envelope of letters that you promised you'd thrown away. Before Sandy was born. How do you think that made me feel, Jack? You promised. So, yes, that night I was in bed with Brad. One betrayal for another. That's how it's your goddamn fault."

Jack was confounded. She had succeeded in putting him on the defensive. "I admit I shouldn't have kept them, but so what? They're only letters. I'd forgotten about them. I only discovered them last week when I was packing up the office. I was going to throw them away." He hated his apologetic tone. His voice started rising. "And how do you conclude that I was going to ruin your life? You're the one who broke things off back then, not me." He thought he remembered it correctly. His memories were confusing, a blend of the actual and the imagined.

Helene seemed to harbor no such doubts about her memory. "You were ready, weren't you? Just waiting for her to give the command. Where was it, Istanbul?" She poured more scotch into the glass and drank it.

Istanbul. Like a punch. Jack knew what she was talking about. It wasn't infidelity on his part. Helene had already walked out; she needed space, she said. And he remembered the dog – Sherlock! – had been hit by a car. Sherlock's death had almost killed him. Then a letter from Cassie had arrived about meeting her in Istanbul. He had wanted to go so badly. The trip would save him, would open up a whole new world, a whole new way of being. He talked with his dissertation adviser about taking a year off. He was just waiting for Cassie to send the details.

Jack dropped his head in his hands. "Yes, I wanted to go. But not for Cassie. For the trip. I just wanted to see the world," he said miserably.

Even as he said it, he realized the statement wasn't entirely true. He had imagined a romance blooming once he saw her again. But it had never happened. All he had gotten from Cassie was that cryptic postcard blowing him off. Not long afterward, a month or two, Helene had come back and moved in; half a year later, she'd suggested marriage.

Helene's rage and sense of betrayal were incomprehensible to him now after what she had done. His own anger resurged. He sat bolt upright on the hard kitchen chair. "And I didn't leave, did I? I married you. I was the faithful and dutiful husband. The cuckold." He took a bigger swallow of scotch than he intended and almost choked, but he needed to wash the bitterness out of his mouth.

"Only because that girl didn't write you back." Helene said it almost triumphantly, as if it was the winning answer in a contest. She must have had this conversation in her head many times, Jack thought with a start, to be so prepared. She leveled her most dispassionate, scientific gaze at him, one that brooked no dissent. "You know it's true."

A troubling thought occurred to him, and he dropped his eyes to the smudged glass of scotch. How did she know if Cassie wrote back or not? In fact, how the hell did Helene know about Istanbul? That he was thinking about leaving? He had certainly never told her.

In an instant, Jack recalled a conversation years before with his teenaged daughter Sandy. She'd been outraged when she discovered that her mother was looking through her emails. "Make her stop," she pleaded with him. He countered with something like "she only does it because she loves you and is worried about you." Sandy had disagreed, even as he had tried to explain it from a parent's point of view. His daughter would have none of that, calling her mother noisy and controlling. Then Sandy said something that had stayed with him, but buried, for all the years since. "She does it to you too, Dad, but you don't notice." He had gotten really angry with her then, even told her to shut up, breaking one of his cardinal parenting rules. Afterwards, ashamed of his reaction, he had put the entire conversation out of his mind. Until now.

Surely Helene had not read his correspondence. Was not reading it now. He was hiding no covert life. She was welcome to read whatever she wanted to; she only had to ask. But going behind his back? Snooping on him? That violated his fundamental sense of privacy.

Jack felt as if his mind had been in a daze for a long time. Puzzle pieces from lost or misplaced memories were only now falling into place. A picture was emerging of that time long ago. He had been waiting weeks for the promised letter from Cassie. Sometime in there, Helene had dropped by his apartment. They had been uneasy with each other; she only wanted to borrow a textbook. Did she stay long? He didn't think so. But the mail might have come in. A letter might have been waiting in the mail box.

He looked at Helene in a new way. "That time you came by, after we broke up. Did you open my mail?"

Now it was Helene who had the presence of mind not to answer. She walked toward the sink and looked out of the window for several seconds. The apricot tree was blooming early this spring. The scene was exquisite: her classic profile, her thick dark hair, framed so beautifully against the delicate pink-white of the apricot blooms. This is the moment, Jack thought, what she says next will determine everything.

Helene turned to face him. Her expression was softer, her tone conciliatory and reasonable. "Jack, darling, it's no one's fault. I'm just saying we're both to blame. We both..."

Jack stood abruptly, startling Helene into silence, startling himself. "I'm sick of your bullshit," he announced, as much to himself as to her. He took his glass and the bottle, and stalked up the stairs.

TOMORROW. HE DREADED tomorrow. Perhaps he would die in his sleep, he thought in hopeful despair. Hours passed; night fell. He stared mournfully at the surface of the old table buried under paper. Gradually, his eyes focused on individual pieces. Various drafts of the conference talk, a file folder of old lecture notes, the stack of multiple choice exams for tomorrow's freshman class. He'd left the presidency papers in his campus office.

He still had classes to teach. Jack's brain began to operate without his volition. Not his limbic system; he knew his emotions were off-line. But the part of the brain that arranges things, solves problems – the frontal lobe – was still working. It informed the rest of his brain that tomorrow was doable. The freshman course was taken care of. He could duck out as soon as the exams were distributed, leaving his teaching assistant to proctor and grade them. His graduate seminar in American politics was Wednesday evening; that was in the far distant future and he would worry about that later. But tomorrow afternoon was the upper division presidency class. He could return their papers - thank heavens he had finished grading - but he really should lecture as well. The students had already lost a day last Thursday when he had canceled class to go to the conference. Yet his mind was too agitated to prepare new notes. He checked the syllabus. They were starting the section on the presidency and congress. The first lecture would be more historical and constitutional. He knew that material well; old notes would do. By Thursday's class, hopefully, he would be thinking more clearly. The following week was spring break. A reprieve.

He couldn't let his personal life upset his professional. He had to keep going. Even if he was a wreck. He glanced at the bottle of scotch, grateful that he hadn't continued to drink. His head was fuzzy enough.

Now he needed sleep. He'd use the guest room down the hall. He would think about Helene and everything else after classes tomorrow.

IT WAS THREE in the morning. The light of the clock penetrated the room's darkness. Jack felt cold, even under the extra blanket he'd thrown over the guest bed. He could not sleep, despite his crushing exhaustion. He tried closing his eyes again and ordering his brain to turn off. Instead, the day's events played in an endless loop in his mind. He thought he would feel furious, but anger was dissipating, leaving in its wake wrenching grief and deep sadness; and, just at the edge, relief.

He gave up on sleep. He went downstairs to the kitchen, thinking milk might help. Once on the first floor, he noticed the light was on. Helene was sitting at the kitchen table, unable to sleep as well.

Standing in the doorway, he asked the question that had been bothering him all night. "Do you love me, Helene? Did you ever?" What was real, he wondered, and what was false in their marriage?

She spoke without looking up. "Of course I did, Jack. I loved you." She didn't use the present tense, he noticed. Glancing up at him, she added, "There were only two. Brad and someone I met at a conference about eight years ago, before we went to that counselor. Both affairs were brief, and didn't mean anything to me. I want you to know that."

He absorbed the information. He was unsure how to respond. Only two affairs, as if that excused the betrayal. Yet somehow, he did feel a little less betrayed. He still did not understand Helene's real motive. Was it anger at some perceived slight? Was it dislike, boredom? Or perhaps her reason had nothing to do with him. Perhaps she was driven by vanity, succumbing to flattery when men succumbed to her beauty. Ego, the belief that she did not have to follow the rules of ordinary mortals. Fear, because she was getting older. Out of this silent litany of possible explanations, one word came out of his mouth, "Why?"

She looked up as he leaned against the kitchen door frame. "I've been wondering that myself, trying to dissect my own heart." Helene smiled ruefully, "I always wanted to do open heart surgery." Serious again, she unconsciously brushed a hand through her loose hair and continued. "I think it's because I wanted you to adore me and you couldn't. I wasn't so special after all."

Her answer disconcerted him. He had always thought of himself as loving and supportive. Her revelation left him wondering how much he really knew about her, the marriage, himself. For the first time, he wondered, "You haven't been happy for a long time, have you?"

She studied him a moment. "No," she replied.

Even though he was expecting it, the word still cut. But she was no longer lying and he had to be grateful for that.

"And you?" she asked.

"Me? For the most part, yes, I was happy. Oblivious, I guess. A clueless jerk." True, she had deceived him, but he had been complicit, assuming everything was all right with her because everything was all right with him. What kind of a marriage was that?

She shook her head no. "Never a jerk. You're a nice man, Jack. A really decent human being."

He shrugged uncomfortably. It sounded like a eulogy, the sort of thing one might say about a deceased friend. In a sense, though, a eulogy was appropriate, he realized. Trust was dead. It was time to mourn.

Helene seemed to read his thoughts. "I don't want a divorce," she said. It was a statement of fact, not a plea or a question.

"I do," he said simply. He hadn't planned to say that. He only realized the truth of it as the words came from his mouth. Everything she had said this early morning hadn't changed that.

She looked at him; he could see the quick flash of surprise and hurt, then the resignation. She dropped her head into her arms. Those lovely arms, covered in the sleeves of a purple silk robe he'd given her last Christmas. He waited. After a minute or two, she raised her head again. "Tell me the truth. Was there something between you and that girl? Did you love her?"

Back to Cassie, he thought wearily. He lowered his head and considered his bare feet on the kitchen floor, pale feet against pale tile. "Let it go, Helene. I didn't love her. I forgot about her a long time ago."

She studied his face and read something else there. "Liar," she said gently. "Maybe you believe that but I don't. All those letters. I saw them pile up on your desk. I saw your eagerness when the mail arrived. How you'd spend hours writing a reply, each one a labor of love." Helene pushed back from the table. "I know you also loved me, Jack. I just wanted you to love me best."

Jack winced at the sadness in her voice. He wondered if she was right, that not only did he love Cassie, but he loved her the most. That thought triggered an ancient sorrow in him. None of that mattered now. He had lost Cassie; now he was losing Helene.

"I gave you all the love I had." He knew this much was true. Implicit was an apology; that he was sorry it wasn't enough.

Helene sighed deeply, then continued, "Well, I guess I should tell you something." She stopped speaking for several seconds.

He dreaded her confession. "Don't, please. I don't want to know about Brad or the other man. I accept some fault for all this."

Stubbornly, she pushed ahead. "You didn't do anything wrong. I did. From the beginning. You need to know."

He held up his hand to stop her; she didn't need to castigate herself, not for his sake. But she kept talking. "I know you thought she forgot about you."

His hand dropped. Holding his breath, he waited.

"She wrote to you. I found her letter just as you said, when I came by your apartment after we broke up. I was miserable. I wanted to come back and needed to see if you missed me, too. Then I saw the letter in your mailbox with an Iranian stamp. I took it. I only got through the first sentence, something about meeting you in Istanbul. I just couldn't believe it. Later on, I realized it was the letter you were waiting for."

He dimly understood what she was saying. "You found the letter and you tore it up."

"Please understand; I was so distraught. I couldn't stand her writing to you. I had to stop her. So I didn't just tear it up. I wrote back, to General Delivery in Istanbul. I told her you were dead." She took a deep breath. "I did what I had to do. What I thought I had to do."

A minute passed as this sunk in. "Oh, Helene," Jack said, his voice a deep groan in his chest.

Her words spilled out in a torrent. "It was a huge mistake. I know that. Not only was it cruel to you and to her. I'll admit that and I'm sorry. But it also made you wonder about her, yearn for her. And you did, the whole first year of our marriage. It was only after Sandy was born that you seemed content. And it hurt me too. I felt I had tricked you into marrying me. How could I ever be certain that you would have chosen me; how could I ever feel secure? And then when I found those damn letters last week...."

Jack could not speak. This news – on top of the other revelations - overwhelmed him. His hands were hot and balled into fists. But the rest of him was ice. One dazed thought broke through: he had to get away so that he would not break down here, in front of her. Blind with anguish, he turned and stumbled up the stairs, going as quickly as frozen feet could, gripping the handrail the entire way.

CHAPTER FIVE

August 25, 1978

Friday

Waking with the dawn call to prayer, Cassie listened for a few moments and considered what she and Ralph could do today. It was a Friday during Ramadan, and most places would be closed. She thought she remembered that Kabul had a history museum; they could try there. But it was much too early, not even six yet. She sighed as the darkness of the room and Ralph's heavy breathing lulled her back to sleep.

Daylight was streaming through the thin curtain when she woke again She checked her watch; past eight already. Ralph, she knew, could easily sleep another hour, but Cassie was ready to rise. Not wanting to disturb him, she slipped out of bed and dressed quickly. *Back soon. Gone to find us breakfast*, she scribbled on a note, signing off with a heart. Then she quietly left the room and the hotel.

Outside, she headed toward Chicken Street. It was largely deserted now, so silent that the previous night's festive crowd might have been a dream. Cassie strolled the length of the street marveling at its transformation. The air smelled clean. Human activity this morning –

even on this usually busy shopping street - was simply too languid to kick up dust.

Cafés were closed until noon and so were the shops. But that didn't discourage her from looking in windows at karakul coats, carpets, antique musical instruments, silks, lapis lazuli –luxuries since the days of Darius of Persia. She wasn't serious about buying. The colors and patterns and strangeness attracted her, but not the idea of ownership. If she owned such fabulous things, she would have to take care of them, a burden she didn't want.

A handful of sidewalk entrepreneurs started setting up. A turbaned man squatted near a large aluminum pot placed on a makeshift burner. Propped against the pot was a hand-lettered sign in Cyrillic and English advertising *shorwa*; the smell of lamb broth and coriander filled Cassie's nostrils. Halfway down the block, a slender young man in traditional brown tunic arranged pears in baskets strapped to a donkey. Another vendor laid out stacks of freshly baked naan. They glanced around, waiting patiently for potential customers to drift past. She hadn't decided yet what to buy for breakfast, and continued walking.

Three men in casual western attire stood on the sidewalk in friendly argument. Short blond hair, erect postures; she guessed they were off-duty Soviet military. They paused and assessed Cassie as she passed, then one made a comment in Russian and the others laughed. Continuing past them made her feel oddly brave and adventurous.

Extending her explorations, she left Chicken Street. A block north was a park with trees and acres of rich green lawn, largely empty this morning. A young Afghan couple in modern dress strolled past, holding the hands of a toddler between them. In the distance rose the blue dome of a mosque, a cobalt sky above. She wished she had brought her camera. A sign pointed to tennis courts and a film theater. She didn't track them down; instead, she found an unoccupied bench and sat in the shade, her body relaxing into the warm morning. Ralph would like this park, she thought. She should get him. Yet she didn't move. She relished these extraordinary minutes alone.

Cassie was out on her own for one of the first times since starting the journey. Invariably, she explored with someone else, usually Ralph, before that Becky in Bangkok. She realized she liked being alone. It opened up options; it affirmed her image of herself as independent and free.

Forty minutes later, she finally stood. Ralph should be awake by now, she thought and walked back to the pear merchant with the donkey. Into her large tote bag she packed several pieces of the ripe yellow fruit. She decided against *shorwa* for breakfast and instead joined the short line waiting to buy bread.

Cassie was passing through the Jam's lounge when she noticed Ralph already dressed and sitting with Danny. She was happy to see them, even Danny. After the grueling day before, she felt a certain camaraderie with him, as if they truly were a company of explorers in a distant land. Breaking bread together reinforced that sense.

She rested the tote bag on the edge of the table and cleared a space for the food between half-empty bottles of Coke and beer. Involuntarily, she thought of Ralph's diminishing travel funds. But this time, instead of frustration with his fecklessness, she resolved not to worry. If he ran out of money, he would be fine; his parents would wire him more. Her folks were not affluent, so that wasn't an option. She had to guard her cash reserves. Except for small luxuries like this shared breakfast.

Ralph smiled and stood awkwardly as she approached. Swaying a little, he pulled out a chair for her, a chivalrous gesture, she thought. Unpacking her bag, she pronounced grandly, "Breakfast is served, gentlemen. Bon appetit."

The men broke into the naan and sorted through the golden pears. Content, Cassie found a perfectly ripe pear for herself.

"Thanks, sweetheart," Ralph mumbled. "You always save the day." She brushed his arm lovingly.

"Yeah, thanks, sweetheart," Danny grinned, food in his teeth.

Without further talking, they quickly consumed the meal. Cassie mildly regretted not getting more; she knew Ralph had eaten very little the day before. But the men seemed satisfied.

Danny belched. A mischievous smirk played along the edge of his mouth. "Say, Cassie, we were talking about the women of Afghanistan. I think they're the most beautiful women in the world. Ralph says Scandinavian women are. What do you think?"

A silly question, she thought, but she'd play along. "I don't know about Scandinavia, but some of the women here are really stunning. At least those I've seen. A lot of women are wrapped up in those burqas and they just look hot."

"My point exactly." Danny rolled his eyes at Ralph.

She lightly chided him. "You know what I mean. Can you imagine what that feels like in this heat? With the full-face covering? They must be roasting under those things."

"Not if they're naked!" Danny almost squealed. "I was telling Ralph this fantasy of mine that women don't wear anything underneath."

His mischievous mood was infectious. Cassie gave a mock scowl, "You've got a dirty mind, Mr. Mack."

Suddenly amused, Ralph chuckled. "What if she's, like, a hundred years old? It's not like you can tell, right? You ask for a kiss and she lifts her veil, and then what?"

Danny laughed too and rummaged through the debris until he located the last pear. He ate in silence a moment, then adopted a tragic tone. "No, seriously. I am so horny. I haven't gotten laid since that temple thing I told you about, Ralph. What's that been, almost a month? Celibacy is ruining my health." He trained large pleading eyes on Cassie.

She snorted good-naturedly and waved him off, "Fat chance! I'm not that much of a humanitarian."

Danny made a comical sad face.

Ralph cocked his head in thought. "That could explain why Marton's so uptight. He isn't getting laid."

"He isn't getting laid because he's a jerk," Cassie said pointedly.

Ralph came to his defense. "He's not so bad."

Danny shook his head, "I don't think he's even tried. In the couple of weeks I've known him, he's never once looked at a woman." Pear finished, he found a few breadcrumbs on the table and scooped them into his mouth. "He doesn't like them," he observed. When he saw Ralph's expression, he quickly added, "Hey, man, he doesn't like guys, either. He doesn't like people in general. He's not gay. I'd know."

Marton walked up at that moment. "What do you know, Danny?"

Ralph and Danny exchanged looks and broke out in hysterics. Marton's lips tightened.

Cassie was getting peeved; what was up with them? Frowning at Ralph, she opted to edit their conversation. "They were talking about the beauty of Afghan women, Marton." She added disapprovingly, "They're drunk. At ten in the morning."

Marton looked again at the two men. "They're stoned," he said and turned to leave the lounge.

Stoned? Cassie regarded Ralph, then Danny. Both men were slumped in their chairs, still giggling. Marton was right, she realized and wondered angrily what Ralph was thinking. It was one thing to smoke dope at home, but here? The legal system was so different and they couldn't even speak the language. And what if the weed was tainted?

"Ralph," she demanded, "Are you smoking pot?"

Examining a pear core, he pursed his lips and shook his head.

"Yes, you are. You're high as a kite."

"It's not pot," was all he said. His words sounded slurred. She hadn't noticed it earlier.

"Okay, hashish." She had heard somewhere it was more concentrated. Ralph only laughed. Then Cassie detected a faint sweet smoke in the air. It didn't smell like marijuana. "Opium?" she whispered. "Please tell me it's not opium. That's poison." Apprehension was replacing anger.

He lifted his gaze from the pear to her face. "*Au contraire, ma chérie*," he asserted in a fake accent. The French backpackers at a table nearby gave hostile glares before returning to their discussion. In a lower voice, he said conspiratorially, "Cassie, this is amazing shit. You've got to try it."

She felt sick. "Opium is dangerous. I'm serious, Ralph. It's addictive." She tried to keep her voice low as well.

He grinned slyly like a boy reassuring a fretful parent. "I'm fine. Better than fine. I feel terrific! And I'm only trying it this once. For the life experience."

For only a moment, she wondered if he was right. He did seem relaxed. She knew so little about narcotics.

Danny had drifted off to sleep. Now, glassy-eyed and dopey, he awoke and smiled at her. "If I said you had a beautiful body, would you hold it against me?"

His clumsy flirtation wasn't funny anymore. "Old joke, Danny. Go back to sleep," she directed him. He clearly was a heavy user; he was to blame for the opium. Was this Ralph's future also? A sharp edge of disappointment scratched at her confidence in him, in their relationship. Who was Ralph, at his core? She had thought she knew.

Last year, she'd gone with him to the Boston marathon and watched, spellbound, his long and easy stride as he passed so many others. Another recollection came, of Ralph entertaining her friends at a French Quarter party with an impression of Darth Vader ordering pizza. Then the memory of him writing all night, in the morning sharing his story: a moving account of a boy accepting his father's death. The Ralph she knew was athletic, funny, gifted. He didn't do drugs. Where was that man now?

She pressed him, "You're such a wonderful writer. It's what you always wanted to be. It's your dream. Opium will destroy it."

Ralph eagerly leaned toward her. "That's just it! Opium is making me see things in new ways. The ideas coming at me are mind-blowing! I'm keeping notes, see?" he brandished a small piece of paper she hadn't noticed before. On it were scratches and hieroglyphics in black ink. "You know what they call it when you inhale the smoke through a straw? Chasing a dragon!" He added significantly, "I've decided to put a dragon in my novel. Brilliant, isn't it?"

A dragon? Before now, he had regarded himself a literary writer, scorning commercial considerations. Even his interest in fantasy and science fiction was intellectual, with Isaac Asimov and Arthur C. Clarke his models. But now he was talking in exclamation points about dragons, and Cassie felt her concern for him morph into alarm. "No, it's not brilliant. It has nothing to do with your plotline or characters."

"I can change my plotline and characters," he replied stubbornly.

She searched for the words to convince him, "That's juvenile stuff, Ralph. Not like the serious work you say you want to write."

Her criticism irked him. He straightened his shoulders and gave her a hard clinical look. "You are so wrong. I suddenly can see the essence of things. And I can see you, too. Uptight and controlling as usual."

Cassie was stunned by the resentment in his voice. "Ralph! I ..."

"Loosen up," he advised in a low growl. "You need this shit more than I do. Ask Danny."

Almost believing that he was right about her, Cassie felt her eyes begin to tear. Almost as quickly, she knew he was wrong. She recalled her quarrel with Becky months before, when her friend said Ralph manipulated people to get his way, and Cassie deferred too much. Becky might have been right after all. Cassie tightened her mouth and glared at Ralph. He didn't notice.

Hearing his name, Danny roused himself and knocked over an empty bottle of beer. Its crash on the floor startled him. "Whoa!" he cried. Then, licking his lips, he scrutinized the table. "Anything else to eat?"

"You know what I miss?" Ralph said rhetorically. "Steak. We had water buffalo in Nepal but I haven't tasted real beef in months. God what I'd give for a cheeseburger and fries right now."

"Shhh," Danny interjected fretfully. "That's evil to Hindus."

After scanning the room, Ralph squinted at him. "There's no Hindus here."

Danny was adamant. "There's me. Cows are sacred, man. I'd never eat a cow. Well, not anymore. And some Hindus even get violent about it, beating people up and stuff." When Ralph made a face, Danny continued. "No, really. Marton and me, we heard about this Muslim guy killed by a mob in India. Beaten to death because of a rumor he'd eaten beef. And he hadn't even!"

Ralph scoffed. "That's ridiculous," he argued. "It's not the Middle Ages. People don't do that nowadays."

"Sure they do. Ask Marton. He heard it too. Almost every bone in the guy's body broken. Marton'll tell you."

Ralph was appalled. "For a burger? God, that's depressing." He dropped his head to the table.

Suddenly subdued as well, Danny agreed, "Yeah, sorry, man."

Leaning back in her seat, Cassie had been listening to their interchange. Her anger had subsided, morphing again into worry. The drugs were to blame, she thought. When the story of mob violence seemed to bring Ralph down a little, she saw a chance to try reasoning again.

"Listen, Ralph. I discovered a pretty park not far away. Let's go there. We can talk, we can get some lunch, just the two of us. We can pick up bus tickets for Herat for tomorrow. Start heading to Europe." He had been excited about seeing Europe.

At first, Ralph didn't respond, but in a minute he lifted his head and looked at her. "I'm sorry, babe. I don't know why I said that shit about you." Then he added, "I don't feel so hot."

Cassie felt encouraged. "I'll get us some tea, okay? It'll make you feel better." Standing up, she turned to Danny. "Tea for you, too?"

"Sure, cool," Ralph said vaguely and Danny nodded.

"Back in a minute." She wove her way through the tables to the makeshift bar and approached the young counter attendant. Remembering him from their first day, she asked his name. He looked a little surprised. To most of the Jam's clientele, he was invisible. To the others, he was the Boy Who Served Drinks.

"Farshad," he answered simply.

"Hello, Farshad," she said, "I'm Cassie. Three cups of chai, please." She glanced back at the table and saw the men talking in low solemn tones. The opium high seemed to have passed. She felt almost giddy with relief.

The attendant carefully poured hot liquid from an aluminum teapot into three tulip shaped glasses. He stirred in cardamom, milk and sugar, and placed the glasses on small white saucers, and the saucers on a tray. With a nod of his head, he passed Cassie the tray.

"How do I say thanks?" she asked. "In Persian, I mean?"

He considered. "There are many ways. You can say *tashakor mikonam, moteshakkeram, sepasgozaram, mamnoon am.*" The words sounded like exotic music. Although they made no sense to Cassie, she loved the lyricism of the language.

"Wait," she smiled. "One word. Just one word for thank you."

"*Tashakor* or *tashakor mikonam.*"

"*Tashakor*," she said slowly. She strained to hear his correction, and then repeated her thanks, "*Tashakor mikonam*."

"Now you speak Dari," Farshad grinned. "Dari is our language. Like Farsi in Iran." Then he replied formally, "*Khahest mikonam, Madam Cassie.*"

When she turned around with the tray, the table was empty. She spotted Ralph and Danny leaving the lounge. For a moment she was confused and considered following after them, bringing their tea. Then she realized where they were heading. Danny's room; more dragons to chase. They had forgotten about her.

She walked toward the table they had abandoned. For some minutes, she simply stood and stared at the mess they had left, and then took the tray to a small clean table on the other side of the room. She hunched over the gentle steam from the tea, unfastened her long hair so it draped around her face. A veil, she thought miserably, not a shield. Disenchantment hit like a physical blow. Quietly, Cassie began to cry.

CHAPTER SIX

March 21, 2007
Wednesday

A ll night the wind howled as it pummeled the house and the adjacent oak tree. The house and tree groaned and sighed but largely disregarded the wind; they had withstood worse beatings through the years. This, too, would pass.

But the howling jerked Jack awake. In the dark, he felt a brush of panic as he wondered where he was. The disorientation passed the next second; he had been in the guest room at Ben and Lana's for a week now. A large and comfortable space, with mismatched furniture collected through the years. It was clean but obviously well-used – visits by their adult children and friends from afar.

In contrast, Jack realized, his and Helene's guest room looked like a photo shoot for an interior decorator magazine. A lovely room, the color scheme set by an original oil painting Helene had hung above an antique oak dresser. The bedding coordinated with the curtains which complemented the towels laid on the foot of the bed, always ready for guests. Yet guests rarely came. Even their children seldom returned home, instead staying in touch via texts, Facebook, and Skype (in fact, he and his daughter had Skyped just yesterday after she heard about her parents' separation). As he showered in the guest bath, Jack wondered sadly about why they never came.

He was up earlier than usual. Ordinarily, he would have read in bed for a few hours to avoid disturbing Lana and Ben, but he had their house to himself. They were in Boston over spring break, plans they couldn't change. But they had insisted he stay. *Mi casa es tu casa*, Lana had said, squeezing his hand affectionately. Such lovely friends, extending this life preserver after he had spent two sleepless nights last week thrashing and drowning in the sheets of his own perfect guest room.

Well, not his guest room any longer. Last Friday morning, with Ben's help, he had packed his Subaru with three suitcases, a laptop and hard drive, two boxes of files, four of books, and a smaller box with CDs, iPod, chargers and some photos. At the last minute, he had taken his running shoes, in case he ever felt like moving again. Helene was at the lab; he left her a note in the kitchen, so she wouldn't worry that there had been a burglary. As he had closed the trunk, the thought struck him that all he wanted from the marriage fit into the back of his car.

That was five days ago. Most of it was still there; only one suitcase and his laptop had been unloaded at Ben's.

He could barely remember last week. He winced now thinking of his poor performance in class. But at the time, try as he might, he didn't care. He gave perfunctory lectures, listlessly answered student questions and then locked himself into his campus office. He had ignored email, faculty meetings, office hours, timid knocks from students. It was irresponsible, but he couldn't help it; he had no energy or heart left. He felt dead. Dead man teaching, he now thought wryly. This was how Ben had discovered him and delicately shepherded him to his and Lana's house. Claimed the body, as it were.

It didn't help that Helene had continued to call him, sometimes pleading, sometimes demanding, other times nonchalant, as if nothing had happened. He answered a few times but the experience hurt so much that he turned off his phone. When she then became furious and left abusive voice messages, he almost felt vindicated. He could justify to himself avoiding her calls and deleting her messages. After Friday, though, the reality of their separation must have hit her, because he hadn't heard from her since.

Now he was the one wondering how she was doing, what she was thinking. Missing her. He knew he should have expected this. Their bond went back thirty-three years, the central relationship of his adult life. He may not have always liked Helene, but Jack had loved her, and he was surprised at the intensity of his grief over the death of their marriage.

That didn't mean he regretted the decision to leave. Making coffee in the predawn kitchen, he understood now that he had no choice. Her actions had triggered an involuntary and primal reaction in his heart, bolting it shut against her. That was unchanged even if she was sorry, even if she could present a marginally plausible rationale, even if he recognized his own role in abetting her insecurity. Emotionally exhausted, all he wanted now was to get far away.

But to where?

As he peered into the refrigerator for milk, blinking against the brightness of its single bulb, he imagined himself a single clear point in the present, with infinite possible paths stretching out from this moment. A sudden terrifying vision intruded on his thoughts: a vast featureless future where he drifted alone and aimless.

He almost dropped the milk carton.

The analytical part of Jack's brain amended his earlier operational metaphor: he wasn't dead; he was adrift. Helene had been his center of gravity. If he wanted to go forward, he had to find other ways to attach.

Little things helped. Mundane activities like making coffee and reading the newspaper were providing some stability, but they were insufficient. As he stared into the early morning, he pondered the problem of creating structure in a void, adding bulk to weightless days. The magnitude of the task overwhelmed him. Jack shook his head to dislodge the grasp of oncoming depression. "You don't need to do this all at once," he chided himself aloud. "One step at a time." Perhaps stacking books and papers into boxes would be a measured next step. He could finish packing his campus office today for the up-coming departmental move. Finishing the chore would feel good. He might as well do it today, he thought, when it's quiet. No one else would be around over spring break, except possibly Estella. He wouldn't mind seeing her.

The sun was just rising when he pulled into the university park-ing lot. At least the wind had stopped, he noted gratefully. His hair was uncombed and he wore old clothes. Campus security would think he was a bum, not a professor, he thought as his key unlocked the building's main door. Maybe that's another possible path, he smiled faintly.

A tower of half-filled boxes awaited him. He shed his denim jacket, turned on a jazz station and got to work emptying the filing cabinets. Determined not to waste time agonizing over which papers to keep and which to throw, he made good headway. For the time be-ing, he'd save everything; he could sift and sort this summer, once the boxes were deposited in the new office. Two hours passed before he heard Estella arriving. Eight o'clock and he was almost finished with the filing cabinets. He allowed himself a silent hurrah, then turned his attention to the book shelves. Again, he made good progress.

Just before ten, when he reached the shelf on political theory, Jack stopped dead. There lay the worn manila envelope, left where Helene had found it. He remembered his resolve to toss all the letters. He should still do it, to prove to himself that her jealousy was insane. Still, he paused. He placed the envelope on the desk next to his jacket;

he would take Cassie's letters back to Ben's place. That would give him time to think about what to do.

THAT EVENING, SITTING at the kitchen table over the debris of dinner, he stared at the manila envelope. Conflicting emotions tore at him: curiosity, longing, regret, disappointment. He hated this lack of clarity; he was used to knowing his own mind. Even though he had deluded himself about the marriage, he had been untroubled by ambiguity. Leaving the marriage was the same thing; he felt in his bones the necessity of it. But now, staring at the stained envelope, he realized he didn't know what he wanted to do. He could end the troubling confusion right now, he thought. He could drop the manila envelope into the shredder. That would ensure no second thoughts once the deed was done. Yet he didn't move.

"Well, then," Jack finally said aloud. He cleared the dishes and wiped clean the table. Then he took a deep breath and opened the envelope. Onto the table spilled almost two dozen sheets, mostly flimsy pale blue paper. Aerogrammes, embossed with postage from Thailand, Malaysia, Nepal, India, Pakistan, Afghanistan. A few envelopes and postcards were interspersed. Here also were three letters that he had sent to General Delivery in Athens, Florence and Paris. They were still sealed shut, stamped with imperatives: *Retour; Al'Envoyeur, Non Reclame.* He set them aside. He knew what was in them: his futile and increasingly frantic efforts to reconnect with her.

A white envelope edged in airmail stripes of red, blue and white stood out from the rest. He picked it up and pulled out two pages. This was her first letter.

Dear Jack:

It was so nice to meet you. Thanks for making the long trip fly by! As promised, here's a letter from Bangkok. I'm staying with my friend Becky. She met me at the airport. What a relief after 30 hours of travel. She teaches at the International School of Bangkok. Yesterday we took a 3-wheeled samlor to the market at the Royal Pramane Grounds. The market is sprawling & crowded; crammed with hundreds of stalls offering opened raw eggs, black noodles and dried squid on a stick. And the strangest fruits. Most are delicious, but one smells like Limburger cheese! Some vendors sell small chicks & mice unaccountably dyed pink. Also for sale are imitation designer clothes and purses, medicines, pots, flip flops, baskets, radios & Buddhist statuettes.

While Becky's at work, I'm exploring. Today I took a river taxi down the klong (canal) behind her apartment building. Two-story teak wood homes stand on stilt legs above the flow. Tiny white temples dot the riverside. Boys jumping in the water, people brushing their teeth, women in sarongs waiting for long boats to bring curry and rice. I hope my photos turn out.

Food's great. Little eateries are everywhere. Becky took me to one with orchids growing up the walls. My favorite place serves fresh seafood, I guess because it reminds me of home. I admit the spiciness takes a little getting used to. It's different than Cajun.

The humidity also reminds me of Louisiana, but we don't have A.C. here. I'm sitting under a half-hearted ceiling fan next to an open window, which helps. We're on the third floor and it's fun to watch life below. In the morning, I wake up to screaming monkeys. Now it's the shoemaker relentlessly pounding a poor shoe. There's a Chinese grocery where we buy ice cream and Singha beer. Next door is a tailor shop that's so poorly lit, the workers cut fabric on a table outside. Across from our building is a restaurant Becky likes; teenaged girls

*are sweeping up now and preparing for the evening crowd.
We'll go there tonight for grilled chicken.*

   *Well, I'm out of space. Farewell from the Village of Wild
Plums, Krung-thep, Residence of the Emerald Buddha.*

   Take care,

   Cassie Robinette

Along the edge, in different colored ink, a postscript had been added:

   *I hope you're okay. Did you finish that international law pa-
per? If you'd like to write back, use Becky's address on front.
I'd really like to hear from you!*

Of course he wrote back.

Suddenly, it struck him: Maybe he hadn't been in love with Cassie. Maybe he had been in love with her letters. They conveyed so
much - visually striking images, pungent smells, humid breath, rau-
cous sounds. He recalled her descriptions of hiking past vivid green
corn fields to a mud-walled guest house in the Himalaya; passing
through the great Mughal gate to suddenly see a rain-shimmering Taj
Mahal; tasting the spices and lemon of Tandoori chicken. He had once
written Cassie that her letters were his Tardis, an extraordinary means
of transport across space and time. She didn't get the reference; she
didn't watch *Dr. Who*. No matter, he thought. The Tardis was a fair
analogy, a portal to other worlds.

   Pouring himself a glass of red wine, Jack decided to try to locate
her, to get an ending to her story. He knew now that she had thought
him dead. That explained why no further letters had come. Of course,
she had still sent that unkind postcard. But that was long ago. Surely
she'd now be as curious about his life as he was about hers. The internet was an amazing tool. Everyone was there. He only had to look.

   Jack flipped open his laptop and typed her name into a search engine. Not many Robinettes popped up, almost none with Cassandra or

Cassie as first names. He found one woman who had died in 1967 and a girl born in 1995. There were many odd paragraphs with the names disconnected, the first in one sentence and the last in another. He scrolled through the possibilities, opening a few files before proceeding. Then he had luck. On Linked-In, he found a Cassandra Robinette who had gotten a J.D. at Louisiana State University in 1985 and now practiced law in Baton Rouge. She could be about the right age, and wasn't Cassie's hometown in that area? He clicked on the account. No photo or further details, but he could send her a message.

Jack stared at the screen and thought. Was this a betrayal of his marriage; was he proving Helene right? He shook his doubts aside and, with pen and paper, the old-fashioned way that helped him think, he crafted a note. Several notes. Each one seemed either insipid or sinister. Best to keep it brief, he thought. Finally, he settled on the wording:

> *Dear Ms. Robinette:*
>
> *I am writing in the hope that you are the Cassie Robinette whom I met in 1978 en route to Bangkok, Thailand. We corresponded for a while and then lost touch. Regrettably, you may have been misinformed of my demise. I am alive and well and would like to correspond again, if you are willing. You may check me out at my university home page (*he inserted the URL*).*
>
> *Best wishes,*
> *Jack Hunter*

He crossed out *demise* and wrote *death*; less pompous. As he typed out the message, his heart pounded: *send it; send it; send it.* When he finished, he refused to stop and reconsider. He hit SEND. And then he waited.

Jack knew he was unreasonable to expect a prompt reply. It was, after all, past midnight in Louisiana. Still, he stared at the screen willing a response. Finally, exhausted, he stumbled to bed.

The morning brought remorse. What would Cassie think when a ghost appeared in her inbox? What had he done, interfering in her life at this point? She might be furious. Or worse, silent. If she didn't reply, he could be back to the agony of three decades ago.

To delay the expected bad news, Jack tried to preoccupy himself, going on a run through Ben's neighborhood, taking a long shower, reading the local paper. Finally, with coffee to fortify him, he turned on his laptop. A message was waiting. His hands shook slightly as he opened it. This was it.

> *Dear Professor Hunter:*
>
> *I am not the lady you seek. We have never met nor have I ever been to Thailand. Further, after viewing your photograph on your college web page, I suspect that the lady in question is White.*
>
> *Sincerely,*
>
> *C. Robinette, Esq.*

Fighting disappointment, Jack read the message twice. He had been so sure. Yet he shouldn't have been. Three decades had passed. Cassie would most certainly have been married by now, perhaps even to Ralph, that boyfriend of hers. Only in his wishful daydreams would she have kept her own name. Jack numbly typed, "Thank you for answering so quickly, Ms. Robinette. I apologize for troubling you. All the best, Jack Hunter."

A few minutes after he sent it, a longer message popped up.

> *You are more than welcome, Dr. Hunter. I can see that this was someone you cared for. You might also be interested to*

know that you are not the first person to contact me regarding this lady. I received a similar email some years ago. That person, however, was not as gracious in his reply. He insisted on proof that I was not she. I naturally took offense and blocked him from accessing my account. That is why my initial reply to you was terse.

Good luck in your endeavors.
Cassandra Robinette

Jack didn't know what to make of this news. Was someone else looking for Cassie? It made no sense. Anyone who knew her would ask the family directly, not scour the Internet as he had to do. It must be a different woman, a coincidence that meant nothing.

His head hurt. As he rubbed his temples, he wondered what he was trying to accomplish. Searching for Cassie was just a way to postpone dealing with his past and thinking about his future. A fool's gambit.

He closed his laptop and stood. Time to get on with life, Jack told himself. Time to finally forget about Cassie Robinette.

CHAPTER SEVEN

August 26, 1978
Saturday

Afghanistan was a crossroads 2500 years before Alexander the Great. Cassie had had no idea. People, priests, goods, animals and armies had passed through, leaving their influences behind. She could see it in the artifacts that filled the Kabul Museum, first in the materials used – from red clay and bone, to lapis lazuli and carnelian, then copper and bronze. She could see it as well in the heads and figurines that populated the rooms. There were crudely fashioned fertility figures, stylized Bodhisattvas, warriors standing guard, and almost comical demons. But there also were faces that seemed personal, representing not abstractions but real people. One lovely face caught her attention: a stucco Buddha that seemed to be smiling, lost in thought. Enchanted, she realized her expression mirrored it. She could become part of the exhibit, another artifact, smiling and lost in thought for centuries. If she stood still long enough, would someone come by to dust her?

A guard came instead and pointed at the clock. It was noon. Rousing herself, Cassie slipped down empty corridors to the front entrance. The building was closing for lunch, even though the staff would be fasting. No matter; she needed to find a post office to mail the letters to Jack and her parents. She emerged on to the sunny crowded sidewalk of Darulman Avenue and was instantly slapped by hot afternoon air. Blinking rapidly, she involuntarily held her breath, keeping the cooler air of the museum in her lungs for a few more seconds.

Too hot to walk. She looked around for a taxi. It was an unusual splurge, this trip out of the city center. But she was angry and upset at Ralph and mad at herself for hanging around the hotel with him and Danny the previous rotten day. Marton hadn't appeared again. She reflected that he was probably dealing with his van and whatever else he did in Kabul. But what did she care? It was best if she never saw him again. Or Danny; she had to get Ralph away from him and his opium. Tomorrow, they would catch the bus to Herat and go on their way. Everything would be back to how it was.

So today, she was doing something for herself. A taxi driver saw her and pulled over hopefully. Through his open window, Cassie asked to go to the post office, but he frowned and gestured, unable to understand. Then he said Kabul Hotel and she nodded. She could get directions to the post office there. She tried to negotiate a price; they settled on 100 Afs, almost twice what she had paid to get to the museum. It was too much, she knew, but she was five miles from the heart of town. She climbed in and moved to the center of the back seat, away from the heat blasting in through the open windows.

Minutes later, entering the air-conditioned Kabul Hotel, Cassie gulped the frosty air. She wandered through the ornate lobby until she saw a uniformed concierge. When she asked for directions to the post office, he politely informed her that there was no need; the hotel would mail the letters for her as they did for all of their guests. This was unexpected luck. She extracted the two airmail letters, a little rumbled from her travel bag, smoothed them on the counter and, with thanks, handed them over.

Cassie was glad she had dressed better than usual today, in black slacks and clean blue permanent-press shirt. Perhaps she really had fooled the nice concierge into thinking she was a guest. Strolling through the lobby, she contemplated extending the fiction and getting lunch there. She wandered toward the hotel restaurant and checked the prices on the menu posted outside its door. She stepped back; lunch would cost more than her room at the Jam. Disappointed but not surprised, she left the hotel.

She wasn't hungry yet anyway, she told herself as she considered what to do next. Cassie felt no rush to be back at the dreary and stifling Jam; no rush to see Ralph, much less the other men. From the large square outside the Kabul Hotel, she began walking south, toward the river. A slightly cooler breeze rose from the river, encouraging her to cross the bridge.

Soon, she found herself in front of a bazaar. All along a cobblestone passageway tiny shops were tucked, some adorned with strips of colorful silk scarves hanging high above, others with bright stacks of brass and copper trays. There were displays of embroidered vests and caps, cases of ornate silver jewelry. As covertly as possible, she took a photograph.

The turbaned shop keepers sitting cross-legged in their doorways were less insistent than those on Chicken Street. Cassie gazed at the silver and gently fingered the fabrics. One shop sold women's clothing; on a hanger outside hung a beautiful blouse: white cotton, artfully hand embroidered in white thread. Cassie felt an unexpected longing. She did not need the blouse and turned away when the shop keeper quoted a price of 200 Afs. She had to be careful with her limited cash; she had squandered too much already today. He followed her. He tried again, pointing at her shirt and gesturing a trade. She raised her shoulders in a sign of regret and shook her head no. Finally he said 150 Afs. She looked again at the blouse. Less than four dollars for such beautiful work. How could she refuse? She paid the shopkeeper and tucked it into her tote bag.

After an hour of drifting past shops and stalls, Cassie left the bazaar and carried her prize back toward the Jam Hotel. Hunger had finally hit her. At the café across from the Jam's entrance, she found a table and ordered tea, bread and a slice of melon for lunch. The meal felt just right; she'd eaten too much meat last night. Satisfied, she leaned back from the table and thought about her trip so far. Perhaps she would go on alone once they arrived in Herat, she mused. There was something to be said for solo travel. Without Ralph, she could have stayed longer in Thailand, even worked for a while at a Cambodian refugee camp. Without Ralph, she could stay here and go to Bamiyan to see the Buddha statues. Then she paused in her reverie. Without Ralph, travel in the region would be risky. She would have to wrap herself in a burqa to look like a local. She lingered over the idea and her last sips of tea.

As she sat, Cassie absent-mindedly studied the doorway to the hotel. She liked the way the light and shadow fell on the old door, so she extracted her camera and checked her film. Thirty-one shots left; she could afford to take a few more in Kabul. She'd buy slide film in the modern city of Tehran. Not here; the boxes of film she found locally were well past their expiration dates. Worse, many were displayed on outside tables, in the sun.

Cassie looked up and noted that sunlight would hit the Jam's entrance in a minute or so. She set up the shot and waited. The light hit, she snapped the shutter. At that instant, Marton walked up to the Jam. He was in the shot, ruining the image she had tried to capture. "Damn," she muttered to herself.

Marton glanced back and saw her. Their eyes met. She involuntarily gave a small wave. He stood still a moment, looking at her, seeming to consider something. Then he turned and disappeared inside.

Seeing him reminded her that she and Ralph still needed to get bus tickets for Herat. She had forgotten. As she stood, she checked her watch; there was still time today. She'd stop in at the Jam and check on Ralph. Maybe he'd come with her to the bus station. Tomorrow or the day after – depending on when they could get seats – they'd finally be on their way.

From the doorway to the hotel lounge, she could see Ralph with Danny slumped nearby. A repeat of yesterday, except this time Marton stood over them, hands on hips, saying something in a sharp voice. She couldn't hear, but Danny appeared to be remonstrating in a strangely placid way, as if he didn't have the energy for a full-blown protest. Ralph was watching, a perplexed expression on his face. Both stoned again. What did she expect, leaving him alone all day with Danny? She couldn't deal with Ralph like this. She'd go to the bus station by herself and get their tickets.

As she turned to go, however, she heard a shout, "Cass!" Ralph's voice. He was waving. The other men looked at her expectantly. Irritated, she walked slowly to where they sat. Ralph tried to stand but his legs refused to support his weight and he fell back on the chair. It didn't seem to bother him. "Where you been, babe?"

"What do you care?" the words shot out.

He blinked. "I care," he said meekly.

She regretted her bitchiness; it wasn't like her. She started over. "I went to the Kabul Museum. Did you know this place was a major highway through the ancient world for thousands of years? You should have come."

"Cool, thousands of years," Ralph said vaguely. She wasn't sure he fully understood her.

"The museum's quite a distance." Marton interrupted.

She glanced at him. "Taxi," was all she said. Turning back to Ralph, she added, "And there's a wonderful old bazaar south of the river."

Marton broke in again. "The Chahr Chatta bazaar? I was there. I didn't see you."

Cassie didn't know its name and shrugged. How did Marton know so much about Kabul?

"Hold on. I'm just gonna rest for a minute," Ralph said as he relaxed against the back of his chair and half closed his eyes.

"Would you like to see more of the city?" Marton suddenly asked her.

"Ralph? Would you like to go?" she asked.

"Already seen it," he mumbled. "Stay here with me." He waved toward the chair next to him.

But she didn't want to stay. He had explored Kabul with Danny; she wanted to explore as well. And she hated being around him like this, too wrecked on opium to even sit straight. She turned to Marton and asked, "Do you know much about Kabul?"

"A little," he replied. "We can go on a drive, if you like."

"The van works?" She was mildly surprised.

He nodded. "Everything's set to go in the morning." Then Marton surveyed Danny and Ralph as if they were on display. "Let's leave the boys to their own entertainment," he advised.

Cassie could hear the testiness in his voice when he said *entertainment*. He was disgusted with them, too, she realized. That helped her make up her mind. "We're going, Ralph. I'll see you later." Then, to Marton, she said, "I need to stop by the room first."

Checking his watch, Marton nodded. "Meet me in front in half an hour?"

It was a question, not a command. Cassie approved of the change in him.

Minutes later, she stood in bare feet in the bath down the hall. She had splashed cold water on her face and neck, washing off the day's dust; unfastened her ponytail and brushed out her hair. Now she stared at the unsmiling face in the small chipped mirror above the sink, and found she had nothing to say to herself. She took a deep breath and returned to her room. From the travel tote, she brought out the white Afghan blouse and studied its delicate designs. Then, after stripping off the permanent-press shirt, she pulled the new blouse over her head. From the bottom of her backpack, she dug out a long black jersey skirt. She would not look drab and dowdy today. At the last minute, she painted rose colored lipstick on her mouth, smudged it on her cheeks.

A few items – her wallet, passport, room key and camera – went into a fringed fabric purse she'd bought in Thailand. It was lighter weight than the travel tote she usually lugged around. Already tucked inside the purse was an apricot-colored silk scarf.

Waiting at the hotel's front door, Marton didn't initially see Cassie arrive. When he did, his eyes widened. "You look lovely," he said softly.

His comment pleased her. "So do you," she said. He had changed also, from jeans to grey slacks, from a tee shirt to a white collared dress shirt, and he carried a sports jacket over an arm. His long black hair was combed back, tucked behind his ears. With his high forehead and delicate mouth, he looked like a nineteenth century poet, like Lord Byron, Cassie thought. Handsome, in a pale poetic way.

They walked to the van, parked in the shade on a side street, and Marton unlocked the passenger door. "Danny and I leave for Herat first thing tomorrow," he said. "Are you coming along?"

Cassie had started thinking about this as soon as she heard that the van was ready. Maybe it was a better plan; maybe she and Marton together could keep Ralph and Danny sober. But she didn't want to get stuck in the middle of nowhere again. "Which way are you going?"

Marton casually replied, "Your way, via Kandahar. It's a safer road, more tea shops and traffic."

"Sounds good," she said, climbing into the van. He wasn't so bad, she thought; she might have misjudged him the day before.

Marton took them on a loop around Kabul, past embassies, mosques and shops, down side roads and through residential neighborhoods. It was a prettier city than Cassie had thought, more verdant and architecturally rich. He seemed to know his way around. "You've been here before," she said.

"Last spring. I'd heard about a business opportunity and came to check it out. By bus, like you."

He turned the van into a park, passing a sign that read *Sher-i-Darwaza*, then another sign in English: Babur's Gardens. Somewhere, Cassie had read about Babur, the Moghul emperor. They drove uphill and parked.

"There's a view," he explained when they got out of the car. They started to follow the markers to the summer pavilion. Away from concrete and asphalt, the air felt cooler. A wind rose, whipping Cassie's long hair into her face. She stopped to tie the scarf around her head, looping the ends loosely around her neck.

"I've been thinking about what you said, about why you travel," Marton commented. "But I still don't see the point."

She thought about it. "To learn, I guess."

"About what?"

"Everything."

"In Afghanistan?"

She shook her head. "Everywhere." It was true, this hunger to know firsthand what the world was like.

Marton studied her. "You're voracious." A judgment, said approvingly.

Cassie didn't know how to respond. Wordlessly, they walked further up the path, through a crowd of school children in uniform, boys and girls running, teachers trying vainly to herd them forward.

"And you're here for business?" she asked.

Marton stopped to light a cigarette. He exhaled before answering. "That's right. Import/export."

"Sales," she said. Cassie didn't probe. She knew it was unfair, but in her mind, business wasn't an idealistic profession, not like teaching or writing, not like Jack or Ralph. She'd spent two years working with New Orleans businesses, making mundane promotional and training films. Maybe that was why.

As they continued on the path, she wondered if she was being unfair with Ralph as well. He could be more susceptible to drugs because he was so sensitive and creative. "Ralph," she said, "he's not usually like this...." Marton stopped and watched her attentively. She tried to explain, "He's smart. A brilliant writer."

Marton dropped the cigarette and crushed it with his foot. "What's he writing now?"

"A novel," Cassie replied. "Well, he was, when we were in Bangkok for a few months. It's harder when we're on the road." She listened to the sound of wind and children's happy screams, and then added, "It's science fiction."

Marton let out a bark of laughter.

Defensively, Cassie shot back, "There's brilliant science fiction. Real literature wrestling with the major themes of our time. War. Deception. What it means to be human."

"And space ships and little green men." The sun was warm despite the breeze, and Marton rolled up his shirt sleeves. He'd left the sports coat in the van.

Saying it that way made Ralph's work sound silly, inconsequential. Marton's remark touched a nerve in Cassie, reinforced her gathering fear that she was being fooled by Ralph. Nonplussed, she quickly walked ahead for several minutes.

Finally she stopped and waited as Marton strolled up to her. They said nothing as they scanned the gardens, just beginning to bud. Then, to foreclose any more comments about Ralph, Cassie asked, "How about you? Any women in your life?"

Marton lit another cigarette, turning away from the breeze to light it. "Sure," he answered. "Some girlfriends. No wife. I don't have time to be married. Someday I will."

Time was an odd reason, Cassie thought, but it didn't concern her. "I don't believe in marriage actually," she said. To Marton's sharp look, she explained, "I do believe in two people loving each other deeply for their entire lives. But I don't think that love has to be licensed by government. Think about what activities are licensed: fishing, hunting, driving. Those are privileges granted by government, not rights. But love? Everyone has a right to love." She stopped herself there. She didn't want to go on and on, as she had in her college dorm room with friends, and with Jack at the airport.

Marton's face lit up. "Exactly! That kind of superior love transcends the petty rules of small-minded bureaucrats. It even transcends time."

He had misunderstood her. She was talking about rights and government power; he about a spiritual link between special lovers. Before she could clarify their differences, though, he spoke again, almost too softly for her to hear. "I loved that way once. A long time ago." He gazed at the valley below, his cigarette forgotten in his hand.

Cassie waited. When he didn't continue, she stayed silent, feeling from his melancholy tone that prying was out of place. He would tell her or not; she shouldn't ask. It was one more mystery about the man.

They climbed to a marble mosque and looked over the city. Cassie dug the camera from her Thai bag and focused. She regretted not having a wide-angle lens even though it would have added weight. She carefully framed and took a shot. Then she stepped back to line up the same scene with Marton in the foreground. But he turned away and held his hand in front of his face.

"Don't," he said.

"It's so beautiful up here. Why not?"

His hand still raised shielding his face, Marton said, "I grew up in the East Bloc. I don't trust photographs. They can get in the wrong hands."

"Really?" She lowered the camera. She was about to reassure him that his photo was safe with her when he held out his hand for the camera.

"Please, let me take one of you," he insisted.

The offer was one Ralph seldom made, so she had few pictures of herself on the trip. "Alright then," Cassie said, retying the silk scarf around her head and smiling at the lens. Marton quickly took three photos and she winced at his profligacy with her finite film.

Handing the camera back, Marton asked, "Would you like a drink?"

"No beer, thanks." She disliked the taste and cloying mouthfeel of the cheap beer at the Jam.

"Of course not. A real drink."

"Real alcohol in Kabul during Ramadan? I can't imagine."

"The Kabul Intercontinental. Rich westerners always have alcohol."

She looked at her watch. It was almost five.

CASSIE HAD THOUGHT that the Kabul Hotel was impressive, but the Intercontinental was in a league of its own. The modern structure was perched on a hill with stunning views in every direction. To the north, a Mughal summer palace and to the east and south, Kabul itself. She spotted the TV tower in one direction, and the Blue Mosque in another. A few miles away flowed the Kabul River, late afternoon light burnishing parts of it pewter as it twisted past the city. In the distance, the majestic Hindu Kush.

Marton parked the van far from the entrance. Cassie understood and did not mind a walk. The van stood out in its shabbiness, not even close to the class of vehicles in the Intercontinental parking lot. As she got out, Marton motioned to her Thai shoulder bag.

"You can leave that in the van."

"Why?" She looked down at it. Black cotton fabric embroidered in reds and yellows, tiny tin coins and colorful beads hanging as fringe. The purse was only two months old and didn't show signs of wear or grime. She thought it complimented her black and white out-fit.

"It stands out. It looks too Third World," he said, putting on his sport coat.

"But this is the Third World," she replied.

"Not inside it's not."

Mildly displeased, she tucked the purse beneath her seat.

"You need your passport." To her quizzical look, he added, "You look so young."

"Ah, for a drink," she understood and retrieved the passport. "I don't have a pocket."

"I do," he said, placing her passport in his inside breast pocket. "Next to mine." He took her elbow and guided her toward the en-trance. Cassie glanced at him, struck by how different he seemed. Not simply better dressed but older and more self-assured.

It felt strange to walk unburdened by bag or camera. Even so, Cassie realized that Marton was right when they entered the glittering and vast lobby of the Intercontinental. Thick white marble columns lined a hall wider than most streets in the old quarter, so polished that they reflected light from half a dozen or more crystal chandeliers. Open lounges to either side offered sofas in blue damask and red silk. She was enveloped in the coolness of air conditioning. Cassie had been staying so long in places like the Jam that she had forgotten the sophisticated ambience of upscale hotels.

Marton guided her past the reception desk and into the Bukhara Restaurant. Very few tables were occupied yet, and a smartly dressed waiter immediately approached. He guided them to a table in the center of the vast space.

Marton looked at Cassie. "What would you like to drink?"

"I don't know," she shrugged. "I guess wine. Gin and tonic? Something with rum?"

"Let me order for you. What taste do you prefer? Salty or sweet?"

"Salty," Cassie replied.

"Do you like olives?" When she nodded, he added, "Have you ever had a martini?" She shook her head no. He turned to the waiter.

"A martini for the lady, two olives, and I'll have a club soda with lime."

The waiter looked at Cassie. "Vodka or gin, madam?"

"Gin," she guessed, because she liked gin and tonic.

He left. He hadn't asked for her identification. Cassie felt worldly and mature.

"You're not drinking?" she asked Marton. Ordinarily, this would make her wary; it seemed like something a college guy might do to get a woman drunk. Marton didn't strike her as a predator, though.

"I'm driving," he responded, then added as an afterthought, "My father was an alcoholic."

The admission startled Cassie. Marton had revealed so little about himself, had even seemed reluctant to disclose his last name. Cassie reached over and touched his wrist. "That must have been so hard for you."

"It was why I left Czechoslovakia. One reason." Marton waved his hand to dispel her sympathy. "So, no, I don't drink. But I don't object when others do."

Another reminder that he had escaped the Iron Curtain. She had to ask, "How did you get out?"

Marton said firmly, "I can't talk about it. If the authorities learn, no one in the future could escape. Do you understand?"

Cassie felt chastened yet increasingly intrigued. Marton's life experiences were so much more serious and daring than her own. She and Ralph were like children in comparison.

The drinks arrived. Cassie tried her Dari and said, "*Tashakor mikonam.*" She hoped she pronounced it correctly. The waiter gave a surprised smile and replied, "*Khahest mikonam.*"

She tested the martini. The strong alcohol taste initially put her off. But by the third sip, she decided she liked it, the spicy tang and saltiness of the drink. She took off her glasses, ran her hand through her hair and leaned back in the plush chair.

Marton was watching her, appraising her. "You belong here, not at the Jam."

"Absolutely, my dear man, if money was no object," she joked and fluttered her hand grandly.

"If money was no object, I would rent the entire place." He was serious. His gaze swept over the gilt and marble and elegantly furnished restaurant. "Definitely."

Cassie considered it. "I don't know. These fancy hotels all look alike. Everything is so western, so modern." She took another sip. "They're like bubbles floating above the real world."

"That's exactly what I like," Marton said. "They're above the ugly world. But they aren't western, they're global, aristocratic. I can't imagine anyone preferring the Jam."

"Good grief, I'm not defending the Jam! This is a beautiful hotel. Certainly I could stay here. But I wouldn't get any sense of the real Afghanistan if I did." She tried to explain. "You asked me why I travel. Robert Louis Stevenson wrote a little book called *Travels with a Donkey in the Cevennes*. Do you know it?" When Marton shook his head, she continued. "At one point he writes that he travels not to go anywhere, but to go. 'The great affair is to move,' he wrote. Most people only know that part. But he goes on. He says he travels" - and here she recited - "'to feel the needs and hitches of our life more nearly; to come down off this feather-bed of civilization and find the globe granite underfoot and strewn with cutting flints.'" She stopped, intensely self-conscious of how theatrical she sounded.

"And that's what you're doing, Cassie?" he asked.

She nodded, "I'm trying at least."

Marton seemed perplexed. "You would trade a featherbed for cutting flints. Why? That makes no sense."

Cassie wanted him to understand. "To feel alive, not lulled into complacency. To experience the real world."

"By suffering needlessly?"

"I'm hardly suffering, staying at the Jam. But I'll take your argument. Maybe we do need to suffer sometimes, at least a little." She never thought about it in those terms before and wasn't sure if this was Stevenson's point. But she liked the idea; it accorded with her religious views, such as they were. "Isn't that what Ramadan is all about? One of the Australians – our first night at the Jam – said Muslims fast because it reminds them of what it means to go hungry. It makes them more aware of the sufferings of others."

"I wasn't there that night."

Cassie remembered. He had been sick. "All I'm saying is that empathy is a good thing. It makes us more open hearted. That's what travel does."

Marton leaned forward, eyes intent. "But you yourself don't need to suffer. You can tour orphanages or poor neighborhoods or brothels during the day. You can write a check, if you feel so moved. Then come back to your feather bed in a place like this."

She scoffed, "That would be treating people as if they're curiosities, like animals in a zoo."

"They are in a zoo."

"Marton!"

"Staying near Chicken Street does not make you one of them, Cassie. 'Elective suffering' – even fasting for a month – wouldn't change that. Local Afghans are just curiosities, to use your words. You know that but you won't admit it to yourself." He softened his tone and lowered his voice. "You can never be their friend. There is too large a gulf."

"No, that's not how I see people at all," she whispered hotly. She turned away, breathing unevenly. The martini abandoned, she crossed her arms over her chest and fumed silently that she was not instrumental about people. He misunderstood her completely.

"I don't mean that as an insult." He leaned toward her. He tried unsuccessfully to catch her eye. "You're a wonderful person, Cassie. You seem to genuinely care about people. The waiter, for example. The problem is that you pretend to yourself that they are your equal. And they aren't, that is what I'm saying. You are smart and beautiful and educated. You've been all over the world. Accept that. It's all right to be better than everyone else. To deserve finer things." His fingertips touched the martini glass and slid it a little closer to her. The gesture seemed to say, *And I can give you finer things.*

A minute passed, two. His naked elitism appalled her. But, as mad as she was, she was not immune to his flattery. As her rapid breathing slowed, she started to wonder if she was using other people, as he implied. If she wasn't being fully honest with herself about her motivations.

"I want to tell you about Katarina," Marton abruptly said.

This caught Cassie's attention. She sensed this was the mystery he'd mentioned in Babur's Gardens.

He glanced around the nearly empty room, the vacant tables, unoccupied chairs. The unfulfilled potential of camaraderie. Marton cleared his throat. "Katarina was a beautiful girl who lived down the hall. Her father was a plumber in the building where we grew up. We loved each other very much. Even though we were so young. That special type of love that transcends time."

Cassie ached to know what had become of Katarina, but she stayed still, not wanting to intrude on this intimate memory. In a moment, he sighed deeply and continued, "She died. That was another reason I left. Without her, I had no reason to stay."

His sorrow touched her. Reaching out for his hand, she whispered, "I am so sorry."

He took her hand and held it for a minute, staring down at the table. "In some ways, you remind me of her."

His remark was so unexpected that Cassie could feel her skin blush.

It seemed to have startled him as well, and he quickly changed the subject. "How's the wound?" he asked as he pushed back her sleeve and studied the back of her wrist.

The bandage was gone. It had fallen off in the shower this morning. She had swabbed iodine on the wound and taped a band aid over it. The band aid was too small, exposing the corners of an ugly orange-yellow gash.

"We need to take care of this," Marton stated simply. "When you're done with your drink."

Cassie had thought they might stay for dinner but she wasn't hungry. When she was finished the martini, they pushed away from the table and Marton excused himself to pay the bill.

As she stood, her head swam slightly, pleasantly. She felt relaxed and light for the first time in months.

They were both quiet on the drive down the hill.

MARTON FINISHED PACKING away the antiseptic supplies. Turning back to her, he said with an artificial nonchalance, "I found something for you today. In the Chahr Chatta bazaar. Destiny, maybe, that we were both there? Anyway," he handed her a small bag. "I hope that you like it."

Curious, she opened the bag and pulled out a belt of woven silver. She caught her breath; she had never seen one like it. A dozen silver threads plaited together into a thick strand; a half dozen thick strands then woven into a flat braid half an inch wide. Every few inches, holding the strands together, was a slender silver band adorned with a small daisy-shaped medallion. The clasp was a tiny screw. There were no adjustments; the belt would fit or it would not.

Slightly inebriated from the martini, Cassie stroked the silver, peered closely at the tiny flowers. "It's lovely. But I can't accept it." She handed the belt back to Marton. It was too expensive; there were unspoken promises intrinsic to accepting such a gift.

He didn't touch it. "Please. I can't return it, you know."

He was right; the bazaar wasn't like the shops at home. She reluctantly accepted the belt. "Well, then, thank you, Marton. But why?"

He shrugged, "You helped me, with the van. And I wanted to." He stood in front of her and took the belt. "Here, try it on."

He reached his arms around her waist to position it. Through the embroidered blouse, she felt the brush of his hands on her back and hips. Then, with nimble fingers, he worked the tiny screw at belly button height. The belt fit. Marton smiled broadly. It was a beautiful smile.

For several seconds, they stood facing each other, foreheads close, breathing deeply, not otherwise moving. Cassie realized with a start that she desired this man. What about Ralph? Wasn't this a betrayal? She tried unsuccessfully to push that question from her mind. Betrayal, an ugly and dishonorable act. No, she determined, not a betrayal. Their relationship was already over, as of this afternoon. She would tell him tonight, or better, tomorrow, when he was straight again. She rationalized that going to bed with Marton would solidify that decision, make it impossible to recant. Ralph would ask about another man but that wasn't it. There was no other man. She wasn't in love with Marton. Sleeping with him wasn't making a commitment, not in this day and age. It would only be sex, nothing more.

As she debated with herself, Marton stepped back and removed his jacket, then carefully removed her glasses. He looked at her. "I won't do anything you don't want me to do." His voice was husky, his breathing shallow. "Trust me." He came closer, and she could smell the lime on his breath. "I want to show you something. I want to show you how beautiful you are to me." His hand rested lightly on her hip. "And to do that, I have to undress you."

Surprised but aroused, she didn't object. He began by slowly unfastening the small side buttons on the white Afghan blouse, then pulling it gently over her head. Not taking his eyes from her, he lay the blouse across a chair. "Ah, as I thought, no bra," he said. "I approve." He pulled her silky undershirt over her head as well. He paused a moment to study her breasts, to touch them delicately, to trace his fingertip around her left areola, then the right. She held her breath.

His gaze dropped to her crotch. She could hear his breathing quicken now, and her own. The jersey skirt had no buttons to unfasten; his hands slipped beneath its elastic waistband, slipping also beneath the waistband of her panties, and in one smooth movement, he pulled them both down. She trembled and stepped out of the fabric mounded at her feet.

Cassie's fingers moved toward the clasp on the silver belt. Looking at it, he shook his head no. "Leave it," he said.

Ignoring the buttons, Marton pulled his shirt over his head in a practiced gesture. Then, taking her hand, he led Cassie to the full-length mirror in the room and positioned her in front of it. He stepped behind her to view her in the mirror as well. "This," he whispered in her ear, "this is what I see when I look at you."

And she saw it too, a striking woman, dark-eyed, hair wild, naked except for a silver belt reflecting slivers of lamp light. Standing close behind her, a man, bare-chested, eyes locked on her own. Her mind, playing tricks, fleetingly imagined the man was Jack Hunter.

It was the most erotic sight she had ever seen.

CHAPTER EIGHT

May 17, 2007

Thursday

The previous evening, Sandy called. Sandy: funny, creative, different. Jack knew he should not feel this way, but she was his favorite child. He posed as the impartial parent, worked assiduously to be fair to both. Even so, she delighted him in ways that her serious and ambitious younger brother Max did not. His son checked all the boxes in terms of accomplishments, but it was Sandy who made people feel special.

Jack was struck that his daughter in some ways was the anti-Helene. She had inherited her mother's dark hair and pale skin, yet not the symmetry of features that accounted for Helene's beauty. Sandy was attractive, but not stunning. Yet, despite having a mother who inspired admiration in her friends, Sandy seemed comfortable in her own skin, even from an early age. She didn't aspire to physical beauty. Instead, she had adopted an alternative persona with tee shirts and jeans, her thick hair short and spiked with mousse. Helene hated the look; Sandy didn't care.

"Hey, Dad. Are you getting settled in?"

He smiled. "All's good. I submitted grades Tuesday so I'm temporarily liberated from the salt mines of academia. How about you?"

She was used to him talking this way. "Are you up for some company this weekend?"

Her question thrilled him. He grinned as he replied, "Frodo returning to the shire? That's terrific." When she was small, he called her a fairy princess. He thought all little girls liked that. At age seven, she had sternly informed him that she did not. Following that humbling experience, he switched to nicknames from *The Lord of the Rings*. Tolkien met with her approval even before she knew what a hobbit was. He hoped Tolkien still did.

She laughed. "I've missed you. You're sounding better. I'm so glad."

"Some days are better than others, but yeah, I am doing better. I can't wait to see you."

"Same here. I should be there about four tomorrow, barring tornadoes and orc attacks." She paused, voice serious now. "I have something important to tell you."

Important to tell you. Through the night and most of today, that phrase had dogged him. What did it mean? That she was pregnant? That she had cancer? That she had joined the marines and was shipping out to Iraq? With Sandy, anything was possible. And that made him nervous.

Hanging up, he realized he had to get ready for her visit. Jack took a hard look at his apartment. The building itself was interesting: a late and unlikely Art Deco structure in the center of town, recently renovated, with a few Art Deco touches inside as well, in the light fixtures and kitchen cabinets. But since his move here in late March, he had done little unpacking. He didn't mind the towers of boxes in every room, but knew he would have to unpack some of them to host his daughter. This morning he finally started.

The apartment had two bedrooms, but one was stuffed with boxes of books and a treadmill he'd bought two years ago and never really used. Eventually, once he bought a desk, it would be his home office. The other bedroom had the bed and antique oak dresser from the guest room in his old house; Helene had decided she didn't want them anymore. Sandy would take the bed, Jack decided, so he threw the sheets in the wash. He dug out another set for himself to use on the sofa. He had a harder time finding which box contained the towels and almost decided to buy more when he stumbled into them in a box he had marked "kitchen." With such accurate labeling, the chaos of moving was going to continue some time into the future, he guessed.

Jack spent the rest of the morning dusting, vacuuming and scrubbing the bathroom. After lunch, he bought enough groceries to last through a snow storm. Finally, the place looked half decent. He checked his watch; she wouldn't be here for another hour. He paced, no easy feat in a living room still occupied by a platoon of boxes.

The doorbell rang before he expected and he jumped to it. There was his girl, his joy.

"Sandy!" he shouted and ushered her in. She dropped her bag and they hugged.

Propping her sunglasses on top of her head, Sandy surveyed the room. "I like what you've done with the place," she teased.

Through her eyes, he saw the bare walls, the haphazardly arranged furniture, the ubiquity of boxes. "The style is called Early Undergraduate. It's very big in New York."

"Your desk!" And she strode up to the oak table now pressed into dining room service. Her hand ran fondly along the surface, caressing the gouges and nicks. "It's smaller than I remembered. But, still, it must have been a bear to get up here."

"Well, I couldn't leave it behind. You know, all those fancy dinner parties I give," he shrugged.

She walked to the trash can he hadn't yet emptied. "Fancy. I see what you mean." In it were discarded work papers, old copies of last spring's syllabus and a few used paper plates. "You do know that paper plates are killing the planet, don't you?"

"I don't have any regular plates."

"You don't have any plates?! We'll go get some."

"No, I mean, I have some, but they're still in one of these boxes." He gestured vaguely into the living room.

"I'll help you unpack." Sandy didn't believe in procrastination. In that, she was like her mother.

"We'll do it later. Meanwhile, would you like a cup of coffee?"

"Your coffee? Absolutely." Sandy followed her father into the kitchen and leaned against the counter as he assembled everything.

Okay, he thought, she's probably not pregnant if she's drinking coffee. He flexed his fingers and intoned solemnly, "This is Professor Hunter's Secret Recipe for the Best Coffee in the Galaxy. I'm passing the time-honored tradition down to you, so that you may pass it to your children, and they to theirs, lo to all the future generations of little Hunter coffee drinkers."

Sandy was silent for a moment. "Dad, that's what I came to tell you."

He stopped dead in his preparations and looked at her.

Smiling reassurance, she waved him on. "In a minute. Once I'm cradling a cup of Professor Hunter's Coffee."

He finished as quickly as he could, mind racing. She looked healthy. Of course, appearances, as he knew, could be deceiving.

Meanwhile, Sandy searched a few cabinets until she found the coffee mugs. "Oh, I like this one," she said. It was emblazoned with pictures of the five conservative justices of the Supreme Court dressed as clowns.

"Clowns it is," Jack said, filling the cup. "Ben gave that to me, after *Bush v. Gore*."

"You and Ben are such political nerds," and she squeezed his arm affectionately.

They carried their mugs into the living room and sat side-by-side on the sofa. Ordinarily, their silences were comfortable. This one felt strained as Jack waited for her to begin. He gazed at her thoughtfully; she gazed at the coffee table. On it was an odd assortment of paraphernalia that he had collected through the years and kept in his old home office. They had come from garage sales, junk shops, curio stands at flea markets. Sandy picked up a small green marble box, with a mother-of-pearl flower inset on its lid. Smiling, she turned it over.

"I used to love going into your office. When I was a kid, I thought every house had a room like that, full of books and all this fantastical stuff. I loved that room. It was like a wizard's tower."

Jack loved the room, too. "Except that it was on the second floor, hardly a tower."

"No," she corrected him primly. "It was up three steps from the second-floor landing. The highest room in the house."

"Quirky architecture in that place," he reflected.

"Ah, the tuk-tuk," she laughed in recognition, picking up the brightly colored plastic samlor, a three-wheeled motorcycle with a bench in back.

Jack smiled also. It had been the first in his collection, its inspiration really. Cassie had sent it from Bangkok. When she was small, Sandy had played with it so often that its yellow roof had long since disappeared.

She put it down and continued to scan the assembled curios. "My favorite was those Russian nesting dolls. Yeltsin on the outside, then Gorbachev, then I forget."

"Yes, Matryoshka dolls. After Gorbachev, there's Brezhnev…"

"Of course," she recalled, "All the way to a tiny bald Lenin."

"Actually, all the way to a tiny Czar Nicholas. Imagine his shock, being stuck for eternity with those nasty revolutionaries. Hold on," Jack stood. "I think I saw it somewhere." He checked in one box near the oak table with no success, but a triumphant smile spread across his face after he rummaged in a second box. "Voila!" He brought the four-inch wood doll to Sandy. "I bequeath him to you."

"Really?!" she clutched Yeltsin to her chest affectionately.

Jack sat next to her, delighted at her presence; anxious about her news. To pass the time, he gestured at it. "The doll teaches us a lot. I mean, in addition to the lineage of Russian oligarchs."

"Ever the professor," Sandy smiled.

Reclaiming the Matryoshka doll, he pulled Yeltsin apart and judiciously lined up seven painted Russian leaders in descending size. "Notice how Yeltsin and Gorbachev are on the outside. That's appropriate; they advocated political openness. But inside, things are different, dark. You have Brezhnev and his repression of democratic movements in the East bloc. And further in is Stalin, responsible for at least twenty million deaths, maybe up to sixty." He picked up the diminutive Stalin, studied it. "Considering only the outside, this Matryoshka doll is fun and colorful. But, inside, it has a heart of darkness." He meant it as a joke, and a rueful acceptance that things aren't always what they seem.

Sandy interjected, "And sometimes, Dad, it's babushkas all the way down."

"Well, yes," he said. He was going to add a quip but stopped speaking when he saw her lean back and bite her bottom lip.

Sandy finally spoke. "But I get the point. Not to be fooled by surface appearances. That's what I've wanted to tell you for a long time. But I couldn't while you were with Mom."

This was it. Jack could hear hesitation and a touch of sadness in her voice; he needed to reassure her. "I would never tell anyone anything you told me in confidence, even your mother."

"I know. But you would have wanted me to tell her." She looked again at the Matryoshka dolls. "I'm not ready to do that yet. I don't know when I might be."

He suddenly had an inkling what her revelation might be, but didn't want to preempt her. Putting down his mug, he looked directly at her. "What is it, Sandy? Tell me. It will be all right."

"Dad." She took a deep breath, then said, "I'm a lesbian. That's what I need to tell you."

Her disclosure made sense the moment Jack heard it. On an unconscious level, he already knew this about his daughter. He scooted across the seat cushion and enveloped her in his arms, hugging so tightly he thought he might cut off her oxygen supply. "Oh, sweetheart." His heart ached with tenderness. "I love you so much."

They sat in a fierce embrace for a few minutes. Then Jack pulled back. "Is there anyone special? Is that why you're telling me now?"

"No, not yet. But," she paused significantly, "there might be soon. Regardless, it was time for you to know."

He nodded. "It's so hard to find love in this world. I don't care who you fall in love with. I just hope you find a wonderful life partner someday."

"Like you did, Dad? Was Mom really a wonderful life partner?"

Jack averted his eyes. He wasn't going to lie to Sandy but he couldn't tell her the whole truth either. Eventually, he settled on equivocation. "We had some good times. We have amazing kids."

"Mom isn't easy to live with. It's okay to admit that. With a few years of therapy, I've come to terms with her." Sandy leaned back on the sofa.

Jack hadn't known about the therapy. "I'm sorry," he responded, "I should have stood up to her more when she gave you a bad time. I'm sorry I wasn't there for you." He stood and paced; so many of the certainties he had had about himself – the loving husband, the supportive father – were only illusions.

"What do you mean? You were there for me." She stood and faced him. "I always knew you would back me up. Or at least hear me out. Remember when she was spying on me? Reading my emails? You got her to stop."

"Did I?" Jack didn't recall that. In his memory, he had snapped at his daughter.

"And lots of other times." A smile played at the edge of her mouth, "Why do you think I've turned out so well? Like father, like daughter." She hugged him again. "We're going to get through this. We're going to let go of the painful stuff in the past, we're going to learn from it, but then we're going to go forward. Right?" When he nodded, she added, "I love you so much, Daddy. So I had to tell you. I've come to realize the importance of honesty. With others, and with myself." She sat on the sofa again and pulled him down next to her. "I'm tired of pretending around you guys. I'm tired of denying something that's central to who I am."

Jack saw his daughter as if for the first time, not as his darling girl, but as a thoughtful and brave adult. It was about time he did; she was almost twenty-four. And she was right about honesty. He was tired of pretending too. "Don't make the mistake I made, Sandy. When you fall in love. Don't think you can change someone once you marry them." That was the best advice he could think of at the moment. "I'm not saying I didn't love your mother. But you're right; living with her wasn't easy. I spent too many years making excuses for her, trying to avoid conflict." He sighed.

Sandy seemed to realize how much this admission cost her father. He was stripping away the dominant mythology of his life: the myth of Perfect Helene. She held his hand. "Someday, Dad, I hope you find a wonderful life partner also."

"Me? Oh, no." He smiled ruefully, "I'm too old. That boat sailed without me a long time ago." He had no illusions on that score.

"What boat? Do you mean love? That it sailed without you?" When he didn't answer, Sandy pursued the question. "Was there someone other than Mom?"

He didn't want to answer. His immediate reaction was defensive: Sandy wouldn't understand about Cassie, would see his feelings for her as Helene did, a betrayal of the family. His second reaction was shame; how could he think that about his daughter? She had been so honest with him. Sandy was not Helene.

Before he could frame his answer, she offered a way out. "You don't need to tell me if you don't want to."

"No, I do need to tell you. In fact, I want to tell you." His own difficult truth was finally coming out. "Maybe I wasn't the best husband. Maybe the problems in our marriage weren't all your mother's fault."

Sandy gasped. "You had an affair!"

He was appalled she would think so. "Absolutely not. This was before we got together, a long time ago."

"What happened?"

"It was someone I met in New Orleans, at the airport. I was heading home from a conference and she was on her way to travel around the world. We talked most of the day, then wrote to each other for a few months."

Sandy waited. "That's it? Hardly a torrid romance," she said, a trace of disappointment in her voice.

He gave a short laugh. "Well, I did kiss her before she got on the plane. Does that count? But, no, no epic romance. I probably did fall in love with her, but I'm sure Cassie – that's her name - never knew it." He only now was realizing it himself. He picked up the empty coffee mugs. "I recently found out your mother has been jealous all these years. She thought I still loved Cassie, if you can believe it." Jack headed to the kitchen.

After a moment, Sandy said, "You called me Cassie once. Do you remember?" Jack returned from the kitchen to look at his daughter. "I was going to Washington for the high school Model United Nations. I was at the airport with the team, and you hugged me and said, 'Safe travels, Cassie.' I never knew who you meant. Now I do."

Jack was startled; he didn't remember. "Oh," he said, abashed. "I don't know why I did that."

"Maybe being at the airport? It doesn't matter, though. My feelings weren't hurt. It's just nice to have the mystery solved, to hear that my dear old dad once had a great love. Quite romantic, actually."

"Well," he said awkwardly, then asked if she'd like more coffee.

"No, thanks, but I wouldn't object to a drink." She stood and stretched. "It was a long drive. How about I make us margaritas?"

In the kitchen, Sandy found ice, tequila, triple sec, lime juice and simple syrup. While she measured and blended, Jack dug out blue-stemmed margarita glasses that Helene thought were tacky. He ran a lime around the rims and then coated them lightly with salt.

As they worked, Jack wondered about his daughter's life, and what role he could play in it. He tentatively broached the subject. Had she encountered bias in the workplace or housing? Did she have a strong network of friends? How could he be supportive?

Things hadn't been easy, she admitted, giving a few examples. Then she added, "I'm lucky to have terrific friends. I'd like you to meet them someday."

"I'd like that too," he acknowledged. "Would it be okay if I visited you later this summer?"

"Absolutely," she beamed as she filled the glasses. "You know, I think I'll tell Mom tomorrow when we meet for lunch. Best to get this over with." She took a tentative taste of the margarita; approving it, she handed the other glass to her father.

Jack agreed. "And she may surprise you, especially if she's in a good mood." They clinked glasses and sipped their frosty drinks.

"She was in a fantastic mood on the phone yesterday," Sandy noted. "She's going to a job interview Tuesday with the CDC."

Jack frowned in thought. "The Centers for Disease Control? I didn't know she had applied there."

Sandy paused and studied his face. "You've got to get used to this, Dad. She's going to do things now without telling you."

"Of course!" he asserted, mildly embarrassed. "I just didn't know she wasn't happy here."

"She was, I think. Well, as much as Mom can be happy. But she didn't want to stay in town and run into you all the time. Then she got the job announcement in an email from a friend of yours. I can't remember his name. She's excited at getting an interview. New beginnings and all that."

Frank Constant, Jack thought. He had sent Helene a job announcement after all. Jack realized he should be grateful to Frank because these new plans were probably the reason Helene was not fighting the divorce or the sale of the house. Still, he felt a small irritation - possessiveness? - lodge in the back of his mind.

Sandy led them back into the living room. Sitting lotus style on the sofa, she said, "So, tell me about this Cassie. What was she like?"

Jack considered the question, then spoke carefully. "She was funny and bright." He looked away now, into the past. "Fearless, too. To me, she seemed so ..." What was the word he wanted? "Free."

His daughter was curious. "Do you still have any of those letters she wrote?"

He hesitated a moment, then went to the guest bedroom to retrieve the manila envelope. Returning, he tried to explain, "I'd forgotten all about them, until I found this envelope during the office move. Your mother thinks I've clung to her memory all these years. It wasn't like that." He stopped, hearing himself, his protests of innocence. "I guess I don't know what to say."

Sandy touched his hand. "It's okay. I'm not sitting in judgment. You stayed true to Mom. It's okay with me if you once loved someone else." She carefully extricated a random letter from the manila envelope.

As she did so, Jack felt a rush of gratitude and relief. He lifted his blue-stemmed glass in a silent salute to his daughter.

Sandy read the letter aloud.

Dearest Jack:

It's 11:30 p.m. and I'm on the train to Jaipur. It's a local, so it stops at all the villages on the way. An hour ago, a dozen rural women from Rajasthan boarded the women's car, all dressed in bright blue and red skirts, black shawls, ornate and heavy silver jewelry. The whole village seems to be on its way to a religious festival. The train's very crowded, so the Rajasthani men are sitting on the roof of our car. The moon is bright and I can see their flickering shadows along the tracks outside.

At first, the women were shy & stayed away. Slowly, they started to lay sleeping toddlers near me, on shawls spread over the hard benches. When I smiled at the little ones asleep, one mother came up and smiled and soon other women gathered closer.

A few minutes ago, the women began to sing-chant a low mournful song, clapping their hands and swaying. In otherworldly voices above us, the men echoed back the song. Now the women are singing more loudly. Two of them – a pretty girl in a pink shawl and a sturdy farm woman, perhaps her mother – are dancing in the aisle, circling around one another, weaving their hands in intricate patterns. [smudge of ink] Sorry about the mess; the train suddenly lurched and the dancers fell over. The older woman fell on me. We all laughed and the dance continues.

The images are so compelling that I regret I'm not taking photos, but the camera feels too intrusive. I need to get over that idea if I'm going to be any good. Or invent a camera hidden in a hat.

Sandy asked, "She was a photographer?"

"No, a film maker," Jack answered. He surprised himself a little; he had not consciously remembered that fact. More solid memories came to him. "She studied film in college, and worked at a film production company before we met."

"Then why not make a movie of her travels?"

Jack chuckled, realizing how young Sandy was. "Lightweight video cameras weren't invented yet. I got one of the early models when Max was small. Must have been about eighty-seven."

Sandy lay the letter in her lap and sat in silence several minutes. "I can see why you saved the letters," she said. "Where is she now?"

He shrugged. "We lost touch." After a brief pause, he said more truthfully, "Actually, I was going to Turkey to meet her, but she suddenly broke everything off. So I don't know where she went after that."

"That's sad," Sandy sipped her margarita, lost in thought. "What happened? Do you know?"

"She didn't explain." Jack picked up the manila envelope and rummaged through its contents. "This is what she sent." He produced the postcard. It was almost pristine, unlike the other letters and cards, which were wrinkled from multiple readings. This one had been read once, maybe twice, before it was hidden away, a secret shame. "This is the last I heard from her. There was another letter but I never saw it. Your mother says she destroyed it. No matter; I'm sure it was just an expanded version of this Dear John."

It was a hotel postcard; the description on the back was in Farsi. Not the sort of place catering to western travelers. Scribbled at the top was *9/5/1978.*

"Where is this?" Sandy asked.

An Iranian graduate student Jack knew had translated the card for him when it had first arrived; Jack struggled a moment to recall. "It's in Iran, Mashhad, close to the border of Afghanistan." He suddenly recalled the hotel's name. "The Omar Khayyám Hotel. Something like that. I have no idea if it's still there."

"Iran and Afghanistan in 1978? That doesn't sound safe," Sandy said as she turned over the card and saw the signature. "Cassandra," she read and stopped. "That's really close to my name." She studied her father. "Am I named after her?"

"No, of course not. We both liked the name Sandra, your mother and I."

"Except Mom didn't know her full name was Cassandra. Am I right?"

"Maybe. I can't recall." Jack's answer was inadequate, he knew. But it was the truth. Then it hit him; it *was* his idea, naming their daughter Sandra. Not intentionally, of course. He knew himself better than that. But, on a subconscious level, he had betrayed Helene after all. Good God, he thought to himself.

Sandy was concentrating on the card, and read the message out loud:

> *Jack, Things are complicated here. I don't know about Istanbul. Don't come now. Explanation later. Cassandra.*

She put stress on the word "now." Jack straightened. In his head, he had always read the sentence differently, to mean that Cassie had now decided he shouldn't come. But Sandy's take implied that Cassie just wanted him to wait. He retrieved the card and reread it to see if he had missed something.

Sandy articulated what Jack was beginning to comprehend. "It doesn't sound like a brush-off to me, Dad."

At the same moment, Jack saw the card wasn't signed in the usual way, with Cassie or the letter C. The rest of the message was obviously written in a hurry, the phrasing truncated, the penmanship rushed. Not even a greeting. Yet she took the time to sign her full name. Cassandra: the woman ignored when she warns of disaster. Sandy was right; it was not a safe time to be in Iran or Afghanistan. Had Cassie been in danger?

A bottomless dread opened before him as he realized how badly he had misunderstood matters all these years.

JACK STOOD IN the dark, staring out at the rain-spattered street, his mind barely registering the few passing cars. Morose and sleepless, he thought over and over about the events of 1978. He didn't hear Sandy slip beside him at the living room window.

"It's late, Dad. Is everything okay?" she asked quietly.

He turned to her dark silhouette. "I didn't mean to wake you."

"You didn't. I got up for a glass of water and saw you standing here. What's wrong?"

Jack stared back outside. "I'm such an idiot."

Sandy took his arm. "It runs in the family. How can I help?" He didn't elaborate, so she pushed a little. "Mom? Cassie?"

"Cassie," he said somberly. "I could at least have written a letter asking what was going on. I knew she'd check General Delivery in Istanbul. I was too busy feeling sorry for myself, while she might have been in serious trouble."

"You never wrote back?"

"Only later, when she was supposed to be in Europe. But the letters were never claimed and were eventually returned." He stepped back from the window and pressed his palms into his eyes.

"Dad, it's all right. Let this go," Sandy urged. "You can't change anything. It's been too long." Minutes passed. When he still didn't reply, she continued, "All right, then. Contact her now. Reassure yourself. I'll bet she has ten children and twenty-seven cats."

Jack didn't move. Finally he said, "I tried several weeks ago. I did an Internet search. She's simply not there." He sighed deeply.

"You gave up after a Google search?"

When he nodded, Sandy glared meaningfully at him. "Is this my father the scholar speaking? The man who never accepts a Wikipedia citation?" She leaned toward him, only partially joking, "What kind of lame research is that, Googling her name and concluding she's lost forever?"

"I...," Jack started to say.

Sandy interrupted her father. "If you're serious, you can find her. I know you can."

CHAPTER NINE

August 27, 1978
Sunday

Marton got up very early, or perhaps he never slept. Cassie didn't know. But when she heard his rustling and opened her eyes, the light was on and he was packing his dress shirt from the evening before. Then she noticed that her large tote and backpack were in the room, propped next to his.

"You got my bags," she stated the obvious. She was not entirely pleased. She had left out a number of things in her rush to get ready the previous afternoon, and she was not confident that Marton had gotten them. More importantly, Cassie had planned to talk with Ralph this morning as she was packing up. She didn't want to end their relationship in front of the other men on the drive. She owed Ralph that much.

Ralph. She felt sick at her betrayal. Why had she slept with Marton? It was a dirty thing to do, complicating the breakup. For the moment, though, Cassie pushed the question aside. She couldn't undo her mistake. Now she had to dress and find Ralph. To explain, to apologize for hurting him, to wish him well in life.

Marton watched her, no expression on his face. Naked, Cassie felt self-conscious as she rose from the bed and rummaged in her backpack for clean underclothes. She noticed in the pack her clothes from the day before. They were neatly folded, by Marton, she presumed; Ralph didn't bother with folding clothes. She pulled out her khaki pants and blue shirt, fingers fumbling as she buttoned it. On the table lay the silver belt, shiny and coiled like a snake. Marton handed it to her; she nodded her thanks and tucked it into the top of the backpack.

"Everything's there," Marton stated, as if reading her mind. "I spoke with Ralph."

"Oh?" She stopped fastening her sandals to look up at him.

"I told him you spent the night with me. So he wouldn't be worried."

"It wasn't your place. I should have done that," she said crossly as she moved rapidly toward the door.

He grabbed her arm as she passed. "He's not there. He's already out in the van, in the back with Danny. You can talk with him later, after he calms down."

Calms down? That alarmed her. She hurriedly hoisted the pack on her back and grabbed the tote bag. Perhaps she could have a quiet word with him before they departed.

A few minutes later, when she approached the van, she peered through the open back door and saw two shadowy forms. Ralph and Danny, one on the seat and another further away, flat on the cot. It was too dark to recognize who was who. No one moved; no one spoke. From the heavy breathing, they seemed to be asleep. Following close behind her, Marton took her backpack, stowing it behind the front passenger seat and shutting the van's back door with a clang. One disgruntled groan from the back, then silence.

"Good morning, by the way," Marton said as he opened the front passenger door for her.

Cassie felt irked with him for telling Ralph. Even so, she shouldn't be rude. "Good morning," she replied as she climbed in. She was instantly struck by the van's awful organic smell; it seemed worse this morning, and she rolled down the window.

Once in the driver's seat, Marton continued, "We'll make good time today, very little traffic on Sunday. We're taking the toll road."

He handed her the roadmap and pulled the van away from the curb. They drove in silence as Marton skillfully negotiated the narrow streets. Enjoying the cool breeze from the open window, Cassie stared out at the predawn city. She was surprised to see so many people in the cafés at this hour. Of course, she realized; fasting wouldn't start until sunrise. After that lay a long hungry day.

The eastern sky had a faint glow by the time they reached the outskirts. Cassie's thoughts kept returning to the previous evening and what she had done. Such a confusion of feelings: anger at herself, sadness and regret that everything was over with Ralph. She hoped they could still be friends, but she didn't expect so.

Cassie shook her head and tried to think of something to talk about with Marton, to take her mind off this incessant brooding.

"How's your business working out?" she asked.

"It's all right," Marton replied, intent on the road ahead. "We'll see what happens when we get to Geneva."

We get to Geneva? He couldn't mean Danny, who had made it plain he was staying in Herat. Unless there was someone else she didn't know about, he must be referring to her. Cassie needed to be clear. "I like you, Marton, but I'm not going to Geneva."

He glanced at her. "You're upset about Ralph."

"Yes. But that's not the reason. I have other plans."

His hands gripped the steering wheel more tightly, but he said nothing.

In the ensuing silence, she studied his profile, considered what it might be like to travel with him. He was different from Ralph, less imaginative, but more worldly and knowledgeable. And where Ralph was blithely oblivious of bills, Marton was generous with his money; she wouldn't have to worry all of the time. But that wasn't necessarily a good thing either, she thought. She was deeply wary of accepting financial help. It created obligations, cost some independence. That thought made her decide to give back the silver belt tonight.

In any event, she knew he wasn't the right travel partner. Marton Zambo did what Marton Zambo wanted to do. Travel with him would never be a shared enterprise.

So, from now on, she'd travel alone. She thought about what that meant. She'd set the itinerary; she could, for example, visit the tomb of the Persian poet and mathematician Omar Khayyám in Iran. And she could focus on photography, maybe start selling her images. The New Orleans *Picayune* might buy some.

Yet, for all of her fantasies of the road alone, Cassie knew herself. She liked conversation, sharing stories and perspectives. Solitary excursions were wonderful when they were brief, but on long journeys like this, she needed companionship.

As they drove, daylight spilled slowly over the silhouette of the mountains, their rocky crests like dinosaur backbones. It washed over fields and fruit trees and ruined caravanserais. She remembered a line from Khayyám her father used to recite: *The hunter of the East has caught the Sultan's turret in a noose of light.* She couldn't remember the rest.

Far ahead in the early morning light was the bus that she and Ralph would have been on if yesterday had been different. It was pulled off to the side of the road. The driver and male passengers were disembarking, spreading prayer rugs on the ground and kneeling toward Mecca. She wondered about Islam; knew so little about it. In Thailand, she had read about Buddhism and gleaned a superficial understanding from talking with a monk once. The same had happened in India with Hinduism. But the truth was that she was ignorant about religion, even of her own. Raised Catholic, she hadn't attended mass in years. Her own beliefs had moved away from faith.

A sudden memory rose of an early conversation with Jack. They had somehow started to talk about religion. He said he was Methodist but his girlfriend Helene was Episcopalian, so he would probably switch. When he asked about her views, Cassie grew uncomfortable. People generally didn't like to hear that someone was agnostic or atheist. She decided to be honest anyway, and told him she rejected the notion of an all-powerful God, that even a benevolent tyrant was still a tyrant. But, she stressed, she did believe in the things Jesus taught: loving others, turning the other cheek, serving the poor. He said she didn't sound like an atheist; she sounded like an anarchist.

She hadn't known if she should feel affronted. "Aren't anarchists violent? Don't they blow things up?"

"That's a misconception," he had explained. "They believe that hierarchy – even in religion - oppresses and distorts the human spirit. In other words, hierarchy creates the real violence."

Cassie guessed she was an anarchist then. And possibly still an agnostic.

When they talked, Jack had been so knowledgeable and non-judgmental. She wondered how Marton would answer the question. She turned toward him. "What do you think about religion?"

"What, them?" He motioned toward the rear-view mirror where he could still see reflections of the men in prayer.

"Any religion. Do you believe in God?"

Marton didn't even stop to think. "I agree with Karl Marx on on-ly two things. 'The idiocy of rural life,' and religion is the opiate of the masses. They're related, of course. Religion is part of the idiocy of rural life."

His answer sounded like a personal grievance. "Are you from a rural area?"

"No, but my father was. I lived in a tedious gray city, huge apartment buildings rising up like tombstones. Modern housing for the dead masses." The disdain in his voice was palpable. He stared straight ahead at the road, "Petržalka."

"Petershall...?"

He shook his head. "It doesn't matter. To return to your question. In Czechoslovakia, maybe especially in the south, villagers still follow Catholic superstition. Even though it violates socialist state policy. I hated going to my father's village. Everyone pretending to be a good comrade, yet burning candles in secret and mumbling Latin spells."

"Maybe they were afraid to be open about it."

"That makes them cowards and hypocrites. My father most of all." He stared hard at the road. Cassie saw his lips tighten.

"Your father was religious?"

"Now he was a real Christian, my father." Unconsciously, Marton brushed the scar she had glimpsed at his hairline. The gesture left her wordless. It spoke of a violent childhood, of pain, anger, terror. Her heart ached for the frightened child.

After several minutes, Marton cleared his throat, "But religion isn't the only opiate. There's alcohol and drugs. And shopping."

"Shopping?"

"The opiate of the masses in advanced industrial societies. Salesmen are priests. Stores are temples, open for worship six days of the week. One day a week is for their other god."

Cassie considered his argument. "Then that's good for you, for your business. You count on people buying things."

He glanced over at her and gave a small smile. "Yes, I plan to push that opiate. Someday, I may even become a High Priest." He laughed but without humor.

"But, in a sense, you're an addict, too. You want the fanciest hotel, the grandest house, the best of everything."

He made a distasteful face. "I thought you understood me better than that, Cassie. I don't want money to buy *things*. I want it to get respect, the respect I deserve."

The conversation was going in a direction that Cassie had some difficulty following. "You want to buy respect?"

He sighed with impatience. "Let me explain equality in the great socialist republic of Czechoslovakia. My family was Hungarian, a minority population there. In school, Slovak students and even some teachers ridiculed me. For years this happened. But I was the best in mathematics so I was sent to a competition in Praha, Prague. And there – lo and behold - Czech students looked down on Slovaks! And looking down on all of us, our great Soviet brothers, the Russians." He regarded her directly. "With money, I'll have power. With power, I'll get respect."

Cassie nodded. She didn't like the idea of pursuing power; it violated her anarchist principles. But she could see how his childhood might have taught him that.

Minutes passed in silence. Cassie looked at the map in her lap. Her eyes tracked the solid line connecting Kabul with Kandahar and Herat, punctuated every inch or so with a dot for a town or toll station. From the legend, she estimated the total distance at five hundred miles. Marton planned for twelve hours. She looked at her watch; about ten hours to go.

They passed groves of trees, villages, melon and grape vines and crumbling watchtowers. Then more brown earth stretching to the distance. Afghanistan in August. It was an interesting place. She looked out at the landscape, taking special note of the ruins of caravanserais, scattered a day's journey by camel all along the route. She imagined traveling by caravan in the days of Alexander. She wondered if Ralph experienced travel this way, half in the present and half in an imaginary past. She glanced back to see if he had stirred yet. In the low light, she could see that Danny was sitting upright, staring outside. That meant Ralph was the immobile form on the makeshift bed.

Cassie shifted her gaze outside, mentally noting the land and life they passed, to use in her next letter to Jack. Since Bangkok, she had often done this. The exercise helped her pay attention to details and provided a way to share her experiences with Jack. She suddenly realized that he was her real travel companion.

In her mind, she wrote:

> *Black blemishes transform into tents of nomads, surrounded by shaggy goat, sheep and camel. We pass a village where the people are the color of their huts which are the color of the earth. Oxen pull wooden plows or trudge in tight circles to thrash wheat. A man shovels dirt into a basket on the back of another; people as pack animals.*

She'd write Jack from Herat. And she needed to talk with other travelers there, to find out more about Istanbul. She wanted to send him details on where and when to meet. In case he decided to come.

Marton spoke. "Are you on birth control?"

"What?" she jumped. He said it so loudly that she flushed with embarrassment; she didn't want Ralph to hear. She whispered back, "Sure, don't worry. I have an IUD." She hoped the engine noise had covered their voices.

He pressed her, "You don't want children?"

"Maybe someday. Maybe not. But certainly not now."

He frowned. "I'd prefer that you…"

At that moment, Danny's voice broke in, loudly complaining of needing to piss. In an aggrieved voice, he added that he was starving.

Cassie was suddenly aware of her own hunger and thirst. It was past eleven already and they'd had no breakfast. Marton abruptly

braked and pulled the van into a dirt lot. A tea house – a *chaikhana* -
stood a hundred feet away.

This is it, thought Cassie, bracing herself. I have to talk with
Ralph. She prepared herself for the painful conversation.

Danny moved quickly to fumble open the van's side door. Cassie
got out as well and walked toward it as Danny stepped out. His eyes
met hers, and his normally open face pinched into a scowl. "You really suck," he told her and pushed past. He strode toward the tea shop.

Troubled at his tone, Cassie looked past him into the van's interi-
or. "Ralph?" she called. With sunlight pouring in, she saw immediately that no one else was there. She didn't believe it and climbed in.
Instead of a man reclining on the makeshift cot, she found two backpacks; they had given the shadows a faux human form.

She scrambled out and confronted Marton, who was just rounding the front of the van. "Where is he?" she demanded. "Where is
Ralph?!"

Marton didn't respond right away; instead, he meticulously
locked the van's passenger door and side door, then tested them.
Eventually, he turned to face her. "Ralph didn't want to come. He said
he might join us later, in Herat or Mashhad."

"And why the hell didn't you tell me?" she shouted. "Why did
you lie?"

He stared at her and then shrugged, "What would you have done?
Stayed behind? Begged him to come?" His own anger was rising now.
"Would he have wanted to see you, do you think? After hearing that
we fucked all night?"

"You told him that!?" She was appalled. She hated the word *fuck*.
Why not *slept with, spent the night together, made love*? She even
preferred the unambiguous *had sex*. To her, *fuck* sounded crude, por-
nographic; it was the ugliest way to have told Ralph.

His voice harsh now, he goaded her. "I said it just like that, Cassie. Because it's the truth. I don't sugar-coat. I'm not some romantic

American who tells pretty lies." His hand shook as he pulled out a
cigarette and tried to light it.

"You're deceptive and mean!" she yelled.

Inarticulate with fury and shame, she stalked away from the van
and into the vast stretch of khaki-colored desert. Her legs trembled;
her stomach roiled. She abruptly dropped into a squat in the gravel.
She hated Marton in that moment. And herself: her vanity and gullibil-
ity in falling for his seduction. Mostly she hated her thoughtless cruelty to Ralph. He would think she had betrayed him and then abandoned
him. And she had. She should have checked to make sure he was on
board and all right. She couldn't blame Marton for that. It was her
fault. There was no way she could apologize to him now; she could
never make it right.

Twenty minutes passed. Eventually, Cassie stood and stumbled
on cramped legs toward the tea shop. She didn't enter; instead, she
found the shed that served as an outhouse. Then she went to stand in
the shadow of the van to wait for the others. Without a hat, she could
feel her face burn from too much sun. She didn't care.

Danny arrived first, and stood silently and awkwardly next to her.
"I didn't know," she told him, "I thought Ralph was in the van." He
didn't respond.

Five minutes later, Marton arrived and opened the front passenger door. Danny climbed in. After he unlocked the side door of the
van, Marton handed her a warm bottle of cola and a small cellophane
package of cookies. "Take it," he said. His voice was softer, placating.
An implied apology.

She wanted to refuse, but her thirst by now was intense and,
without a word, her hand took both offerings. She crawled into the
back of the van for the rest of the journey.

LATE AFTERNOON. CASSIE finally started to feel calmer. Her sharp anger was dissolving into the haziness of remorse. Perhaps it was the influence of the somber vista beyond the smudged window: a lonely limestone mountain, vast empty desert, only mirages of water.

She leaned against the glass and stared. Between the road and distant Hindu Kush lay a fog of dust. All dirt and rock here, sun on stone. Far away, along the jawline of the mountain, ancient fortresses jutted up like broken black teeth. Cassie squinted at dark blemishes against the pale earth. People? A town? No references to determine how close or far they were. The apparition finally came closer: a family in caravan, belongings wrapped in colorful blankets, loaded on camels. As the van passed them, a little girl riding on top of one bundle noticed her and waved. Cassie, smiling despite her pain, gave a small wave back.

At supper time, they stopped once more for tea and petrol. This time, Cassie joined the men. She had little stomach for food but nonetheless ordered rice with her chai. They sat around a low table without speaking. Once outside, she scanned for toilet facilities but saw none. The men walked a little way into the desert to relieve themselves, but Cassie felt too self-conscious to follow. As she considered her options, a slightly older French couple emerged from the *chaikhana*. The French woman also looked around, saw her and then motioned for her to come along. They posted guard for one another as they pissed behind a collapsed mud wall behind the teahouse. The French woman smiled and bid Cassie *au revoir*. The small act of normalcy made her feel slightly better.

Finally, after fifteen hours of driving, they pulled into Herat. It was late evening. Marton parked under a weak street lamp and strode down the street to find accommodations. Danny and Cassie stayed behind to unload the packs. Cassie hauled out her own; Danny easily carried his and Marton's.

As they did so, Cassie confided in a low voice, "I'm so sorry I hurt Ralph. I never meant to leave without him. I thought he was with you. That's what Marton said. But I should have checked." Assuming that Danny knew, she added, "And I shouldn't have slept with Marton. I don't know why I did."

Danny nodded. His mood had tempered through the long afternoon. "He can be really persuasive. I know." He seemed more alert than she had ever seen him. But more downcast and anxious also, glancing around at the shadows just beyond the lamplight.

"How will I ever explain it to Ralph? I'll never see him again." She felt close to tears.

Danny faced her. "Hey, no worries. He'll get here. And remember I'm staying in Herat, so even if you guys have to leave, I'll see him. I'll tell him what you said. How you're sorry."

Spontaneously, Cassie stood on tiptoes and kissed him on the cheek. "Thank you." She noticed then that he was sweating and had a runny nose. "Are you all right?" she asked.

Danny nodded. "It'll pass." He wiped his nose on his tee-shirt's sleeve.

A minute later, Marton rejoined them. "I've got rooms for us at the Behzad Hotel. There," he pointed in the direction of a large hulk not far from where they stood. "Local style, but clean. They have a good restaurant, free breakfast and indoor plumbing with hot water." At that, he gave Cassie a small private smile. "They only had two rooms available. I made reservations for us for five days." After they each shouldered a backpack, Marton gave Danny a room key. "You're next to us," he said.

"I want my own room," Cassie protested. When Marton and Danny both looked at her in alarm, she took a step backward but didn't concede.

"Please," Danny entreated.

"I'll sleep in the chair," Marton assured her.

Cassie said nothing. She felt too drained to argue or find another hotel tonight. For this one night, she would stay, but she would find some way not to sleep with Marton.

They checked into adjacent rooms on the third floor. Cassie and Marton's room had a double bed, along with a table and chair and a short stiff sofa where Cassie decided she would sleep. The bathroom, Marton said, was on the next floor down. Wordlessly, she grabbed her bag of toiletries and a towel and headed down to shower.

By the time she returned, Marton was walking out the door. "I'll be gone for a few minutes," he said. "I need to use the hotel phone to arrange things for tomorrow. The next few days will be busy."

Alone, Cassie looked at her backpack and considered what to do. Marton had unpacked part of his bag and stacked his things on the table; he'd left half the table clear for her. She knew she wouldn't use the space. For tonight, she only needed her oversized white tee shirt and cotton drawstring pants. Tomorrow, she'd find another hotel and rest for a day before catching the bus to Tehran. Then she stopped to reconsider. She might stay longer in Herat; after today's grueling drive and emotional strain, she wasn't anxious to keep going. And Ralph might show up.

She heard a noise and glanced up; Danny stood in the doorway.

"Where'd he go?" He seemed in pain, his shoulders hunched around his ears, his face awash with perspiration. "When's he coming back?"

"Sit down," Cassie ordered and guided him to the chair. "I think you're coming down with something." She opened her tote bag and retrieved a small medicine kit, then she popped the lid on an empty plastic film canister and shook out two aspirin.

Danny weakly protested. "I'm okay. Really. I just need to see Marton." He pressed his palms into his eye sockets.

She tried to sound reassuring. "He'll be back any minute. He's downstairs making a phone call." She kept her hand extended with the pills and Danny eventually took them, placed them in his mouth and swallowed. Closing his eyes and leaning back in the seat, he seemed resigned to wait.

Cassie replaced the medicine kit in her tote bag and noticed the aerogramme paper. Her last two sheets; she'd have to use them soon because they had Afghan postage and would be useless once she crossed the border into Iran. She would use one to write to her parents and the other for Jack. She pulled them out of the bag and placed them on the table next to where Danny slumped.

He opened his eyes and saw them. "Can I have one?" he pleaded. Cassie paused. She didn't want to give one away; then again, she didn't want to say no, not after his offer to help with Ralph. She could buy more airmail stationery tomorrow. Or a postcard; her parents liked getting postcards because their longtime neighbor used them as inspiration for painting watercolors.

"Sure." she handed him the flimsy blue sheet. Danny carefully folded it and stuffed it into his shirt pocket for later. He mumbled his thanks.

"Girlfriend at home?" she asked. She wouldn't be surprised if he had a dozen; he seemed to be quite a womanizer.

"Kid sister." Danny suddenly grinned, his shoulders relaxing a little. "Debbie's her name. She's terrific - really cute and really smart. Much smarter than I am," he bragged. He sat up straighter. "Two years ago, she learned how to sew in Home Ec and now she makes her own clothes. Most of them, anyway. Coats are hard, so I bought her one last year." He glowed with pride.

This was a side of him Cassie had not imagined. "Sounds like you're really close." She envied Debbie; she missed her own older brother.

"She's the best," he continued. "I wanted her to come along but our folks said no, absolutely not." He pinched his lips together, and mimicked in a high-pitched voice, "'Don't be ridiculous. She's too young.'" Probably the mother, Cassie thought. Danny fidgeted in his chair and continued, "They think I'm a bad influence. They're pretty conservative, religious, you know. But Debbie's mature. She's been working every summer for ages. Jeez, she sent me fifty bucks in her last letter, after I told her I was broke. Fifty!"

Cassie was moved. "How old is she?"

"Sixteen going on twenty-six," he said. "She's had it pretty rough with our folks so she's grown up fast. They don't get her. She likes miniskirts and halter tops, but they want her to wear these shapeless polyester double-knit dresses. They fight with her all the time. Once I heard Mom say she looked like the whore of Babylon." He hunched over at the memory. "That made Deb cry. How can parents be so mean?"

Cassie couldn't answer; her own parents were nothing like that.

A moment passed and his expression softened. "I was six when she was born. I went to the hospital with a neighbor because Dad was at work. I looked through the glass window they have, you know? And this tiny baby in a pink knit cap smiled at me. Right at me. It was like POW," he smacked a fist into his palm, "instant love. This perfect little being."

She studied him a moment. He was not callow after all. Not simply a druggie pushing Ralph into oblivion. She wondered briefly about his story, what had really brought him so far from home. She also realized that he was younger than she was, only twenty-two. It shifted her feelings about him, made her feel protective. The big sister to a big brother to a little sister.

Danny cleared his throat. "So, tell me about this professor guy that Ralph says you're always writing to. Was he your old boyfriend or what?"

"Gosh, no. And he wasn't my professor either. He's just a friend, a nice guy I met at the airport in New Orleans."

"Really?" Danny thought about this. "But he *is* a professor."

"Soon to be. He's finishing his doctorate. His dissertation thesis is that the imperial presidency in foreign affairs didn't end with Vietnam and Watergate and Nixon's resignation. That, despite the War Powers Act and other new laws, presidents will assert extraordinary powers again and threaten the constitutional system. He thinks it's inevitable because of nuclear weapons and other modern technologies. So Congress and the people have to remain vigilant."

"I have no idea what you just said," Danny groaned. "I hope he doesn't write this boring shit in his letters."

Cassie felt a little stung; she thought Jack was fascinating. She quickly added, "He's funny, too. He once wrote as an alien visiting an earth grocery store. Another time, he described the sights and sounds of walking through Haight-Ashbury on a Saturday night. It was amazing, like I was there." It inspired her own descriptive letters.

"The Haight? What a coincidence! Me and Debbie are going to move there once I get back to the States. A friend of mine has a record store, says a job's waiting for me anytime I come."

Cassie smiled; Debbie seemed to be a good influence on her brother. In the short term, however, he was moving nowhere. Danny was leaning back in the chair, eyes closed now, energy depleted.

Marton still wasn't back. A good moment to start a letter, Cassie thought. It might be awkward to write to Jack with Marton in the room. She roused Danny, "Why don't you go and get some sleep?"

"Sure, sure, sure," he said and stood abruptly. The move made him dizzy and he grabbed the table's edge to steady himself. Then he turned to go. Cassie knew she would have to write quickly. She claimed the chair he had vacated, found her pen and scribbled a salutation.

"Hey, Marton," she heard Danny say from the doorway, and she looked up. Marton had returned.

He brushed past Danny and approached the table. "What's this?" he asked mildly as he picked up the page in front of her. "Who's Jack?"

"A friend," she replied, reaching for the paper.

He held the largely blank sheet held away from her, waiting.

Danny interjected, "A professor. That's what Ralph says." Cassie noticed that he didn't give Marton the full story.

Marton kept his eyes on her. "Your professor?" She worked to keep her expression neutral. She didn't like this curiosity of his. It felt like jealousy.

"Give me the letter," she insisted archly and reached for it again.

This time, he handed it to her with a mock flourish. Then he frowned. "Please don't write any letters," he ordered. "That goes for you, too, Danny. There are SAVAK agents all around, even on this side of the border. We have to be careful the next few days, until we're out of Iran. Do you understand me? No letters. It's too dangerous."

Danny asked the same question that had come to Cassie's mind. "What's SAVAK?"

"The Iranian secret police."

Cassie didn't understand how any letter she would write could interest the secret police. Further, they were miles from Iran. Marton was being paranoid, she realized with a start. Nevertheless, under his stern gaze, she folded the aerogramme and slid it into her tote bag. She would finish the letter later when she was alone. He couldn't command her not to write.

A DISTURBING DREAM startled Cassie awake, but now she couldn't remember much. Mashed up visual images: the Grand Palace in Bangkok but in the dream it was Geneva. A man with a blue face accosted her and tried to sell her opiate of the masses. Then she was watching Jack and Ralph try to stab each other with pens.

Cassie huddled deeper under the covers. The air here was drier than in Kabul, making nighttime temperatures cooler.

Marton had refused to sleep on the bed; it was hers, he insisted. She ignored him and dragged a blanket and pillow to the sofa. He spread another blanket and pillow on the floor. No one slept on the bed.

The sofa was lumpy and short. Half asleep, she shifted her weight for the thousandth time searching for a comfortable position. A lost cause. She opened an eye, noticed that Marton was no longer on the floor. She could see his silhouette standing at the window.

"Everything okay?" she asked sleepily. She imagined him keeping watch for elusive SAVAK agents.

He turned toward her. "You're awake," he said. "Good. I want to apologize for yesterday. For telling you that Ralph was in the van."

Cassie was not expecting this. She made no reply; she wasn't sure she should forgive him for it.

He explained. "I was angry. At Ralph, not at you. Early in the morning, when I went to get your backpack, I told him you were safe and not to worry. I think I also said you were my girlfriend now, but nothing crude or vulgar. And do you know what he did?" She could sense Marton studying her intently, as if she could guess. "He shrugged," and Marton shrugged to make the point. "He didn't hit me, or even curse. He lost you and did absolutely nothing." He turned away, looking again out of the window. In a matter-of-fact tone, he reflected, "I would have killed him, if it had been reversed. What an inconsequential man. So I told him he couldn't come with us. I couldn't stand the idea of him in the van." With palpable scorn, Marton added, "Now *that* upset him." He paused in thought. "He didn't deserve you. He never deserved you."

Cassie still said nothing. His story reassured her in some ways; he hadn't been nasty with Ralph and Ralph hadn't been as angry as she feared. But it hurt also, to think how easily Ralph had dismissed her from his life; she felt mortified for believing she had mattered. Regardless, now that she could visualize the morning's encounter, she felt her burning sense of shame cooling down. Her anger at Marton still simmered, though. For telling Ralph in the first place. For blowing up at her in the desert instead of telling her this.

Marton didn't seem to need a response from her. "I'm not like him, Cassie. I fight for what I want. I have always had to fight."

He moved toward the sofa and sat on the floor next to her. "Ten years ago, when I immigrated to Canada, I spoke almost no English. I found a job in a hotel. Housekeeping - mopping floors, scrubbing toilets. Dirty work, but I did what I had to do. Later I worked other jobs around the hotel. When I wasn't working, I studied English and practiced speaking with guests. Late at night, I worked out in the hotel gym. That's how I survived. Finally - because I work hard and I'm good with numbers - I got promoted to night manager. I like working at night when no one is around."

Silence for several moments as Cassie studied his profile in the dark. "It sounds lonesome," she offered.

"Not really. Guests sometimes like to talk. And sometimes a quick fuck with a lonely woman traveling through. It's not a bad life." Marton leaned his back against the sofa. "The hotel management, they liked me. I don't drink; I don't take drugs; I don't steal. I stayed there two years, then moved to a better hotel, then a better hotel, until I worked as night manager at a top hotel."

It sounded like a classic rags-to-riches tale, with a boy hero from Czechoslovakia. "Is that where you work now?"

In the darkness, she could see him shake his head no. "Last December, I met a man who told me about an excellent opportunity here. I came last spring, did a little business and everything checked out. So

I quit my job, took all my savings and came back." His shadowy form shifted so that he faced her. "It has to work out, Cassie. It has to."

She got his meaning. He was risking everything. That could explain his quick temper, his paranoia, his intensity. That didn't excuse his lies about Ralph. Even so, she felt sympathy mixed with admiration and concern. His risk-taking elevated him in her eyes, made his business venture sound valiant and brave.

"I don't have an education, not like Ralph. I don't have family or rich friends. But I do have experience. I have ambition. I have dreams."

He stopped speaking. Finally, Cassie filled the silence. "Having dreams is a good thing." She thought about herself and this trip.

In the dusky light from the street, she could see his grin. "I'm glad you said that. When I met you, all of my dreams started to become real. For the first time in my life, everything is coming together. Our meeting was destiny."

He couldn't be serious; she smiled at his melodrama. "You can't say that, Marton, that stuff about destiny. You don't even know me. We just met a few days ago."

His voice in the dark was earnest and firm. "I feel as if I've known you my entire life."

Taken aback by his certainty, she didn't know what to say. Quiet minutes passed. Finally, Cassie stood, gathered her pillow and blanket and walked to the bed. She lay down and watched as Marton picked up his bedding and came beside her. They did not touch. Even so, Cassie felt the warmth generated by his body and listened to his breathing. In moments, Marton was asleep.

But she couldn't rest. Instead, lying still, she wondered what he meant, if he cared at all about her. She wondered if she should leave in the morning or stay a while longer. He wasn't like Ralph. In fact, he wasn't like anyone she had ever met. He was an enigma, a mystery. And some deep part of her wanted to solve it.

CHAPTER TEN

May 21, 2007
Monday

Jack had spent much of his adult life doing research. He considered it detective work. He was in full detective mode now. He knew the importance of considering what questions to ask and why and where to look for evidence. He knew the necessity of background and context. Beyond that, social scientists needed certain personal traits: patience, focus, rigor and intellectual honesty. They had to be willing to accept when a hypothesis was weak or disproved by the evidence. For Jack, that meant he had to be brave enough to admit he might never find Cassie; even that Cassie could be dead.

Until her death was established through hard evidence, though, he would proceed with his hypothesis that she was not. And the corollary hypothesis that she could be found.

But there was a major difference between this research and his professional studies. Unlike his work on foreign policy and presidential power, this was a deeply personal quest. The question of her whereabouts was not abstract or theoretical.

134

Jack felt energized and optimistic, thanks to Sandy. All weekend, she had helped him unpack and organize his space. Books were on the shelves, towels in the linen closet, dishes in the cabinets, pictures on the walls. He was amazed at how much better these changes made him feel about the apartment, about his new life as a single man. And when Sandy happily reported that the lunch with her mother had gone well, he felt genuine relief as well; he had not been able to predict Helene's reaction to Sandy's news.

Now, with his daughter gone, he had no obligations but to the investigation. "The Cassie File," Sandy had called it, a wry reference to the *X Files* because Cassie had seemingly vanished. "Don't discount extraterrestrial abduction," she had advised when she left. "The Truth is Out There, Dad."

The truth indeed. With his morning coffee in hand, he stared at the world map he'd tacked to the wall in the dining room, his base of operations. "Where in the world are you, Cassie Robinette?" His finger traced the line of her journey as far as he knew it: from Bangkok to Nepal to India to Pakistan to Afghanistan to Iran. From there, she could have continued as planned to Turkey, Greece, and the rest of Europe. Or, instead of Turkey, she could have headed due west from Mashhad to Iraq. Or she could have turned around and gone back to Kathmandu; she had loved it there. She might have joined a Buddhist monastery or a Hindu ashram. Or started working at a refugee camp on the Thai-Cambodian border; she'd mentioned that possibility once. Or she could have come home.

If only he had the last letter, the one that Helene had destroyed. It hadn't mattered to him before, since he had expected only hurtful news. Now he felt its loss keenly. According to Helene, the letter had started with a reference to Istanbul but she said she had not read the rest before burning it. He fought the feeling of searing recrimination against Helene, against himself, concentrating instead on what he did know. "Where are you now?" he whispered again at the map. To find out, he would need to work both ends of the question: 1978 and 2007.

On-line, he had found and printed out a 1978 calendar. He also had signed up with several newspapers for archival access so he would understand the geopolitical context in which she was traveling. And he registered with an internet company that compiled government databases, everything from arrest records to marriages and divorces.

Now Jack cleared the big oak table. There, he dumped the letters out of the crumpled manila envelope and organized them by date, stacked them according to locale. With smooth jazz playing in the background, he settled down to reread Cassie's letters, making notes, compiling lists, looking for clues. As he read, he filled in her likely itinerary on the 1978 calendar.

He was also looking for her birthdate to eliminate false leads. He remembered that she had been born in the same year as Helene, 1955, but what month? Then he came across a letter he vaguely recalled.

It's my birthday! Dinner on the terrace of the Oriental Hotel with friends of Becky's parents, visiting from Chicago. It's an elegant, traditional place, tranquil & cool above the serene Chao Phya River. We're loud & underdressed, surrounded by other loud & underdressed farongs (foreigners). But the Thai waiters are unobtrusive & impeccable. We're like crass coloni- alists from a Somerset Maugham short story, blundering through the country without a clue.

The date was June 8. He wrote it down.

Names of friends, family? She mentioned Ralph a lot, but never his last name. Jack scanned the letters and nothing jumped out. Had she told him when they met? It was twenty-nine years ago, and he simply couldn't remember.

In addition, she provided no first names of her parents or hometown, although he knew it was in southern Louisiana somewhere. Didn't she go to college in New Orleans? He thought he remembered that. She must have mentioned it in conversation since it wasn't in the letters. He knew she had studied film. In the airport, they had talked about their favorite movies. For years, he thought of Cassie whenever he watched *Casablanca.* She said he reminded her of Humphrey Bogart in the film. He thought it was a compliment but wasn't sure.

Jack kept scanning the letters. In Bangkok, Cassie had stayed with a former college roommate named Becky. Again, no mention of a last name. This was getting frustrating.

He suddenly remembered seeing the names of the two men Cassie had met in Kabul. He found her last letter: the men were Danny Mack and Marton Zambo. He wrote the names down, and their nationalities. Then he tried a quick internet search. Nothing on either one. It was as if all three of them, perhaps Ralph as well, had stumbled into the Bermuda Triangle and disappeared. He would try a more exhaustive search on them later.

Then an idea came to him. He had written several letters to Cassie in care of her Bangkok friend. There had to be a return address on at least one of the envelopes.

And there it was: Care of Becky Dehart. His eyes scanned the Thailand letters searching out Cassie's references to Becky. She taught third grade at the International School in Bangkok. Perhaps he could find an old roster of ISB teachers somewhere. Becky had a new boyfriend named Raul; he worked for the Mexican embassy. No last name for him either. Even so, details like these might help him find Becky, and she would know where Cassie was.

He turned again to his laptop, trying various search engines with the name Becky Dehart; again, no luck. He wasn't surprised. Women often changed their last names when they got married; even Helene had. Maybe he could search Facebook for an American woman who attended college in New Orleans named Becky or Rebecca, who also had taught at the International School of Bangkok in the late 1970s. He picked up one of Cassie's last letters from Thailand and glanced over it again.

Then he stopped at a sentence he had skimmed several times. Becky had gotten engaged to Raul. Cassie thought it was a funny co-incidence that he had the same last name as her hometown.

Her hometown had a Spanish last name! Jack raced to the under-ground parking garage and found a road atlas in his car. Impatient to know, he spread the atlas on the hood and flipped the pages to Louisi-ana. By the dim overhead light, he drew his finger across the state's southern tier. Other than for large towns, though, the print was too small to read; he brought the atlas upstairs and grabbed a magnifying glass. Lots of French names: Baton Rouge of course, Lafayette, Thibodaux, Ville Platte. Strange ones like Opelousas and Ponchatoula. And then he saw it, south of Baton Rouge. The town was Gonzales. That was where Cassie was from. He knew it the instant he saw it.

Becky Gonzales. That had to be the right name. He prayed that she hadn't married someone else after all, or long been divorced or dead.

This time searching the web, Jack had luck. The smiling face of an older woman was attached to a Facebook account that claimed more than a hundred friends. Not much was available for public view-ing, but she did list some of her past affiliations. One of them was the International School, and the years were exactly right – 1977 to 1979.

Jack hurriedly typed a Facebook message.

Dear Ms. Gonzales: You don't know me but I was a friend of Cassie Robinette's, your college friend. I would like very much to reconnect with her and hope that you can help. I know that she stayed with you in Bangkok in 1978. Do you know where

she went from there? Any help would be most appreciated.
Thanks, Jack Hunter.

As he had with Cassandra Robinette, Esq., he provided his university URL, so she would know he was legitimate. He did not have
high hopes of a quick response, but he hoped for something. Meanwhile, he would have to be patient.

To feel productive, Jack decided to scan news stories from 1978.
From his own research, he knew how political upheaval could upend
ordinary lives. Events in Afghanistan and Iran thirty years ago could
account for her disappearance and still be complicating his ability to
find her. He checked the listing of headlines. One piece of good news
that year: Anwar El Sadat and Menachem Begin signed the Camp Da-
vid Accords. But most headlines were grim. Plane crashes, terrorist
kidnapping and murder in Italy, two popes dead, a mass murderer of
young men, mass suicide in Guyana.

Jack stopped. He had forgotten about Guyana. More than nine
hundred members of the People's Temple – including hundreds of
children – had been urged to drink poison by the group's fanatical
leader Jim Jones. A related memory rose, that Jones had been a community leader in San Francisco when Jack lived there; had befriended
Mayor Moscone and gay supervisor Harvey Milk. Jack had liked both
Moscone and Milk and had voted for them; later that same year, both
were assassinated. Now he wondered how he had blocked these tragedies from his memory. What else did he not remember that he thought
he would never forget?

Overall, 1978 was a terrible and disheartening year, and he started to close the laptop. Then, at the bottom of the screen, he saw the
subheading he was looking for. Central Asia. Jack clicked on the links
to read the full news reports on Afghanistan.

Within months of criticizing the Kremlin's increasing domination
of Afghan affairs, the Afghan president had been murdered and re-

placed by a pro-Soviet group. That was in April 1978. By the time Cassie arrived four months later, much of the country was in rebellion. She had mentioned tanks and troops, even a soldier holding a gun to her head, yet her letter treated it simply as an interesting episode. Jack pondered: travel for an American in Afghanistan was risky. If something bad had happened, would anyone know about it? The decades that followed remained tumultuous: war with the Soviet Union, the rise of the Taliban and civil war, the U.S.-led invasion after September 11, 2001, ongoing war.

Then there was Iran. He reviewed the news accounts with increasing concern. By late 1977, opposition to the autocratic regime of Shah Reza Pahlavi sparked nation-wide labor strikes and protests. Things came to a head on September 7, 1978, when the Shah imposed martial law. The next day – called Black Friday - thousands of protestors in Tehran were reportedly shot by soldiers. Jack quickly flipped to the 1978 calendar. Her postcard from Mashhad was written on the fifth. He swore under his breath. She had been on her way to Tehran. Had she gone? Had she been hurt? Who would know? He wondered if the CIA or State Department had reports. Perhaps Frank Constant could use his connections.

Brooding and anxious, Jack opened Facebook again and checked for a message. Seeing none, he closed his laptop. "Hell with it," he said and put on shorts and running shoes. He needed to run.

As he was trotting down the steps of his apartment building, his cell phone rang. It was Estelle from the office. Since he wasn't teaching summer school, he wasn't expected to be on campus. He considered ignoring the call, getting back to her later. But he felt a little curious. He consciously adopted a light tone when he answered. "Hi, Estelle. How's life in the trenches? The department move going well?"

"Hello, Dr. Hunter. Sorry to bother you at home. The move is a real pain in the posterior, as it happens. You're about the only one whose stuff is all packed up. But that's not why I called." She paused, "You just got a strange phone message. I thought you might want to know. The woman said she was Becky, a friend of a friend from Bangkok. Nothing else, and no last name. Does that make sense?"

"Yes!" Jack realized Becky Gonzales must have found his office phone number on the web site and decided to call. "I've been hoping to hear from her," he added to explain the enthusiasm in his voice.

"She left a number. Are you ready?"

Jack asked Estelle to hold for a moment as he ran back upstairs to the apartment. As he scribbled the number, he recognized a Houston area code. "Thanks a lot, Estelle," and he hung up.

He dialed the number nervously, hopefully. "Is Becky Gonzales there, please?" He found himself fidgeting from foot to foot in his running shoes, and had to will himself to stand still.

"Yes, speaking. How may I help you?"

"Hello. I'm Jack, Jack Hunter. I left you a message on Facebook?"

"Yes, of course. I thought you might call. The woman in your office was very nice but she absolutely refused to give me your personal phone number." A warm voice with a southern accent.

"Sorry about that. It's university policy."

"Well, it's not a problem." The woman added reassuringly, "I understand."

Jack leaned his elbows on the table. "Thanks for calling, Ms. Gonzales."

"Call me Becky, please. I thought I should call because I don't have good news, I'm afraid. I haven't heard from Cassie in ages. Really, not since she stayed with me in Bangkok."

Jack had braced himself for this possibility, but even so felt deflated. "Well, do you know anyone else I might contact?"

"Have you tried her old boyfriend Ralph? He might know."

"I don't know his last name. Cassie never mentioned it. I only know yours because I wrote to her at your address in Bangkok."

"You wrote to Cassie there?"

"Yes, several times. We had met in the airport in New Orleans."

Then came a drawn-out silence on the other end of the line. Finally, she announced, "I know who you are. You're C-3PO."

"Excuse me?" The neurotic droid in *Star Wars*? He was dumbfounded.

"Now how did I remember that when I can't remember my own cell number half the time?" Becky sounded amazed at herself.

"C-3PO?"

Chortling, she said, "Let me think a moment what it stood for. It was Cassie something. Ralph made it up to annoy her. He thought he was being witty. Oh, I've got it! Cassie's Pen Pal Professor...," she paused to think. "Obsession. Pen Pal Professor Obsession! Ha!" She sounded so triumphant that Jack imagined her high-fiving herself. "He'd call you that whenever Cassie said she had to write you a letter."

"Obsession?" This conversation wasn't getting any clearer to Jack.

She explained, "From Ralph's point of view. An hour she spent writing to you was an hour she wasn't focusing on him. He was jealous. She was half in love with you, you know."

In a rush of unexpected pleasure, Jack felt his face coloring, his mouth open. He was relieved there was no visual. Quickly regaining composure, he asked, "So, can you help me?"

"Actually, we really haven't been in touch since then. I have no idea where she is now. We argued about Ralph. I thought he was arrogant and self-centered and told her so. She deserved better."

"Was he violent? Could he have hurt her?" Jack needed to consider the possibility that Cassie was not the victim of geopolitical events, but of someone she trusted.

"Ralph? Good Heavens, no. He wasn't mean, just manipulative. That's what I meant. Cassie just couldn't see it." Then her tone softened and she mused thoughtfully, "But it wasn't a big fight."

Jack waited for her to continue. When she didn't, he asked, "Did she ever write?"

"No, that's the point. Well, I didn't expect a letter while she was on the road, but I did once she arrived in Europe. We had plans to meet in Madrid over Christmas break. A mutual friend was there on Study Abroad. But Cassie never got in touch, either with me or our friend. And she never showed up. I realized then she hadn't forgiven me."

As she spoke, Jack recalled something. "She told me about your Christmas plans, in a letter from Delhi. So I don't think that's the reason." He didn't want to alarm her, but had to be frank. "I think she got into trouble. And that's why she never showed up."

Becky was silent for several moments. Then she murmured, "Oh, God, no. What could have happened to her?"

It was a rhetorical question. He answered it anyway. "From that September on, I don't know. The last letter I got was from Kabul dated late August, 1978."

"And nothing after that?" Becky started to sound frantic.

"A cryptic postcard from Iran arrived about a week later. I misread it; I thought she was ending things with me, such as they were. I didn't put two and two together until now; that she might have been caught up in what was happening at the time in Afghanistan or Iran." He thought back to the ominous news articles he had just read.

"I didn't even think…. I'm so stupid." she said.

"I know how you feel, but I don't know what we could have done at the time." Then, with urgency in his voice, Jack added, "That's why I feel I have to find her now. I have to know."

Becky agreed instantly. "Yes, of course. Talk to Ralph. He was with her, wasn't he? He was supposed to be looking out for her!"

Jack picked up the pen again. "Do you know Ralph's last name? How I can reach him?""

"He pronounces it Ralph now."

Jack blinked. "You mean like Ralph Vaughn Williams?"

"Yes, honey, Ralph like in Safe. It's Ralph Johnson. Lord, the only reason I remember is because he's sometimes mentioned in book reviews. He's a pretty famous fantasy writer."

Jack sat up straight. "*That* Ralph Johnson?" He knew his work. His son Max read a lot of it.

"I know. Who would have guessed, right?"

So Ralph had succeeded as a writer after all. Cassie had believed in him from the beginning. Surely Ralph would help him find her.

"I don't have a phone number, but I'll bet you can reach him through his publisher." She added, "Meanwhile, I'll contact other friends from the old days, to see if they've heard anything."

"Terrific idea." Jack was getting excited, eager to start his search for Ralph Johnson.

"Well, I've got to go. Keep in touch, and I'll do the same. It's nice to meet you after all these years. Bye now."

Once they disconnected, he flipped open the laptop and started searching Ralph's name on-line. As he clicked on the publisher's web site, his phone rang again. It was Becky.

"Listen, Jack dear, I just had an idea. I'm active with the alumni association at Loyola."

When she said this, he couldn't help but interrupt. "Loyola University! Of course! I'd forgotten."

Barely pausing, she continued, "I'll see if I can get an address for Cassie or her folks through the alumni office."

"You can?"

"No promises, of course. There are all sorts of privacy laws now. And no guarantee that the address on file is still any good. But I'll be in New Orleans in a few weeks and will drop by Loyola. Being face-to-face makes it harder for them to turn me down. I'll let you know what I find out, regardless. Okay?"

"Great, thanks." Jack said, then repeated more firmly, "Really. Thanks, Becky."

"No, honey, thank you. I feel awful about Cassie. If you think of anything else I can do, you just let me know. And you've got to promise to tell me what you find. Even if it's not good news."

"I promise." His elation tempered when he understood fully what she meant: *even if it's not good news.* But he refused to consider this possibility, not yet. As he hung up, he felt only optimism. He now knew Cassie's hometown and college. He had a lead on Ralph, who surely knew something. And he had an ally in Becky Dehart Gonzales. How could he not find Cassie?

CHAPTER ELEVEN

August 28, 1978

Monday

Marton hummed softly as he dressed. A comforting morning sound to Cassie; her mother used to hum when she cooked breakfast. Opening her eyes, Cassie watched him pull on a torn tee shirt and pants. His good shoes tucked under the table, he took a worn pair from his backpack.

"Hey, there," she said, sitting up in bed and wrapping her arms around her legs. "Pretty casual for business, isn't it?"

Marton considered his attire. "We're inspecting merchandise today, and the factory's filthy. In fact, most of the factories are. It'll be dirty work all week, unfortunately. Unpacking, sorting through things, repacking."

She scooted to the edge of the bed, dangled her feet. "What types of merchandise? Carpets and things?"

He glanced at her, then returned to tying his shoes. "Someday, yes. Now, wool cushions, ceramics, lapis lazuli boxes, some tourmaline. A few rough-cut emeralds. And silk, when I can find good quality. Things easy to transport in the van."

"Oh, you're not shipping them?"

146

He shook his head. "We'll have half a dozen boxes or so. Plenty of room in the van."

Plenty of room, she thought, now that there were only three of them. Actually only two, if she continued to travel with Marton and Danny stayed in Herat. "Danny," she said, remembering him. "Is he working today too? He looked pretty terrible last night."

Marton shrugged. "He seemed okay when I checked. We're meeting for breakfast. Come along, if you like," he said.

Just as he was about to leave the room, Cassie called his name and he stopped. If she was going to travel with him, she had to be absolutely clear. "Please don't ever lie to me again," she said.

For a moment, Marton didn't move. Then, with a slight dip of his head in acknowledgement, he turned and left.

She dressed and combed her hair and soon was downstairs as well. The hotel breakfast room was on the first floor. By the time she arrived, Marton was just sitting down with hardboiled eggs, dates and bread. Danny was still at the buffet table. His clothes were in better condition than Marton's, a tee shirt emblazoned with an image of the Taj Mahal and a pair of loose cotton trousers, both white but slightly soiled. He hadn't come to Afghanistan prepared for dirty work, she mused as she moved to his side.

"How are you feeling this morning?"

He gave a weak grin. "Hanging in there." His face was still pale and his hands shook as he carried his tray of food to the table. But he managed not to spill anything.

Cassie filled a plate and sat next to Danny, across from Marton. As she ate, she studied the contrast between the two men. Danny, though taller and more muscular, seemed fragile somehow next to Marton, whose movements were so sure and precise. Theirs was a strange relationship, she thought, somewhere between a friendship and a business arrangement. But it wasn't equal. Any stranger could see who was dominant.

"What will you do today?" Marton asked her, finishing his tea.

"I don't know. Look around the town, visit this famous mosque Danny talked about." She was no longer certain she needed to find a new hotel. She was feeling more relaxed this morning, and decided to take things one day at a time. "When will you be back?"

"Not before five. Today's factory is out of town, so we won't come back for lunch. Will you be all right?"

"I'll be fine," she assured him.

The men finished their meal and hustled noisily out of the breakfast room. In the sudden quiet, Cassie was surprised at the relief she felt. The entire day alone, a luxury of time, no obligations but to explore. She finished a second cup of tea and returned to the room for her camera and tote bag. At the last minute, she tied the apricot scarf around her hair. Then she pushed through the hotel's double doors and randomly opted to turn left.

A few steps away, in a large display window, was posted an artistically lettered sign in English: the Afghan Tourist Office. A good place to start, she thought, and went in. The room featured a long counter, a few chairs, a book shelf and rack of brochures. Along one wall, a large map of the city was posted. But she was drawn to an enlarged colored photograph posted on another wall; it showed an impressive minaret looming against a backdrop of towering desert mountains. With a cap of stone, it reminded her of an elongated chess piece, a bishop. Cassie approached to examine it more closely.

A dark-eyed man stood behind the counter and watched; initially he had appeared a little taken aback when she entered, a lone woman. Now he inclined his head in greeting and, in very correct English, said, "The Jam Minaret, madam. Very old, eight hundred years. Perhaps the tallest in the world at sixty-five meters."

She didn't know how to convert that height into feet, but the man's expression told her enough: it was extraordinarily tall. She asked, "Is it far from here?" She wanted to go, to stand at the base and gaze at the medieval stone finger pointing the way into the heavens.

"Not far but, alas, difficult to reach on rough roads. It is in a high mountain valley. There are tours, however," and he pointed to one of the brochures in the stand. "The journey will take two days, maybe three, depending on conditions of the road. Truly, it is magnificent, if you have the time."

She couldn't answer; she honestly did not know if she would have the time. But she decided to raise the possibility with Marton. "What else should I see?" she asked. "In town?"

He walked to the brochures and picked up several, then handed them to her, with a mimeographed map of Herat. On the map, tourist hotels and historic points of interest were marked and identified with a key in English and French. The Tourist Office itself was number fourteen. Even the Behzad Hotel was noted.

This would help a lot. She smiled as she took the material. "*Tashakor mikonam*."

The man's eyelid flickered before he responded, "*Khahest mikonam*." He added, "Pardon me, madam. Do you speak Dari?"

"No," she confessed, "A word or two. I wish I knew more."

He paused only a moment. "You are American?" When she nodded, he continued, excitement rising in his voice. "My son is an engineering student at Herat University. He knows English and he would like to learn American-English. You are here for a few days? Then you must meet him for tea. He can teach you Dari, and you can speak to him in American."

She planned to read this afternoon, take a nap, continue her letter to Jack. But this opportunity was too appealing and Cassie replied at once, "I would like that."

The man stepped back and bowed his head slightly. "Pardon my presumption, madam. I became carried away. First, I must ask your husband."

She almost said that she wasn't married but then reconsidered. She decided to invent a husband for safety's sake. Otherwise, she might seem dangerously immoral. Despite the trappings of modernity in the cities, Cassie sensed a deep traditional reserve in Afghanistan. She reassured the man, "My husband is working but he will not mind. He has asked me to visit the sights in Herat. If your son would like to meet, I can come this afternoon."

"Excellent. At two o'clock then, when he is free from class. You will please come here first?" When she nodded, he made a small gracious bow.

A few minutes later, clutching map and brochures, Cassie took her leave. On the insistence of the man in the Tourist Office, she decided to visit first the Friday Mosque, Masjid-I-Jami'. It was only a block away, south of the hotel. Reading the map as she walked, she saw that the fortress she passed was the one where Genghis Khan and later Tamerlane had battled. They were part of a history she had never studied in school. She squinted in the bright daylight to read the inscription posted high on its wall, but the dates and unfamiliar names didn't hold her attention.

That changed when she arrived at the mosque. Surrounded by a vast wall, it wasn't initially visible. But when she stepped through a gateway, she could only stop and stare. Masjid-I-Jami' was unlike any structure she had ever seen. Two high towers crowned with blue domes framed the mosque's imposing face. Recessed within the face was an arched entrance rising at least three stories high. The entire structure was covered in glazed tiles of blue, violet, green, gold, orange and ivory, laid out in mesmerizing designs of Arabic script, floral figures and abstract geometrics. Cassie wandered around the vast paved courtyard eying the mosque from various angles. Finally, she saw an image she wanted and took a photograph; a few minutes later, a close-up of intricate tile work; then a panorama that – she sadly realized – would not do justice to the colossal structure.

She finally pulled herself away to return to the hotel for something to eat, taking a circular route back. On the way, a glint of blue light in a window distracted her. A small sign in the window advertised a glass bazaar and workshop. Curious, Cassie held her hands around her eyes to block out the sunlight and peered through the dusty window. Within was shelf after shelf of blue glass. She tried the door but it was locked, the shop closed. She would come back, she decided.

BY TWO THAT afternoon, Cassie had returned to the Tourist Office. Waiting for her was the man she met that morning with a much younger man, who introduced himself as Saaleh. At a wave of his father's hand, he and Cassie left the Tourist Office for a *chaikhana* across the street.

Saaleh was about twenty, Cassie guessed. As they walked, he asked politely where she had been in Afghanistan, what she had thought of Kabul, where she was from in the United States. His English was fluent, she thought, with a distinctive British accent.

They sat at a small table, and, at a gesture from Saaleh, a waiter brought Cassie mint tea. She turned to her new pupil. "Aren't you having any?"

He lightly waved his hand. "I will later. It is Ramadan." Then he thanked her for meeting him. Leaning forward in his chair, he explained, "I want to learn American English because I hope one day – *Inshallah* - to work with U.S. firms doing business in my country."

"Are many American companies here?"

"Some, and more are coming. The British have been here longer than a century but I think - . Well, we have a ... complicated history with the British."

Cassie asked, "Do you like English? As a language?"

He laughed. "It sounds like barking dogs to me," he admitted. "And American English makes no sense sometimes. What does it mean, tongue in cheek? Bend over backward? Ball park figure? Kick the bucket? These phrases are absurd."

She felt a little self-conscious sipping tea when he had none, but the taste was excellent. So she drained her cup as she explained those idioms and many others.

For his part, Saaleh taught her basic phrases. "*Baleh*, yes. *Nah*, no. *Salaam*, hello. *Khodahafez*, goodbye. *Lotfaan*, please. *Inshallah*, God willing." She made notes, inventing a phonetic vocabulary along the way to help her remember pronunciation. The hour went quickly and, as they stood to leave, Saaleh asked if she would like to meet again the next day. Cassie promised to try.

Walking across the street toward the hotel, she repeated the words over and over, like an incantation. "*Baleh, nah, salaam, khodahafez, lotfaan, Inshallah*." In a sense, it was an incantation; the words could open doors to the culture, connect her with people she met.

Then she heard a man singing from somewhere down the street near the hotel. The sound was so unexpected that Cassie stopped to listen. The melody didn't sound Central Asian, but it had an unusual rhythm. Intrigued, she walked toward it. The man's voice wasn't loud but it carried in the still air. It was a hot afternoon in the third week of Ramadan and the sidewalks were largely deserted. The singer was not expecting an audience, she guessed.

Cassie turned a corner and immediately saw Marton's dusty van, the side door open. The scene surprised her; she thought he was working at the factory out of town. Reasoning that he had left Danny behind, she paused to watch. His shadowy form appeared to be scrubbing the van's interior. As he worked, he sang in a language she didn't recognize. His voice was rich and deep, but it was the tune - haunting and sad – that unsettled her. Deeply moved, she considered approaching him to ask about it. But she sensed that her presence might embarrass him; it would certainly break the spell. So she listened for a few more minutes and then slipped quietly away.

Hours later, she heard Marton's step outside their door and was startled to notice her heart racing. He smiled when he saw her; she had not noticed before how engaging his smile could be. Perhaps his singing had altered her brain's chemistry, enlarging her sympathetic awareness of him.

His forehead was streaked with sweat and dirt, his shirt soaked through. But his mood was expansive, despite his worn appearance. "Let me shower," he said, "and we'll go to dinner here at the hotel. They say the Behzad is famous for boiled sheep rib. The restaurant opens at seven for foreigners."

Business in Herat must be going well, she thought as she combed out her hair and twisted it on top of her head. Around her neck she tied a black cord holding a decorative metal pendant from Srinigar.

When Marton returned, he glanced at the tin pendant. "I have pretty jewelry in the van. Let me give you a lapis necklace."

"No, thanks. This is just for fun. I don't like jewelry, actually."

"All women like jewelry," he replied gravely.

"What can I say?" she shrugged.

At seven fifteen, they left their room and were passing Danny's door just as it opened.

"Hey," Danny said, stepping into the hallway. "Where you guys going?"

Cassie felt Marton's hand on her elbow, trying to guide her forward and down the stairs. But she couldn't very well ignore Danny. "Dinner, here in the hotel."

"Can I tag along?" he asked as he locked his door. His face was drawn and his energy seemed low, but Cassie thought he looked a little better.

Marton didn't reply, so she smiled, "Sure."

At dinner, though, Danny's hands began to shake again, and he only ate half of his sheep rib. When the waiter informed him the

Behzad did not serve beer, he slumped back in his seat, apathetic and downcast.

Concerned, Cassie tried to cheer him. "Tell me, Danny, what's your happiest memory?"

"What?" he roused himself and looked at her.

"You know, what was a really happy time for you?"

He was silent several moments before he suddenly grinned. "Oh I know! When I learned to surf. It was awesome. I was fifteen." As he spoke, his voice became louder and more assured. "The waves were so powerful. I almost drowned a half a dozen times, but when I finally caught a wave, man, I flew! Fucking amazing! Girls on the beach were watching me …." He laughed, more like his old self again. "Yeah, I was totally happy. No troubles, no complications. Just flying over the ocean." He moved his hand smoothly over imaginary waves, then turned to her. "What about you, Cass?"

Her mind was busy evaluating her memories. She felt elated the day she finally embarked on this journey, the day she also met Jack. But the memory was mixed, especially the sad farewells to her parents. Then she thought of the afternoon she met Ralph. He invited her out for coffee after his poetry reading; she was excited but anxious as well. She loved filming her senior project; the cast and crew – all students like her - grew tight, like family. But then the film wrapped up, people graduated and everyone went their separate ways. None of these counted as her happiest memory.

Then, one purely joyful recollection came to her.

"When I held an alligator," she said. Talking about it brought her back to that day: the July humidity and the slow progress of the boat winding through the bayou. "I was eight. My parents took us to a farm that bred alligators. Some of them were huge, so I had to stay close to the grownups. But Jason, my big brother, saw how frustrated I was, so he brought over this baby alligator." So many memories of Jason were heartbreaking, since his death almost a decade before. But not this one; his car accident was still years in the future. She continued, "He showed me how to hold it, and then handed it to me. I was so scared and thrilled. I can still feel its slick leather skin, kind of a charcoal black with yellow stripes down its back. It had a tiny snout and teeny sharp teeth. But it didn't bite me. It let me hold it for several minutes. I begged my parents to let me take that baby alligator home."

Danny's eyes were wide. "Did you?"

She laughed. "Baby 'gators grow up to be big bad 'gators. So no."

Marton was watching them. When Cassie turned toward him, she met his gaze. "I don't have many happy memories," he told her. "But once I went to the High Tatras, on the border with Poland. My uncle took me and his son. We hiked part way up to Lomnické štit, then rode the cable car to the very top. It was early spring; snow covered all the peaks. There was a café, and my uncle and cousin stayed inside with hot chocolate. But I wandered around and found a pirate's plank, a meter wide and several meters long, sticking out of the mountain side." His expression grew distant; like Cassie, he was back in that day. "It had a metal fence around it, to keep people from falling off. Still, it was terrifying to stand at the very end, suspended hundreds of meters up in the sky. I made myself stand there until I wasn't frightened anymore." Then he lit a cigarette and took a drag, roused from his reverie. "I was always afraid as a boy. Of my father, of bullies in school, of Party apparatchiks who bossed people around. But that day I realized I had more power than they did. I could stay on the platform, or I could jump off. I had the power to choose life or death."

Neither Cassie nor Danny said anything. Finally Danny grunted, "How's that happy? That story's freaking weird, man. It doesn't make sense. Those assholes could still beat the shit out of you."

Marton frowned thoughtfully. "But from that moment I could choose not to be afraid."

Cassie suddenly saw the similarities in their stories. "Did you notice? We all mentioned the power of nature, living in the moment and confronting our fears."

Marton studied her and nodded. "Yes, we're alike, you and me. But Danny ..."

In that moment, Danny lurched out of his seat and, clamping his mouth shut, rushed to the restaurant's back door, toward the toilet. His dash startled them. Watching him disappear, Cassie urged Marton, "We have to take him to a doctor tomorrow. He's really sick."

"Why do you worry so much about him? He'll be fine." Marton replied mildly and stubbed out the cigarette. "He's just going through withdrawal. Give it a few days."

Of course, she thought, drug withdrawal. Danny no longer had access to opium. She wondered if Ralph was going through it as well, alone in the Jam Hotel. She shifted uncomfortably in her chair. Should she feel guilty? She could do nothing now to help Ralph. It had been his choice. And he really could take care of himself; he didn't need her.

Danny returned, apologized and retired to his room. Cassie and Marton sat a while longer, finishing their tea. Then they climbed the stairs as well.

As Marton closed the door and she turned on the lamp, Cassie said, "I thought you would say the day you escaped from Czechoslovakia was the happiest. The day you were free."

Marton walked toward her. "I left someplace unbearable, but I didn't know what I would find. Someplace worse? There's no happiness in escape." He folded his arms around her, held her tightly. "There's only uncertainty, and a little hope."

She rested her head against his chest and heard his heartbeat. She thought back to his melancholy song, his damaged childhood, his love of Katarina, the girl who died. He wasn't Lord Byron; he was more like a Brontë hero, Cassie decided, like Mr. Rochester. Wounded by the past, he pretended not to care. But he did, she was certain of it. He may disparage romantics, but he was one himself. The realization aroused in her both tenderness and desire.

Moving behind her now, keeping her encircled in his arms, Marton kissed the tender flesh behind her ear and moved his lips to the nape of her neck; her skin prickled with pleasure. They were so close that, against her lower back, she could feel him becoming hard. Without hurry, he unbuttoned her blouse and lay a warm hand flat against her belly. "I want to make love to you." he murmured. "Yes?"

"Yes," she whispered, surprised at the intensity of her desire. She turned to face him and they kissed again and again. Everything around her receded: the outside sounds, the room, even the heat itself.

No lover, even Ralph, had ever aroused such passion.

ON TUESDAY MORNING, eyes still closed, Cassie stretched luxuriously and reached for Marton. The bed was empty, she realized with regret. She glanced at the clock. It was almost eight and she had overslept. A glass of mint tea, long since tepid, was waiting for her on the table, with his note: *My Angel - Good morning!* She rose and showered, smiling as she thought about him and the night before.

The hotel dining room was almost deserted as she ate a late breakfast. Upstairs afterwards, she hummed cheerfully as she straightened the room and hand washed a few clothes. She knew she didn't love Marton, but she simply couldn't get sex off her mind. The mood stayed with her as she scribbled a few travel entries in her journal. Finally, she left the hotel and found a small café near the Friday Mosque for lunch.

Fortunately, by then, the thick fog of arousal had lifted. Alone at her table, she reviewed her Dari language notes from the previous day and, at two, wandered back to the tea shop to meet Saaleh.

This time, though, he wasn't alone. With him was a young woman dressed in a boxy jacket and dark skirt, long black hair uncovered. Cassie turned to leave; she didn't want to intrude on an intimate moment between Saaleh and his lovely girlfriend. But Saaleh saw her and rose to bring her to the table; it was his sister Azadah who had insisted on meeting her.

After the introductions, the young woman asked shyly, "Please forgive my curiosity. I have never before met an American woman. Did you go to university?"

"Yes. I studied film," Cassie answered.

"Ah, Hollywood," Azadah told her brother knowingly.

"No, no." This was a common misperception. "I'm interested in the aesthetics of film and its cultural impact. I hope to make documentaries someday."

"I see," the young woman said. "Have you made any films?"

"A few in college. Since then, I've worked on several small films. Not as the director or cinematographer though. I was a production assistant for a company in New Orleans before I started this trip."

"And your husband lets you work," Azadah said nodding.

"You should make a movie about Afghanistan," Saaleh effused. "It's a beautiful country with an ancient culture."

"Yes, a very interesting country, both ancient and modern," Cassie observed, thinking about men in business suits and women in burqas.

Saaleh seemed to understand. "In our country, modern ideas are sometimes under attack. Not in the cities, but rural areas, where tradition is strong. Many people distrust and fear what is modern, many mullahs, too. They would roll back Time if they could. But, of course, they cannot."

"A good thing, too," Azadah rolled her eyes. "Or I could not study medicine!"

MARTON AND DANNY arrived back after five, again dirty and sweaty. In passing, Marton gave her a tight smile and slight nod before heading downstairs to wash. Cassie's gaze tracked Marton's feline movements as he gathered a clean set of clothes and his kit. His mere presence triggered a flush of erotic anticipation. She wished the shower was en suite instead of a different floor. She would have joined him under the hot water.

But he seemed preoccupied and a little distant. It was simply fatigue, she reasoned. Danny hung around their room, leaning against the door jam. When Cassie motioned for him to sit, he shook his head and gestured at his stained clothes. Despite looking exhausted, however, he seemed more alert.

"You're feeling better?" Cassie asked.

"Yeah, thanks. Not a hundred percent yet, but I'll live. I don't want to go through that ever again."

"Stay away from opium." She tried to make it sound like friendly advice, not a scolding.

He nodded. "You got that right." He made a face. "Disgusting bitter shit. Still." He sighed, "That feeling.... I can't explain. Like surfing high above the ugly world."

His remark touched her; he seemed so innocent in that instant. "It's an illusion, Danny."

"I know. But sometimes an illusion's fun." He chewed on his lip and added, "I'm sorry. For giving that shit to Ralph. That's why you broke up with him, isn't it?"

She considered. "Yes, but it would have happened sooner or later. We weren't a good fit." She understood more clearly now, not only things about Ralph but about herself. She had twisted herself into someone she thought he wanted and, in the process, lost both herself and him. "We were like fictional characters written by different authors, stuck in same book," she said. Until Kabul, however, she hadn't seen it.

Danny interrupted her thoughts. "Well, be careful with Marton."

"What?" she blinked. Danny's remark startled her. She thought the two men were friends. "What do you mean?"

"He's a user." For a brief moment, she thought he meant opium, but then Danny elaborated, "He uses people. He has his own agenda. Just be careful, okay?"

A warning against romance; that Cassie guard her heart. But that's not how she felt about Marton. It was physical attraction, mostly; she knew that much about her feelings.

Before she could reassure him, though, Marton entered the room, towel draped over his shoulders and hair wet. He seemed startled to see Danny still there.

"Don't you have a room of your own?" he asked sharply.

"Yeah, sure," the younger man replied. Saluting Cassie, he said, "See you later, alligator."

She didn't like Marton's tone and, as soon as they were alone, she pointed it out, "He's just being friendly."

"He screwed up today. He doesn't pay attention. He's starting to get on my nerves."

The friendship was fraying, she realized. Both men were on edge. "It's only a few more days, right? Then we'll be on our way to Iran." Without Danny, she thought. The realization made her pensive; she'd come to like him.

Briskly rubbing the towel through his hair, Marton considered. "Unfortunately, I'll need him in Mashhad."

"Really? Have you asked him?" When Marton shook his head no, she observed, "I don't think he'll do it. He wants to stay here a few more days and then head back to India."

"It's only for one day, and I'll pay him extra. He'll come."

"Why do you need him anyway?"

"Insurance," Marton said. "I'm carrying valuable merchandise, the gems especially. To travel safely across the border, I have to make arrangements with local contacts on both sides. Some of them are rough men, corrupt. I need Danny as my body guard."

She scoffed. "Danny's no body guard. He's too gentle."

"They don't know that." He explained, "All he has to do is stand with his arms crossed and frown. He looks convincing enough."

"Why do you need to work with these men in the first place? What about the police? They'd protect your shipment."

He gave a sharp laugh. "Sometimes my local contacts *are* the police. They're often the most corrupt."

"This sounds dangerous, Marton." Cassie frowned, thinking about possible risks they were all taking.

He backtracked. "Not really. I'm simply cautious. That's my nature. And it's worth a little risk. The payoff in Geneva will be huge."

"I've been wondering, Marton. Why Geneva? It's only a few boxes. Why not ship them directly to Canada?"

Cassie thought he seemed guarded when he answered, "My distributors are in Geneva. I don't have the contacts I need in Canada. Not yet, anyway." He checked his watch. "It's time to go to dinner."

DANNY JOINED THEM on their walk to a restaurant near the Herat Museum. He dawdled behind Marton and Cassie, staring in shop windows and making funny faces at children he passed, causing them to laugh and squeal. Cassie took his high spirits as proof that opium was out of his system at last.

She glanced at Marton's profile, wishing she could restore his passion from the night before. She almost took his hand, but even that level of intimacy felt inappropriate on a city street in Afghanistan. "Rough day, huh? You both look pretty bushed."

"Oh, that," he replied. "The factory today wasn't ready. We did more heavy lifting and opening crates ourselves. No air conditioning. Some items were broken and I argued with the supplier. I lost my temper." He paused. "I don't like to lose my temper."

She remembered that about him, when the van broke down outside Kabul. Wanting to ease his tension, she asked, "By the way, did you know this town is famous for blue glass? The workshop is close to our hotel. You could import that."

He shrugged. "Not glass. Too fragile."

They continued to walk in silence. Cassie decided to ask about the song. "The other day, I heard you singing. You were cleaning out the van. I couldn't catch the words."

Startled, he exclaimed, "I didn't see you."

"I was down the street. I didn't want to interrupt, so I just walked away. What was that song?"

Offhandedly, he said. "It's Hungarian." Then, looking at his feet, he softly added, "My grandmother used to sing it."

"Were you close to your grandmother?" She hoped so; she wanted to imagine someone cared for him when he was small.

He hesitated a moment before a terse answer, "Close enough."

Not the happy response Cassie was hoping for. "Well, it's a beautiful song. What's it called?"

"It translates to something like 'Gloomy Sunday.' Some people call it the suicide song because it's about a man killing himself after his beloved dies. The man who wrote the song later did."

Cassie frowned. "How tragic."

"It's only a song," he observed.

She wanted to hear it again, now that she knew what it was about. "Would you sing it for me sometime?"

Marton scrutinized her face, then nodded. "Certainly. If you like." They continued their walk. A minute passed and he stopped. His expression was serious but his blue eyes shone, like shards from the glass bazaar.

Then he spoke so softly that she had to lean toward him to hear. "I love you, Cassandra," he said. "I will for the rest of my life."

LOVE. CASSIE AWOKE Wednesday morning thinking about what Marton had said. At the time, she had been too stunned to reply to his quiet declaration. Since then, neither of them had spoken of it. Now it was seven and Marton was already gone. He and Danny must have left early to avoid the heat of the day.

After so misjudging her feelings for Ralph, she was wary of love. Certainly she cared for Marton, felt tenderness, concern, and at times desire. But she didn't fool herself that those emotions were love. She regretted she couldn't love him in return; he seemed so in need of it. But she had to be honest about her feelings; she had to tell him. The last thing she wanted was to deceive him.

To clear her head, she went walking. Eventually, she passed the places she had seen on her first day in Herat and so found herself again in front of the glass bazaar. This time it was open, and she pushed through the door into its mysterious interior.

Cassie caught her breath. Arrayed around her, on dozens of shelves, was blue glass: from cobalt to sky blue, pale turquoise to ice. Some objects were exquisitely encircled in golden swirls; others unadorned. Saaleh had told her that blue glass traditionally was used for donkey beads and water dishes for bird cages. Now those traditional pieces were interspersed with stemmed glasses, long-necked vases and bowls with fluted rims. She wandered the narrow aisles clutching her clumsy bag to her chest and admiring the colors and craftsmanship. She told herself she was only looking. The objects would be too expensive and difficult to carry home. Then she saw a blue-green cup.

She held it to the window, ran her fingertip along its smooth rim. She imagined herself sipping mint tea from it in some faraway future.

The shopkeeper – the owner or craftsman or brother –greeted her. Hesitating only a moment, she asked the price. When he told her, she quickly calculated the cost as only a few dollars. Then the shopkeeper found its partner. Should she splurge on two? She could wrap the cups in several socks, buried in the middle of her pack. They might travel safely enough.

She intended to bargain; she knew shopkeepers expected it. But she had no heart for the game and reached for her wallet to pay the full amount. For a few moments, her hand flailed around in her tote bag. Where was it? She peered inside, panic rising. The wallet was gone. Had she dropped it? Had she been robbed?

Heart pounding, Cassie held up a hand in apology and rushed from the shop. She retraced her steps through the bazaar, up the road and back to the hotel, scanning the ground and trying to remember when she had last seen it. Not since lunch a few days before. Saaleh had insisted on buying her tea. Marton had paid for everything else, and she had let him. This was her punishment for being inattentive.

It wasn't a huge amount of money, about thirty-five dollars. But here that was a fortune; it could cover five days of travel: hotels, meals, transportation. She had to find her wallet. Cassie rushed into the Behzad, heading for the stairs to search the room. As she passed the lounge, she heard her name called. It was Danny; he and Marton were waiting for an early lunch in the hotel dining room. They had just come from work, clothes sweat-stained and dusty. But their faces and arms were damp and reddened, scrubbed clean from their morning labors.

Without any preliminaries, she walked up to them and spoke rapidly. "I was going to buy something at the glass bazaar. But my wallet's gone!" She looked at Danny with a mixture of accusation and plea: "Did you take it?!"

Danny scowled and shook his head vehemently. "No way."

Cassie fell into an empty chair. "I'm sorry, Danny. I'm just in a panic. Maybe the hotel staff? I can't imagine who would take it."

"Well, it wasn't me." Danny looked hurt.

Marton had been watching without a word. Finally he reached into his back pocket and pulled out her wallet. "I have it," he said simply."

She grabbed it and glared. Confused and angry, she blurted out, "Why the hell did you steal it?"

He didn't flinch. "I didn't steal it. I took it for safekeeping. You're so careless sometimes, Cassie. You leave your purse slung across the back of your chair, and when you go to the toilet, anyone could take it."

He sounded so reasonable, so concerned, but Cassie wasn't mollified. She defended herself, "I only do that when you and Danny are sitting right there."

"At dinner last night, you and Danny were gone at the same time. What if I had to leave? What if I looked away? You must be more careful."

The timing hit her. He had taken her wallet within an hour of professing love. Was this his idea of affection?

He added, "That's why I put your passport in the hotel safe, with mine."

Her passport. She hadn't remembered to ask for it back after their evening at the Hotel Intercontinental; hadn't even missed it. She agonized: he was right about her being oblivious. What was happening to her brain? This absentmindedness was new. With Ralph, she felt responsible; she had to be alert. But Marton took charge so naturally.

"I want it back," she demanded, angrier with herself now than with him.

"Of course." Marton stood and looked down at her. "Shall I get it now? It may take a few minutes. The hotel safe is in the manager's office." At that moment, their food arrived, but Marton did not take his eyes from Cassie.

She instantly felt she was being irrational. After all, the passport was secure. And his meal was getting cold. She stood up next to him. "No. Later is fine." Danny invited her to join them for lunch but she declined. She needed to be alone to think things through. Excusing herself, she left the dining room and the hotel.

Cassie went straight to the glass bazaar but it was closed again, so she circled back through the old town. On the next street, she entered a kebab shop on the ground floor of a youth hostel; she joined the backpacker clientele. The meat was tough but prices were cheap. After she finished, she sat and reflected on her feelings about Marton. Last night's confession of love was strange enough, but learning that he had taken her wallet triggered a deep unease. Intellectually, she could understand his need to control; it grew out of insecurity, probably a product of the abuse he'd suffered. But even if he meant well, even if he loved her and wanted to protect her, she could never accept such control. It felt too constraining, even demeaning. If she was foolish and naïve sometimes, so be it. She would live with the consequences.

When she returned to the glass shop, the door was wide open to the afternoon breeze. The man who kept the shop grinned broadly as Cassie entered. He handed her a small paper with the cost of the two cups. She noticed he had lowered the price, and she smiled in appreciation as she handed him the Afghani bills. From under the counter, he produced a small package, carefully wrapped in brown paper and string. She placed the treasure in her bag, thanked him and left.

In the few minutes to spare before her meeting with Saaleh, Cassie stopped at a small kiosk and bought a postcard of the Friday Mosque. She had to let her parents know where she was, despite Marton's exaggerated warning about Iranian secret police. The woman at the counter pointed toward the post office. Once there, she dashed off a few lines.

> Dearest Mom & Dad,
>   I'm well. In Herat with Marton & Danny (we met in Kabul). They have a van, which makes travel a little safer. Ralph comes soon by bus. By next week, we should be in Iran.

No need to alarm them with the news about Ralph, she thought. She still hoped he was on his way. Her parents believed she was safer with him.

> I visited this mosque a few days ago. It's magnificent! I thought Miss Millie might like to paint it. I'm also learning to speak a little Dari (like Farsi). A nice college student is teaching me every afternoon. His father heads the tourist office here.
>   I hope all is well. I love & miss you all so much!
>   Cassie

She gave the postcard to the postal official and immediately felt better. It was time to finish Jack's letter as well. She hadn't written anything since Sunday night. She checked her watch; it was almost two. She would have to wait until after the meeting with Saaleh.

When she saw her earnest young friend waiting at the café, she felt a small twinge of disappointment that Azadah had not come. She had met so few women in her travels. Perhaps Azadah didn't want to intrude on her brother's sessions, Cassie thought and settled into her chair. Within a minute, a glass of mint tea was before her.

Cassie decided she wanted to learn practical vocabulary: how to ask for directions, order food, reserve a room, buy a bus ticket. Saaleh was patient and clear. She labored over her phonetic notations until she was satisfied she could mimic his sounds.

In exchange, she tried to answer his questions about the American and British political systems. She wished Jack was here; he knew so much more about such things.

In an hour, they took their leave and Cassie hurried back to the hotel room to write. She found Jack's aerogramme where it was stashed in her tote. The minute she saw the blank page, she knew what she wanted to write.

> *Have you thought any more about coming to Istanbul? I really hope so. I'll be there by Sept. 18. We could arrange to meet in Hagia Sophia at high noon on Sept. 22, just like in a movie. Let me know if you can come and if the date works for you.*
>
> *By the way, I'm not with Ralph anymore. I'll explain the whole melodrama later.*

A screech of brakes and loud thud outside made her jump. Cassie pulled back the curtain to scan the road: two cars had collided. Neither seemed badly damaged, and the drivers were already out of their vehicles and shouting. Then she noticed Marton approaching the hotel. He was back early. Determined to avoid an argument with him, she folded the aerogramme and tucked it into a paperback novel, then opened the book and pretended to read. Her pulse, she realized, was racing.

A few minutes later, without a word, Marton entered and walked to where she sat. He placed her passport and a small wrapped package in front of her. She slid the passport into her tote bag and studied the package. The wrapping paper and string were familiar. Before she opened it, Marton explained, "This is for you. A small gift for telling me about the glass bazaar. I've decided to order a few items after all. I watched how carefully they pack everything."

Cassie still burned from his earlier stunt. Yet, despite herself, she was pleased he liked the glass bazaar, pleased the shop would have more business. She felt vindicated somehow. Besides, she had her passport back. No harm done.

Slowly, she unwrapped the parcel: inside was an exquisite water dish fashioned for a bird cage, in sky blue glass decorated with gold, like early morning light on wisps of cloud. She held it up to the window to admire it. But mixed with admiration was resentment. Responsibilities came with owning delicate and valuable things. Keeping it intact would not be easy. But to refuse the gift, especially from a lover, felt ungracious and mean. She wrapped her fingers around the dish and thanked him. Marton kissed the top of her head.

"Marton," she said slowly, "we need to talk. About what you said yesterday when we walked to the restaurant."

In an ambiguous gesture, he held up a hand. Cassie paused.

"I know," he said. "It was premature. I spoke too soon and you're not ready. I understand and it's all right."

Relief flooded through her. "I care about you, I really do. I just don't know …"

He interrupted, "Please, forget that I said anything. I become too impatient sometimes. I know I need to give you time." He looked down at the blue glass ornament in her hands. "For the moment, we'll pretend it never happened. All right?"

"Yes, all right," she echoed.

The next day followed the usual pattern of her life in Herat. After the men had left early for work, Cassie explored the city, ate lunch alone, and then joined Saaleh for their lesson. This time, Saaleh had a surprise. "Today," he announced, "we'll visit Jami."

She thought Jami must be a friend, but as they walked to the taxi stand near the Friday Mosque, Saaleh explained. "Jami is a great Sufi poet. He wrote in the fifteen century, a philosopher and theologian. And he served in the Timurid Court. Both a practical man and a mystic." His respectful tone told Cassie this was his highest compliment.

The taxi deposited them at a smaller mosque nestled in a garden. The driver promised to wait. Together Cassie and Saaleh walked to a tomb shaded by a pistachio tree. Saaleh talked about Jami's life and pointed to his epitaph. In a gentle voice, he translated:

When your face is hidden from me,
Like the moon hidden on a dark night,
I shed stars of tears
And yet my night remains dark
In spite of all those shining stars.

The yearning and anguish in the poem stirred her. Jami wrote of spiritual loss, but Cassie heard human grief as well. Her own grief. For her brother mostly, and half dozen other deaths and regrets in her life. Ralph and their dreams together. Jack.

In silent contemplation, they walked around the grave. Saaleh stooped and took a pinch of soil. "As a blessing," he said. "You can take one too."

The feel of the warm earth in her fingertips only heightened Cassie's sense of loss.

As the taxi returned them to the city center, Saaleh chatted with the driver and Cassie thought again about Jack. Surreptitiously, she slipped a photo from her bag, the picture of Jack and his dog. Seeing his face triggered a rush of emotion. Was this love? Should she tell him so? Did she love Marton as well? As she put the photograph away, she realized she wasn't ready yet to finish writing the letter. She had to consider carefully what she wanted to say.

FINALLY CAME FRIDAY. Her melancholy mood had eased slightly, so Cassie dressed to join the men for breakfast. Marton confirmed that they would leave for Iran on Sunday. Other than that, they said little. When the men left, she wondered briefly how they could work with so many businesses shut. It was the last Friday of Ramadan, and she thought everything except the mosque would be closed. Her meeting with Saaleh was canceled as well; they had made plans to meet one last time on Saturday.

To prepare for their Sunday departure, Cassie used the morning hours to wash out underclothes and shirts, lightweight items that would dry quickly. Then she started rounding up her shoes and shampoo and other items scattered around the room. Packing lifted her spirits, because travel would bring her closer to Tehran and news from Jack.

She was glad when Marton didn't return for lunch. Alone, she ate a hard-boiled egg and naan left over on the hotel breakfast buffet. Afterward, she returned to the room finally ready to write, finally ready to tell Jack how she felt. Sitting at the desk, she pulled the last aerogramme from its hiding place in her paperback.

A heavy tread on the stairs made Cassie pause. Probably other guests; it was much too early for the men to return. Even so, she decided to check and opened the door a crack. There was Danny, hunched against the doorframe to his room, searching the pockets of his filthy white cotton pants for the key. He looked drained.

"Hey," she called to him, fully opening her door. "Can I get you something to eat? Or some tea?"

He shook his head but smiled weakly in appreciation. "I'm okay. Rough day. Just going to lay down for a little while."

"I'll knock later. In case you want anything," Cassie offered.

"Thanks." He found the key and turned to go.

Just as Danny was closing his door, Marton stormed up the stairs two at a time, and headed straight for Danny. Rage had turned his face almost purple. Eyes wide, Danny rushed to close the door. He wasn't quick enough; it wouldn't have withstood Marton's assault in any case. Marton shoved Danny into the door frame.

"What the hell did I tell you?!" Marton demanded, waving a sheet of light blue paper like a knife at Danny. "Not to write any fucking letters! And what's on the counter downstairs, waiting to be picked up?! A fucking letter! And when I open the fucking letter, what do I read? Fucking bullshit!"

Danny winced. "I had to write my sister. She sent me money and I had to let her know it arrived." His voice sounded pathetic.

Marton's explosive fury stunned and frightened Cassie. She stood frozen in the door of their room and wondered frantically what she could do to intervene, how she could calm him down. But before she could react, he balled up the blue paper and threw it at her. "Burn that," he ordered. Then he pushed Danny into his room and shut the door. The hall was suddenly silent.

Heart pounding, Cassie returned to her room and rapidly pulled things out of her backpack, dumping them on the floor. A box of matches was here somewhere. Finally she found it. She opened the box and, that same moment, knew she couldn't burn the letter. She had to know what it said. Glancing nervously over her shoulder at the door, she quickly flattened out Danny's letter, folded it into thirds and stuck it at the bottom of her pack, beneath a pair of rough woolen gloves she had bought in Nepal. She would retrieve it later, when Marton went out.

Meanwhile, she needed him to think she had destroyed it. Without reflection, she picked up her letter to Jack, wadded it up and dropped it into the ashtray. She tried to strike a match but her hands shook too much and the flame died. Concentrating, she tried again, and at last touched a meager spark to the corner of the page. It crept slowly across her handwriting. "Hurry up," she muttered. If Marton returned and saw that she had disobeyed, what would he do? She had never seen anyone so angry. "Come on," she urged the little flame as it slowly ate the page. She glanced furtively over her shoulder at the door and jumped; Marton was standing there.

Wild eyed, she looked down at the burning page; it was finally aflame. Marton walked up to the table and put an arm around her; she flinched. He didn't seem to notice, studying the flame with her as if they were admiring a campfire together. Eventually, only a nondescript corner of pale blue remained.

"Good," he said.

She could not meet his eyes. He lifted her chin and examined her face. He must have sensed her terror, because he became calm, almost affable. "Danny and I had a talk," he said. "He knows now how important this is. For all of us." When Cassie didn't respond, he continued. "The lies he wrote could have gotten all of us arrested, thrown into prison. You included."

"What lies?" This didn't seem like Danny.

Marton shrugged. "He wanted to entertain his sister. So he made up some crazy story about us. As a joke, you know Danny. The problem is the police don't have a sense of humor. He shouldn't endanger our lives. Right?"

Cassie didn't answer. She was too confused. What had Danny written that made Marton so furious and afraid? What had he written that could get her arrested?

"Right?" Marton repeated, more forcefully now.

"Yes, okay," Cassie said, purposely not echoing his language, a small assertion of independent thought. Just as purposely, she added what she sensed he wanted to hear. "You had no choice."

He nodded. "I had no choice."

That afternoon and evening, Marton never left her side. He insisted on helping her repack items she had tossed from her backpack in her search for matches. Each time he approached her pack, she held her breath but he never discovered the contraband letter. Then he started to pack his own things, softly singing *Gloomy Sunday*. He was kind and attentive, yet she sensed he was watching her every move, gauging her reactions, trying to read her mind. Perhaps she was being paranoid. Regardless, she had no chance to retrieve the letter to read in secret. They had a quiet dinner downstairs. Danny was nowhere to be seen.

On Saturday morning, Cassie awoke aggravated with herself for sleeping through the night. She had intended to slip out to the bathroom to read Danny's letter while Marton slept. Now, she couldn't. He wasn't here this moment, but he was close by. Sitting up in bed, she could see on the table a cup of mint tea sending off a wave of steam; a second cup for her nearby, its saucer on top to hold in the heat. He must have just left for the toilet. Then she noticed a piece of paper next to them, with writing both in English and Arabic script.

Intuitively, she saw the aesthetics of the scene and wanted to take a photograph. Sunlight angled through the thin curtain, creating a line of light between the different alphabets. Quickly and quietly, she grabbed her camera and impulsively picked up Marton's passport from the dresser. Its dark red edge complemented the palest green of the mint leaves. She carefully positioned it, focused, adjusted the aperture and took one shot. Then she heard Marton in the hall, talking with Danny. He sounded amiable. Good. He had been too rough on Danny the day before; he had terrified them both. She hastily replaced his passport and returned to bed.

Before lying down, though, she stole another look at the note. Below the crudely written foreign script was a phrase in English: "Please help me. I am an American and I am lost. Where is the bus station?" She recognized Marton's handwriting.

By the time he entered the room a few seconds later, her eyes were closed in feigned sleep. She heard him shuffle the papers on the desk. She could imagine him folding them; putting them away. As she pretended to sleep, she ruminated about the phrase. Why had Marton tried to copy it out in Arabic? He could have asked someone to help; Saaleh would have. And why identify as American and not Canadian?

She considered; maybe he planned to give the note to Danny, in case he ever needed help. The whole thing didn't make sense.

Five minutes later, Cassie pretended to wake. Marton smiled when he saw her and put aside the road map he had been studying. "Breakfast?" he said.

She made no objections and dressed quickly, hoping he would go to work as soon as the meal was finished. But even then, he did not leave. Instead, over empty dishes in the hotel dining hall, he said, "Show me the sights of Herat. I have Afghani cash to spend before we leave the country tomorrow. Let's have a nice lunch, a splurge. Like ordinary tourists."

"Don't you have to go to work?" She hoped her voice didn't betray her anxiety.

"This afternoon," he replied. "Danny can handle things this morning."

Cassie returned briefly upstairs to finish dressing and Marton followed. At last, he excused himself to the toilet. She quickly found Danny's letter and tucked it into the waistband of her slacks, under her shirt.

Carrying along the tourist brochures and map, Cassie showed him the Citadel, Masjid-I-Jami', the museum. As they passed the glass workshop, the shopkeeper emerged and smiled at her, shook Marton's hand. At noon, Cassie steered Marton to the backpacker kebab place but he insisted on finer dining. He flagged a taxi and they drove to Hotel Herat on the outskirts of town. There, on a shady patio overlooking a swimming pool, they ate baked chicken and French pastries. Marton told her stories about working in Canadian hotels.

Finally, at 1:30, the taxi returned them to the Behzad. They stood a moment on the sidewalk before Cassie thanked Marton for the lunch and walked across the street to the café. Once inside, she peered furtively through the window to confirm that Marton was not there, still watching. She claimed a corner table in the back. While waiting for

Saaleh, she carefully drew Danny's letter from her waistband and read.

> *Hey Debbie!*
>
> *I can't believe you sent $50!!! You are really the best. I don't need it now because I have a job, so I'll use it to buy you the best gift ever.*
>
> *The job is with a businessman I met in India, Marton Z – (I call him Zorro). He paid me $100 last week to pose as his body guard, if you can believe it! He promised me $500 for this week cause the work is so shitty. I also scored something in Kabul called Black Russian; a real head trip! But I had to go cold turkey and almost died!! I'm okay now. Never, ever do drugs, Debbie. Seriously. I'll tell you about it someday.*
>
> *Zorro's leaving tomorrow for Iran, then Geneva, but I'll stay here in Herat for a few days and then head back to India to a different ashram. The last one didn't work out. Met a girl and you can guess the rest!*
>
> *I don't really like Zorro (he's a control freak) but his girlfriend's nice. Her name is Cassie. I liked her old boyfriend a lot more. He's a writer I met in Kabul. I think he'll be famous someday so remember this name - Ralph Johnson. Cassie should get back with him. Or maybe I'll find him and get him to go with me to India.*
>
> *I know what you're saying – sounds like a soap opera! So I'll just shut up for now. But I want you to know that I think about you every day, even if I'm really terrible at writing.*
>
> *Your handsome big brother,*
> *Danny*

The letter made Cassie confused and angry. This wasn't some fairy tale, as Marton had said. Nothing in it implicated her at all. Why had Marton lied about that? The letter did seem to implicate him, though. Black Russian, she surmised, was opium. Did Danny mean that he'd used his salary to buy it? Or that Marton had given it to him? She didn't want to believe it. Marton was so straight; he didn't even drink. And he bought legitimate things for his business, like the blue glass. Further, if Marton was a dealer, wouldn't Ralph or Danny have warned her?

On the other hand, she thought, dealing in opium would account for needing a body guard. Could he also be smuggling opium in the van, hiding it in ordinary merchandise? Was she just being hysterical? She glanced again at the letter. That reference to shitty work in Herat mystified her. What did Danny mean?

Regardless, she had to mail the letter to his little sister. She knew what her brother's letters had meant to her. Rummaging in her tote bag, she found a roll of clear tape to repair and seal the torn aerogramme. At the last minute before taping it shut, she took out a pen and scribbled on the bottom of the page: *Danny really loves you*, and signed it *Cassie*. Danny hadn't said it explicitly, but it was true. This was her small gift to the girl.

She glanced up and saw Saaleh arrive, weaving his way through the tables to her. He smiled as he sat across from her. They talked briefly about his studies, about his sister.

Then Cassie sighed. "It's set. We leave tomorrow for Mashhad."

His expression turned serious. He looked over his shoulder at the others in the café and whispered, "Be careful in Iran. Don't let people know you're American."

"I don't understand. I thought Iran was pro-Western."

"Reza Pahlavi is a very bad man. There are protests every day, all over the country," he continued softly.

"What does this have to do with my being American?"

"Don't you know?" he asked, genuinely astonished.

Cassie felt embarrassed at her ignorance. She kept up with the news when she was home, and now read the *International Herald Tribune* when she could find it. But she still didn't know much about Iran, about the world really.

Saaleh continued in a low voice. "Because the British and Americans support Pahlavi. They put him in power. They helped him depose an elected prime minister who wanted to nationalize petroleum. They didn't protest at all when he named himself king of kings, the Shah of Iran. He's a ruthless autocrat, with a brutal secret police and corrupt family. And still Britain and the U.S. support him." Saaleh explained, "They want his oil, and they're afraid of the Soviets."

This was a history she didn't know. She wasn't sure how accurate it was, but Saaleh clearly believed it. "And now?" she asked.

"And now, there will be a revolution, I think." He leaned forward. "So you must be very careful."

Later, on the sidewalk outside, they said goodbye. She fought the urge to hug him, as departing friends did in Louisiana. Instead, she bowed her head and held her hand over her heart. "You have given me a great gift this week," she said earnestly. "Thank you."

Saaleh nodded in agreement. "For me as well, Mrs. Robinette. Travel safely, *Inshallah*." As an afterthought he added, "And think of me sometime and Afghanistan."

He crossed the road to the tourist information office where his father was outside waiting. Cassie waved at them both and watched sadly as they entered the office, their lives now on different paths. She would miss Saaleh.

One last wave at the window and then she walked away, taking a circuitous route to the post office. Paranoia again: was she being watched? Against the hammering of her heart, she made herself walk slowly and casually, stopping periodically along the way to gaze in shop windows. At a small produce stall next to the post office, she bought a bag of dates. Then she entered the post office and nonchalantly dropped Danny's tattered aerogramme in the outgoing mail box. Only when it left her hands did she realize she had been holding her breath.

More walking and thinking and walking and thinking. She arrived at the Herat bus depot. It was crowded, and Cassie joined a long queue at the ticket counter. Ordinarily, she would have engaged herself by discreetly observing the other customers. Today, however, her mind was too turbulent. Only one idea was clear: Not knowing if she could trust Marton, she had to find her own way forward.

She stood at last before an agent and used her rudimentary Dari to ask for a ticket on the next day's bus to Mashhad. Regrets, he said, it was full. And the day after. And the bus back to Kabul. In every direction, for the next few days, the buses were already booked. The agent shrugged in a gesture that said, what could one do? Monday was the end of Ramadan and everyone was traveling to celebrate with family and friends. Perhaps, Cassie realized, there really was a seat somewhere. But she was non-Muslim and her claim – against the dozens of devout waiting behind her in line – was weak.

She seemed to have only two options, to stay in Herat, or travel with Marton to Mashhad. Gripping the bag of dates, Cassie retraced her steps to the hotel. She had to find Danny.

CHAPTER TWELVE

May 22, 2007
Tuesday

What kind of person was Ralph Johnson? Jack was inclined to trust Becky's sense that he wouldn't have hurt Cassie, but Ralph was there when Cassie disappeared and had to know something. Jack didn't know if Ralph would agree to talk, or be honest if he did.

Anticipating Ralph's wariness, Jack decided to frame his initial request for an interview in a way that appealed to the writer's interests and vanity. He looked for clues about the man in book reviews, interviews and news stories.

What he found was of limited utility, focusing on Johnson's work rather than his biography. But shortly after the start of the war in Afghanistan in 2002, the writer had been interviewed several times about his time in Kabul in 1978. Jack recognized the entrée he needed.

He sent an email to Ralph through his publisher:

> *I'm a political scientist studying the situation in Afghanistan just before the Soviet invasion. In articles I've read, you had*

some cogent insights. Would you agree to an interview in person?

A small lie, Jack told himself, then he attached his cell number and C.V.

He had no idea how the system worked. Assuming publishers actually forwarded emails to their authors, did authors always respond? Those inundated with fan mail might take months to read an individual message. Jack again had to lecture himself to be patient. In the meantime, he decided to call his son for more insight about Ralph Johnson.

"Hey, Dad," Max answered.

Jack could hear road noise in the background. He had admonished his son before about talking on the phone while driving. This time he just said, "If you're driving and can't talk, I can call back."

"Chill, Dad. Carly's driving." Then in the background, Jack heard a faint feminine voice say, "Hi Dad!"

Carly was his son's girlfriend. More than a year now, Jack thought. He hadn't met her yet but they'd chatted on the phone a few times when he called his son. Maybe they were serious. Jack hoped not; he liked Carly but Max was only twenty-two. He hoped his son would experience more of the world before settling down. Jack knew firsthand that you don't always meet the right partner when you're young.

"Tell her hello from me." Jack could hear Max convey his greetings. Then he said, "Listen, is this a good time to talk?"

"It's okay. We're heading to a movie. Are you calling about Sandy? Did she tell you?"

Jack hadn't intended to mention Sandy; after all, it was her news to share. But he was happy she felt comfortable enough to tell her brother. "Yes. I'm proud of her. It took some courage for her to reach out."

"I've known for a while. I'm glad it's out. Amazing about Mom, isn't it? That she's cool with it."

"Yes, I suppose it is," Jack said. He tried to sound casual when he added, "I'm also calling to ask you about Ralph Johnson, the writer. I know you've read a lot of his work, and I'm interested in any thoughts you might have. I'm trying to meet him."

"Seriously?" Max sounded genuinely surprised and impressed. "You're meeting Ralph Johnson? And you want my help?"

"Well, yes, I hope to, anyway." Jack considered how to explain. "He knows – or knew – an old friend of mine, and I'm trying to reach her and I think he can help."

"Whoa, can you repeat that again?"

Jack did, and then added, "You know that he traveled in Afghanistan in 1978?"

"Sure, everybody knows that, Dad. His first novel, remember? When he writes about the desert planet of Ghoridi? The plotline comes straight out of Afghan history."

"Oh," Jack didn't know that. He missed that in his research. "What's he working on now?"

"The Zoroaster series. Book four will be released in the next few weeks. It's a big deal." Max paused. "So who's this old girlfriend you're trying to find?"

"She's not my old girlfriend. She was Ralph Johnson's. They were in Afghanistan together. I only met her once." Which was technically correct, he reasoned.

Jack realized he must have sounded apologetic, because Max replied, "Hey, it's cool with me. Sandy gave me a heads up about your search." The light banter suddenly was gone. "I guess that's what happens when people get divorced," his voice a mixture of wistfulness and disappointment. "Besides, Mom's seeing someone, too."

Jack frowned. So she was still seeing that postdoc asshole. Then he reminded himself he had no right to be jealous. The divorce was inevitable; just a matter of months. He breathed deeply to control the irritation in his voice. "Yeah, I know."

"He's some guy who works in the Bush White House. How weird is that?"

Now Jack had to struggle to contain his sense of betrayal. Frank, he thought, his so-called friend and former student. "How can she be seeing Frank Constant? She hates his politics."

Max cleared his throat and - gently, awkwardly - replied, "Uh Dad, I don't think they talk much about politics."

WHEN JACK FINALLY hung up, he fell back in his chair and stared into space for several minutes. He realized he was not as free of Helene as he had thought. His feelings were messy, still entangled with her. He stood and shook his limbs; did some stretches to release the tension. Helene was his past; he didn't yet know about his future. He realized that was why he was so focused on finding Cassie.

Now it was a matter of waiting for Ralph to respond. Jack discovered something new about himself: he hated the waiting. Where was his renowned patience and perseverance? He used to love getting lost for weeks at a time in research. In fact, he never thought of himself as a man of action. He was a thinker more than a doer, most comfortable with books and a life of the mind. He and Cassie had talked about it in the airport. She told him he should travel overseas, if he was going to teach foreign policy. He tried to explain how one did research; that experiencing foreign cultures wasn't the same as analyzing political, legal and economic data, and then theorizing about what it all meant. He remembered her doubtful look.

Jack spent an hour following up on other clues. Knowing that the Robinettes were from Gonzales, Louisiana, helped. He sent emails to those he could find in the southern part of the state. The name was unusual enough that he hoped they knew one another. The first two replies were regretful; they did not know a Cassandra Robinette. A third contact replied that she had been dead a long time and to stop harassing him. Jack convinced himself this was a different Cassandra; probably the one whose obituary he had seen back in March. He received no other replies. He considered giving up. Cassie was no doubt happy somewhere. Thinking him dead all these years, she might not appreciate him suddenly showing up.

Then an idea came to him: maybe Frank could help. In Jack's mind, Frank owed him that much. He hadn't caused their split, but he was certainly taking advantage of it. Deciding not to mention Helene, Jack dashed off a text asking his former student to discover what the State Department knew about American tourists in Iran in early September 1978. The U.S. embassy would have still been open; it wasn't seized by Iranian militants until November of the following year. Were there any extant records of citizens disappearing or needing help? In particular, any American women?

BACK TO WAITING, back to killing time. He stared at his computer screen and considered polishing the paper he was slated to present at a major national conference in August. With little enthusiasm for the task, he debated starting something new related to his search for Cassie, perhaps a study of Iranian-American relations during the late seventies. That didn't inspire him either; he knew the subject had already been done. He leaned away from the table, bored with himself.

In films and books, action unfolded quickly. Characters didn't have to sit around and wait for something to happen. They were bold, proactive, risk-takers. Not just in fiction but in real life also. Even some presidents fit the type, he reflected. Teddy Roosevelt famously extolled "the man who is actually in the arena." Even if he makes mistakes, even if he fails, at least he dares greatly.

Teddy Roosevelt settled it for Jack. He was finally in the arena; he wouldn't give up.

He found his shoes. As he readied himself for a run, he had another idea. He was in pretty good shape; his cardio was excellent. But he could use strength training. He would join a gym, work with a personal trainer. That's what he could do with his time and energy. Prepare for a future in the arena.

ONLY FOUR DAYS after sending his email, on Friday, Jack opened his laptop to find a cursory response from Ralph Johnson asking for more clarification on what he wanted to talk about.

Jack wrote back immediately. He considered how to explain.

I read that you traveled in Afghanistan & Iran in '78. Would like to talk w/ you about your experiences.

Ralph must have been on-line at the exact same time. He replied immediately.

Not Iran. Afghanistan & Pakistan. What specifically do you want to know?

So Ralph had not traveled to Mashhad with Cassie. That's interesting, Jack thought as he typed, "Wasn't it dangerous for Americans at the time?"

Ralph answered, "Situation was tense, with Soviets already in country. But ordinary Afghans friendly."

Jack nodded to himself, took a sip of coffee and typed back, "That's part of what I'm researching, attitudes of ordinary people. Are you free for an interview anytime soon?"

Now came a longer pause before Ralph's response. "Sorry, no time. I have a book tour coming up."

"Yes, I know," Jack typed. "Book four in the Zoroaster series, right?" Bless Max for cluing him in. "It's a big deal to your fans," he added.

"Thanks, I think so too. It's called *Cult of Fire*," came the reply. Then, clearly reconsidering Jack's request, Ralph typed, "We can meet after the tour, in six weeks or so."

Jack wondered: would Ralph be willing to meet earlier if he knew Jack's true purpose? Or would he decline to meet him altogether? He opted for a fishing expedition.

> *I'm also interested in gender relations at that time, given the rise of the Taliban and their draconian treatment of women. I read somewhere that a young woman traveled with you. I'd like to explore if her experiences with local people were the same as yours.*

No reply from Ralph. Jack stared at the screen for a full minute. Then came Ralph's response: "Where did you read that? I've never mentioned it in any interview." His tone was guarded.

To be honest or not to be honest, that is the question. Jack couldn't think of a plausible lie, so he typed,

> *The woman herself told me many years ago. She triggered my interest in this subject. Unfortunately, we've lost touch.*

"Who are you?" Ralph's message demanded.

Jack knew it wasn't his name Ralph wanted; he already had that. It was his connection to Cassie. He considered a moment and then typed, "I'm Cassie's professor friend." He added, "C-3PO."

A pause, then the reply, "What do you really want?"

Jack wondered what he should say. He hadn't intended on being so candid this early in their conversation. Too late to fabricate something now, he thought.

To be frank, I'm looking for answers about Afghanistan, about Cassie. I'm trying to find out what happened to her.

Ralph replied immediately: "Can't help you."

And nothing else.

He must have signed off. Jack typed "Please" but still got no response.

Minutes passed. Jack sat back in his chair, aggravated with himself for blowing this chance. Tomorrow, Jack promised himself, he would send another email, apologize for lying and beg for some answers. He hoped Ralph would be more open to talking by then.

Just then, the phone rang. It was Becky Gonzales.

"Hi there, Jack. I wanted to touch base, let you know I'm still trying to reach some of our old friends."

"Has she contacted anyone?"

"Well, no. That's why I'm calling. Because it's so strange. It's as if she vanished into thin air. Except for a call I got this morning from her cousin whom I know because he once dated my sister." Becky paused briefly, then said softly, "He told me that she never came home; that his parents believe she's dead."

Jack said nothing. He couldn't digest this news. It lay like a rock in his belly.

Becky added quickly, "That doesn't mean she is, Jack. From what I gather, there was never any formal notification from the State Department. And an old friend of ours thought he saw her a few years ago outside a Baton Rouge shopping mall. She was crossing the parking lot; he shouted at her from his car, she didn't hear. By the time he parked, she'd walked into the mall and he lost her."

Jack clutched at the straw eagerly. "When was this?"

"Not long before Hurricane Katrina, so I'd guess late 2004 or early 2005. But no one else reported seeing her about then."

"So it may or may not have been Cassie?"

"It's a mystery, this whole thing. Nobody just disappears. Not nowadays."

Becky's last comment stayed with Jack. That evening, running through the neighborhood, he mulled it over. People used to be able to invent new identities for themselves and disappear. The frontier was full of people pretending to be someone else. It was an ancient plot line; didn't Shakespeare use it? He wanted to believe she had disappeared; he just couldn't accept the alternative explanation.

Jack slowed to a walk as he approached his apartment building. At the base of the stairs, he bent over to catch his breath and considered the possibility: Cassie could have easily disappeared if she did it many years ago, before the advent of the Internet age. But why would she? She wouldn't have cut connections to cousins or old friends casually. Something must have triggered her action.

Early the next morning, Jack was roused awake by Brubeck's *Take Five* on his cell phone. He grabbed it from the night table and glanced at the caller's ID. It was a number he didn't recognize. He sleepily said hello.

Without preliminaries, a male voice said, "This is Ralph Johnson. You said something yesterday. That you're trying to find out what happened to Cassie."

Jack sprung awake. "Yes. She seems to have disappeared in Iran. I thought you might be able to help me find her."

A thoughtful pause, then the voice resumed. "I honestly don't know what happened to her after Kabul. Didn't she go home?"

"Not that I can find. Her family and friends say they don't know what happened to her." Jack didn't mention Becky's grim news from the day before.

"I didn't realize that." The voice was somber.

Jack made his pitch. "You might have a clue from those last few days with her. Couldn't you help me?"

There was a long pause. Then Ralph said, "I don't think I can, but I'll try. But not over the phone."

They made arrangements to meet at Ralph's home in San Francisco on the Friday two weeks from then, during a break in the book tour.

"Oh, and one more thing," Ralph said as they were signing off.

Jack waited.

"Don't ever lie to me again, you fucker."

"You got it," Jack replied, a little stung. He was sorry he had lied.

He immediately booked a flight for the Thursday before their meeting, then a rental car and hotel. He started to write the flight information on his calendar when he noticed the date of the meeting. June 8, Cassie's birthday. She'll be fifty-two, he thought.

RALPH LIVED IN the northwest corner of the city, in a neighborhood not far from the Pacific. Jack left his car at Sutro Heights Park, then walked a block and turned right. He didn't want to park in front of Ralph's home. He wanted – needed – time to think. He had mixed feelings about Cassie's old boyfriend, and he wanted a few minutes to prepare himself. The day was pleasant for San Francisco, in the mid-fifties. But against a cool ocean breeze, Jack zipped his jacket and raised the collar.

The homes were pleasant and well appointed: single family, two story. Not ostentatious but, Jack surmised, probably worth a lot given their prime location in one of the most expensive cities in the country. He hadn't realized fantasy fiction paid so well.

Soon he was standing outside an English Tudor style home. Gazing at it from the sidewalk, Jack wondered if the heavy exterior beams were structurally needed or just for show, like a movie backdrop. A brass plaque mounted above the doorbell declared "Built 1925." Structurally needed, he guessed. It made him like Ralph better. He rang the bell and was mildly surprised when the writer himself opened the door.

Each man surveyed the other for several seconds. Ralph was tall, with a slender almost youthful face and delicate hands. But a thick torso and gray thinning hair revealed his age. His was a body that had sat at a computer or dinner table for long hours. Even so, he was good looking, dressed with casual sophistication in khaki slacks and a burgundy cashmere sweater. Jack wondered absently how he appeared to Ralph. His body might be in better shape – he was speculating here – but he knew his face showed every one of his fifty-six years. His salt and pepper beard probably didn't help, he suddenly thought. And his old leather jacket and jeans suggested a bank account more meager than the well-known author's.

Ralph ushered him inside. The foyer was as stylish as its owner, boasting a fresh spray of flowers on a side table, reflected in a large antique mirror on the opposite wall. Jack's quick glance into the mirror confirmed his assessment of his appearance. He looked like an aging professor. He sighed as he unzipped his jacket.

Ralph politely offered to take his jacket and, when Jack politely declined, Ralph escorted him up a flight of stairs to a large office with a bank of windows looking out on the Pacific. The view stopped Jack momentarily; it was simply stunning. Motioning for him to sit, Ralph positioned himself behind an impressive teak wood desk situated in front of the windows. He made no offer of coffee or water. Jack wasn't surprised; this wasn't a social call.

Jack's eyes took in the room. Other than a bookcase, the desk, Ralph's chair and his own, the room was fairly Spartan. No collection of odd miscellany crowded the shelves, no old sweaters tossed over furniture, no stacks of books on the floor. The large desk was clean except for a computer and large monitor. Beneath his feet was a Persian style carpet in pale green, lavender and beige. Ralph's office was austere yet refined. The only concession to the personality and profession of the owner were framed prints of every book cover that Ralph had published. There were more than two dozen.

"Thanks for seeing me," Jack said earnestly. "I know you're very busy and ..."

"Can't talk long today, sorry," Ralph intoned. Seeing Jack reach into his briefcase, he added, "And please no tape recorders."

"Of course not." Jack extracted a notebook and placed it on his knee. "This won't take long," he assured Ralph. He weighed the man across from him, his seriousness, his coolness, his self-importance. Ralph had seemed more interested in Cassie's whereabouts two weeks before; his concern had evidently waned in the intervening days. Realizing he needed to reengage him in Cassie's cause, Jack said, "She often wrote about you." He noted Ralph's quizzical look; eyebrow raised. He decided to add something complimentary which was mostly true. "She was excited about traveling with you."

Ralph nodded. He seemed to believe Jack.

Jack made another move calculated to flatter. "And after our interview, if you don't mind, my son Max would really love an autographed copy of *The Oracle's Apprentice*." Thinking it would be a nice surprise for Max, he had packed a copy in his briefcase. According to a published interview, Ralph considered it his best fantasy work.

Ralph gave a polite smile. "My pleasure," he said. The blandishment seemed to be working. "Tell me more about yourself," he asked. "And why you want to find Cassie after all these years. I'm curious."

Jack was bored with his own story and anxious to elicit Ralph's, but he recognized the need to establish bona fides. He talked about enjoying her letters and wondering why they had stopped. Leaving out any mention of their planned rendezvous in Istanbul, he said he hadn't pursued the matter at the time because he assumed she and Ralph were busy traveling. Then years passed: he finished graduate school, married and started a family, landed a teaching post. "By then, I didn't know where she was. I guess I put her out of my mind until recently when I was packing up my office for a move, and ran into a batch of old letters. I started wondering how she was. But my ... curiosity was really piqued when I could find no trace of her." In reality, he was not just curious; he was anxious, even alarmed. But he opted to use Ralph's earlier word. He didn't want to activate any latent jealousy.

"No trace at all?" Ralph's face registered disbelief, so Jack outlined his exhaustive Internet searches and inquiries. Despite his misgivings about mentioning Becky's name, he spoke about her recent phone call, the fact that some in Cassie's family believed her dead.

At this, Ralph met Jack's eyes for the first time. A frown line appeared between his dark brown eyes. "And how do you think I can help?"

"The last letter I received was postmarked in Kabul. You were with her then. I'm trying to piece together where she went from there."

Ralph paused. "Do you know about the two men we met there? Danny and Marton?"

"She mentioned them in her last letter. Said Danny was all right; that you and he were friends, but Marton was an asshole. Something like that."

Ralph barked out a bitter laugh. "That's rich. I mean, she's right, he was. But she certainly seemed taken with him."

"How so?" Jack looked up from his notebook.

"Well, she went on a date with him when we were still *ostensibly* a couple."

This didn't make sense to Jack. "A date?"

"One afternoon, I was sitting in the hotel lounge in Kabul. Danny and Marton were with me. She came in. Marton asked her out in front of me. They left the hotel together."

This didn't fit Jack's sense of Cassie at all. She didn't seem like someone who played the field and broke hearts. "Where did they go?"

Ralph hedged, "I don't know, actually. I stayed in the lounge with Danny." He shifted uncomfortably. "Listen, it's been a long time and my memory is a little fuzzy. All I know is that I didn't see her again. She and Marton left together," he repeated, still confounded by it. "You should talk to him."

Jack checked his notebook. "Marton Zambo, right?"

"I don't recall his last name. But I do remember he made a big fucking deal about it being Marton with an O. The jerk." Then Ralph added, "I do remember Danny's last name, though. Danny Mack. Nice kid. I think he was working for Marton. His sister contacted me a few times to see if I knew what had happened to him. He disappeared too, evidently. Maybe he and Cassie ran off together."

Jack was noncommittal. "Maybe," he said, thinking he might pursue this later. But now he needed more clarification about the date. "So one afternoon Cassie left with Marton. Was she okay when she come back?"

"She didn't come back. That's what I'm telling you. At least not to me. The next day, she left Kabul with Marton. No warning. Nothing." A sour note in his voice. He swiveled his chair and scowled at the ocean.

"What happened? I'm a little confused...." Jack stared at him.

Ralph took some time before answering. "Marton pounded on my door in the middle of the goddam night. I scrambled out of bed and that's when I realized that Cassie wasn't there. I opened the door, Marton pushed past me, switched on the light. He started packing up her things. I just sat on the edge of the bed. I remember feeling really fucked up. My brain wasn't working right. Finally I asked him what the hell was going on."

He turned back to face Jack. "He said they were leaving right then for Herat. So I stood up and told him I'd hurry, and I started to stuff shit into my pack. The next thing he said I remember very distinctly. His words, his tone, his expression. He said, 'You're not invited.' I was garbage left on the curb. Then he told me Cassie was going with him. He said something corny, like from a Western, that she's his woman now. That memory is weird; I may have imagined those words. But I got his meaning. I felt furious and hurt and confused. And then Marton did something I can never forgive."

Jack leaned forward, his face etched in concern.

"He gave me a week's worth of opium." Ralph stopped.

This wasn't what Jack had expected Ralph to say, but the whole episode started to make awful sense. Ralph was probably stoned when Cassie left. Marton was probably a drug smuggler; after all, he had opium to give away when it suited him. What about Cassie? Jack had to ask, "Did she use also?" He didn't want to think of her that way, but he knew that addicts had a talent for disappearing and self-destructing.

Ralph shook his head vehemently. "No way. She always wanted to be aware, on top of things. She didn't even drink much beer. I don't think she ever tried anything stronger than marijuana. And, even then, just a handful of times."

Jack sighed with relief. But Ralph's comment just raised other questions. "She went with Marton anyway? Even though he was a dealer or smuggler?"

"I'm sure she didn't know, now that you ask." Ralph got lost in thought. "She was funny that way. Worldly in one sense. Smart. She'd read a lot, talk to people, pick up some of the language. But she was naïve in another sense. Clueless about the underbelly of life, if you know what I mean."

Jack nodded. He did know what he meant. He felt it about Cassie as well, her trust in people, her optimism. It was one of her appealing attributes. And it made her vulnerable. "Didn't you tell her your suspicions about Zambo?"

Bristling in self-defense, Ralph glared. "I didn't know at first. I thought it was Danny's shit. Sure, I figured it out later, but by then she was gone."

"I don't understand. She was still there when Marton gave you the opium, right? So what happened after that?"

A brusque laugh, humorless and angry. "What the hell do you think happened? I got wasted."

"No, I mean immediately after Marton came to your room. Didn't you follow him out to see Cassie, to see if she was all right?"

"Hell, no. I was too upset."

Jack dropped his pen in his lap and sat back to look directly at Ralph. "By then, you knew the guy was a drug dealer. Yet you didn't see her at all. Not since the afternoon before." He was edging out on thin ice, he knew, but he couldn't stop himself from observing, "So you really don't know if Cassie left with Marton. Or was kidnapped. Or worse." It was a cruel thing to say, but he felt a mounting anger he couldn't control, and a deep fear.

Ralph stared at him. He had clearly never considered these possibilities. Then slowly, slowly his face crumbled as he absorbed Jack's meaning. He dropped his head into his hands.

Minutes passed. Jack sensed he was hurting and didn't care. Eventually, Jack swallowed hard and eased the conversation back to the aftermath of her departure. "When you got to Herat later, did you hear anything? Do you know if Cassie was still with Zambo?"

Ralph roused himself. "I didn't go to Herat. I got sick as a dog. I thought more opium might help and went to ask the kid that served drinks in the lounge, figuring he might know a dealer. But then I saw this little girl, the owner's daughter, I think. Maybe four or five. And she was clutching this cheap plastic doll, the one Cassie had carried with her for weeks. Maude, she called it. I remembered then that she had ditched it when we left with Marton the first time. And that doll, with its painted eyes and mouth...." Emotion threatened to overcome him and he had to pause. In a moment, he continued, "That doll reminded me of Cassie and everything good we had together. Until that moment, I'd kept myself too numb to feel anything. But that doll ripped me apart. I think I even started sobbing. The young guy in the lounge brought me back to my room, made me tea and basically looked out for me for a few days until I was feeling better. Then I called my folks, and they wired enough money for me to fly out of there."

"You never went to Herat."

"Nope. Got to the Kabul airport and adios Afghanistan."

Jack stood. He was infuriated with Ralph but he knew it was unfair. Ralph believed Cassie had deserted him; hadn't Jack made the same assumption, on flimsier evidence? And hadn't Jack also failed to follow up to see if Cassie was all right?

The interview was over as far as he was concerned. Ralph seemed finished, in any case. Jack extended his hand. "Thanks for your time."

Standing, Ralph confirmed, "Not for publication, right?"

"Definitely not for publication."

"I hope it helps." Ralph sounded sincere.

Jack smiled tightly. "Oh, yes, I'm sure it will." He wasn't sure at all, but Ralph seemed to need the affirmation. He opened his briefcase to pack his notebook.

"Well, memory, you know. You have to take it with a grain of salt. But that's what I recall." Then Ralph added, "Some of it came back when Danny's sister contacted me. The first time was about ten years ago, and things were fresher in my mind. Oh, and she asked about Cassie then too, come to think of it."

Jack stopped. He'd forgotten about Danny's sister. "Do you happen to have her contact information?"

"I should. We met for coffee last year. I like to keep business cards," he replied and dug through the top desk drawer. "Here somewhere," and he produced a card engraved with the name of Deborah Mack. "But I have to warn you. She's a conspiracy-theorist. A little cracked in my view. Just so you know."

Jack pocketed the card, shook Ralph's hand again, and took his leave. "I'll find my way out, thanks." He opened the office door.

"Wait," Ralph said, picking up a Mont Blanc pen, "didn't you want me to autograph *The Oracle's Apprentice* for your son?"

RAGE WAS STILL new to Jack. He had spent most of his adult life assiduously avoiding getting angry. But the past few months were colored with strong and contradictory feelings. Fury and joy, remorse and hope. This rollercoaster ride was giving him psychic vertigo, he thought as he stared out at the crashing waves of the Pacific. Part of him wanted to reclaim that former self, the man who got pleasure from teaching, long talks with friends, a glass of wine with his wife, reading a play. Admittedly, not everything was calm beneath the surface in those days. He recalled feeling irritated when students plagiarized; pissed off when administrators bullied; exasperated with Helene's unforgiving judgments of others; mildly depressed that his kids didn't call. In retrospect, however, his life had been a serene watercolor. Now it felt like a garishly colored collage.

The ocean's fury helped tame his own. He finally returned to his rental car. Inside, he retrieved the card Ralph had given him and dialed the number for Deborah Mack. He sincerely hoped she wasn't a little cracked.

She answered on the second ring.

"Hello, Ms. Mack. My name is Jack Hunter and ..."

She interrupted, "Yes, what do you want?" She must have thought this was a sales or survey call.

Worried that she might hang up, Jack spoke more quickly. "I'm looking for Cassie Robinette and I understand you're looking for Danny Mack. I think they were traveling together in Afghanistan and Iran. Ralph Johnson gave me your card."

"Oh God oh God oh God," the woman's voice replied.

"I thought we might meet and compare notes, see if we can figure out what happened to them."

"Jack Hunter," she said, "You will never know how happy you've just made me."

CHAPTER THIRTEEN

September 3, 1978

Sunday

Cassie hoisted her pack on her back and slowly negotiated the stairs in the dim early light. Here she was, going to Mashhad with Marton after all. And Danny as well.

Danny had objected vehemently last night at dinner when Marton brought it up, yet eventually he'd acceded. She'd been away from the table for a few minutes. When she returned, she heard Danny stressing that it would be for only one day; then he would return to Herat. She had been surprised and wondered how Marton had convinced him so quickly. With Danny leaving, she began to rethink the option of staying alone in Herat.

She hadn't seen Danny since Friday afternoon's ordeal. He looked strained. When Marton briefly left them alone to pay the dinner bill, she whispered that she had mailed the letter to his sister. Danny looked incredulous, then relieved. With a catch in his voice, he thanked her twice. Then he swallowed and whispered back, "I have to tell you something."

At that instant, she caught Marton watching her from across the restaurant and subtly signaled Danny to stop talking. Marton walked up to her and said, "They told me you already paid for our meal." His voice was cordial but his lips were pursed; she could tell he wasn't pleased.

Since reading Danny's letter, Cassie knew that she could no longer be Marton's lover. She had to reclaim autonomy, and that included paying her own way. So she affected a casual air and shrugged, "No big deal. It was my turn." She pretended to survey the other diners as she tried to figure out what was really going on. She felt ignorant and vulnerable. Danny was key; she had to have a chance to talk with him.

None came.

Getting ready for bed that night, after Marton left for the bathroom, she made a pallet for herself on the carpet of their room with a pillow and one blanket. She lay down and tried to make herself sleep. It was useless. Instead, her mind recited the risks of traveling with Marton the next day: crossing a heavily guarded border with a man she didn't really know and could no longer trust; heading straight into political turmoil, according to Saaleh; and possibly carting along a cache of illicit drugs. Restless and irresolute, she had not yet made up her mind when Marton returned from the bathroom and saw her. She read the puzzlement and offense on his face and consciously ignored him.

He walked past her to his backpack and stowed his toiletry bag. "You're angry for some reason," he said, his back to her.

Cassie blurted out. "Marton, are you smuggling drugs in the van?"

His turned toward her, his expression shocked. "Did Danny tell you that?"

"Danny didn't tell me anything." She needed an answer, so she slowly repeated the question.

"Is that what this is about?" He gestured at the pallet. When he reached down to take her hand, she pulled it away. His eyes held hers for a long minute. "No, Cassie, I am not smuggling drugs; I don't like drugs. You know that." Gently, insistently, he added, "Now stop this nonsense and come to bed. You won't sleep well on the floor and we have an early start tomorrow." She didn't move and, in a less cajoling voice, Marton said, "Come to the bed. Don't worry; I won't force myself on you." Arms crossed, he stood waiting.

She felt too exposed on the floor at his feet, and stood up. "Are there *any* drugs in the van? On top of the van, under the van?" She had to be precise. He might be playing word games.

"No. Other than aspirin, there are no drugs in, on or around the van." A definitive answer. His voice didn't waver, his eyes stayed steadily on hers.

Surely he wouldn't lie to her face. Maybe there had been drugs but they were gone now, sold or sent by a different carrier. She needed to believe him, that Danny would be safe when they crossed the border. As for herself – assuming she did decide to go along - she had no intention of staying with the van as it passed through the border checkpoint, drugs or no drugs. She would walk through on her own; Marton couldn't stop her. But she doubted that Danny would agree to join her. Marton had some sort of hold over him, and it wasn't simply that Danny was young and trusting.

Still, she felt overly melodramatic with the pallet. Accepting Marton's assurance that he would leave her alone, Cassie picked up the pillow, wrapped herself in the blanket and sat on the far edge of the mattress. Then she lay down as far as possible from Marton's side. The light went out. She felt Marton lay down as well. True to his word, he didn't touch her.

Cassie stared at the dark wall a few feet away trying to think things through, trying not to be impulsive. She debated staying in Herat for several more days waiting for a bus. Travel with Marton carried risks, but so did being alone in western Afghanistan.

If she stayed, Saaleh and his family might help her. An uncomfortable thought arose: she would be intruding on their holiday celebrations. An unpleasant one followed: they would ask what had happened to her husband. What could she tell them? How modern were they, really? Even at the hotel, she might face questions.

If she went, she could look out for Danny, and he could look out for her. She remembered Saaleh's prediction about imminent revolution in Iran; if he was right, she had to cross the country as soon as possible. She needed to get to Istanbul, not be stuck here, on the wrong side of the revolution.

As exhaustion began to overtake her, she knew her decision. She would go with Marton to Mashhad.

SHE FELT AS if she had barely slept when Marton rose, dressed and grabbed his pack. She soon followed, but he moved quickly and, by the time she reached the sidewalk, he was already there, his gear stowed, waiting for her. Unfazed by her silence, he seemed energized and ready to be underway. He took her arm and she shook him off. She didn't need help to step into the back of the van. It was filled with boxes now, except for the bench seat and a narrow path leading to it. She negotiated the obstacle course, rested her pack on the seat and clambered over it to sit beside the window. Then she glanced to the side at the cardboard box nearest her, curious and fearful about its contents. Silk, spices, something terrible? The box – like all the others - was heavily taped.

Finally, Danny arrived. Also in a strange and quiet mood, he only glanced at her as he pitched his pack on top of one of the boxes, then climbed into the driver's seat. Marton, after closing the van's side door, climbed into the front passenger's. They rolled out of Herat just as dawn broke.

In addition to the boxes, something was different about the van, but initially Cassie couldn't place it. Several minutes into the drive, she realized what it was; the pungent smell no longer permeated the air. Marton had been cleaning the van, she remembered, when he sang that haunting song. She was relieved that the rotten earth smell was gone; it had been a bad companion on the journey through Afghanistan.

Staring out the window now, she imagined with dread her upcoming confrontation with Marton, when she left the van at the Iranian border station. Since Friday and his rage at Danny, her uneasiness had grown, mutated into apprehension. He was so volatile. How would he take it: as an insult, a rejection? It didn't matter; she had to do it. She was brave, wasn't she? But her palms were wet with sweat and her breathing shallow. She wasn't brave at all. Marton had opened her eyes to that and other hard truths about herself. She wasn't faithful, not after what she did to Ralph. She wasn't independent, she wasn't smart. Marton had exposed her true self: vain, unfaithful, cowardly and credulous. She had fewer illusions about herself; she had to give him credit for that.

They arrived at the border more quickly than Cassie expected. It was now full morning, but the day was not yet warm. The Afghani border checkpoint at Islam Qala was housed in a ramshackle structure that seemed stressed trying to accommodate the scores of bus travelers waiting to be processed through. They stood patiently in a line that streamed out the door on to the warming pavement. Unlike the bus, the van as a private vehicle was directed toward a door on the side of the building. Marton motioned for Danny to park next to an empty taxi.

Checking out of Afghanistan was easy. Only four people stood ahead of them, presumably from the taxi. The line moved quickly.

Danny was in front; Cassie moved to stand with him, hoping for a word, but Marton stepped in-between. None of them spoke. Soon,

Danny reached the counter, giving his passport to a middle-aged agent in a khaki uniform. After a perfunctory examination, the agent stamped it and handed it back. It was Marton's turn, but before he approached, he conspicuously touched Cassie's forearm and smiled brightly at her. The gesture seemed odd, not characteristic of Marton at all. Then she saw the border agent watching them, and understood immediately that this was theater. Marton was playing a role. He wasn't a suspicious character traveling alone; he was an ordinary businessman with a young girlfriend. Cassie was his disguise.

The realization appalled her. A second realization then hit: An ordinary businessman didn't need a disguise. That meant his cargo wasn't innocent. He had lied. Again. The goddamned bastard, she thought. In that instant, her fear of the upcoming confrontation vanished.

Finally Cassie reached the counter and relinquished her passport. Not even looking at her, the agent gave her documents a cursory perusal before stamping the Afghan visa. No one was in line behind her, so the agent stood and followed the three of them to the van.

Once outside, Cassie noticed that a quarter mile stretch of gravel lay between the Afghani border office and a modern white concrete structure. That must be the Iranian border checkpoint, she thought. The Herati bus passengers were crossing the gravel on foot, hauling shopping bags and suitcases and infants. In the opposite direction came bus passengers from Iran. For some reason, the buses didn't cross the national borders, leaving passengers no choice but to awkwardly portage their belongings across the wasteland. With a backpack, though, Cassie knew she wouldn't have a problem.

Her attention returned to the Afghan agent as he finished circling the van and peered into its dark interior. In heavily accented English, he asked Marton questions about his load. Marton obligingly produced a box cutter and handed it to the agent, who sliced the tape on the two closest containers.

Cassie was alarmed; she hadn't expected a search in Afghanistan. Why hadn't she left the van earlier? It was too late now. She held her breath as she watched the agent pull a ceramic vase from one container, a lapis lazuli box from another. He poked briefly around in each container and seemed satisfied. Facing Marton again, he snapped his fingers and held out his hand. Marton handed over the vehicle registration papers; tucked beneath the top page was a twenty-dollar American bill. Cassie observed the agent inconspicuously pocket the gift as he returned the papers. Then he said, "You are free to leave," as he turned to go back to the counter.

Cassie moved quickly now. She hopped in the back of the van and grabbed her backpack and tote. As she alighted, Marton moved to her side and said softly, "What the fuck is this?!" He glanced quickly at two Afghan soldiers squatting in the shade of the building, to ensure they hadn't heard him.

That's good, she thought. The soldiers will keep Marton from overreacting. She suspected they wouldn't care if he hit her or dragged her into the van, but the racket might alert the border agent to conduct a more thorough search. Cassie assumed a light tone, as if leaving the van was a perfectly reasonable thing to do. "I just feel cramped in the back and want to stretch my legs. It's not as if you need me in the van." She gave a good impression of a grin. "Danny, why don't you come along?" she added as she buckled the pack around her waist.

Danny's eyes twitched from Marton to her and back again. Marton was glaring at him. "That's okay, Cass," the younger man said. "I'm driving. But I think *you* should go."

Marton didn't say a word as she headed down the dirt path that paralleled the road. His anger only confirmed her own. In a minute, the van sped past her; neither man looked in her direction. If Marton was angry enough, he might order Danny to drive to Mashhad without her. In that case, she would try to get a seat on the Iranian bus. Regardless, it was too late now to reconsider.

The walk to Iran's border office took just ten minutes; she joined the patient bus passengers waiting to get inside. They were all locals: shopkeepers, students, whole families. At last she was at the glass double doors. As she pushed through them, air-conditioning smacked her. She caught her breath; she had not experienced such cold air since her drink in the Kabul Intercontinental. She shuddered at the memory.

The line of supplicants filled a long corridor; at the far end hung a life size portrait of the Shah of Iran, mounted high on the wall. The photographer had angled the shot upward, so that Reza Pahlavi's head appeared wreathed in sun-lit clouds, a saint on a medieval icon. His hand waved in beneficence, but Cassie knew now the friendliness was a ruse.

Beneath the Shah's portrait, three crisply uniformed agents manned a massive counter. Each traveler's face was scrutinized; each bag methodically searched. Along the left side of the corridor were glass cases with museum quality displays of all the ways travelers had tried to smuggle drugs into the country, and all the years they were now serving in Iranian prisons. The line moved so slowly that Cassie had time to examine each item. Hollowed out heels of shoes, false bottoms of luggage, empty shaving cream cans, fake gas tanks. The effect was intimidating: Iran boasting it could catch anyone trafficking illicit drugs.

She started to panic. Danny and Marton, in all likelihood, would get caught. Marton might deserve it; it was his van and his cargo and his duplicity. Further, he had the wiles and the cash to redeem himself from a bad situation. But not artless Danny. She had a clear idea what would happen if he was caught. Months ago in San Francisco, Jack had told her that Americans couldn't count on U.S. legal protections if they were arrested for breaking another country's laws. The embassy could contact your family and help you find an attorney, but that was about it. In much of the world, there would be no presumption of in-nocence, no right to counsel, no protection from coercive interrogation. Even torture was possible. Danny's U.S. passport would not protect him.

Brooding on this, she finally reached an unsmiling agent. She placed her passport on the counter and hoisted up her backpack and tote bag. The agent opened the passport, studiously comparing her face to its photo. Then he flipped through pages to read where she had been. She could not see what he was reading, why he was frowning. For a moment, she worried that he might turn her away, but then his fist came down hard on her passport, fixing an Iranian entry stamp. As she tucked the passport into her shirt pocket, he opened the tote and dumped its contents clattering on to the counter. Her camera, her wallet, the journal, three pens, a paperback, the package of dates, a water bottle, a roll of toilet tissue, the head scarf. He examined the small bags of miscellany: lipstick, comb, mirror, aspirin, band aides, tampons. The intimacies of her life exposed; she flushed with embarrassment. The agent saw nothing interesting and swept the pile back to her. As she quickly repacked the tote, he opened the top of the backpack. He reached in and pulled out her shawl, then the small down pillow she used on hard bus and train benches. He stopped. He stared at the pillow in his fist, at her and back at the pillow. Then he roughly stuffed it and the shawl into the pack and pushed it toward her. Over her shoulder, he gestured for the next traveler to approach.

Cassie rapidly gathered her things and moved aside. Everyone else in line was still undergoing a thorough search. She scooted out of the building, relieved but surprised that the infamously meticulous Iranian authorities had given her a pass. Marton's instincts were right: she was a great disguise. Without her, the van would be more suspicious. Danny's presence probably helped a little. It gave Marton a cover story; they were just friends in transit through Central Asia. But an even better cover story would have featured a trusting young woman carting a down pillow. Cassie felt gullible for believing Marton and guilty for abandoning Danny.

An Iranian bus pulled away from the curb as she stepped outside, and a long queue waited to board the other one. She realized there was no possibility of getting on, even if she wanted to. But where was the van? She scanned the area, worried about Danny. There it was, parked a little further down the road. They had gotten away with it; he was safe. Her knees felt weak. Still in the driver's seat, Danny saw her and waved through the window. With a grim set to her mouth, she crossed the distance and got back in. Danny's eyes met hers in the rear-view mirror but no one spoke.

Negotiating the border crossing had taken an hour. It was mid-morning as the van pulled on to the highway, heading west. Cassie remembered Marton's map of Iran; less than 200 miles to Mashhad. There, she knew, things would come to a head.

AT THE FRONT desk of the Hotel Khayyám, Cassie spoke in Dari to ask for three rooms. Both she and Danny needed space away from Marton. She would cover it, cost be damned. Behind the desk, the owner, a portly bearded man in a business suit, shook his head and said something. He spoke too quickly for Cassie to comprehend. Standing next to him, his teenaged son repeated in English, "Sorry, madam, only one room is available." She frowned and shook her head; one room would never work.

Marton overheard just as he approached the front desk. "That won't do," he said sternly. He wanted Danny gone. "We need two."

The young man replied in an apologetic tone. The hotel was packed, he explained, with the upcoming holiday. The hotel had only one room open, a family suite. One of the best in the hotel. Four rooms and a bathroom. Very comfortable.

This was their third try; the other two hotels were booked solid, or else did not want to rent to Westerners. Mashhad seemed to be a conservative town, Cassie had thought as they walked from hotel to hotel. She saw virtually no women on the streets or in the shops, even in burqas. Her own bare face elicited stares from local men.

Now, making a decision for all of them, Marton nodded and extracted his wallet. Cassie almost grabbed her bag to find another place but then reconsidered. It was getting late in the day. A four-room suite meant she would have her own bedroom. It would only be for one night, she told herself. The deciding factor, though, was the hotel's name: Omar Khayyám, her father's favorite poet. It had to be a good omen.

To cover her expenses, she pulled out her wallet as well, but she had no Iranian rials. She chided herself for forgetting to exchange money in Herat. Marton hadn't forgotten though. He paid for two nights and the older man handed him the room's single key.

The suite of rooms was light and airy, the nicest rooms Cassie had stayed in during her journey from the east: three bedrooms and a living room, high windows looking out on to a main street. Even the luxury of a bathroom. She took her backpack into one of the rooms and shut the door. Her own space. Solitude. She sat on the bed and reveled in this greater luxury, one she had not even realized she missed.

Still, she couldn't relax long; she had to get cash so she could travel onward. Rousing herself and grabbing the tote bag, she moved swiftly through the unoccupied living room and returned downstairs to the front desk. The teenager remained at his post.

"Pardon," she continued in Dari. "Where is a currency exchange?"

Replying in English, the youth told her it was closed and would be closed for several days. It was the end of Ramadan.

"Oh, no! We're traveling tomorrow, and need rials," she said urgently.

He considered this, then made a phone call. As she waited for him, Cassie noticed a stack of hotel postcards on the front desk.

"Lucky news," he smiled when he hung up. "My uncle has currency exchange in the market on the next street. It is open for you and your family until five." He added, "Please take a postcard of our beautiful hotel. It is free."

"Thank you," she smiled, slipping the card into her bag. "The hotel is named for Omar Khayyám, isn't it?

"You know Omar Khayyám?! Yes, madam, he is buried in Nishapur, not far away."

Cassie wished she had the time to visit, for her father's sake, but first she had to get away from Marton. "A great poet," she said wistfully, turning to leave.

"Yes, madam," he beamed after her. "A great Sufi poet!"

Cassie quickly walked to the next street and found the uncle's exchange booth. En route, she debated how much Iranian currency to get. She was, after all, just traveling through. Yet Tehran was said to be expensive. In the end, she exchanged her remaining Afghani bills, plus two twenty-dollar traveler's checks. That gave her almost sixty dollars' worth of rials, surely enough for bus fare, meals and rooms until she crossed the border into Turkey. In a pinch, she could cash more in Tehran. And she had a credit card tucked in the bottom of her backpack with her Louisiana driver's license. She hadn't used it at all on the trip; she didn't want her parents to be stuck paying the bill.

Walking back, Cassie realized Marton might need more rials as well; even driving quickly through Iran would require several nights lodging, and he favored nicer accommodations. If he wanted to exchange more, he would have to hurry, though.

Back in the room, Marton was staring out of the window of the main room. "Where have you been?" he asked as Cassie pushed through the door. To a casual listener, his voice would have sounded merely curious, but she heard a demand.

She told him about holiday closures and the currency exchange. It was the most she had said to him in almost two days.

Marton nodded brusquely in reply. Through the bathroom door, he called for Danny to hurry up and come along.

"I'm busy in here," Danny yelled. "And I can't hurry the fuck up!"

Cassie sensed Marton intended to wait. She looked at her watch. "Only fifteen minutes until closing," she informed him. "If you need rials, you have to go now."

She could tell he was disgruntled as he rushed out of the door. The second he was gone, Danny emerged from the bathroom.

"I need to talk to you, and Marton said he'd kill me if I did. So I've been waiting. This may be our only chance." When Cassie started to reply, he held up a hand. "Most important: you've got to get away from him. He's fucking crazy. You figured out about the drugs, didn't you? When you walked through the checkpoint? I was really glad you did that."

Cassie nodded. "It's opium paste, isn't it?" she asked somberly.

A stricken look came over his face. "Heroin. It's fucking heroin, Cass. I'm so sorry. I should have told you earlier. That's what we were doing in Herat. Opium's bulky and it stinks; heroin's easier to hide."

"Oh, Danny," was all that Cassie could say. All along, she had assumed it was opium.

"I didn't think he'd go nuts, though," Danny explained. "He seemed to really like you. I figured you'd be okay; you could leave whenever you wanted. But he's really, really pissed now and I don't think he'll let you go."

"Why do you say that!?" The idea of being captive alarmed her.

"Because now he knows you know about the heroin. Even though you didn't know. Not then. But that's why he got so pissed off when you left the van. And he thought it was disrespectful, that you didn't trust him."

"Of course I don't trust him!" Cassie shouted, stunned by Marton's gall. She paced, trying to disperse the electricity of rage and terror.

"He also thought the van wouldn't get searched if you were there. Especially if you didn't know. Because you look so innocent."

"Yeah, I figured out that part."

"That's why I wasn't supposed to tell you anything. Marton said you'd be safer if you didn't know. That if we were caught, you could claim ignorance." Danny reached out and took her hand. "Come with me tomorrow morning, back to Herat."

"I don't know. Maybe." She was thinking hard about it. Even though she'd be headed in the wrong direction, traveling with Danny had the advantage of safety; Marton would be less likely to stalk her. She sighed deeply. "I bet you regret coming along today."

"Well, it wasn't like I had much of a choice."

Uncomprehending, Cassie frowned.

Danny looked away and swallowed. "The thing is, he told me…" His voice caught; he had to start again. "Last night, he told me he'd hurt my sister if I didn't do what he said. He'd have her killed. I know he was exaggerating but Jesus!"

Shocked, Cassie stared in disbelief. Marton threatened to kill little teenaged Debbie. Even as an empty threat, it was unforgivably malicious. She felt sick to her stomach and dropped to the sofa.

Danny sat heavily next to her and said hopelessly, "He said he saw her address on the letter I sent. So he knows where she lives. It's my fault." He dropped his head into his hands.

Cassie was shaking her head, trying to reassure Danny and herself. "No, it's not your fault. And he can't know her address. He didn't have time to write it down," she insisted, replaying the awful scene in her mind. "He read the letter, then ran up the stairs to get you and threw the letter at me to burn, remember? He didn't have time," she repeated with less certainty.

"I don't know. He could have a photographic memory. I just don't want to take any chances when it comes to Debbie."

A step on the stairway alerted them. "Get ready to leave with me tomorrow," Danny instructed as Cassie rose, headed to her room and closed the door.

She sat on the bed, thinking about what he had said. Leaving Marton wouldn't be easy. She had to prepare. The first step, she now knew, was getting rid of anything that might provide a clue about where her loved ones lived, any clue that could give Marton leverage to make her stay. Quietly, Cassie dug through her bags and collected the letters, her journal, Becky's boyfriend's business card, scraps of paper with addresses – even the airport napkin with Jack's contact information – and hid them under the far corner of the mattress. She'd burn them when she had the chance. She was unhappy to lose the letters, but at least she knew most of the addresses by heart.

Second, her credit card; she pulled it and her driver's license from the deep recesses of her pack, glad that Marton didn't know about them. Near them on the bottom was an envelope of photographs of family and friends. She brought that out too and made certain each photo carried no identifying information. The photos went into her tote, the card and license into one pants' pocket, her wallet in the other. The money belt was around her waist; she opened it and slid in the passport.

What else? She racked her brain. She could buy a burqa; that was the perfect disguise. Except it wouldn't work if she traveled with Danny. So maybe she shouldn't travel with Danny; maybe she was putting him and his sister at risk if she did. In a burqa, she could continue on to Tehran. But then she couldn't carry her backpack; dead giveaway if Marton followed. Without it, what would she take? What was essential? She did a quick inventory. One change of clothes and her sweater and shawl. Toothpaste, etc. The camera, obviously. A few small mementos from her travels: the necklace from Srinigar, a fabric

Christmas ornament from northern Thailand, the blue glass cups, and
… She had to stop. This was too disheartening. She shouldn't have to
leave anything behind.

In anger, she decided to confront Marton. She would tell him this
evening, and tomorrow she would be on her way, either to Herat or
Tehran. There was nothing he could do to stop her, not with Danny
around.

Cassie suddenly realized that she had to alert Jack before he
bought his air ticket to Istanbul. Her plans were in flux. She might
need to meet him elsewhere or on a different date. Extracting the hotel
postcard, she quickly scrawled, *Things are complicated here. I don't
know about Istanbul. Don't come now. I'll explain later.* She really
wanted to tell him everything but didn't have the space. Or the time;
she heard Marton talking with Danny outside her door. Nervously, she
signed the card *Cassandra* and hid it in her back pocket. She promised
herself she would send a long letter in a day or two, once she was
safely away.

She picked up her camera and, taking a deep breath, quietly
opened the door. In the living room, Marton sat smoking at the table,
concentrating on a sheet of paper in front of him. Through an open
door across the room, she spied Danny, sprawled on his bed reading a
paperback. She paused, removed the lens cap and snapped a picture.
Part of the story, she told herself, a horrible part like the breakdown of
the van.

Replacing the lens cap, she strolled up to Marton and glanced
down at the paper; it looked like a city map written in Persian. He
turned around in his chair. "Where are you going?" he asked in that
deceptively neutral voice she was coming to hate. She was prepared
for the question and gestured at the camera. She was learning from
him how to deceive. He tilted his head slightly but said nothing more
as Cassie walked out. As she passed his door, Danny moved his fingers slightly in a subtle wave.

The teenager was still at the front desk. She bought a stamp and affixed it to the postcard. "Can you mail this for me, please?" It would save her a trip to the post office. She smiled when he took it. "*Tashakor*," she said.

The boy smiled back. After tucking the postcard beneath the counter, he introduced himself as Jahwed. He was fifteen. "You are the first western woman I meet!" He sounded delighted at the discovery.

Cassie smiled. "You speak English well. Did you learn it in school?"

Jahwed smiled broadly. "No. My uncle teach me, the man at currency exchange. Mostly I learn from movies."

"You get English movies here?" The disclosure surprised her a little; perhaps the town wasn't as conservative as she had thought.

"Some English, some American. And, of course, Persian. I love movies." Then, lowering his voice, he confided, "My father thinks they waste time. But my mother and sisters love me to tell the stories. I must be careful, though. Many things are not right for women to hear."

Tactfully shrugging, Cassie shifted the subject. "What's your favorite American film?

Jahwed laughed, "That's easy! *Rocky*, of course!"

Not what I would pick, Cassie thought, but it made sense; after all, he was a fifteen–year-old boy, not that different from her cousins.

"What is your favorite American film?" he asked her eagerly.

She thought about it. *Citizen Kane* always topped the list of the best; classmates had argued in favor of newer films, *The French Connection* and *Dr. Strangelove*. Great movies, but not her favorite. She loved *Lawrence of Arabia*, but technically it was British. Then she said, "*Treasure of the Sierra Madre*." Like *Lawrence of Arabia*, a story of outsiders in harsh terrain. "Hard to say really. I studied so many in college," she explained.

"You went to college?!" The idea shocked him.

"Yes, I was a film major; I love movies too. After I graduated, I worked as a production assistant with a film company." He looked both impressed and puzzled, so she explained, "I helped the director."

"Ah." This role seemed appropriate to a woman and Jahwed nodded. In a reverential tone, he said, "Then you must know Masoud Kimiay, a great Iranian director. He makes many movies, but my favorite is *Qeysar*. Surely you know it. Very exciting. But very sad too. Maybe he wins at the Cairo International Film Festival."

Iranian director? A film festival in Cairo? This was a new world for Cassie. She realized suddenly how parochial her education had been, focused on North American and European cinema, except for Akira Kurosawa.

Jahwed disappeared for a minute through the curtained doorway behind the counter, and returned with a glass of white liquid full of small green specks. "This is Doogh, from my mother, because you like Omar Khayyám and movies, like me. Doogh is very good," he assured her.

She took a tentative sip at first, before she recognized the taste as yogurt and mint. She nodded appreciatively. "It *is* delicious," she agreed and finished the glass in silence. Standing there in the hotel lobby, in the presence of the teenager and the invisible presence of his mother, she felt her shoulders starting to relax.

When she was done, Jahwed shyly asked, "Is that your camera? Can I see?"

Cassie nodded and pulled it from around her neck. "First, we turn it on," she said. After removing the lens cover and flipping the dial, she handed him the camera and watched him peer through the viewfinder. "Turn this to focus," she instructed; he pointed the lens toward the sofa and exclaimed when the image sharpened. When he looked up, she continued, "Here's where you set the aperture, or the size of the window for light to enter. It's called the f-stop." To demonstrate, she made a window with hands. "The smaller f-stop makes the window larger, good for low light situations. And here you set shutter speed, or how long the window stays open. You use a slower shutter speed when you're inside, like we are, because the camera needs time to gather more light. You adjust both to get the exposure you want." She assessed the light in the room. "Let's try f2.8 and 1/60." Jahwed gave her the camera and she adjusted the settings, checked them in the viewfinder, and handed it back. "See the thing with the plus and minus sign, on the left side? It's a light meter. When the settings are good, the line will be in the center. Try moving the f-stop here and see what happens."

Grinning, Jahwed moved the f-stop back and forth, staring through the viewfinder as he revolved around the room. He pointed the lens at Cassie. She gave a small smile and looked to the side, a little embarrassed. He took the shot and beamed. "My first photograph!" he exclaimed. "I make a photograph! Please wait," he called to her as he disappeared again. "I must tell my mother!"

The moment of discovery. Cassie recognized it and felt his thrill. But she felt a little anxious, too, about the safety of her beloved camera. Nothing to worry about; he was soon back and ceremoniously returned the camera to her. "I really really thank you, Mrs. Zambo."

She froze. As she was showing Jahwed her camera, she had forgotten about Marton. *Mrs. Zambo* brought him back. The name, the idea of what it represented, turned her stomach. She would never be *Mistress of* Zambo. Admittedly, the title had worked as a subterfuge in Herat, and would work here as well, where her unmarried status would be even more scandalous. But she couldn't let the deception pass; she was bone tired of pretense.

"I'm not married actually," she informed Jahwed. "Marton Zambo is not my husband."

Jahwed looked aghast. "Then who is he? Your brother? And who is this other man!?"

"Neither is my brother, but the tall man is like family to me. He's good. But Zambo…," and here she paused, wondering how to explain. "He's dangerous. Stay away from him."

"Oh, no! He attacks you?!" When Cassie shook her head no, Jahwed continued urgently, "Then you must go away before he does! The tall man must help. Do not let the man who pretends to be your husband dishonor you and your family anymore."

"I won't. I'll keep away from him tonight; I'll block my door," she told him. "And I'll leave tomorrow, to meet my brother." My brother, she reflected sadly. She had said it to reassure the young man; in this culture, brothers were important protectors, of both women and honor. But for the briefest moment, it was as if Jason was alive and coming for her.

"Good," Jahwed said earnestly. "Otherwise, you will have to kill yourself and then your brother will try to kill that man Zambo, and your brother will die too, and it will be just like *Qeysar!*"

The plotline, Cassie presumed, of the Iranian film.

Just then, behind her, Marton spoke, "We're going to dinner." She flinched; how long had he been standing there? She hadn't seen him and Danny emerge from the stairway. "Come along, Cassie." Like a dog, she thought. He was calling her to heel.

As she turned from the front desk, she caught a glimpse of Jahwed, his eyes wide and mouth open. Seeing the scene through his eyes, she reddened with shame. Head down, she followed them out.

Dinner was quick and unusually quiet, lamb kebabs at a neighborhood café. Toward the end of the meal, Marton turned to Danny and said simply, "We leave for the meeting at eight sharp. I'll knock on your door at seven thirty."

"No need," Danny replied gruffly. "I'll be ready. Afterward, we come back to the hotel, and then go to the bus station, right?"

"And then you go to the bus station, yes."

Cassie saw Danny look at her for a signal but she didn't respond. She hadn't told Marton yet that she was leaving. She was afraid that if he knew, he'd find some way to stop her. But time was running out and she had to tell him soon.

Just thirty minutes later, the time came. Danny had said good-night and retired to his room, leaving Cassie and Marton alone in their living room. "Can we talk?" she asked.

He stared at her. "And what would you like to talk about, my angel?" He said the last word sarcastically. Sitting at the table, he motioned for her to join him.

She chose a chair on the other side and cleared her throat; her mouth felt incredibly dry. "Things aren't working out between us, Marton. It's no one's fault but it's over, our ... relationship." She disliked her imprecision.

"What are you talking about?"

"I'm leaving tomorrow. By myself."

A full minute passed before Marton replied, "So you were lying before, when you said you cared about me."

"No, I meant it. But we're just not good together."

Annoyed, he snapped, "That's crap. Danny put you up to this, didn't he?"

"No, Marton. You do things that scare me."

"Such as?"

"Such as making me burn Danny's letter. And taking my wallet. And lying to me."

"Like what? When did I lie to you?"

She paused, not daring to mention she had read Danny's letter, not daring to utter the word heroin. "You lied about the drugs. You're smuggling opium. I smelled it in the van." A credible lie, she thought to herself. She didn't want to implicate Danny.

"That was Danny's, not mine. Before we left Herat, I made him get rid of it. You don't smell it now, do you?"

"Then why did you want me to stay in the van when we went through the border?"

Marton's eyes narrowed. "Danny told you, didn't he? That little shit. What lies did he tell you? That I'm some major drug lord?"

It bothered her that he kept blaming Danny. "He didn't tell me anything. I figured it out on my own. I'm not stupid."

A pause. He stared at her for several moments and then lit a cigarette. Face impassive, agitation showed in his fingers; the match flickered in his shaking hand. He took a drag, exhaled. "So, where do you plan to go now, free as a bird?"

"I don't know. Probably Tehran. Eventually on to Europe."

"Same route I'm taking."

She ignored him. "Maybe back to Herat. I think there's an airport."

"Ah, Herat! Now I get it. You're going with Danny." His mouth twisted in an ugly smirk. "You used me, Cassie. Used me to get away from Ralph. And now you're using Danny to get away from me. I thought you were special but you're just another slut."

Fury dissipated her fear, turned it into steam. "That's bullshit. You tricked me into leaving Kabul without Ralph." A sudden realization hit her, "You hooked Ralph on opium. And Danny, too. It was you."

"I don't know what you're talking about."

"The whole thing – your profession of love, that sad song - all of it, cheap carnival tricks. And I fell for them. You don't love me. You need me as cover. I'm an investment in your goddamned 'business.'" She was breathless when she finished.

Marton stood suddenly, chair clattering to the floor behind him. With fists clenched, he struggled to restrain himself. Cassie didn't wait; she stood as well, stormed into her room and slammed shut the door.

Calm down, calm down, calm down, she repeated to herself. The worst part is over. Now he would sulk and insult her, but she was halfway home. Tomorrow morning, when Danny returned for his backpack, she'd be ready to go with him to the bus depot. Once there, she would make up her mind about the direction, east or west.

An hour passed. When her breathing finally slowed, Cassie carefully opened the door. The main room was lit but deserted; Marton had gone. She slipped quietly to the bathroom. With face washed and teeth brushed, she retraced her steps. Then she checked her room to ensure he wasn't hiding behind the door, under the bed. All clear. Crazy paranoia, she told herself.

She laid out clothes for the morning: jeans, striped shirt, walking shoes. She transferred her wallet and credit card to her jeans. Then she unfastened the fabric money belt from around her waist and sighed with relief. With the passport inside, the belt had been stiff and uncomfortable all evening. Now everything inside was damp with sweat, her traveler's checks, even the passport. She pulled everything out and lay them on the top of the dresser to dry out overnight. She would repack them in the morning.

In her drawstring pants and tee-shirt, she was ready for bed. But when she climbed under the sheet, she studied the closed door. It had no lock. She rose and propped the backpack and heavy tote against the door. They wouldn't stop anyone, but they should make enough noise to awaken her. She didn't think Marton would force his way in, but if he did, she'd scream and Danny would come.

Everything was secure; she turned out the light and lay down.

An hour later, when she finally started drifting off, she heard a light knock. She jolted awake. Heart racing, she stood, turned on the lamp and stared at the door. Another light knock. She moved her bags aside and opened the door an inch. There was Marton, still dressed, holding a pot of steaming tea and a single cup. She could smell the mint.

"I was being unreasonable. Of course you can leave tomorrow if you want to. I would like to stay friends." His voice was conciliatory. He lifted the pot. "A peace offering."

The gesture confused and annoyed her. What was his angle? Did he think she'd let him sleep with her? Did he think she would stay? But she also felt a small measure of optimism; Marton was letting her go. Just maybe, everything tomorrow would be fine.

When she said nothing, he continued, "Let me put it down, all right? The tea is quite hot."

With bare hands, she couldn't take the aluminum pot herself, so she opened the door. Marton walked to the dresser and deftly set down the pot and cup. She watched him closely, but he touched nothing. Turning to her, he gave a small smile. "Good night, angel," he said as he left.

His sudden appearance unnerved her. There was little chance she could fall asleep now. Maybe some tea would help her relax. She stared at the pot, wondering if it was drugged. She took a cautious sip. The taste was perfect, just the right amount of mint and sugar. Even so, she hesitated. She put the cup aside and picked up a book instead. In five minutes, her mind drifted from it to the tempting pot of tea. In ten minutes, feeling no adverse effects from the first sip, she poured a full cup. She was proud of herself; she had stood up to Marton, she had not been bullied. Best of all, she would be on her way tomorrow. She would be - what were his angry words? - "free as a bird."

Around three in the morning, an intense urge to urinate woke her. She tried vainly to ignore her bladder. Eventually, resigned, she slipped out of bed in the dim light. Quietly pulling her pack and bag away, she left the room and fastidiously shut the door behind her. The main room was dark but she remembered well enough the location of the toilet. Walking slowly to avoid colliding with furniture, she finally reached it. In less than two minutes, she was back in bed, body happy and luggage restacked against the door. She relaxed into sleep.

CASSIE WOKE SUDDENLY. The room was full of light. She sat up, checked her watch. Almost eight, later than she wanted. The men would be starting their so-called business meeting soon; Danny might be back within the hour. Good thing she was mostly packed. She jumped out of bed and quickly pulled on her shirt and jeans. Before zipping up the pants, she reached for the money belt on the dresser. Something was wrong: the belt itself and the traveler's checks were there but where was the passport? She looked under the tea pot, on the floor around the dresser. Nothing.

She fought to keep down her fear. Think logically, she told herself. The luggage was still stacked against her door. No one could have gotten in. The passport must be here somewhere. On hands and knees, she searched under and behind the dresser and bed. She remembered taking the passport out of the money belt, but checked there just in case.

"How the hell …?!" and then she knew with dreadful certainty what had happened. She could visualize it, Marton waiting in the dark in the living room. Waiting to hear her tiny mouse movements, poised like a cat to slip into the room when she went to the toilet. He had seen the top of the dresser when he brought in the tea; he knew the passport's exact location. She was gone such a short while, but he could have done it in seconds.

She slumped down along the wall next to the dresser and weighed her options.

CASSIE COULD HEAR Danny's quick step on the stairs. He rushed into the living room. "Are you ready to go?" he asked as he pulled his backpack up. "Marton finally paid me and he says there's a bus to Herat at eleven and we still need to get tickets. He won't drive us, though. We've got to walk." He flourished a map, the city map that Cassie had seen Marton brooding over the previous afternoon. An X marked the hotel's location and a black circle had been drawn to the southeast. "It's not far. Get your stuff and let's get out of here."

She didn't move from the table. "I can't. I don't have a passport. Marton stole it."

"What? I'll make him give it to you."

"How? I've already searched his stuff and can't find it. He probably has it on him. Or hidden it in the van. He's incredibly good at hiding things." She paused in thought. "But I'll get it back, don't worry. I'll go to the proprietor and ask him to call the police. Marton has to give it back to me."

"Well, hurry up, then. Let's do it!"

"I already tried. The proprietor's gone this morning. Only the teenaged son is around and I don't want to involve him with the police. His father's back at eleven thirty, I'll talk to him then. But you'll miss the bus to Herat if you wait, especially if you've got to walk. Go on," she urged when Danny looked doubtful. "Really. I'll be fine."

"He's such an incredible asshole." Danny set down the pack. "I'd better wait with you. I can go to Herat tomorrow."

Cassie thought back to Marton's ugly accusations about him. "Actually, I think you being here will only make things worse. He blames you for me leaving. I don't think he'll be as difficult if it's only me."

Clearly torn, Danny stared hard at her. "I hate to leave you alone with him."

"You won't be. I'll catch the bus to Tehran later today. I asked Jahwed; he says there are two departures, one at twelve thirty and another tonight. He says they shouldn't be full because most people are already with their families. I'll be on one of them. I promise. Go."

Danny reluctantly agreed. He slowly lifted his backpack again.

She stood now and hugged him tightly. "I've really enjoyed getting to know you." Had it only been a dozen days?

"Me, too. You got my number. Give me a call when you get home. Better yet, come see me. I'll teach you how to surf. You'll love it. And you'll get to meet Debbie."

"You got a deal," she said. "Happy trails, Danny. Take care of yourself, okay?"

He bent down and kissed her cheek. "See you later, alligator," and he was gone. Just like that.

Tears formed along the lower rims of her eyes. Sitting again at the table, she brushed them from her eyes.

"Danny." Marton's unmistakable voice in the hall outside. "I'm glad I caught you. I want to give you something. Hold on a minute."

Marton entered, went to his room and briefly rummaged around. In a minute, he passed her again on his way to the hallway. His voice said, "Here, take this in case you get lost. You can ask for directions with it."

She couldn't see Danny, but heard his subdued reply, "Gee, thanks, man." She wondered if it was the note she had photographed back in Herat. Good, she thought. If he wouldn't give Danny a ride, it was the least he could do.

"Have a good trip," Marton said.

Cassie couldn't catch Danny's muffled reply, but she heard his heavy tread on the steps. And then Marton was standing next to her. He pulled out the chair close by and sat.

"So, you're not going with Danny." He casually lit a cigarette.

"You know why. You stole my passport. Again."

"What an accusation. I don't have your passport. You must have lost it somewhere." He exhaled smoke.

"Give it back to me, Marton. I'm serious." She held out her hand toward him, palm upwards.

He took her hand. "Tell you what. I'll give it back to you tomorrow, when we leave for Tehran. You don't need it before then. I'll keep it safe. I always do."

She yanked back her hand. "If you don't return it right now, I'm going to the hotel proprietor, and he'll report it stolen. The police will come. They'll search all over. Even the van, I imagine." She paused to let that sink in. "Stealing a passport is serious business."

"Interesting idea, the police," he said casually. "I see one of two things happening. Either they will believe me as your husband, or they will believe you, search the van, find what they will, and arrest both of us." He knocked ash from his cigarette. "At the very least, you're an accomplice. That's what they'll believe." He looked at her directly. "Prisons here are brutal, especially for women. The guards are all male."

His counter-threat seemed credible, and it infuriated and frightened her. She came to a decision: she didn't need the passport. She would leave today regardless. Once in Tehran, she'd go to the U.S. embassy for new documentation. Cassie stood.

Marton seemed to sense the change in her. "Okay, I'll give you back your passport. In a moment. But first let's talk. Please." She sat again, glaring at him. "It's in the hotel safe," he said, drawing on his cigarette. His eyes seemed hooded and impossible to read. "Are you certain you want to go?" He took her hand again. His voice was sad and his touch gentle.

This time she did not pull back. His behavior puzzled her; she half expected him to proclaim his love again.

Instead, he gazed at the back of her wrist, the one with the wound he had dressed all those days ago in Kabul. His finger tenderly traced the scar, a jagged white line along the wrist bone. It was healing well. "Scars are good to have," he mused. "They remind us of things. Souvenirs, as the French say." Then he turned her hand over, and brushed the inside of her wrist. It was a highly sensitive area, and the stroke produced a sensual thrill.

Aggravated now, Cassie tried to tug her arm away. His grip was strong. She tried again, without success. "Let me go," she demanded.

Suddenly, Marton brought the cigarette from his mouth and pushed the burning tip into the soft sensitive flesh he had just stroked.

Cassie screamed, a strangled yelp of sound. She desperately jerked her arm but he tightened his hold.

Calmly holding the cigarette in place, he said slowly, "Don't ever threaten me again."

The flesh continued to burn. Searing pain incited tears; her vision blurred. She blinked rapidly, trying to clear her eyes, trying to see.

Finally he raised the cigarette back to his lips and looked down at the scorched hole on her wrist. "See what you made me do," he said mournfully. He looked into her eyes.

Her entire body shook; her breath was ragged and shallow. She looked away, hating him.

He repeated, less sadly, "See what you made me do, Cassie. It's because you don't trust me. You always want to have your own way. You don't accept that I know best."

He finally released his grip. She yanked her arm back protective-ly, clasped it securely to her breast. Panting in pain, she couldn't speak.

He stood and went to his room. Seconds later, he returned with the first aid kit. Sitting again, he reached across the table for her wrist. She frantically scrambled back out of his reach.

Marton sighed. "Fine. But take care of that." He nodded toward her wrist. He carefully placed the first aid kit between them. "And clean up. We're going out to dinner at the best restaurant in town. You'll like it."

Just then came a knock on the door. Without another look at her, he rose and opened it slightly. Cassie could hear Jahwed. "There is a phone call for you, sir. Urgent, he said."

Without a glance back in her direction, Marton stepped out of the room. As the door was closing, she heard him instruct the teenager. "Madam is not feeling well. Please see that she is not disturbed." Then the sound of the key turning in the lock.

Cassie grabbed the first aid kit, rushed to the bathroom and locked the door. Avoiding the mirror, she turned on the tap to cool and wash the wound. The touch of soap and water triggered such intense pain she had to stop to catch her breath. Then, grimacing, she dried the burn with a clean tissue and ever so gently applied a dab of antiseptic cream. With only one hand, she carefully positioned a band aid over the wound. It was not easy to do; her hands were shaking violently.

Then she sat on the closed toilet seat and squeezed her eyes shut against tears of pain and outrage.

She would escape. Or she would kill him.

CHAPTER FOURTEEN

June 9, 2007

Saturday

I know you're out there somewhere, somewhere, somewhere.
I know I'll find you somehow.
And somehow I'll return again to you.

Jack heard the familiar lyrics on the radio this morning as he drove through the fog to the San Francisco airport. The Moody Blues, late 1980s maybe. For years, the song had left him feeling bereft, even though he was not consciously missing Cassie in those days. But this morning, it triggered an optimistic defiance against the Fates. He *would* find her.

This trip to southern California would put him a step closer to that goal. Deborah Mack had offered to fly up to meet him on Sunday, but he felt too impatient and booked a seat on a noon flight south. He arrived at the terminal two hours early, paced the concourse, picked up more coffee, stared outside at planes refueling and carts delivering luggage. Finally, he parked himself at the departure gate and let his mind wander.

San Francisco International Airport, his old home port. It was also where he had last seen Cassie. She had had a three-hour layover before her flight to Bangkok. He could have said goodbye and left, but he stayed instead to keep her company. They had been basically inseparable since meeting in New Orleans. Their flight to Dallas hadn't been full, and after takeoff, Jack had moved to sit next to her. The subsequent flight to San Francisco was crowded, and they were seated four rows apart. But by then they seemed to be a couple, and Jack's seatmate had offered to switch places with Cassie.

They had talked the entire day. Jack learned about her friends and family and childhood. She described her schooling and final film project; outlined her professional hopes. By the time they had reached Dallas, she had shared her thoughts on politics, religion, ethics, and art. On the flight to San Francisco, she disclosed deeper feelings — dreams and disappointments and hurts, including the emotionally wrenching death of her brother. And she knew as much about Jack; the conversation had been truly reciprocal. He was amazed at how candid and comfortable he felt talking with her.

Waiting for her flight, he had asked what she'd do when she got back to the States. She had shrugged. "Maybe I'll go back overseas, depending on what I find there. Or maybe I'll move here."

"To San Francisco?" Her answer had startled him a little.

She had sipped her coffee. "Why not? Ralph would love to be in the Bay Area. And, well, *you* live here."

Ignoring a rush of pleasure, he told her that he would probably have to move in the next year, when his research assistantship ended. "I need a temporary teaching post while I finish the dissertation," he explained.

"Do you know where?"

"I'll start looking this fall. I'd like to get an adjunct position here, but academic jobs are tight right now. I may not have a lot of options."

"But you'll keep me posted, right?"

Jack had grinned; it was the first time they had talked about staying in touch. "I'll write if you will," and he scribbled his address on a coffee-stained napkin.

Cassie had tucked it into her travel tote. "I'll send you a card as soon as I land. Unfortunately, I left Becky's address in my backpack."

"With the dead body," he had joked and Cassie had laughed.

Half an hour before her departure, they had strolled to the gate. "I feel that I've known you for years," she told him. "Isn't that strange? Would you even consider coming with me? Or meeting up somewhere?"

Jack had taken her hand; twenty-nine years later, he imagined he could still feel it. He hadn't answered; he didn't know what to say. He wanted to shout yes! But he wanted to finish graduate school and he wanted to be with Helene and he had responsibilities.

As if she read his mind, Cassie answered her own question, "No, never mind. It's a crazy idea. It's expensive and uncertain and you have a lot on your plate. Maybe our next incarnation," and she had smiled reassuringly.

Looking back, he realized this was the moment which crystallized something in him, a feeling that today he recognized as love. At the time, though, nothing seemed crystallized. His feelings bewildered him, and he stumbled over his words, "Thanks for asking though. Perhaps in the future, something will work out." In his own ears, his remark sounded insincere and unconvincing.

In those days, Jack now recalled, anybody could join air passengers at the departure gate. With a handful of other well-wishers, he had stood next to Cassie. Her flight number was called; passengers lined up to board. Farewells and hugs around them. For the first time all day, Cassie and Jack had stopped talking. The line shortened. Finally, she said goodbye and stood on her toes to kiss his cheek. But Jack at the last moment put his mouth against hers, and kissed her long and hard. The kiss shocked and aroused him. He wondered what she thought of it. She didn't pull away.

"Stay," he pleaded. He hadn't intended to say it, but the word elbowed out.

An almost imperceptible shake of her head. She countered, "Come with."

Rational thought abandoned him. "Write to me. I'll meet you someplace, I promise."

She squeezed his arm and then ran past the waiting airline staff to board the plane, the last one on. She looked back once to wave.

Then she was gone.

FIVE MINUTES TO boarding and his phone rang. It was Becky.

"Bad news, Jack." She spoke without her usual Southern preliminaries. "Cassie's parents both passed away. Her dad's been gone a long time but her mother died just three years ago. We missed her by just three years!"

Jack could hear the frustration and hurt in her voice. He felt disappointed too, and oddly bereft, as if they had been old friends of his. He thought back to the middle-aged couple he'd seen in the New Orleans airport. "I'm so sorry to hear that." As an afterthought, he added, "Do you happen to know their first names? It might help me narrow the search."

"Certainly. Pernina and Ulysses. He went by Hank. We met a few times but they were always Mr. and Mrs. Robinette to me, of course. Cassie thought the world of them. It's awful they died never knowing what happened to her."

Jack remembered seeing Pernina's name during his online search of government databases, but Ulysses must have died before records were routinely digitized. That was a name that Jack would not have missed.

After a pause, Becky asked, "How did it go with Ralph? Did he help?"

"Marginally. I'll tell you about it later. But he did give me the name of someone in southern California who may help. The sister of a guy that Cassie met in Afghanistan. I'm catching a plane there now and will call tomorrow with an update." And with that they signed off.

Another obstacle in the search, he thought. But he wasn't as disheartened as he might have been. Deborah's search for Danny would provide an alternative path to Cassie.

He turned off his phone and boarded the plane. After a ninety-minute flight, he arrived at the Ontario airport, emerging into a crowd of waiting family and friends. He scanned faces but had no idea what Deborah Mack looked like.

"Are you Jack?" The question came from a tall, handsome woman in a tailored white blouse and trim slacks. He guessed she was in her forties, with short blond hair in spiky tuffs and a complexion tan but not damaged by the sun.

"Deborah?!" He didn't know what he had expected, but not this fit and vibrant person.

"Call me Deb." She took his hand in a firm grasp. "I can't tell you how pleased I am to meet you. I've been looking for Danny for so long that I'd about given up." She added quickly, "but not really."

"I hadn't realized your brother disappeared too, not until I talked to Ralph and he told me about you," Jack explained as he carried his bag to her car. "Cassie mentioned him in her last letter, so he was next on my list to contact. I think they traveled together from Kabul to Herat."

Deb nodded thoughtfully as she started the engine. "That fits with what Danny wrote as well." She paused as she pulled out of the parking garage. "Danny didn't write much, so I'm glad you have her letters. They may fill in some gaps."

Jack discreetly studied her profile as she spoke and, with relief, decided that Ralph was wrong. Deb seemed serious but not crazy obsessed.

She recounted her background as they drove to Riverside. She was an attorney, loved tennis and yoga, had been divorced several years, no children. He told her a little about himself as well. In the late afternoon light, they arrived at her home, a 1940s bungalow, shaded by an ancient orange tree in the front yard. The place was small but recently renovated; stylish yet unaffected. Like its owner.

Deb poured them each a gin and tonic and settled across from Jack at a walnut dining table. Nearby was a matching walnut buffet, with a two-drawer filing cabinet standing next to it. The filing cabinet's top drawer was labeled Household, the bottom one, Danny. She was organized, Jack thought appreciatively; he fought the urge to open the lower drawer.

She saw where he was looking. "I was still a teenager when we got the letter from the State Department, but I knew even then it wasn't true."

"Wait," Jack said. "What letter from the State Department?"

She rose and opened the drawer, returning with a file folder. From it, she extracted a single sheet of State Department letterhead stationery. He scanned the letter. Dated September 21, 1978, it was addressed to Mr. and Mrs. George J. Mack, regretfully informing them that the body of their son, Daniel Ezekiel Mack, had been found in a neighborhood of Mashhad, Iran, apparently the victim of armed robbery. While there was no identification on the body, his passport had been found in a black-market stall not far away. Regrettably, due to the summer heat and the delay in finding the body, local authorities had ordered the body buried immediately. In case the family wished to have the body exhumed and cremated for repatriation, the letter provided information on a British-owned funeral home in Mashhad to make the arrangements. Sincere condolences. The letter was signed by a man named Richard Porter.

A heart-rending letter; Jack imagined the distraught family reading it. Terrible from his point of view as well; he had harbored a small hope that Danny and Cassie had fled Iran together, that she wasn't alone.

Deb handed Jack a passport and he flipped through it, then paused to study the earnest young face, big grin, shaggy hair shading his eyes. "Daniel Ezekiel Mack," he read aloud.

"Daniel Ezekiel, Old Testament. I'm Deborah Esther." She took the passport and, like Jack, gazed at the face of her missing brother. "Our parents bought the whole thing. It fit their narrative about his life: the wages of sin, reaping what you sow. They thought he was sinful and a terrible influence on me. They certainly didn't approve of his gallivanting around the globe, as they put it. And his interest in Hinduism! Well, you can imagine. They were so mad at him, they didn't even want to pay to have his remains returned to the States." Deb was still bitter about it; Jack could hear it in her voice.

He finally found the words, "Danny's dead."

Deb was quick in reply, "No. I'm sure he's alive. Or, rather, I'm sure the body they found wasn't Danny's."

"Why not?"

"I pretended to be the family lawyer and wrote a letter to this Porter guy and asked a lot of questions. He provided a few more details, and two of them jumped out at me. First, to make the identification, State Department folks had matched police photos with the passport they found. They never actually saw the body. And remember, it had already been days since the man was killed. Second, the man wasn't killed in a robbery; his body was robbed later. Witness reports said he was killed to stop a sexual assault. Local police were investigating, but the killers were unlikely to be found or prosecuted. As far as the police were concerned, the victim deserved what he got."

Deb leaned toward Jack now, solemn and intense. "That's when I knew for sure it wasn't Danny. My brother was sweet and gentle, and he loved women. He would never, ever, sexually assault someone."

Jack was not so sure. The State Department, as a rule, was cautious and would not have sent the condolence letter without a very high degree of certainty. It was more likely that the body was Danny's; that the young Californian – perhaps innocently - had flirted with a neighborhood girl, oblivious of religious taboos, and had been killed for it. However, instead of expressing his doubts to Deb, he asked, "What do *you* think happened to him?"

"I think he stayed in Afghanistan, that his passport was stolen there and used by someone else to get into Iran. From there, who knows? He said he wanted to get back to India. He obviously didn't have a passport but he was pretty resourceful." She retrieved another file folder, carefully pulling out a taped and wrinkled aerogramme, blue paper that Jack knew well. "Here's his last letter. It arrived not long before the State Department's."

The letter was postmarked Herat, September 2, about a week after Cassie's letter was sent from Kabul. Danny said Marton – whom he called Zorro – had provided room, board and a small paycheck in exchange for his work as a body guard. Reading between the lines, Jack believed Marton had also given him the Black Russian opium; it fit what he had learned about Zambo from Ralph. Jack's heart sank when he reached the reference to shitty work; it had to mean heroin production. He knew from his research it was not uncommon in western Afghanistan at the time, and a week-long stay in Herat was about right. In all likelihood, then, Zambo was producing heroin and smuggling it to Geneva, and that meant serious danger for Cassie, especially if she crossed the Iranian border with him.

Jack kept reading and saw Danny's mention of her and Ralph. This was how Deb had gotten their names. Finally, Jack's eye traveled to the bottom of the page, and he caught his breath. Even without the signature, he knew the postscript was Cassie's – her handwriting, her sensibility. Clearly, she and Danny had been friends.

He sat quietly for several moments, unsure what to say. He didn't think he should mention his suspicions about heroin production and smuggling to Deb, not yet. It would contradict her idealized image. "So," he said, "you found Ralph."

She leaned back and crossed her arms. "It wasn't easy. I had his full name, but no address or even a hometown. I searched every phone directory I could find in the library, More Ralph Johnsons than you can imagine, and none of them the right one. By the early 1980s, he had started to publish. I got the name of his publisher and sent them letter after letter to forward to him but I never heard anything back. Finally, with email, I managed to reach him directly. That was about a decade ago. He wrote back, said he couldn't help. Then I got busy with other things and forgot about him. But a year ago I decided to contact him again, and I convinced him to meet with me."

"How?"

"I said that Danny had mentioned him in a letter, and he was curious. I flew up and we met in a restaurant near Fisherman's Wharf. A tourist place, lots of people around. Maybe he thought I was a stalker. Anyway, he read the letter and said some nice things about my brother, about how funny he was, a great guy and all that. But he said he hadn't seen him or Cassie since Kabul. They both had left with this guy Marton. Ralph said he made a big deal that it was Marton with an O. He didn't know the last name, though."

"I do," Jack said. "It's Zambo. Cassie mentioned him, said he was Czech Canadian; I presume she meant he had emigrated from Czechoslovakia to Canada. I'd wager that would have been in the late 1960s. When he met Danny and Cassie, he was probably traveling under a Canadian passport. That's all I have."

She sat bolt upright. "That's more than I've ever been able to find! Hold on," and she dialed her cell phone, quickly relayed the information to someone, and then hung up. To Jack's quizzical look Deb said, "My P.I. His name's Tony, former LAPD detective. I met him when I worked in the D.A.'s office. Then, when he retired a few years ago, I heard he was opening an investigative office here in town and I hired him."

"Has he found anything?"

"Nothing more than I already knew. He did contact Richard Porter again. Porter remembered the case, said it had always haunted him because it was the first time he had dealt with an American murdered overseas. He told Tony the victim's face and body had been severely beaten. I guess he hadn't want to share that grim news with the family. But to me, it proves my point. If the face was badly beaten and the body not discovered for days, how could they have made a positive ID that it was Danny? From police photos, no less? It was someone else. I know it was."

Jack felt sick. The idea that Danny might have been beaten to death was dreadful to contemplate. He realized he had to be clear with Deb about the very real dangers Danny had faced. "He was involved in risky business, you know. Opium, possibly heroin production, smuggling. It's all implied in the letter you showed me."

Deb didn't seem fazed. "Yes, Tony and I talked about it. And if the man in Mashhad had died of an overdose or in a botched drug deal, I'd have to admit the possibility he was Danny after all. And Zambo would be to blame. But hammered by locals for raping a woman? Not my brother."

"So, you don't think Zambo's to blame for your brother's disappearance?"

She shook her head. "He might know something, though. At minimum he can confirm that my brother didn't go to Iran. And what about you? Is he to blame for Cassie's disappearance?"

"Honestly, I don't know." Jack stared at his hands against the table's walnut grain. "But I have a bad feeling about him."

She nodded grimly. "Then let's find Mr. Zambo."

TWO IN THE morning, and Jack was at his laptop still searching for any sign of Zambo. Deb had finally given up and gone to bed. Before retiring, she had given him sheets and a down pillow for the sofa. That was forty minutes ago and he was still perched at the table. Surfacing from a web search was like coming up for air. He was groggy, sore and stiff. Rubbing his eyes and stretching, he considered calling it a night. Alternatively, he could rewarm a cup of coffee, but then he would never be able to get to sleep. "Hell, with it," he muttered to himself, "time to take a break." He brushed his teeth, turned out the light and lay down.

Marton Zambo, Canadian companies, Czech émigrés, the search terms ran tediously along a Mobius strip in his brain. A question formed at the edge of Jack's barely conscious mind. Had Zambo changed his name? Is that why they couldn't find him? If so, he was beyond reach.

Lying in the dark, Jack now thought of a skinny bare-chested teenager standing next to a surf board. Deb had shown him that photograph of Danny, the only family picture on her living room walls. She described her brother as sweet and gentle. The police report said sexual assault. Danny's own letter referred to opium and possibly heroin. The mystery of his death troubled Jack, and he found himself wondering if Zambo knew about the death and if it troubled him too. After all, Danny was probably working for him at the time.

Maybe there was something to that. Jack sat up on the sofa, letting the idea develop. Maybe, if Zambo had changed his name, he had kept some reference to Danny. Not directly, given the illegal nature of their work together. But Zambo might have used an oblique reference. Maybe Marton Dan? Dan Marton? Or Marton Zorro, Danny's nickname for him?

Jack thought it was unlikely but even so got up and turned on his laptop. In the dark dining room, his eyes took a few minutes to adjust to the bright screen. He blinked and tried variations on Marton Dan and Dan Marton. Nothing stood out. Then he typed Zorro into the search engine. Hundreds of entries popped up; Jack scrolled past references to the novel and television show, Wikipedia and costumes. Then, near the bottom of the screen was a listing for a company called Zorro Boards. Thinking of Danny at the beach, he clicked on its web site: a surf board manufacturer in Santa Monica, founded in 1981. In his picture, the company president, Jack was disappointed to see, was a youngish guy. Nothing suggested a link to Zambo but Jack had a hunch. He turned on a reading light and wrote a note for Deb, in case she rose before he did in the morning.

"See if Tony can find anything out about a company called Zorro Boards in Santa Monica. Who founded it, present owner, any corporate ties, that sort of thing."

Propping the note on the coffee maker, he returned to the sofa and this time fell into a deep sleep.

Jack awoke to the smell of roasted coffee. When he opened his eyes, he was startled to see Deb already dressed and sitting at her laptop. She smiled when she saw him sit up.

"What time is it?" he said groggily as he tried to pull on his jeans under the blanket.

"Past ten," she said amiably. "I called Tony."

This woke him up. "And?"

"Zorro Boards advertises itself as locally owned, but it's a subsidiary of a company out of Panama, which in turn is part of a holding company in the Cayman's. And that holding company is a small part of an enormous multinational called Z.I., based in Vancouver. The man who owns *that*," and here she paused for effect, "is a naturalized Canadian citizen. His name is Marton Zane. Marton, with an O."

ZANE WAS AMONG the richest men in Canada; indeed, he wasn't doing poorly when stacked against the world's wealthiest. But he was no celebrity. A highly private man, he seemed allergic to publicity, particularly reserved about having his photograph published. At least that was Jack's conclusion by lunch time. By then, he and Deb had tracked down a few news articles about him – *Forbes, Fortune, Businessweek* – but they were either brief mentions or promotional pieces aimed at people interested in investing in his company, Zane International. There were few personal insights, except that he was a self-made man who had fled Soviet oppression when he was young.

Images of him also were rare. In one staged photo taken years before at an anti-drug charity event, he had posed with his elegant wife and another equally elegant woman, along with two Hollywood celebrities; all of their faces were clear except for Zane's, which was turned away from the camera. A photo dated last year showed him at a cocktail party hosted by a business consortium in Ottawa; a different wife was next to him. Again, his features were difficult to see. Even when Jack magnified the images, the most he could discern was that Zane was of medium height, slender to medium build, with a full head of silver white hair. He was the rare man who looked at ease in a tuxedo. Except for that and his hair, there was nothing remarkable about him. Jack wasn't sure he could recognize him on sight.

Tony continued to call with bits of information throughout the day, newly energized by success in finally tracking down a Person of Interest. He discovered that Zane had emigrated from Czechoslovakia in 1969 and was naturalized in 1977. Nothing yet about any name change but it was, after all, Sunday. Tony assured Jack that he could find out more once government offices reopened Monday.

Thanks to his research, they also had Zane's personal email address. Given the possible link between Zambo and Cassie's disappearance, Deb deferred to Jack on making first contact. So he spent

Sunday afternoon considering how to craft a message that would elicit a response from such a man. After several discarded drafts, he settled on an oblique approach, similar to the one he had used with Ralph.

> *Dear Mr. Zane,*
>
> *I am interested in your travels in Afghanistan and Iran in 1978. I believe we have some friends in common. Please call at your convenience.*

Before sending it, he showed it to Deb.

Her eyes grew wide. "He was smuggling drugs then, remember? It sounds like you're going to blackmail him," she pointed out.

"Yeah?" He read it again, "I suppose you're right." He deleted the message and stared at the laptop's blank screen. No ideas came.

"My advice? Don't be coy. Tell him upfront that you're a former friend of Cassie's and were wondering if he had heard from her since they traveled together in seventy-eight. That's the truth and it doesn't sound too threatening."

Jack typed the message, but he didn't feel optimistic about it. Honesty might not be advisable with someone like Zambo.

Deb tried to reassure him. "We don't need to tell him the entire truth. Just pieces of it, to bait the hook."

He hit SEND.

"WE GREW UP in Ventura," Deb told him over enchiladas and beer. Dinner was at a Mexican restaurant a few blocks away. "Our father was pastor at a little Baptist church and Mom was the produce manager at the supermarket. Not a bad childhood, overall, but when we got to be teens, they panicked and became really strict. Especially with me. Well, it was the seventies, you know. Sex, drugs and rock'n'roll. And surfing; Danny was an avid surfer."

Jack remembered the photograph she had shown him, imagining what might have led the young man to leave the beach life behind.

"After my divorce, I moved to Riverside. Too expensive to live on the coast, and I had a job offer. So here I am. I worry sometimes that Danny will go back to Ventura and not find me. I still keep in touch with our old neighbors, to see if they've heard anything. They really liked Danny."

"Your folks are dead?"

"No. They're in assisted living in Ojai. They moved away from Ventura long before I did. We don't talk much; a phone call at Christmas. And we exchange birthday cards."

"You don't talk to your parents?" Her admission stunned him. He still missed his parents, dead for more than a decade.

She read the dismay in his face. "We don't have much to say to each other."

"Still...," Jack stopped. How dare he start moralizing about parent/child relationships? He was chagrined when he thought how distant he'd let his relationships with Sandy and Max grow while he was with Helene. "I'm sorry. Never mind."

Deb was silent a moment. "Maybe you're right. Maybe it's time to get in touch."

Later that evening, they compiled material for Jack to take home with him; copies of the State Department correspondence and Danny's last letter, the front page of his passport, Tony's report, a photograph of Danny with hair pulled back in a ponytail and his face clearly visible. In turn, Jack left a copy of Cassie's last letter with Deb.

"I'll call the minute I hear anything from Zane," he promised. If Zane didn't respond within a week, they made plans to brainstorm other possible steps. They said goodbye in the morning, Deb leaving for the office and Jack for the airport.

The flight was dull, just as he liked it. By mid-afternoon, he was back in his apartment, eating a late lunch, when he opened his email.

A reply from Frank Constant's personal account. Finally, progress on Iran, he thought. The message was characteristically chatty:

> *My sources at State tell me that there's no record of a missing American woman at the time you mention. However, all hell broke loose about then in Tehran, so who knows. When the embassy was seized the next year, lots of documents were shredded. There's a report of an American male found dead in Mashhad. I don't suppose that's related. By the way, what's this about?*

Jack feared the death was related, but didn't yet know how. Hearing about the murder again depressed him. He typed a quick thanks and then added on a whim,

> *Is there any way I can get into Iran?*

He probably would find his answers here in the States, but he wanted to be ready if the mystery took him to Mashhad.

An hour later came Frank's reply. Jack could read the agitation in his words.

> *Are you kidding me?! Didn't you read the news about the American who disappeared there not long ago? Asking questions can get you in a whole lot of shit in the Islamic Republic of Iran.*

Jack wanted to argue: the man who disappeared - Robert Levinson - was on Kish Island in the Persian Gulf, not the mainland. And there was speculation that he was former FBI or DEA or both, according to news accounts. But Frank's last sentence did hit home. Asking questions was probably what got Levinson into trouble; and asking questions was exactly what Jack intended to do.

He would have to think about how to answer.

THE CALL HE was waiting for came Monday evening, sooner than he had dared hope.

"Dr. Hunter," said a smooth male voice on Jack's cell phone, with just the slightest accent. "This is Marton Zane. You sent me a curious email."

"Yes, yes," Jack replied, scrambling to grab a pen and paper. "Please call me Jack. Thank you for returning my call, Mr. Zane. Or may I call you Martin?" A purposeful slip.

Almost instantly, the other voice – peevish - broke in. "It's Marton. Not Martin."

He half smiled to himself. "Indeed, my apology, Marton."

"Apology accepted, Jack, although I have to say I'm confused by your message."

"I'm looking for an old friend named Cassie Robinette. We lost touch some time ago. I thought you might have heard from her. You traveled together in 1978, through Central Asia."

"So you said in your email. However, I have never been in Central Asia. And why would you think I know your friend?" The last was said slowly, carefully.

"Cassie mentioned you in a letter. I believe your name was Zambo then." It was a guess; he hadn't gotten confirmation from Tony yet.

Silence. Jack could almost hear Zane's calculations, if he should continue the subterfuge or not. Legal name changes were a matter of public record.

"Interesting," he said at last. "I knew a Marton Zambo once, a long time ago. What did she write in this letter?"

"That you and another man named Danny Mack befriended her and her boyfriend Ralph Johnson in Kabul. That she was traveling with you to Herat." When Zane didn't respond, Jack added, "I'd like very much to find her."

"Would you? And who might you be?"

"A friend from the old days, before her trip." Jack decided to push a little harder. "Ralph Johnson thinks you know where Cassie went, after she left Kabul with you."

"Your friend is wrong." The friendliness was gone.

Jack kicked himself; he shouldn't push, he should just let the conversation unfold. He didn't want Zane to hang up.

Then, after a brief pause, Marton's voice returned on the line. It had resumed its genteel charm. "I think we'd better meet, Jack. Say, at three next Sunday afternoon in my office in Vancouver. Check in with ID at the front security desk. And, Jack, bring along those letters you have to help me refresh my memory."

The meeting was set. Jack hung up and immediately called Deb with a report.

"Pretty strange, him suddenly changing his mind about meeting you," she said.

"I think he's curious about what I know," Jack reasoned. "He asked me to bring the letters."

"Curious? Or afraid that you know something about his drug smuggling?" She mused, "I think I should come."

He tried to dissuade her. "Not a good idea, Deb. He'll probably be less candid if there are two of us. And he's not *just* a drug smuggler. He could be complicit in Cassie's disappearance. I'm serious; it could be dangerous."

"That seals it, Jack. I'm coming. I've dealt with bad guys for a long time and I know what I'm doing. Besides, we're a team now, you and me." In her frank tone of voice, the matter was settled. "Oh," she added eagerly, "Tony found something else today. In 1979, a man named Marton Zámbó legally changed his name to Marton Zane. He's definitely our man."

CHAPTER FIFTEEN

September 4, 1978

Monday

Cassie stood at the open window, calculating the drop to the sidewalk below. The distance wasn't far, just one story up. But even if she dangled from the windowsill, her feet would still be eight feet above the ground. Further, she wasn't sure her damaged arm could hold on. She could sprain an ankle or worse.

She had to try. Holding tight to the Thai purse looped bandolier style across her chest, she lifted one leg on to the sill. She tried to force herself to hurry. Marton could return at any time and she didn't want to miss the Tehran bus. At least Danny had gotten away, she thought.

A soft knock roused her. She jerked in alarm, heart pounding. Surely it wasn't Zambo; he would have used the key. On weak legs, she tiptoed to the door and put her ear to the wood. She tried to quiet her rapid breathing so she could hear. Then came Jahwed's voice, urgent and low. Relief surged through her.

"Madam, are you all right? Madam, I unlock the door now." The sound of a fumbled key, a click and there he stood, eyes wide. "I hear you scream," he said. "He attacked you?"

She understood him to mean a sexual assault, so she shook her head no. "He did this," she said and held up the underside of her arm. The band-aide was hanging loose, exposing a ruby crater on the white flesh.

He barely glanced. "You must hurry then. There was a phone call and he went away. But only for a little while, I think."

"You'll help me?"

"I will try."

Cassie moved rapidly. In addition to the Thai bag, she grabbed her camera and scarf. A burqa; she needed to buy a burqa to hide her form and face. Then she caught sight of her pale hands and, thinking quickly, found the wool gloves from Nepal. Her shoes might give her away, but she had no good alternative; she would simply have to be careful when she sat. She hoped the market near the currency exchange was open on the holiday.

Jahwed motioned for her to follow.

She had an idea. "One minute," she told him. "I'll meet you downstairs."

He nodded and disappeared.

She rushed back to her bedroom. She would ask Jahwed to tell Marton she had gone to a clinic to get the wound dressed. If he believed she was coming back to the room, she would have more time to escape. Pulling clothes from her backpack, she arranged the Afghan blouse, silver belt and black skirt on the bed as if ready for their dinner out. Her brush and lipstick were conspicuous on the dresser. The large tote bag was open and sitting at the base of the dresser next to her backpack; sandals lay nearby. She often left with her camera, so its absence would not alert him. At the last moment, she grabbed the silver belt. It might be handy as a gift or a bribe.

She checked the hallway and stairs for any sign of his return. No one was about. She ran down to the front desk where Jahwed was waiting.

"I need to buy a burqa and get to the bus station. I must get to Tehran." Words tumbled out, almost incoherent. Marton would kill her, she thought, he would kill her if he caught her. She awkwardly wrapped the scarf around her head, as if it might hide her identity.

The teenager understood. "To meet your brother," he said.

Cassie nodded. "Yes, my brother." She suddenly found speaking difficult; her throat seemed to be closing.

"My mother and sisters can help. But first we need permission from my father."

Her nascent optimism faltered. She remembered the father from her first evening, as they checked in. While not a traditionalist, he wasn't a modern man and would hesitate to embroil his family – especially the women of his household – in the sordid troubles of an unmarried woman traveling with two unrelated men.

Jahwed misread her dismay. "We have time," he assured her. "The bus to Tehran is at nine."

She had missed the earlier bus; eight hours to wait and hide, Cassie thought anxiously. Where could she go if the father refused to help?

Jahwed guided her through the curtain and into a windowless hallway. Halfway down the hall to the left was the open door to an office.

The father, a stout man in his forties, sat behind an immaculate desk. Dominating the wall behind him was a framed photograph of the Shrine of the Cloak of the Prophet Mohammad in Kandahar; the family, Cassie remembered learning from Jahwed, was originally from Afghanistan. With a new silk turban and embroidered waistcoat, the older man was dressed more elegantly and traditionally than he had been the day before. It was the end of Ramadan and he had been at prayers this morning.

Jahwed explained her need for help. When his father said nothing, the teenager spoke more urgently. Finally he paused and the older man replied in a curt tone, watching his son but pointing at Cassie. He crossed his arms; the matter seemed settled. She felt the edge of a fatalistic despair. Then in a soft voice, Jahwed said a few more words. He spoke so slowly that Cassie found she could understand. "Beloved father, it is *Eid al-Fitr*."

The holiday was not simply the end of a month of fasting; it was a time of forgiveness and atonement. She wondered if Jahwed was implying they had a responsibility to protect her honor. She had, after all, wanted her own room. Instead, they had put her in the suite with the men. Perhaps, she hoped desperately, that would convince the father.

Jahwed stood silently and respectfully. Cassie stayed motionless two steps behind, her hands clasped in front of her like a prisoner awaiting sentencing. She hated being silent and opened her mouth to press her case, then rapidly clamped it shut again as she read the father's expression. She saw his distaste for her, even scorn. She dropped her eyes to the polished desk surface, uncomfortably aware of how brazen and unworthy she seemed. She dare not treat him as an equal, meeting his eyes and mounting an argument. The only way she might garner his help, she thought fearfully, was to elicit his paternal sympathy.

Pulling the envelope of photographs from her bag, she drew out one of her parents in front of their home. She loved the photograph; both were laughing. It had been taken the week before she left, on their anniversary. Against unseasonably chilly weather, her mother had a headscarf and both parents wore coats. "My mother and my father," she said simply in Dari and slid the photograph across the desk.

The father studied it. He asked if this was her parents' house; once Jahwed had translated, Cassie nodded. She imagined the house through his eyes: white trimmed in blue, a flowering pear tree in the side yard. Then the older man reached for the envelope in her hand and examined a few other photographs. Cassie identified them. At the photo of her girlfriend Becky she said, "My cousin." Then her venerable neighbor whom she called Miss Millie. "My aunt." The fourth photo was of Jack and his puppy. She had brought no photographs of Jason, so she said what came to her mind: "My brother." These didn't feel like lies; they felt like some deeper truth about love and family.

The teenager was peeking over his father's shoulder at the pictures. He pointed at the photograph of Jack and said something; the father nodded, studying again the photograph of her parents. The teenager whispered in English to Cassie that he told his father about Jack looking for her. "As he should," Jahwed added.

Finally, the father looked straight at her and asked something. Jahwed translated. "Your family wants you back?"

The question filled Cassie with shame. What was she doing to them, leaving them for so long, traveling recklessly around the world? Pure selfishness. Eyes lowered, she answered as honestly as she could. "They are sad I am away. I am their only daughter."

Silence filled the room. Still deliberating, the father shifted in his seat, the stern family judge.

Cassie sensed he had connected with her parents, with the love and fear and pride and hope parents feel. Yet, despite any connection, she knew the cultural chasm between them was deep. Even granting her an audience was highly unusual. His primary duty, she knew, was to protect his family. Her very presence here threatened that.

How could she show that she respected him and would not harm them? By being modest, yes, but something more? She thought of the silver belt, brought it out and laid the gleaming woven band on the table. "A gift," she said quietly to Jahwed. "To thank your father for his willingness to hear my request. Perhaps it can be sold to help feed the poor during *Eid al-Fitr*." Jahwed translated.

His father looked startled at her gesture. He picked up the silver belt and inspected the fine work. When another minute passed, he looked at his son and spoke again. Hiding any emotional reaction to the news, the youth translated, "My father says it is good to remember the poor. My family will help you, *Inshallah*."

An involuntary cry escaped her lips. She had almost given up hope. She wanted to kiss the father's hand, his cheek. Instead, she said a simple thank you in Dari, her hand over her heart.

The father nodded, accepting her gratitude graciously. He said again, "*Inshallah*." As she and Jahwed left, he rose and firmly shut his office door behind them.

Everything happened quickly after that. She followed Jahwed further down the hall and turned right into a kitchen where four women sat in front of low tables and a stove. They stared at her, their faces bare in the privacy of the home. Jahwed spoke rapidly to a handsome woman that Cassie took to be his mother. She stood and said, "*Eid Mubarak*," a holiday greeting, Cassie realized. She echoed the greeting. Then the woman pulled her into a small room in the back.

The mother looked through a stack of burqas and pulled out a dark gray one near the bottom, well-worn but clean. Another mature woman joined her and together they drew it over Cassie's head and adjusted the face covering so that she could see. The women conferred briefly; one of them chuckled. The mother mimicked walking as an old woman, bent over and crippled. Cassie understood instantly and nodded. The women were smart; she had to walk differently for the disguise to work. She hobbled arthritically across the room and the second woman laughed in approval. Cassie saw this was an adventure for them, like one of the stories that Jahwed recounted from the movies.

They pulled her back into the kitchen and positioned her in a corner. The mother of Jahwed noticed her shoes and quickly pulled the fabric over her feet. Cassie tugged on the gloves. Looking as ancient and tiny as possible, she watched the other women begin preparing the evening meal.

A minute after she sat, the outside door to the hotel banged open. Sound traveled easily down the hallway, and she could hear Jahwed greeting the guest. A low grunt followed and then a heavy tread on the stairs. In a moment, the guest was back down.

"Where is my wife?" Marton's voice loudly demanded.

Jahwed replied in exaggerated poor English. "She gone, sir."

"Gone where?"

"To clinic for doctor. She hurt." Cassie could imagine Jahwed gesturing at his arm. Marton would not be pleased, but he couldn't dismiss the legitimacy of the excuse.

"Where's this clinic?"

Jahwed must have pointed, because Cassie heard the hotel's front door open. "If she's back before I am, make sure she is safely returned to the room. She is not to leave again, not without me. Do you understand?" And then the sound of the door closing.

She strained to hear more but there was only silence. He was gone again. The women, who had paused in their work to listen as well, now turned their attention back to food. They were in high spirits making a feast to celebrate the end of Ramadan, and they laughed and chatted as they worked, a few times peeking shyly at Cassie.

Jahwed's mother approached and squatted next to her, motioning for her to lift the face covering. Then she pointed to herself and said "Habibeh." Cassie said "Salaam," and repeated Habibeh's name several times. Then, recalling her lessons with Saaleh, she added in Dari, "My name is Cassandra." The older woman raised her eyebrows in mild surprise and repeated "Cassandra" until it sounded almost perfect. Both women grinned in delight, and the other women – watching closely – smiled also.

Cassie tried a rudimentary conversation of "How are you? I am well, thank you." Earlier, with Jahwed and his father, she had been too terrified to remember anything, but phrases and words started to come back to her. When Habibeh offered her tea, she accepted with "*Baleh lotfann*," Yes, please, and added, "*Tashakor mikonam*," when she was handed a tulip shaped glass. Finally, through gestures and a few words, she asked if she could help with the meal. Habibeh pointed to a platter and bags of dates, pomegranates and dried apricots. By then, Habibeh's youngest daughter had arrived in the kitchen and sat next to Cassie, showing her how to properly arrange the fruit.

One young woman cooked rice; another mixed bread dough and molded it into triangular shapes. They seemed to be sisters. Habibeh and the other older woman were preparing an elaborate chicken stew. Cassie stole looks as they toasted and ground up walnuts, chopped and sautéed onions, browned the chicken and finally added a rich red paste. "*Khoresh-e-fesenjān*," Habibeh told her when she caught Cassie looking, and she gestured at the pomegranate in Cassie's hand.

There were dishes of spices and herbs, a plate of white cheese, and platters of sweets made in advance: clover-shaped cookies, cakes, fried sweet dough coated with honeyed syrup. The fragrant smells and ordinary act of cooking calmed Cassie. This was real life, not the erratic days she had spent with Marton.

The bread was almost ready to be dropped on a hot stone when Cassie suddenly remembered what she had hidden upstairs: the addresses, letters and journal that had to be destroyed. They were still tucked under the mattress in her room. She jolted upright and all of the women stopped to look.

She couldn't find the words to explain, so she simply dashed from the room and down the hall, sprinting up the stairs with the robe hiked up so she wouldn't trip. As she approached the door, she panicked that she had no key, but the door was unlocked and the handle turned easily. In seconds, she was in her room again. Everything was as she had left it. Marton had not searched her things, not yet.

Cassie lifted the mattress and there they were. Grabbing the stack of papers, she turned to leave, but when she saw her backpack, she paused. The bird water dish, blue glass and gold, a gift for Habibeh? It was buried deep in the pack, wrapped in a tee shirt. She would only need a moment to dig it out. She stepped toward the pack and was about to lay the letters on the dresser when a low sound or a deep intuition alarmed her. He's coming back, she suddenly thought, get out of here now.

Rushing, she was halfway through the living room when she heard his tread on the upper stairs. He was close. Almost blind with terror, she stumbled into the bathroom to hide.

Breath ragged and heart thumping, she felt dizzy and weak as she looked for a way out. No windows in the bathroom, no escape. She could hear him now turning the knob of main door. He would come in and find her. Maybe he would kill her. She had a sickening insight: maybe that's what had happened to Katarina, the girl he had loved. Maybe he really was capable of anything.

Then Cassie caught a glimpse of herself in the mirror. A veiled stranger stared back. It was a bizarre but thrilling sensation. Escape was possible after all. If she didn't recognize herself, he might not either. Her determination returned. She could do this.

She gathered an armful of used towels to hide both the papers and her shaking hands, and emerged from the bathroom just as Marton entered the room. Not daring to look at him, she kept her head down and back bent. She shuffled past.

Marton didn't notice her; she was a grey ghost. He brushed by to search her bedroom, then the other rooms. Cassie forced herself not to run, not to hasten at all. Instead, fighting her terror, she continued her slow and agonized progress to the room's door. Finally, she reached the stairway and, with a gloved hand, grabbed the handrail. She was negotiating the third step down when Marton shoved her out of the way, hurrying to the front desk. She stopped on the steps and listened as he berated Jahwed.

"She's not at either of the clinics I passed, she's not in the pharmacy and she's still not in her room. Where is she?! Have you hidden her? I demand to know!"

"Sorry, sir, I make mistake. She is at doctor's office, not clinic. It is two streets that direction. Halfway up road."

"On the left or right side of the road?" Marton pressed impatiently.

From the top steps, Cassie could see only the men's bodies and legs, but Jahwed's shrug was unmistakable. A sign that he did not understand, forcing Marton to illustrate by raising his left hand, his right. "Oh, sir, right side," Jahwed replied.

Cassie watched Marton's legs disappear. Only then could she make her own legs finish descending the stairs.

Back in the kitchen, she handed the bundle of dirty towels to one of the younger women. Then she lifted her face covering, took the papers and, under the curious gaze of the woman at the stove's open flame, carefully fed each page into the fire. She bit her lip and concentrated on keeping her hand steady, all the while listening. Within five minutes, her cherished letters were gray ash on orange coals. She took a small breath in relief and sadness.

She heard the hotel door slam open and forceful steps approach the front desk. The voice was his, agitated and insistent but words indistinct. In reply, Jahwed calmly asked if he wanted tea. Without waiting for a reply, the teenager entered the kitchen and instructed his mother to prepare tea. While he waited, he gave a quick glance and shy smile at Cassie. Tea would fix everything, his expression seemed to say. Then he carried out the tea tray.

Cassie had just resumed her seat along the wall when she heard the crash of glass, the clang of a metal tray careening off a wall. Then the voice, clear and furious. "I don't want your fucking tea. I want my fucking wife! Where is she?!"

"I not know sir."

"Is she here?" Marton demanded. Cassie could hear him push past the boy and enter the hall. The women in the kitchen also heard his approach and, as one, they quickly dropped their face coverings. The second before Marton appeared, Cassie managed to drop hers as well. Even with the warning, his presence in the kitchen doorway was so shocking that no one moved. He encountered only cloth walls and silence.

Through her face screen, she could dimly see him scanning the room, posture rigid and hands on hips. "Cassie!" She almost jumped when he shouted her name. "I know you're here. Come out right now," he ordered. She tried to shrink into invisibility.

Then his eyes fell on her. In alarm, she imagined he could see right through the burqa. Any second now, he would rip it off, twist her arm, drag her away. She fought the compulsion to flee, even to breath. But just as quickly, he discounted her, shifting his attention to the other adult women. He must have recognized her as the old woman from upstairs.

Habibeh, the matriarch, stood then and crossed her arms in angry defiance. She shouted at him and pointed to the door, but Marton discounted her as well, shifting his concentration to the three women seated behind her on the floor. Cassie saw his hands twitch, aching to strip them of their head coverings. Jahwed, who had been frozen in the doorway, rushed out.

Marton's eyes settled on something. She followed his gaze. A chef's knife – blade still smeared with chicken fat - lay on the low table in front on the other older woman. Cassie instantly understood that he was calculating the steps. Horrified, she knew she had to alert the women; they didn't know his capacity for violence. She had to give herself up before he got the knife. Whimpering in terror, Cassie started to unfold her legs and stand, her eyes still fixed on the blade. Then she saw the older woman grab the knife and point the blade's tip at Marton; she must have seen his greedy gaze as well. "Just try," her gesture said, "I have known this knife for many years and can handle it well."

Marton rapidly shifted tactics and scanned the shielded faces again. Voice low but dense with rage, he said, "If you don't come right now, you'll regret it. I'll hunt down everyone you know." Still no one moved.

To demonstrate his ability to stalk her, he pulled out her passport and brandished it. He started to read, "Cassandra Robinette." He paused a second to savor the unusual name, a name easy to track down. "Date of birth: 8 June 1955. Birthplace..." He seemed unsettled for a moment. "West Berlin." His voice exposed a hint of doubt.

In the same moment, Cassie saw it too. Marton knew almost nothing about her, even with the passport. He had never asked about her background, her hometown or college major, her friends and family. He did not know her parents lived in West Berlin only briefly, when her father had been stationed there with the Air Force. For all Marton knew, her family was still there.

She mentally reviewed all that she had said to him, all she had left behind in the room. There were no clues; she had been thorough. She permitted herself a flicker of hope.

"I know about your brother, Jason."

His comment yanked her back to the moment. Of course; the baby crocodile story. It was a meaningless piece of information though; Jas was gone, killed in a car accident a decade ago.

"And your friend Jack the professor. Danny told me all about him." His voice regained its confidence. "He or Jason will tell me where you are. I'm sure I can persuade one of them." Involuntarily, her head shot up in horror. But he wasn't looking in her direction when he announced to the room, "You can't get away, Cassie, so stop playing games. You'll only hurt Jason or Jack."

Jack. Danny might have mentioned him, but in enough detail to be tracked down? Would Marton really hurt the people she loved?

Surely these were empty threats. But still. She now understood on a visceral level how Danny had been coerced into coming to Iran. She felt it too.

At that moment, Jahwed rushed into the kitchen with his father. The large man's imposing form filled the doorway. Sensing the presence, Marton turned. Face flushed, the father bellowed at Marton; Jahwed did not need to translate for the gist of the message to communicate. The father took a menacing step toward Marton; his rage was magnificent.

Marton rejoined. "My wife is here, hiding." Even so, he retreated two steps.

The father looked disgusted. He must have said something insulting because Cassie could hear one of the younger women softly chuckling. Then, in commanding tones, he shouted again at Marton and pointed at the door. The teenager translated, "Go now. My father demands you leave hotel forever. These are women of his household, under his protection." There was a pause. When Marton made no move, the father roughly pushed him toward the door, and Jahwed, dashing through it ahead of Marton, shouted back, "I get police!"

In that instant, Marton must have realized the implications. Cassie surreptitiously watched his reaction. His body remained tight, but he withdrew through the doorway, just beyond the reach of Jahwed's father. Even Marton feared an interview with the police, with his van full of heroin. His eyes skimmed the shapeless cloth bundles squatting on the floor before him, surrounded by cooking pots and implements. He shouted one last time, "I'll find you, Cassie. I won't stop until I do."

Then he stormed out.

THAT NIGHT, AT eight, Jahwed came to lead her to the bus depot. He whispered in English. "It is not far, but you cannot walk fast, grandmother," A reminder that her part was not yet over; Marton could be watching.

"The back way," Jahwed said, guiding her through a small court-yard and past the toilet to a narrow alley. Cassie hadn't known there was a back way; surely Marton didn't know either.

The camera and Thai bag hung around her neck under the burqa, moving gently against her chest as she walked. In one gloved hand was a bag containing food from Habibeh and a water bottle filled with lukewarm tea. Her stomach churning with anxiety, she had eaten little of the feast and still was not hungry. But the mother had insisted on the food; the trip to Tehran would take fourteen hours.

Cassie tried to calm her breathing. Surely Marton was long gone from Mashhad. Twenty minutes after the confrontation with Jahwed's father, he had stalked out of the hotel, noisily dragging his pack and hers down the stairs. Yet her heart still beat violently as they left the alley beside the Hotel Khayyám and moved into the main thorough-fare.

"This is Emam Reza Road," Jahwed whispered. "The bus station is not far." They turned to the left. Cassie thought it odd; from Dan-ny's map, she would have guessed the opposite direction. He kept her hand on his arm, maintaining a slow steady pace. "Do not worry. We will be there soon."

Every shadow and every sound seemed a threat. Suppressing a fierce need to look all around, she kept her head still and down. She crushed the urge to run as well, hobbling slowly beside the young man, her hand gripping his arm tightly.

The bus depot was crowded with passengers and their families, but there was no sign of Marton Zambo. Cassie felt relief when she saw police wandering through the crowd, stopping men, asking for identification; no wonder Zambo wasn't there. She cautiously gazed around the station. Placards in Arabic and Latin lettering announced destinations she had never heard of: Ashkhabad and Krasnovodsk,

Kerman and Quetta. She followed Jahwed who followed the signs to the ticket window for Tehran and Tabriz. A note posted on the window listed several stops along the way, with an estimated mid-morning arrival in the capital. That was fine with her. The embassy would be open by then.

Jahwed bought the ticket with money she gave him. He handed her the change. She took it reluctantly; she wanted to leave the money with him, but she didn't dare. She might need it for the long journey. What could she give him instead? She owed him her freedom, possibly her life. How could she ever thank him? As soon as she framed the question in her mind, she knew. Carefully extricating it from around her neck and pulling it out through the burqa's wide sleeve, Cassie handed him the precious camera. "For you," she said in English. "Thank you for saving me."

Jahwed beamed in surprise. "*Moteshakkeram*, Lady Cassie." He cradled the camera like an infant. "I always will remember you. And I always will remember f-stop, the window for the light."

She blinked back tears. "I hope we meet again someday," she said. "Goodbye, my friend." And she climbed up into the night bus to Tehran.

AN HOUR INTO the drive, Cassie finally felt free of Marton. She had been closely watching the highway and had not spied his old van following along. He was furious, she reasoned, but he was also greedy and ambitious and anxious to avoid the police. In the end, his business concerns would trump personal ones, she was sure. He would continue on his way to Geneva without her.

Meanwhile, she would get a new passport at the American embassy in Tehran. Then she could go anywhere in the world, except possibly Geneva. He would never be able to find her. And she had learned her lesson about taking up with strange men. The burn scar –

his souvenir – would always remind her. "Bullet dodged," she said grimly to herself. Though still shaken at how close she had come to danger, she felt stronger from the day's trauma; she had survived.

As the bus drove through the darkness, Cassie watched her spectral reflection in the window and thought hard about her choices in men. They hadn't been smart, on the whole. Initially, Ralph had seemed different, someone with his act together. But in the end he wasn't capable of sustaining an adult relationship. Through much of the trip, he had behaved like a kid – enthusiastic and sometimes charming, more often heedless and insensitive. Then her veiled eyes accused her; she had helped. Hadn't she repeatedly handled boring logistics like buying bus fare and keeping track of their luggage? His dependence had been partly her fault.

Ironically, Marton had pulled her in the opposite direction, and she had let him. The master planner making all decisions and solving all problems. Ha, she thought bitterly, the master liar and bully.

Bad choices; how could she trust herself in building any future relationship?

At that moment, she thought again of Jack, his humor, his kindness, his intellect, his kiss. His kiss; how close she had come to abandoning this whole enterprise when he whispered for her to stay. She was glad that she hadn't. She was learning so much about other people and places, about culture and geography and art, about herself. Even so, in the quiet of the bus, Cassie allowed herself to imagine how different her life would be right now if she had stayed. A surge of yearning swelled through her, carrying the certitude that he was the one, the love of her life. She had known it since visiting the poet's tomb in Herat. Really, much earlier than that she had known it, in the oceanic depths of her heart.

A message from him should be waiting for her at Tehran General Delivery. She could hardly wait. Tomorrow, after she read it, she would write him that long overdue letter. She would tell him everything.

HOURS AND MILES passed. It must be after midnight, she thought, burrowing into the thick folds of the burqa against the cold air. Loneliness enveloped her as well, a melancholy denouement to the drama and euphoria of her great escape. She had often romanticized the notion of solitary travel, but she didn't feel the romance now. She wanted the night to be over; she wanted to be out of Iran, heading to Istanbul and Jack.

The burn throbbed painfully, keeping her awake. To pass the time, she peered around at her fellow passengers. Behind the full-face veil, in the dim interior of the bus, she could see little beyond indistinct lumps. She listened attentively and heard only the deep breathing of sleep. Cautiously, she lifted a corner of the veil to look around. No one was stirring.

The night bus had drawn only one family; parents and three children, including an infant. They had been on the bus when she boarded, and she had chosen a seat close by. The other passengers were all men, ranging widely in age but most in traditional garb. She speculated they were middle class businessmen and students, teachers and young engineers. Western-oriented elites did not ride the bus. In the back, though, sat another foreigner, a pale young man with glasses and fuzzy blond hair. He slumped in the seat as he slept. Perhaps, she thought hopefully, he spoke English; perhaps they could talk a little at the next rest stop.

Soon, the bus pulled off the road, crunching gravel under its tires. When the diesel engine died, the sudden silence was startling. The driver opened the door and let himself out. Gradually rousing themselves, the passengers stood and headed sleepily down the aisle. Cassie sat, waiting patiently to follow the family out. The man with the fuzzy hair passed her. Through her window, she saw him enter the brightly lit tea shop with most of the others.

Cassie didn't want more tea. Instead, once she was outside, she walked to the dark side of the bus to survey the highway and black terrain beyond. No other traffic; no van. Then she heard shouting, aggressive and loud. Oddly, it sounded like English. She looked around the bus toward the tea shop. The fuzzy haired man was outside, surrounded now by a group of youths who were chanting, "Death to America! Death to America!" One youth pushed him to the ground, and she heard him curse in German. Just then, two police officers and the bus driver emerged from the shop and broke through the circle. The police roughly dispersed the angry crowd while the German scrambled to his feet and hurried back to the bus. This time, he moved to the vacant seat behind the driver.

Cassie reboarded soon after he did, but said nothing to him as she passed. Better not to complicate his situation any further. Better that she stay huddled and hidden. She thought about what Saaleh had told her and wondered if this was the start of the revolution.

MIDMORNING AND THE bus pulled into the terminal in central Tehran. By now, the air was hot, and she was even hotter inside the oppressive thick robe. Cassie had come to hate it. Yet it was the stuff of fantasy, an invisibility cloak shielding her from monsters like Marton and those men at the rest stop. As she stepped down from the bus, she furtively surveyed the waiting crowd. Marton wasn't there. She wasn't expecting him, but his absence hardened her resolve to dispense with the disguise. She spied a ladies' room across the cavernous hall; she'd take the burqa off there.

Sweating and tired and stiff with immobility from sitting so long, she limped away from the bus, her ragged walk no longer feigned.

Two other buses had arrived with hers, and another one was preparing to depart. She hobbled clumsily through the milling crowd.

Soldiers were everywhere, she noticed. They were stopping people, asking questions, checking papers. What if they checked hers? Other than a Louisiana driver's license, she didn't have any. What would they do? She decided it was better if she appeared as she was, an American woman. They might even take her to the embassy. She continued to the restroom.

But halfway across the station, she froze, profoundly shocked. There he was, sitting on a bench and staring hard at each female form that passed. Marton Zambo hadn't given up; he never would give up, she realized now. Even the presence of soldiers hadn't dissuaded him.

A large group of veiled women passed on his left just as Cassie slipped by on the right. She reached the safety of the restroom a second before he turned his head.

Her heart thudding, she tried to think of a plan. She could try hiding all afternoon in the restroom; he had to leave the station eventually. But what if he didn't, and she made the mistake of emerging when no buses had arrived? In an empty hall, she would be easy to spot. At least now there was a rush of travelers to hide among. Clearly, she could not relinquish her costume while he was out there. As an American woman, she could not count on soldiers intervening if she was accosted. Dressed as an elderly Muslim woman, they might. Or Marton might think so and hesitate long enough for her to get away. So far, fortunately, he had not noticed her. Even if he did - she told herself - she was invisible. He'd never recognize her. After all, he had already passed her a number of times without making the connection. She just had to stay cool.

To compose her nerves, Cassie lifted the veil and splashed water on her face, dabbing it dry with a tissue. Then she checked the wound, now circled by bruises where he had gripped her wrist. The burn mark looked raw and inflamed. She struggled to change the bandage, wincing with the effort and the pain.

An Iranian woman stood next to her, chic in a violet suit and pink silk blouse. As she was applying lipstick, her gaze inadvertently moved to Cassie's white face. She stopped mid-movement. Then her eyes traveled to the ugly wound and worn burqa before returning quizzically to her face.

Cassie met her eyes and said, "*Eid Mubarak.*" The woman was too startled at first to reply, but finally managed the holiday greeting as well. Giving her one last look, the woman left.

Cassie waited a little longer. Finally, she replaced the veil and peeked out of the restroom door. Marton wasn't in sight; now was her chance. She shuffled out and turned toward the station's exit, considering how best to get to the embassy. She had to find it quickly, before he had a chance to get there first. But where was it? Was it close enough to walk or should she take a taxi?

A movement to her left drew her attention. Her heart stopped. Across the wide expanse of the terminal, Zambo was staring at her. She was no longer invisible. For a moment, she was too frozen with fright to react. She could only watch as he walked briskly, purposefully, toward her. At that moment, a busload of passengers emerged from the side door and engulfed his form. She lost sight of him, and only then could she move. In panic, she rushed out of the station. On the sidewalk in front, she stopped. Which way should she run? She searched frantically for a shop or café where she might hide. Or a taxi, except none was close enough.

Then she saw the Iranian woman in the violet suit, standing on the curb next to a Mercedes. The trunk was full of luggage, and the driver was chatting with a teenaged boy, her son perhaps. Cassie recognized the boy as a fellow passenger from Mashhad. The boy got in the front seat. As the driver closed the trunk, Cassie rushed up to the woman, practicing a sentence over and over in her head. "Excuse me, madam," she said in childish Dari, hoping the woman understood. "I need help. The American Embassy. Please." She glanced over her shoulder. Marton had just emerged from the building and was swiveling his head. In an instant, he spied her. With greater urgency, she begged, "Please."

This time the woman's face registered no surprise. Without a word, she took Cassie's elbow and guided her to the car's rear door. Giving a quick comment to the driver, she almost pushed Cassie inside.

Just as Cassie scrambled into the rear seat, she looked up. Twenty feet away, Marton had broken into a run. He was staring straight at her, his expression hideous.

"Oh no, oh no, oh no," Cassie cried, unconscious she was making a sound.

In the next second, the Iranian woman was beside her and the car door slammed shut. The engine purred just as Marton's face reached the window.

"Cassie!" he roared, slamming his fist on the car's roof.

The Mercedes drove away.

CHAPTER SIXTEEN

June 16, 2007

Sunday

I talked with my parents yesterday," Deb said as she settled into the passenger seat of the rental car. Jack's plane had arrived in Vancouver an hour before hers, giving him time to pick up the car and meet her in front of the airport terminal. "They told me something I never knew. It may be relevant."

Jack waited, inwardly glad that Deb had reached out to her parents.

"In the months after the State Department letter, several of Danny's friends called the house, looking for him, including a few old girlfriends. One girl was especially upset when our folks told her he was dead. She asked a lot of questions and they told her what they could, which wasn't much."

Jack nodded. He didn't really see the point of the story.

"I knew this, of course," she continued. "It was one of the reasons I got so angry at them, telling everybody Danny was dead. Anyway – and here's the part I'd never heard before – the girl who got really upset also asked about me. By name. Isn't that strange? She asked if I was all right." Deb stared now out of the window. "My mother never told me. Or maybe I didn't listen."

Jack spun around to look at her. "You think it might have been Cassie?!" The news stunned and thrilled him, evidence she'd come back.

"I don't know, but who else could it have been? I can't imagine any of his old girlfriends asking about me."

"Why would she ask if you were okay?" he pondered aloud, not expecting an answer. "What was the connection, I wonder?"

They drove in silence for several minutes before Deb asked, "Do you think Cassie could be in hiding?"

Jack nodded. He had started to think that, too.

Deb speculated, "Maybe she's hiding from Marton Zane. After all, she would know he started out smuggling drugs."

"That's no big deal," Jack answered. "Statute of limitations. He can't be prosecuted for it."

"No, but he still wouldn't want the world to know."

That was true, Jack conceded. Bad for business, bad for his reputation. He remembered the photo of Zane at the anti-drug fundraiser. But would the threat of exposure be enough to send Cassie into hiding for twenty-nine years? It didn't seem likely.

Deb had already agreed not to attend the meeting itself, but she nevertheless warned Jack. "He'll pump you for information, you know. Even a small slip could expose Cassie. This interview could put her in danger."

"I know," he said, griping the wheel tightly. He had realized the same thing. Zane was too eager to meet him, too eager to see the letters Cassie had sent. Something was there, even if they didn't know what it was. Jack hoped talking with Zane in person might give him a clue. Turning to meet Deb's eyes, he replied, "I need to be very careful about what I tell him." He returned his attention to the almost empty expressway. "Here," he said, reaching into his jacket pocket. He handed an oversized envelope to Deb. "Her letters. I brought them to read again on the plane. You hold on to them."

Deb tucked the large envelope into her purse. "Well," she sighed, "I don't know what he can tell you."

"He's already told me two things. First, that he doesn't know where she is. Second, that he believes she's alive, or at least was alive the last time he saw her. If I can learn where that was, I may be able to pick up her trail."

"You said he lies. That he lied when you spoke with him on the phone."

"And I expect he'll lie today. But you can learn a lot from what someone cares to lie about." He smiled grimly. "You said it yourself: bait the hook."

Another few minutes passed before Deb spoke again. "In that case, don't forget to ask about Danny."

"I won't forget. I promise."

DOWNTOWN VANCOUVER WAS quiet on Sunday, a city abandoned under a clear summer sky. They drove down West Georgia Street and passed the Zane International monolith; a block and a half away was the entrance to a hotel coffee shop. It was open, and Deb motioned that she would wait there. Parking nearby wasn't a problem.

There was still time before the meeting, so Jack joined her at a window table in the almost empty coffee shop.

Deb stirred sugar into her latte as Jack checked his pockets. The only documents he carried were copies of Danny's photograph and the one Cassie had sent of herself from Thailand. Then he looked at his watch, briefly squeezed Deb's hand and stood. At the last minute, he handed her his mobile phone. "Now you've got me feeling paranoid. Maybe Zane can remote access my phone's directory. I don't want him to find you or Becky. He already knows about Ralph Johnson, but that's okay; Johnson's clueless about Cassie."

Deb frowned. "What if you need to call me?"

"I'm only a block and a half away," he reassured her and then headed down the street.

Like the city itself, the lobby of the office tower seemed largely deserted. Then Jack saw two young executive types chatting with a uniformed guard, who ushered them through to the bank of elevators. The guard turned to watch Jack as he approached.

"Good afternoon. I'm here to see Marton Zane."

The man held out a hand and said, "Your ID, sir."

Jack considered giving him his driver's license, but it had his home address. Instead, he extracted his passport and, in a conversational tone, remarked, "Pretty quiet around here on a Sunday, I expect."

The guard said nothing. He scanned the passport and handed it back. Then he typed a few keys on the computer and made a phone call, speaking too softly for Jack to overhear. When he hung up, he looked at his watch and waited. Minutes passed slowly, quietly. At length, he stood and motioned for Jack to walk past the line of dormant security screeners. There, he asked Jack to lift his arms and, when Jack did, he patted him down. Once that was done, the guard escorted him to an elevator that stood by itself, and he used a key to unlock the doors. Then the guard returned to the security desk and made another phone call. Jack entered the elevator car and looked around. It was not as large or brightly lit as ones commonly used for ferrying employees and ordinary clientele. The door closed whisper quiet behind him and began its smooth ascent without him having pushed any buttons. When the doors opened a few seconds later, Jack encountered a tall black man in a pale yellow polo shirt, arms crossed.

"Hello. I'm here to see …"

"Please follow me, sir." They walked down a wide hall, thickly carpeted, past a reception area and glass walled conference room and finally entered an enormous office, white and stark and sophisticated. Jack swung his head around looking for Zane but no one was there. The man in the polo shirt held up a hand. "One minute, sir." Then he disappeared through a door in the far wall that Jack had not seen.

Jack wandered to the huge window, mesmerized by the panorama of the city below. The building was so high that he could see over the heads of its neighbors to the sun-glittered waters of Broward Inlet. The light was almost blinding; he blinked hard and turned away. To the left of the window stood a massive granite sculptural piece that didn't interest him, but on the opposite wall was an oil painting of a reclining nude in the style of Ingres's famous *Grande Odalisque*. Startled, Jack realized it was a very specific woman; he recognized the facial features of Zane's current wife. The pose was tame by contemporary standards, yet the painting's soft eroticism seemed out of place in an office. Puzzled, Jack wondered about Zane's motives. Ego and pride of "ownership"? Or a business strategy to divert and unsettle male visitors? He studied the lovely face. What did she think about having her naked portrait hanging here? She might consider it a compliment, but he knew Helene would hate it, and probably Cassie, too. To Jack the painting's placement objectified the woman, serviced her sleek beauty to a crass business advantage. He disliked Zane for doing it.

After a few minutes, the secret door opened again and Jack was ushered through. The polo-shirted guard followed him in but stood just inside the door as Jack entered a different space and time.

He was immediately seduced.

Thick maroon draperies cut off the Canadian summer sky, so seconds passed before his eyes fully adjusted, but even by the single light – an ornate desk lamp – he took in dark polished wood and arm chairs upholstered in gold and maroon brocade. Book cases rose to a second floor, with a catwalk served by a carved spiral staircase. Hanging above the fireplace, a gold-framed mirror reflected the room's somber rich colors. Overhead, a crystal chandelier was dark, and shadows hung in the high corners. Only a laptop and phone on the highly polished desk countered the impression of a nineteenth century library.

Behind the desk stood its curator, Marton Zane, dressed in black tee shirt and jeans. He still held a pen, and papers were scattered in front of him. This was the real workspace, Jack determined. The first room was theater. He guessed that few were invited backstage and was somewhat surprised that he was among them.

Carefully laying down his pen, Zane circled his desk and approached, moving with a confident grace. He wore his white hair very short now, head almost shaved, which accentuated his high forehead. With a strong brow, cheekbones and nose, his face almost seemed sculpted in stone. A memorable face; a Roman emperor's. The thin line of his lips formed a small sardonic smile as his eyes met Jack's; startling eyes: almond shaped and an electrifying blue.

"Dr. Jack Hunter." Zane said it with a soft significance. Without shaking hands, he motioned to a gold brocade armchair. "Please, sit. May I offer you something to drink?" That slight accent again.

"No, thank you." He settled into deep upholstery as Zane returned to his desk.

"Are you sure? I'm told I have a superb single malt scotch."

A curious way of phrasing the offer, Jack thought as he demurred again and swept his eyes over the bookshelves surrounding him. "Quite an office," he said admiringly. He strained to read the titles, to see what sorts of books his host read, but the shelves were too distant and the light too low.

Zane gave a captivating smile. "Yes, it is. Like the Ervin Szabo Library in Budapest. But with better Wi-Fi, of course."

This side of the man was so unexpected that Jack was intrigued, "Any particular focus to your collection?"

The smile vanished, the eyes narrowed slightly. "I'm not certain I know what you mean." Zane replied carefully.

"Oh. You know, biography, ancient history, French Romantic poets," he smiled and confided, reader to reader, "For example, I like reading plays. In fact, that's how I first became acquainted with Václav Havel. His plays are a little difficult but that could be the translation. I'd be interested in your view of his work."

Zane's shoulders tensed and he looked away. "Havel's all right," he said noncommittally.

His indifferent response seemed unusual to Jack. Even if Zane hadn't read or liked Havel's absurdist plays, surely he had read something of the man's and had formed an opinion. Havel, after all, was a hero of the Czechoslovak independence movement; he had even served as the first freely elected president in more than forty years.

But perhaps Zane wasn't really a reader. Jack leaned back in the plush chair and considered the Roman emperor across from him. Perhaps the library was another stage setting, with the books - like the nude portrait – simply strategic props.

Discomfited with how easily he had fallen for the library's allure, Jack steered the conversation back to why he had come. "Thank you for seeing me. And on a Sunday. I know you're a busy man." He surveyed the stacks of documents on the desk, passing over a crystal ashtray and pack of Davidoff cigarettes and finally settling on a delicate blue glass ornament flecked with gold. Its curious shape caught his attention.

Zane followed his gaze and silently moved the blue ornament out of reach. "Tell me about this girl you're looking for."

He made it sound as if Jack wanted to buy her. "A long-lost friend, actually. Not a girl. She'd be about my age now, a little younger."

Zane consulted a piece of paper. "Cassie Robinette?" He took the photo Jack offered and examined it. "I think I do remember this face. She was traveling with a tall man. What was his name?"

"Ralph. I mentioned him to you on the phone."

"Yes, Ralph Johnson, that's right. He became a writer, I believe. Have you read any of his work?" Before Jack could reply, Marton asked, "Do you mind if I keep this?" He had already started to put the photo into his desk drawer.

"Yes, actually. I need to have it back." Instinctively, Jack lied; he had copies but he was disinclined to share one with Zane. He held out his hand.

The men stared briefly at one another.

Jack gambled. "Of course, if you were close friends, I could make a copy for you."

Marton's eyelid flickered for a moment, then he handed back the photograph. "Never mind then. We weren't close at all." He fixed the blue eyes on Jack. "But I do seem to recall she had a professor friend she corresponded with. Is that you?"

Jack didn't intend to answer, but he inadvertently gave a quick smile. He could read Zane's pleased expression at his tacit admission.

"So, you're Cassie's professor. Well, tell me about your search so far. And what has led you to me."

Jack cleared his throat. "I know you were working with another American, a young man named Danny Mack, in August of 1978." At this, he showed him the picture of Danny.

Marton merely glanced at it. His tone was firm. "Not working with. Traveling with. For a short while."

First lie, Jack thought as he pocketed Danny's photograph. "You and Danny met Cassie and Ralph in Kabul, and you invited them to go with you to Herat. But your van broke down and you had to return to Kabul."

Zane studied him for several seconds before replying. "You got this from the letter you mentioned on the phone?"

"And Ralph confirmed it."

"Did he? I'd like to see the letter. To help my memory."

Jack absently brushed the jacket pocket where the letters had been, glad that Deb had them. "That's all the letter says. Ralph told me he stayed behind in Kabul when the three of you left for Herat a few days later."

"Did he say anything more? About why he stayed behind?"

Jack realized Marton was fishing, to see if he knew about the opium. "Why no. Was there something he should have told me?"

Marton parried with his own question. "What did you find out about Herat?"

Jack feigned ignorance. "That's why I want to see you. I only know that the three of you stayed there for a while."

"Not long. A few days."

"Oh, I understood it was about a week." He watched Marton's face but could read nothing.

"What makes you think that? Was there another letter?" Marton gave an innocent smile as he probed.

Better to keep him uncertain, Jack thought. "I also understand that you and Cassie traveled to Iran together." He almost mentioned Mashhad and the Hotel Khayyám, but decided that detail was better left unmentioned. "What happened to Danny? Did he go with you?"

Silence ensued, broken only by Marton tapping a finger on the highly polished surface of the desk. Finally he said, "You're mistaken, as I told you on the phone. I don't know what happened to the girl. Or to this Danny Mack you keep talking about. I stayed a few days in Herat, then flew directly to Istanbul. By myself. The girl – Cassie – left very early the same day I did. I saw her leave for the bus station right after breakfast."

"To go to Iran."

"I presume so, yes. She had talked about it."

"But weren't you lovers? Ralph believes that you were." It hurt Jack to say it.

Marton was matter-of-fact. "Then he's an idiot. She wasn't my type. The painting in the other room? That's my type."

Jack recalled the voluptuous beauty, blond and uniformly tan. The photograph of Cassie, in contrast, showed a pale, slender woman gazing directly at the camera, glasses perched on top of her head and sandy blond hair in a ponytail. A pretty girl, but no fashion model. Cassie's magic was in her movement, voice, intellect. It wasn't easily captured in still photographs. "So you weren't lovers." He didn't believe that for a moment, but he found himself wanting to.

"Oh, no. We were friends. Acquaintances, really. One of those brief, chance friendships that form when fellow English speakers meet in the far corners of the world. Seriously, I haven't thought about her in decades, not until you called. Now, of course, you've made me curious. I'd like to know what happened to her."

"How about Danny? Do you know what happened to him?"

"Not really. He was nice enough when he was sober, a little dim-witted. But he could turn violent when he was drunk." Zane paused. "He seemed obsessed with your friend but she wasn't interested. In fact, I just remembered something. The night before I left, I found him in her room, pinning her down on the bed. She was struggling to get up. I pulled him off and knocked him to the floor. When I shoved him out of the room, I told her to lock the door."

Yet another lie, Jack was sure of it. It conflicted with Danny's letter, as well as Cassie's friendly notation on it. Further, he doubted Marton had the physical strength to toss the taller man from the room. Still, Jack tried to keep an open mind; the tale wasn't inconsistent with the State Department's report.

"And that's when she left for Iran. Alone."

"Yes. Although, come to think of it, Danny was packing to leave Herat also. I'd given him the van, you see. I've always assumed he returned to Kabul, but he could have followed her. You should find him and ask him about her."

Did Marton not know that Danny was reported dead? It was possible but unlikely. Marton seemed like a man who kept tabs on things. Opening his notebook, Jack played along. "Do you know where I might find him now?"

Zane leaned back, appraising Jack. "Why would I know that? I barely knew the man."

"You gave him your van," Jack pointed out.

"A piece of junk that kept breaking down. As you said yourself." He picked up the blue glass object and continued, "Cassie was an interesting girl. She came from somewhere unusual, but I can't quite recall the name. What was it again?"

A casually launched query that Jack dodged. "A small rural town. But it doesn't matter. She never came home. Her immediate family is gone now and everyone else seems to think she's dead."

"You don't believe them, though, do you?" Zane asked softly.

Jack shrugged. "Maybe I do. But I'm an academic. I like to have evidence."

The splendid smile returned to Marton's face. "I do, too, Jack Hunter. I do, too." He scribbled something on a slip of paper and handed it to Jack. "To defray expenses for the search."

Glancing down, Jack saw it was a check for one hundred thousand dollars. He was astounded; it was more than his annual salary. His voice coarse, he insisted, "Thanks, but I don't need it," and tried to hand it back.

"Take it. We both know you don't make much money as a professor." Zane stood abruptly, signifying the end of the meeting. His eyes bored into Jack's, and his thin hand captured Jack's in a vise-like grip. "What I need is your assistance. Now that you've piqued my interest, I really would like to see Cassie again. I'm counting on you to keep me informed."

Before Jack could respond, the man in the polo shirt was at his elbow, escorting him out.

JACK WAS DEEPLY shaken as he stood in the elevator, his left hand still holding the humiliating check. His mind replayed the discussion, but locked on the last minute in particular. Until that point, he had prided himself in besting Marton, getting more information than he had given out. Marton's lies had all but confirmed that he and possibly Danny had been in Mashhad with Cassie. But Jack couldn't stop thinking about his last remark, his condescending belief that Jack could be bought.

He had been so unnerved that he had even forgotten to toss the check on the desk as he intended. Irritably, he stuffed it into his pants pocket just as the elevator doors opened. He'd shred it later.

On the sidewalk again, he felt disoriented and uneasy, the sort of apprehension that clouds a morning after the nightmare itself has been forgotten. He anxiously looked around for the coffee shop where Deb was waiting. Then he walked briskly toward it.

Preoccupied, he didn't hear the soft-soled footsteps behind him, so he didn't realize he was being followed until he felt a rough push on his shoulder. Then a stronger push and he tumbled down the entry ramp of an underground parking garage. He was trying to regain his footing when a burly white man in a hooded sweatshirt came up and kicked his feet out from under him. He collapsed on the concrete. A kick in the ribs and he curled into a fetal position. His brain wasn't working right. He kept thinking about the stupidity of a sweatshirt on a warm day like this, and the mugger's shoes. There was something not right about the shoes. A third kick and he was out.

He became conscious seconds later as he felt ham-sized hands riffling through his jacket pockets. Then, from far away, he heard a voice that seemed familiar.

"Police! Help! Someone's beating a man in a parking garage on West Georgia. It's called All Day Parking, a blue sign. Hurry! I think he's killing him!"

The thug stood suddenly, and Jack was dimly aware that he was turning to approach the voice, but then he heard the voice shout, "God, you guys are fast! Quick, down there." Evidently thinking better of an encounter with law enforcement, Jack's assailant turned instead into the dark parking garage and ran.

Jack remained curled defensively as Deb rushed to him. "Are you all right?" she cried frantically.

"Police?" he gasped as he painfully regained his feet. "Catch him, must hurry." He had difficulty breathing and couldn't straighten all the way.

Deb didn't reply. Instead, she grabbed him around the waist and held him upright as he moved awkwardly up the incline. When they paused on the sidewalk, she whispered, "There are no cops. There wasn't time to get my phone out of my purse. I just held my fist to my ear and faked it."

His cough-like laugh caught on the excruciating pain in his side.

They awkwardly stumbled three-legged back to the coffee shop, now so crowded they had difficulty finding a seat. Finally, in the back, Jack eased himself into a booth as Deb put in their order at the counter. Swarming around him were dozens of conference attendees from the adjacent luxury hotel, sporting badges and carrying conference totes. Jack had never felt more thankful to be caught in a crowd of conference attendees.

Returning with coffee and water for them both, Deb said, "You're right. We have to call the cops. Even with the hoodie, I can give a partial ID. White guy, black jeans, grey sweatshirt, big and square like a refrigerator."

Jack pushed the coffee aside and sipped carefully at the water. Feeling a little better now, he shook his head. "Too late. He's long gone."

"We need to file a report. He might mug someone else." She waved toward the out-of-towners around them.

"I don't think so," Jack replied thoughtfully. "He wasn't a typical thug." He remembered the odd shoes. "Loafers. He was wearing loafers with tassels." He felt for his wallet, still there. As were the rental car keys and his watch. He was glad he'd left the phone behind. He patted his jacket pockets, patted them twice. "He got the photographs. I think he also was looking for the letters."

"Zane must have sent him," Deb muttered. "Asshole."

Jack grinned in relief, imagining Zane's fury when the thug returned without the main prize. Then a sobering realization broke into his muddled brain. The assault demonstrated Zane was fully capable of violence. Things weren't funny at all. Somber now, Jack took Deb's hand, "Thanks for being paranoid. And for thinking fast with that fake call to the police."

She smiled. "No problem. It's how I'm wired. Too many years in the D.A.'s office." She finished her coffee, then stared into the empty cup for several seconds before asking, "Tell me about the meeting. What did he say about Danny?"

The conversation was still fresh enough in his mind that Jack could repeat most of it verbatim. Toward the end, he told her about Zane's sexual assault allegation about Danny.

"No way!" She was mad now and ignored the stares of coffee drinkers close by.

"A lie, I know. Totally inconsistent with the letters and what you know about your brother. So what does that tell us about Zane?"

He watched his companion's eyes as she concentrated. "That Danny's the fall guy. That Zane is blaming him for something he did." Excitement rising, she started to rush, "That it was Danny who stayed in Herat, not Zane, which means the body in Mashhad isn't Danny's. Just like I thought."

Jack didn't believe that last part, but he had come to much of the same conclusion about the rest. It could explain Cassie's disappearing act, if Marton had tried to rape her as well as smuggle drugs.

Deb interrupted his thoughts. "What now?"

"Mashhad, Iran. We know Cassie went there, and Marton's lies convince me that he went there too. I think something happened in Mashhad, and that's why she disappeared." He looked steadily at Deb. He wasn't going to discount her assistance ever again. "You want to come, too?"

She shook her head no. "But I'd love to get into Afghanistan, especially Herat. I can't see that happening in the next year, though, not until the war ends." She chewed her lip in thought, then asked, "How are you going to get into Iran?"

He had considered this already. "I've got a friend in the White House," and he gave a small smile.

DINNER WAS LIGHT, salmon and salad. Jack was still in pain and queasy. As he reached into his pocket for his wallet, he felt the folded paper. The check; he had forgotten about it. Pulling it out of his pocket, he showed the check to Deb.

"He gave it to me either as an insult or to buy me off," he fumed, "or both." Then he started to tear it in half. She immediately touched the check to stop him.

"Why shouldn't I?" he asked angrily but he put the check on the table.

Coolly, Deb held up two fingers. "Number one: He meant the check as an insult, right? If you cash it, you confirm his disdain for you. You're an academic, poor and naïve about the so-called real world. He'll think he can fool or co-opt you. I say let him. Let him underestimate you." She dropped one finger, leaving the middle one raised. "And second, let's use the money to spy on the bastard."

The symmetry was beautiful. Jack was nodding now. "Okay, we'll put Tony to work. Let's see what he can discover about Marton's henchman, Mr. Loafers. I have a feeling we'll be seeing him again. Oh, and there's a body guard, too. Tall black man, early forties. Former military, I'd guess. Then, find out what Zane was like as Zambo, back in his old hometown. He doesn't strike me as a dissident idealist who fled because of the Soviet crackdown on Prague Spring. Why did he really leave Czechoslovakia?"

Deb was already texting Tony.

Despite the sharp pain in his ribs, Jack felt righteous and joyously angry. Going after Zane felt good.

HIS APARTMENT SEEMED small and mean after Zane's fantasy library, but Jack put that out of his mind and began reviewing files. He was waiting for Frank to get back to him; he had to get into Iran.

Frank called. He was upset. "Listen, Jack, this isn't smart. All sorts of shit could be coming down soon. I can't give you any details, but there are some in the Administration who really want to kick Tehran's ass."

"Over Iran's nuclear program?"

"Well, that and helping the Iraqis kill our soldiers. I mean, a military strike isn't off the table. And you don't want to be stuck on the wrong side of the border if, or when, it happens."

"Okay. I'm forewarned. Thanks. Now, will you help me get in?"

Frank signed audibly. "I may be able to. But I don't like this, Jack. I don't like this at all." He hesitated. "You got a pen? There's this group, the American Iranian Association. I've met the director at a few D.C. functions. I just called her and she says they may be able to fit you into an upcoming trip."

"The American Iranian Association," Jack repeated as he wrote.

"It's a nonprofit educational-business group aimed at improving relations between the U.S. and Iran. Right up your alley. They're sponsoring a visit to Tehran next month, so you'll have to hustle to get a visa."

"Perfect. I can give a guest lecture or whatever."

"You're not going to like the whatever."

Jack paused. "Meaning?"

"Meaning that you'll be going with a trade delegation of cigarette manufacturers." Frank must have heard his groan, because he added, "You could put this off. Next year, AIA is sponsoring a trip for American academics and media. You'd get to meet Ahmadinejad."

The president of Iran. The scholar in Jack was tempted, but he demurred. "The wait's too long. I'll go with the cigarette salesmen." He wrote down the project director's contact information. "I really appreciate this, Frank. I'll let you know…"

His voice anxious and perplexed, Frank broke in. "What's got into you? A few months ago I had to drag you out of your hotel to see Las Vegas. You like routine; you hate gambling. But this whole thing's a dangerous gamble. What's changed?"

"Nothing's changed. It's just that I'm trying to piece together a puzzle. A puzzle with high stakes. It's actually a lot like doing research."

"Helene thinks you're going through a midlife crisis."

Jack could almost hear her saying it, but he was surprised at his calm reaction. The mention of her name didn't upset him, nor did her flip assessment of his state of mind. He simply said, "Well, it's a little more complicated than that. By the way," he added, "how is she?"

"Good. She likes Atlanta. She's been there a week, getting settled. The new job starts tomorrow." Frank chuckled nervously.

Jack hadn't realized that she had already moved. After so many intense years together, he was struck by how quickly their lives had gotten disentangled. "I hope she's happy" was all he could think to say, and he meant it.

"Jack, I feel like a real bastard about Helene. I didn't intend to start anything with her …. Things just happened…"

"It's okay," he said quickly. He didn't need a confession. "Really. I'm over it. I wish you both the best." He paused pensively. "Life moves on. Affairs begin, they end. When it comes to emotions, we don't have as much control as we think we do."

Now Frank laughed in relief. "You're a prince, Jack Hunter. For a man who hates the monarchy, you are a real prince."

INITIALLY, THE AIA director wasn't thrilled at having him join the delegation at such a late hour, but someone had just dropped out of the trip, leaving an opening. She warmed up when Jack explained that he was trying to locate two friends who had disappeared in Iran in 1978. It was a human-interest story that, if successful, could be a great public relations piece for AIA.

"You'll have to pay your own way," the director clarified. "But we can help with the paperwork and expedited visa, if you hurry."

"Of course," he assented. "How can I get to Mashhad?"

"You'll need permission. I'll speak with our contacts in Tehran about it. There's no guarantee. You could be stuck in the capital the entire time. If you do get permission, you'll need a government-approved interpreter. Probably a driver as well. So bring lots of cash."

"Got it," Jack said. That was the best they could do for him, but he was satisfied. He could work with that.

"We've spent a lot of years building up a good rapport with a handful of higher ups in the Iranian government," the director said and then took a deep breath. "What I'm saying, Dr. Hunter, is please don't do anything stupid while you're there."

CHAPTER SEVENTEEN

July 22, 2007
Sunday

What the hell was he doing, going to Iran? Jack's eyes were closed, seat belt unbuckled, seat reclined, to all appearances a man in repose on the long transatlantic flight. But he couldn't doze; he couldn't shut up his damn brain.

Sandy had argued with him. He remembered the timbre of her voice, the urgency when she begged him not to go. He realized he shouldn't have told her about his beating in Vancouver. And she had told her brother, who was almost as insistent that Jack stay home. He knew they were worried they would be the faces of the family left behind, if he was killed or taken hostage or accused of espionage. The ones on CNN, begging Iranian officials to release their father, begging U.S. officials to rescue him. Their concern wasn't unreasonable. Levinson, the American, was still missing. And Frank's warning about a possible U.S. strike on Iran - while Jack didn't think it was likely to happen - was not impossible either.

He felt unsettled by guilt - knowing he was responsible for their distress – coupled with an unacknowledged fear that they might be right; something terrible could happen to him.

Yet he had to go. Rationally, he didn't believe the journey was dangerous. He was with an American trade delegation. Protocols were in place, memoranda of understanding. He would be fine with the group. But that was the problem: he had no intention of staying with the group.

"Damn your quest!" Sandy had stormed on the phone.

On the long flight, he thought about her remark. He hadn't thought of the search as a quest. He considered it an investigation, something thoughtful and methodical. Quests, in contrast, were perilous, and people on quests were obsessive. He didn't think he was obsessive. After all, he had done plenty of other things this summer. Like that trip to visit Sandy; phone calls with Max; dinners with Ben and Lana. He'd finally healed enough from the beating to return to weight training and running.

Admittedly, he had spent an afternoon or two annotating Tony's preliminary report on Marton Zane. He'd learned that Zane was on his third marriage and had four children, three grown and one in boarding school. His two bodyguards were a former marine named Lawrence Williams and a college dropout named Todd Brill, or Mr. Loafers as Jack still thought of him. Jack had paid Tony from his own savings account. He simply couldn't bring himself to cash Zane's damn check. It was still tucked in his wallet somewhere.

Other than that, he had gotten on with his life.

Except that he hadn't. He had stopped working on his research paper; he had canceled his presentation at the political science conference in late August; he had not yet read a new text he'd ordered for his graduate seminar. His mind and his heart weren't into it. Instead, Jack spent restless days reviewing his notes and Cassie's letters, intent on finding any clue he might have missed, anxious for the day of his departure. If he was truly honest with himself, Jack knew that the search was distracting him, drawing him away from his professional duties. Perhaps he was on a quest after all.

As dawn broke, the plane landed in Munich. He had a two-hour layover before the flight to Tehran's Imam Khomeini airport. Jack hauled his well-worn book bag down from the overhead compartment, shouldered it and headed into the sprawling terminal. The men's room first, where he brushed his teeth and splashed water on his face to wake up. Then coffee; lots of good options in the international terminal. There wasn't time to explore, so he located the departure gate and found a seat. He pulled a paperback from his jacket pocket and settled back to read.

"This seat taken?"

Jack glanced up at a youngish white man in business attire, average height, average weight, ordinary in every way except for his red hair.

"Not at all," Jack offered, drawing his book bag a little closer.

"Thanks," the man said as he sat down. Cluttered around his legs were a large carryon bag, a duty-free shopping bag and a trim leather attaché case. "First time going to Tehran?" To Jack's nod, he added, "Me, too. I'm a little nervous actually. I was a kid during the hostage crisis. Remember the count on the nightly news? Day 382 in captivity and so on?" Again Jack nodded. "Well, I guess those images stay with you a long time."

Jack did recall. Everyone had been focused for so long on the Soviet Union as the enemy that most Americans were blindsided by the Islamic revolution in Iran, even more so by the seizure of U.S. embassy personnel months later. A new type of fear pervaded the country's psyche; the fear of a world where totally unexpected threats could erupt at any time. The days-in-captivity count had fed that fear.

The man continued, "I don't think we have to worry, though. Some guys I know have been there and they say Tehran's a modern city. Friendly people. Well, some of them."

"Yes, that's what I understand as well," Jack said. "On one hand, those who would like to open up to the rest of the world. On the other, hardliners who still see the West as a hegemonic threat, the Great Satan."

"You nailed it." The man held out his hand. "Clive Riley. I'm in telecom."

"Jack Hunter. I'm on a trade delegation with the American Iranian Association."

"Huh, trade? You don't strike me as a business type. You look more like a," he paused a moment, "a journalist or a professor."

The accuracy of the assessment mildly surprised Jack. Clive Riley hadn't struck him as someone who was especially astute. "Yes, I am a professor. How could you tell?" After all, he was wearing a sports coat, khaki slacks and an open-necked button-down shirt, similar to that of other travelers, including Clive Riley.

Riley grinned. "The way you talk, and your bag and shoes."

Jack glanced down at his scuffed leather shoes and slouching book bag. He smiled, "What if it's a disguise and I'm really an international spy?"

The man's grin briefly faltered, then lit up his face again. "Ha! Good one, Jack. So, what brings you to Tehran? Giving a lecture or something?"

An innocent enough question, but Jack wasn't sure how candid to be. "I'm doing some research, actually." That was close to the truth, he thought to himself.

"Cool. What are you researching?" When Jack didn't answer right away, Clive Riley apologized. "Sorry, I know I ask too many questions sometimes. That's what my girlfriend says."

Jack deflected. "Are you going to Tehran on business?"

"Yeah, a few meetings. Lots of potential customers in an untapped market." His words sounded like a memorized pitch to investors. "My company's been laying the groundwork for a while. Baby steps to get to a big deal someday." Riley leaned confidentially toward Jack. "Do you mind if I ask for some advice? I don't mean about business. I want to get my girlfriend a nice gift. What's Iran famous for? What are you getting your wife?" Riley seemed so young and earnest in that moment that Jack was inadvertently reminded of his own son, except that Max seldom asked for his advice any more.

"I'm not married," Jack replied, thinking how strange the admission sounded. "But I think you can find about anything. Jewelry, carpets, ceramics, I imagine." Riley's question reminded him he should look for gifts for his children. "There's a souvenir place called Dustoe that you might check out."

"Great, thanks. It sounds like you know Tehran."

"Only what I read in the *Lonely Planet*."

"Are you spending all your time in the capital? For your research, I mean. Any trips to see the countryside?"

"Just Tehran." He didn't mention Mashhad. In an uncharacteristic flash of superstition, he didn't want to jinx his chances of getting there.

Their flight was called. Jack's boarding zone was before Riley's. As Jack turned to head toward the line, the younger man stuck out his hand again. "See you on the other side," he said cheerfully. An afterthought: "Oh, and what hotel are you staying in?"

When Jack told him, he seemed extraordinarily pleased. "Me, too! Let's grab dinner sometime. What do you say?"

He's lonely, Jack realized, maybe even a little scared. Feeling avuncular, he smiled, "I'd like that." And it was true: an evening with Clive Riley could be a welcome antidote to what he was afraid of finding out in Iran. The man was so open and uncomplicated.

With that, they parted.

BY TUESDAY, HIS second full day in Tehran, Jack was restless and concerned. It was early evening already and still no call to confirm a trip to Mashhad. Tomorrow was his last full day in the country, then an early morning departure Thursday for the States. He wondered how difficult it would be if he simply went to Mashhad on his own. He wondered if the authorities would think he was CIA.

Sunday, when they landed, had been too full to be worried: getting settled at the hotel, contacting Sandy and Max to let them know of his safe arrival, chatting with a few other members of the trade delegation at the welcoming dinner. He had seen Clive Riley in passing once or twice; they had waved. Then he crashed post-dinner with jet lag.

Most of yesterday, with other members of the delegation in meetings, he largely kept to himself, waiting for the call. He essentially moved into the lobby, since it had the only internet connections. At least there he could check email and read newspapers online. Mid-afternoon, he had coffee with fellow delegates Stan from Miami and Reyes from Scottsdale. Dinner was at the hotel with Riley. A nice enough time but Riley's verbosity was beginning to wear thin. All he did was talk about his life and ask questions about Jack's. Jack had hedged his replies, telling Clive only about his teaching and his children. Mentioning Cassie and his quest had felt too personal. He had declined an after-dinner drink and went to bed early. Much later last night, suddenly wide awake, he wandered back to the lobby and chatted for an hour with the solitary hotel desk clerk.

Today was much the same. A late breakfast on his own; a workout in the empty hotel gym; emails and on-line newspapers in the lobby. Riley had found him at lunch time but he begged off since he had just finished breakfast. Besides, the American Iranian Association had organized a tour of the city's highlights in the afternoon, dinner at a local restaurant included. He had gone with the group, nervously checking his phone throughout.

At the end of the tour, the bus dropped them off at the hotel. It was almost seven. On the pavement outside, Jack checked his phone again, just in case he had missed the call. Nothing. He passed through the glass doors. Around him, en masse, the delegates swarmed through the lobby talking about their impressions of the city. Suddenly, Jack's mobile phone rang. He dug it out of his pocket as another guest brushed against him. To hear better, he went back outside to take the call.

"Professor Hunter? Please meet your interpreter at six tomorrow morning in the hotel lobby. You are scheduled for a 7:30 flight."

"Thank you."

"Do not bring a camera or recording device. Do not take photographs."

"I understand. Do I need to bring anything? An overnight bag?" He considered what would happen if he missed his flight home on Thursday.

"There is no need. You return to Tehran on a flight later in the day. Goodnight."

That easily, the trip to Mashhad was set.

The next morning, Jack was in the lobby by 5:45. The friendly night clerk was on duty again and brought him a welcome cup of coffee. They were exchanging pleasantries when a man with glasses, dark hair and neatly trimmed beard walked through the automatic glass doors. Heavy set, he was dressed in a dark gray business suit with a white shirt; the collar was open and he wore no tie.

"Good morning, Professor Hunter. I am Mohammed, your interpreter." He held out a large hand.

Jack noticed that he gave no last name. Shaking his hand, he replied, "*Salaam*, Mohammed."

His interpreter motioned toward the glass doors. "You are ready to go? We will return this afternoon, *Inshallah*."

In the reflected light from the lobby, Jack could see a waiting taxi. "Yes, I'm definitely ready to go." In his pockets were his passport, a small notebook, the Hotel Khayyám postcard from Cassie, and photographs of her and Danny and a poorer quality one of Marton Zane enlarged from the one taken at the charity fundraiser. He wished he had surreptitiously snapped one when he was visiting Zane but he hadn't thought of it. Besides, he didn't have his mobile phone with him. He didn't now, either. He had left it in his room, because it had both a camera and a recording device. He hoped he wouldn't regret leaving it behind.

The sun rose as they pulled away from the hotel; the drive to the airport took only minutes. They were waiting with boarding passes when Mohammed asked him about his interest in visiting the hotel owner in Mashhad.

Jack understood in that moment that Mohammed was more than an interpreter; he was a minder and a spy. He envisaged Mohammed writing a report about the day for some intelligence agency. As succinctly and clearly as possible, Jack explained about his search for Cassie, a long-lost family friend. He then brought out the postcard. As the Iranian studied Cassie's message, Jack asked if it was possible to see if there were any official reports on an American woman by that name.

Instead of answering, Mohammed shook his shoulders regretfully. Holding up the card, he then asked, "You do not know this hotel owner? He did not contact you?"

"No."

"You have never communicated with him?"

"Never." Uneasy, Jack realized the government suspicions that must have fallen on the poor man once an American expressed interest in meeting him. "I don't even know his name. Or if he was at the hotel in 1978. I'm here because of the postcard. It's the only clue I have."

Mohammed didn't speak again for several minutes. When he did, he startled Jack. "The man was there in 1978," he stated. "He was a boy. His father owned the hotel."

Hopeful news, Jack considered. The boy might remember Cassie. As they took off, he felt a surge of adrenalin, difficult to contain during the ninety-minute flight. Finally, they landed and he bounded down the steps of the plane, Mohammed close behind.

Jack barely registered the sights of Mashhad as a taxi took them directly to the Hotel Khayyám. They walked into the lobby; the place was crowded. Mohammed spoke quickly to a harried man behind the front desk, then quietly explained to Jack that the group checking in were pilgrims who were visiting Haram–e Motahare Razavi, the shrine of Imam Reza, for purification. The two of them would have to wait for the owner to be free. He then led Jack to a half empty dining room where they took a table looking toward the lobby. They could observe the milling crowd and two teenaged boys who carted luggage of every shape and size toward a staircase. When a waiter arrived, Mohammed ordered mint tea and breakfast for them.

They ate in silence. The crowd in the lobby was dwindling.

"Have you been to Iran before, Professor Hunter?" Mohammed had finished eating and was daintily sipping hot tea from a tulip glass.

His fingernails were immaculate, Jack noticed. Self-conscious of his own roughly manicured ones, he slipped his hands off the table.

"No, this is my first visit." he weighed his words carefully. "I haven't seen a lot so far but my impression is that this is a beautiful country." He was about to add that he enjoyed meeting Iranian people, but checked himself. Mohammed might take too keen of an interest in his casual acquaintances. He didn't know how much he could trust the Iranian.

"Do you speak any Arabic or Farsi?" Mohammed's tone was gently inquiring, as if asking if Jack had slept well the night before.

Jack gave a low chuckle at the thought. "Saying *salaam* is the extent of my vocabulary."

Finally, the man from the front desk walked to their table. He was middle aged and wore a dark suit coat over a long white tunic and trousers. On his head was a cap. He and Mohammed conversed for a few minutes. While Jack could not understand the words, he caught the man's deference to the interpreter. Turning to Jack, Mohammed introduced the man as Jahwed, the hotel owner. Jack said *salaam*, and introduced himself.

Jahwed led them through the doorway behind the front desk, down a hall and into a small office. They all sat. Jack's eyes took in the space, austere except for a large yellowed print of an ornate shrine of some sort, with several small framed prints on either side, artistically rendered images of archways and domes. The office furniture and carpets were worn but well-kept and clean. A photocopier dominated one corner.

The hotel owner seemed to be expecting them, nodding as Mohammed spoke. Jack caught the word for American. He assumed his guide was explaining the purpose of their trip because Jahwed gave him an expectant look.

"Thank you for seeing me," Jack said as Mohammed translated. "I am looking for a woman named Cassandra Robinette. She sent a postcard from your hotel in September 1978. Here it is, and her photograph."

Jahwed scanned the postcard and nodded; it was from his hotel. Then he studied the photograph for a long time. He frowned at Jack and said something. Mohammed translated. "He says that he well remembers your sister. She was kind to him and his mother."

His sister. She must have told Jahwed that for some reason, and he would play along. Before he could respond, however, Jahwed added more and Mohammed translated, "She was in terrible trouble and you should never have let her travel alone."

Terrible trouble – what was it? The news hit Jack hard.

Jahwed's reproachful voice continued. Mohammed said, "She was traveling to meet you in Istanbul. But you should have come here to meet her." As he translated, Mohammed also frowned in disapproval at Jack. "She was alone. Where was her brother?"

Jack looked down. All of these years, Jahwed had been angry at him, the negligent brother. His contrition was genuine. "Yes, I should have come." It was patronizing; Cassie would not have approved. But he said what he knew the men needed to hear. And, in some deep unreasonable part of his mind, Jack did blame himself. "I'm very sorry I didn't. Now, I want to find her." He paused and took a breath, dreading to hear the answer to the next question, "You said she was in terrible trouble. What do you mean?"

When the question had been translated, Jahwed paused and looked away. Jack tried to read his expression. It was sad now, not angry and accusatory. Then he spoke at length, and Mohammed stopped him several times to ask further questions or clarifications. Finally, Mohammed turned to Jack and explained.

"She arrived during *Eid al-Fitr* with two men. One man acted like her husband, taking charge of things. She asked for her own room, very unusual but not unknown among pilgrims seeking purification. But the hotel was full for the holiday. Only the large suite was free, and the husband agreed, so they stayed there for one night. The woman was unhappy but what could she do? Jahwed and his father did not know until later that the man was bad and was not her husband."

Mohammed paused and Jack presented the other photographs. "Were these the two men?"

Jahwed nodded immediately when he saw Danny's face. "This one, yes. She said he was like her family. He was also bad but not to your sister." Then he stared and scowled at the picture of Zane. Mohammed translated, "This other one, he cannot tell from the photograph."

Suddenly, Jahwed seemed to remember something and he hurried to a gray file cabinet. A few minutes of searching brought a weathered book, securely closed with string. Untying it, he flipped through the pages. Jack saw what the book was: a guest register. Most was in Arabic script in different ink and handwriting. Then a page opened with Latin lettering. Jahwed showed Jack; the names jumped out: Marton Zambo, Danny Mack, Cassandra Robinette, along with their passport numbers and nationality. The date was 3 September 1978. Beside Zambo's name was a note for two nights. Cassie's handwriting was immediately recognizable, and Jack ran his finger over the long-dried ink.

"May I have a copy of this page?" he asked. Mohammed must have asked for one as well, because Jahwed made two copies and gave each of them one. Mohammed folded his and put it away, while Jack continued to stare at the page. "You said she stayed only one night? This entry says two."

Jahwed nodded, and then spoke at length, staring intently at Jack as Mohammed translated. "Danny Mack went away the first day. Cassandra Robinette also tried to leave then, but Marton Zambo locked her in the room and burned her arm."

Jack winced involuntarily.

Mohammed continued, "Jahwed heard her scream. When Zambo left for a while, he unlocked the door and brought her to his father in this very office. He begged his father to help her before Zambo could dishonor her. She showed them photographs of you and your parents. His father knew what it was to worry about one's children, so he agreed to help." He paused in his translation and asked Jahwed a question. Turning back to Jack, Mohammed said, "His mother disguised her and hid her in the kitchen until nightfall, when Jahwed took her to the bus depot." Another memory came to Jahwed, and Mohammed translated. "When she was hiding there, Zambo forced his way into the kitchen, and threatened his mother and aunt and sisters. He and his father forced him to leave."

Another brief exchange between the two Iranian men, then Mohammed concluded, "That is the entire story. Your sister got on the bus."

"The bus to Tehran?"

"Yes, the bus to Tehran." Mohammed now looked into Jack's eyes. "He feels very badly about this. He always thought that she escaped, but now you tell him that you did not find her in Istanbul and she never arrived home. This saddens him."

Jahwed's sincerity was evident. Jack met his eyes, briefly sharing the sorrow. He pretended to himself that he could pick up her trail when he got back to Tehran, but he began to fear that he couldn't; that his search was over.

Finally, Jack asked the question that Deb needed to know. "So, the other man, Danny Mack. You said that he left the same morning that Marton Zambo hurt Cassie."

"He was a terrible man, also."

Puzzled, Jack asked Mohammed if Jahwed could explain.

"Danny Mack said he was going to Herat, but instead he went to the shrine of Imam Reza, far away from the bus station. He desecrated the sacred place and dishonored the devout, and they grew very angry. He was beaten."

"He died, didn't he?" Jack found he couldn't say the word murdered; he was too upset to hear that his instinct had been right, that the dead man was Danny, and he would have to tell Deb.

The hotel proprietor gave a curt nod and spoke softly. Mohammed repeated, "He had liked him, but his father was right. Unbelievers are like that. They seem good on the surface, but there is evil in their hearts."

"Surely not all unbelievers," Jack softly protested.

Jahwed thought before he replied and Mohammed translated. "Not your sister. She was kind and pure. She gave him her camera when she left. A gift for helping her. These photographs around us, Jahwed made them with the camera."

Looking with renewed interest at the framed prints, Jack said, "They are very fine."

Jahwed reached into a bottom drawer of the desk and extracted an old-fashioned film processing envelope, the type once used to hold prints and negatives. He handed it to Jack as Mohammed explained that these were the photographs on the roll of film when she gave him the camera. Jahwed had saved them, in case she ever returned.

Jack flipped through the dozen or so prints. Three were of her smiling in the wind, with a city stretching below her in the background. Two photos were taken of a massive mosque someplace. A few other travel images. Then came a still life of a steaming cup of tea and a piece of paper. Another of an alleyway with a man approaching a door. Cassie was experimenting with composition and light, Jack noted. The next one in the stack showed two men next to a blue van, neither man looking at the camera; Jack immediately recognized younger versions of Marton and Ralph. He showed it to Jahwed, who shrugged regretfully. The next image was of Marton and Danny in a hotel room. This time, Jahwed nodded vigorously and said something. Those are the men, Mohammed translated; the photograph was taken here, at the Hotel Khayyám. Jack realized its import. With the guest book signatures, the photo confirmed that both Danny and Zane were in Mashhad. He paused and decided to look through the images again, this time carefully studying each one.

The still life caught his attention. Something was written on the paper. He held the photo beneath Jahwed's desk lamp and read the English portion aloud, "Please help me. I am an American and I am lost. Where is the bus station?"

Unaccountably, Jahwed glared at him and grabbed back the photograph. He too read the note and spoke angrily to Mohammed, who took the picture and said slowly, "In Arabic, the note does not say this, Professor Hunter. It is disgusting."

"What does it say? Please, I need to know." Jack insisted.

Frowning, Mohammed read, "I am a rich American and I want …" He paused and cleared his throat. He seemed uncomfortable speaking the words aloud. Finally, he continued, "I want sex with your daughters. I will pay you well."

"What!?" Jack was flabbergasted. This made no sense. Why the hell would Danny …? But Danny wouldn't.

Jahwed said something and Mohammed translated, "This is the note found in Danny Mack's hand, this terrible note written in the language of the noble Quran. This is why he was beaten."

Jack barely heard. He was holding the still life against the names printed in the guestbook. He was almost too angry to speak. "See this?! The handwriting matches. Zambo wrote the note. I bet he gave it to Danny. He set Danny up."

Mohammed leaned in close to examine the handwriting.

Extremely agitated, Jack stood and paced. "Didn't anyone see this? Obviously Danny didn't know what the Arabic part said. He thought he was simply asking for directions."

Mohammed looked troubled. "I doubt the police could read English." He asked Jahwed a question, and turned again to Jack. "Our friend Jahwed cannot. He only recognized the note in the photograph from the description of the crime."

Jahwed interrupted again, highly disturbed. He spoke at length. When he finished, he slumped in his chair and look down at his hands as Mohammed finally was free to speak. "He remembers something else. The police reported that the American was carrying a city map. The hotel was marked with an X and the shrine circled. Jahwed says he made those marks and gave Zambo the map after Zambo asked him what place in the city was the most sacred. Jahwed always thought Danny had stolen the map from Zambo. But now he realizes it is his fault that Danny Mack went to the shrine of Emam Reza and not the bus station."

"No," Jack protested weakly. "Jahwed could not have known. No one could have imagined...."

All three men sat in silence. Jack felt sick at heart.

Mohammed looked at his watch and signaled that it was time to go. First, he excused himself to go to the toilet. Jack reluctantly gathered his things.

Jahwed leaned forward on his desk, eyes penetrating Jack's. In strongly accented English, he said. "I thank you for coming at last, Mr. Professor. You find your sister. She is so kind."

Jack was startled. He had no idea that Jahwed understood any English. "Thank you so much for seeing me, and for helping her escape. I believe you and your family saved her life." After all, he thought, if Zambo had Danny killed, he would not have hesitated to kill her. Thanks to Jahwed, she left Mashhad alive; that was something to cling to.

"Please?" Jahwed gestured at the processing envelope in Jack's hand. "A photograph?"

Jack understood and opened the pack. He extricated one of the photographs of Cassie on the windy hillside and, with his right hand, ceremoniously handed it to Jahwed.

The other man smiled as he studied it. "This is Kabul, you know? She come here from Kabul. I never forget her." The photo went into his desk.

Both men stood just as Mohammed returned. Jahwed walked around the desk and embraced Jack.

"I will let you know, Jahwed, when I find her. I will let you know."

Only after Mohammed translated did Jahwed nod, a sign that he did not want to let Mohammed know he could understand simple English. Evidently, he didn't completely trust Mohammed either.

In minutes, they were driving away from the Hotel Khayyám. Jack glimpsed the famous golden dome of the shrine, one of the holiest sites in Iran, where Deb's carefree older brother had been killed. "Is Danny buried near here?" he asked.

Mohammed spoke with the driver and the taxi turned right, away from the dome. "It is not far. We can visit the grave if you wish. But only for a brief stop."

"I'd appreciate that very much," Jack confessed. Since he didn't have a camera, he would try to memorize every detail to share with Deb.

Bright sunlight flattened the perspective of the graveyard, glinting off stone and erasing shadows. Jack put on his sunglasses as he followed Mohammed. Against the July heat, he had already removed his sport coat, leaving it in the waiting taxi. Now he absently rolled back his cuffs. Most of the headstones were marble and granite, carved with western names. The place looked neglected, even a little wild. Now any European who died in Mashhad was flown home for burial, Jack thought, not left in a foreign land.

Mohammed must have asked the driver for directions to the grave, or perhaps he knew already of its notoriety. He quickly led Jack to a mound at the edge of the graveyard. It was marked with an unobtrusive plaque with the initials D.E.M. 1956 – 1978. Probably due to Richard Porter, Jack thought, the State Department guy. Someone had defaced the plaque with orange paint; someone else had ineffectually scratched at the plaque's surface with a nail. But the vandalisms were years old; even those who had hated Danny had now forgotten him.

Jack was overcome with sadness. All along, he had expected this; he had considered Deb's insistent optimism an exercise in self-deception. Yet while his brain had understood, his heart had refused.

He had wanted desperately to share Deb's hope; it was so tied to his own. Even when he heard Jahwed's horrific tale today, Jack still resisted. Now, faced with the grave and its sad little marker, his heart finally knew. And it hurt like hell.

Danny Mack had been so young, his son's age. When Jack thought about the sustained brutality of a beating death, he couldn't get that fact out of his mind.

Mohammed stood silently a few steps behind him. As they turned to leave for the taxi, he said, "Please tell his family I now do not think he was guilty of the crime." Without looking at Jack as he walked, Mohammed added brusquely, "It was the other man who defiled the holy place."

It was a melancholy drive to the Mashhad airport. Neither man spoke. They had boarded and buckled their seat belts before Mohammed turned to Jack. "Why did you tell me that she was a friend and not your sister?"

Startled, Jack didn't know what to say. Either way, he would have to admit to a lie.

Mohammed answered his own question. "I know. The shame." He said it sympathetically, as if he had some experience with family shame.

Jack cautiously asked, "Do you have a sister as well?"

The large man sighed. "I will tell you a story, not unlike your own in some ways. I was a boy on the cusp of manhood when the revolution came. Our family was very modern. I went to the American school, read books in English, and ate at the Colonel Sanders restaurant – yes, in Tehran. My sister was at university then, engaged to a man she had met there. She and I were alike. We protested together against Reza Pahlavi, who was a brutal colonial puppet, and celebrated together when he fled. But when the Ayatollah Khomeini returned from exile in Paris and established the Islamic Republic, she and her fiancé continued to protest. We argued; Islam is the true revolution, I told her. It is the only way to reject colonial corruption and follow the true path. Then her fiancé was arrested. We heard he was tortured." He paused for a minute, frowning at the memory. "When that happened, my father was frightened for her, his only daughter, and urged her to marry another man, high up in the revolutionary police. She did. It was not a happy marriage. She would come to our house, bruised and crying, and my father would send her back. Once she came and her arm was broken. He sent her back again. He had to. Then, one day, she disappeared. No one spoke of her. My heart stopped beating; I thought she was dead."

Mohammed stopped speaking as the air steward handed each of them a small packet of cookies. In silence, he waited for his tea and Jack's coffee to be poured. Then he took a delicate sip, cleared his throat, and returned to his story. "A week later I learned that she had escaped. She had abandoned her country, the revolution, her family. Her husband was very angry. So, of course, her old fiancé was executed as an enemy of the revolution. My father was arrested and interrogated. Where had she gone? How had she escaped? My father insisted he knew nothing, and eventually they believed him and let him go. I was furious that my sister would do this, and bring such dishonor and pain to the family. From that moment, I decided she was dead to me."

"How did she get out?" Jack couldn't stop himself from asking.

Shrugging, Mohammed explained, "I think that my mother helped her. My mother came from a wealthy Tehran family, and some of them had already left Iran. But I didn't tell this to my father. How could I? It was my mother. That compounds the shame."

In the ensuing silence, they sipped their coffee and tea. Then Jack ventured another question. "Did she ever return to Iran? Did she ever see her parents again?"

Mohammed shook his large head no. "The curious thing is that I cannot forget my sister. I still wonder how she is doing."

"Would you see her again, if you could?"

Mohammed carefully took his last bite of a cookie and chewed thoughtfully. "That, I am not prepared to say." Then he brushed crumbs from his tray table into the empty tea cup and wiped his fingers on the small airline napkin. "Perhaps when I am older, your age, I will feel as you do and will try. That is why you interest me, Professor Hunter."

The revelations startled and moved Jack. He had looked at Mohammed as an actor in a stereotyped part: the government agent whose driving motive was to serve the state. Now he saw the man's complexity and glimpsed how principled stands and passion could tear apart an ordinary loving family caught in political turmoil.

When their inflight refreshments were cleared away, Mohammed asked to see the photograph of the note again. He squinted at the two divergent messages, frowning and shaking his head.

"May I keep this?" he asked at last.

Jack agreed. He had the negatives; he would print out another.

Mohammed tucked it into his suit coat pocket and then made a few notes on the back of his copy of the guest book page. He noticed Jack watching and explained. "I have a friend from school who works in the office of the prosecutor. I will ask him about this case."

Jack nodded solemnly. Ultimately, that was the only solace, the pursuit of justice. He thought of another photo that could help the prosecutor, the one of Danny and Marton in the hotel room. He laid it on Mohammed's tray table. Then he added, "If the prosecutor decides to investigate, this is how to reach Zambo now." On the back of his university business card, he clearly printed the name Marton Zane and his Vancouver business address. "He's a very rich and powerful man," he advised as he handed over the card.

"Perhaps. But we are not without resources." Mohammed smiled slightly at the understatement, and gave Jack his card. "I hope that you find your sister. If you do, please have her contact me. Her assistance in this matter could be most helpful."

BY THE TIME they had arrived back at the hotel in the late afternoon, Jack felt a cold rage rising against Marton Zane, in its force unlike any he had experienced before. He controlled it as he shook Mohammed's hand and disembarked from the taxi. He held it tightly in as he entered the hotel and passed quickly through the lobby, even as he gave perfunctory nods to several members of the trade delegation working on their laptops. He continued to grapple with the rage as he walked toward the coffin-sized elevator, praying he could keep it in check until he reached his room.

As he pushed the UP button, he noticed a man rapidly approaching, clearly aiming to board as well. Glaring at the presumed intruder, Jack did not stop the doors from closing.

Finally, in the security and silence of his room, Jack released himself to the furies - punching, punching, punching the mattress until, exhausted, he finally fell on the floor by the side of the bed and buried his face in his arms.

JACK STARED AT the small screen of his mobile phone. What could he say to soften the news of her brother's death? Nothing. Yet he didn't have the heart to keep Deb in hopeless hope another day. He typed:

> *I have a lot to tell you about today. Main news is that I got confirmation it was Danny who was killed here. I paid respects at his gravesite. Danny was innocent; you were right about that. I am so very sorry. I wish I was there with you.*

He glanced at his watch; it was morning in Riverside and Deb would be awake. Good; darkness tended to magnify despair. He sent the message. She would be devastated, but at least she would finally know.

A knock on the door. Jack didn't want to see anyone, but he peered through the peep hole. Clive Riley stood there, looking concerned. Another, more insistent knock. Jack sighed and opened the door a crack.

"Hey, buddy, I haven't seen you around today. Where'd you go? Were you able to get out of town?" he asked eagerly.

Jack didn't want to talk about his day. "I've been around," he said. "No place special."

"Oh. Well, want to grab some dinner? We could hit the bar first. My treat," Clive grinned. "I have an expense account, remember?"

The thought of food made Jack nauseous. And he didn't have the energy to engage with Clive right now. "I appreciate the offer, but I can't. I'm going to just work in my room tonight, start packing up for the trip home tomorrow."

"Are you okay? You don't look okay."

"Actually no. I'm not feeling all that well. But thanks for coming by." The younger man didn't budge; uncharitably, Jack thought him obtuse.

"I could bring you hot tea, or a whiskey," he said solicitously. "You seem kind of down. Maybe I could cheer you up."

Jack felt guilty for his unkind thoughts about Riley. "No, but thanks again. I'll be fine after a good night's sleep. Have a nice dinner."

"Okay then. But call me if you change your mind. Room 304," Clive Riley said as he finally turned away.

Jack smiled weakly in acknowledgement of the offer and then gently closed the door. Maintaining normalcy even for the brief conversation exhausted him. He leaned his forehead and elbows against the door and stood for several minutes concentrating on breathing. Finally, he felt himself recover. He made his way to the bathroom and picked up the miniature bottle of shampoo. A shower was what he needed. It would cleanse away the stink of the day's heat and his emotional rawness.

As he showered, he realized he had to send Deb another text. He drafted it in his head as he dried off. With the towel around his waist, he sat on the bed and typed it out:

> *MZ set up Danny's murder. I'm bringing evidence. Iranians may investigate. Talk to your friends in DA's office about extraterritorial jurisdiction. Maybe they can build a case. Or at least investigate.*

Going after Zane could be the anchor Deb would need after losing Danny for certain. He remembered too well the awful feeling of being unmoored in the days after his marriage ended. And Deb was experiencing something far worse. Somehow, Zane had to be exposed as the monster he was.

Then Jack read a little, watched CNN on the room's television and finished packing, including small ceramic cups from the hotel gift shop for Sandy and Max. He sat on the edge of the bed. He simply wasn't sleepy. Admitting it, he dressed again and decided to head down to the front desk to settle his hotel bill.

The same friendly night clerk was there, grinning as Jack approached. The paperwork was settled quickly and the clerk wished him a safe trip home.

"Oh, and sir," he added. "A man has been asking about you and I did not know what to say."

Jack was puzzled. Perhaps Mohammed had returned. "Was he an Iranian? The same gentleman as this morning?"

"No sir." The desk clerk was firm on that point. "Another western foreigner."

"Canadian?" Could Zane have sent someone to track him? His eyes swept the empty lobby.

"No sir, American. My friend on the day shift thought he saw him following you. But he could be mistaken."

"Following me?! Today?!" He remembered a man moving closely behind him the evening before, when his mobile phone rang. A man also rushed to catch the elevator this afternoon. Was that him? This was alarming news; Jahwed could be at risk. Jack would have to let Mohammed know, to alert local law enforcement to make sure Jahwed was safe.

The clerk shook his head no. "Not today. Before. He said today the man was very agitated when he could not find you, and he asked my friend where you had gone. My friend did not know of course. He told me about it when I came on duty."

Jack weighed the news; it wasn't totally grim. Zane had correctly guessed that Iran was his next destination. He had Jack's passport information and a top investigative team; tracking his movements would not require heavy lifting. Yet Zane and his spy evidently didn't know where in Iran Jack went. He hoped they thought he was still in Tehran. He was glad now that he had left his mobile phone behind, just in case they could access his GPS.

The clerk wasn't finished. "An hour ago, the man came to me and asked if I knew and I said no. Then he offered me six hundred thousand rials to find out where you went. I have never been offered a bribe before. It is deeply insulting."

Twenty dollars U.S. must have been tempting, Jack thought as he concurred.

The desk clerk continued, "I told him that it was none of my business. He could ask you himself if he had to know."

Jack smiled with sincerity for the first time in days. "Thank you for handling that so well. You have done me a great service." He pulled out his wallet and extracted his remaining Iranian bills, almost fifty dollars' worth. "Please accept this as a small gift." He discreetly slid the money across the counter and watched as the clerk smiled in acceptance.

"So, will you tell the man where you went today?" the clerk asked.

"Not in a million years. But I'll tell you, if you'd like to know."

"Best not, sir. Because, if the red-headed man comes back, I would have to lie."

The red-headed man. Clive Riley, whose affable manner invited confidences. Jack rebuked himself for underestimating him, for being taken in so easily. He tried to remember everything he had said to the man. He thought he had been careful with Riley, even reserved. Garrulous people tended to do that to him, at least early on. He was profoundly relieved he hadn't had a drink with him this evening. Given his anger and distress, he knew he would have been tempted to talk.

SEVEN HOURS LATER, Jack was back in the lobby, waiting with the other delegates for the airport shuttle. Standing with Reyes while Stan paid his hotel bar bill, Jack was ready to be on his way. Stan rejoined them and started a friendly argument with Reyes. Jack turned away as he heard his name called. There was Riley, hailing him as he worked his way through the gathering, side stepping luggage and briefcases.

"Great to see you again!"

Jack could hear the insincerity in his voice; he hadn't noticed it before.

Clive continued," I was supposed to fly out Saturday, as you know, but last night I got word that the company wants me back right away. So I'm on your flight. Isn't that great? We can get seats together. I can keep an eye on you since you aren't feeling so hot."

The thought of spending almost twenty hours with him almost made Jack choke. "Not possible," he managed to say. "I'm coming down with the flu. Hotel doctor said so. And the early stages are the most contagious."

"But I could…"

Shaking his head regretfully, Jack interrupted, "I already decided to pay extra and get a seat by myself. I appreciate your offer to help, but I wouldn't dream of sitting with you, exposing you to my germs. Your girlfriend would never forgive me." With a fake regretful smile, he added, "Have a safe trip home. It's been something getting to know you."

Jack moved away from Clive Riley just as the shuttle arrived.

CHAPTER EIGHTEEN

August 2, 2007
Thursday

It's weird what the mind thinks about on a two day drive by yourself, Jack reflected. Abu Ghraib, Keith Jarrett at Carnegie Hall, drought in the countryside he passed through, Helene at the CDC, Helene and Frank, subprime mortgages and his retirement savings, shootings at Virginia Tech, his kids, Obama's chance of winning the nomination over Clinton. He didn't mind driving, although this was the longest solo road trip he had taken in decades. In fact, he got into a rhythm with the road, disliked having to stop. Stopping meant he had to do something. Driving itself made few demands once he'd settled on the destination.

A musical beat sometimes moved him along. Delta blues and Zydeco on local radio; his own stack of C.D.s. A few times he played the newest one, a mix of classic New Orleans - the Neville Brothers, Irma Thomas - that Sandy had made for him. Upbeat rhythms that ordinarily energized him. But the music wasn't working this time, and he found he preferred to sit hunched over the wheel and drive in silence. His brain was filled with enough noise.

And too much of the noise was about Iran.

314

Since the long flight home, he had been brooding. Less now about the savagery of Danny's murder than what its pitiless and careful planning revealed about the murderer. Against the backdrop of Mashhad's geo-political tensions, Zane had been able both to choreograph the killing and conceal his hand. He would have had no scruples about doing the same to Cassie. True, Zane acted as if Cassie was alive; in fact, seemed eager to find her. But that meant nothing, Jack now knew. Zane had acted that way about Danny as well. His pretense was easy to explain: he was using Jack to discover if his ancient crimes were coming to light.

On the other hand, Zane's cruelty and duplicity, his heroin operation and violence against Danny could have easily terrorized Cassie into vanishing. That meant she would have been alive to receive the letter he sent to Tehran General Delivery confirming his plans to meet her, and later the terrible letter that Helene had sent to her in Istanbul. Who knew where Cassie might have gone after receiving that one?

Jack replayed in his mind the few clues he had that she wasn't dead. Jahwed had confirmed that she had made it on the bus to Tehran, so she had survived Mashhad. It was a direct bus; an attack or accident en route would have been difficult for Zane to arrange at the last minute. In Tehran at the time, the State Department had a significant presence, and some record would have been made and sent to Washington if an American woman had died there. Yet Frank's inquiry had found none, and Becky had confirmed that there had been no State Department letter to her family. And there was that friend that Becky had mentioned, the one who thought he saw Cassie in Baton Rouge only a few years ago. It was about the same time her mother died, Jack suddenly realized. Surely that meant something.

So he wasn't ready yet to give up on the quest.

Ready or not, though, he had come back from Iran with little hope. Emotionally drained, he sensed he was at a dead end. Every trail had brought him tantalizingly close only to disappear, leaving him with more questions. Deb, in contrast, finally had answers, tragic as they were. She had closure, and he secretly envied that.

His lowest point occurred the previous Sunday, at Danny's memorial service in Ojai. Jack had flown into Santa Barbara and rented a car, but road construction slowed him and he arrived a few minutes late to the service. As unobtrusively as possible, he slipped into an aisle seat next to an elderly couple. After the service, the couple introduced themselves: they were from the old neighborhood. For years they had been looking out for Danny on Deb's behalf, in case he ever showed up.

And Jack had an epiphany: Neighbors. Someone who had lived across the way or down the street from Cassie's parents would know something about her. Even if she was in disguise with an invented name, they would have seen her visit. Even if she had died, they would know where she was buried. You can't keep secrets like that from old friends next door.

A few weeks earlier, such an epiphany would have triggered a shout of joy. This time, Jack's reaction was muted, guarded. This trip to Cassie's old neighborhood could be a fool's errand. Neighbors move away, they forget, they die. But this was all Jack could think to do. And so he was driving through southern Louisiana, the heavy August humidity outside fogging the air-conditioned glass of the car.

This time, though, he had taken precautions. He would no longer recklessly expose others to danger as he had with Jahwed in Iran; he had to assume Zane was tracking him. He mistrusted flying or taking his own vehicle, but the alternatives – bus or rental car – were also easily traced. He had mordantly joked with his friend Benjamin about hitch-hiking, when Ben insisted he borrow his car. Then Deb bought him a prepaid mobile phone, and Sandy sent the CD. Other than those three people, he told no one else about his plans, even Max. Making no advance hotel reservations and paying cash for food, gas and lodging, Jack was as far under the radar as a modern man could get.

Now he was getting near the end of his journey. Pine and cypress trees elbowed close to the interstate highway, suggestively draped in Spanish moss. Sprinkles of rain turned into mist on the hot pavement. A stork flew overhead. He left the interstate and drove through rural towns of chiropractor offices and beauty salons, churches, coffee shops and gas stations. He passed dozens of clapboard cottages with boats in their driveways. Finally, beyond the towns, came sugar cane fields, oil refineries, levees and loading docks. It was late afternoon when he came to the place he was looking for: Gonzales.

The internet had provided detailed directions to Rome Street. An aptly named road for Cassie the traveler, he thought, driving slowly past modest but well-kept homes, green lawns and carports with swings. He didn't need to check the street address; he knew it by heart. And there it was. With his heart racing, Jack parked Ben's car and just sat looking at the house. A large pear tree shaded one side; red lilies grew in wild profusion along the other. He imagined Cassie outside on the front steps, or picking pears, or washing the family car. This was where she did her homework, dressed for Sunday mass, dreamed her *National Geographic* dreams. But the house, once painted white and trimmed in blue, was aging; the grass was overgrown as well. The current occupants spent less time caring for the place than Pernina and Ulysses did, Jack could see. Then he noticed a tricycle and two kids' bikes on the lawn. Small children; no wonder the occupants didn't have time.

Small children, so probably no one associated with Cassie. Still, he had to ask. He unbuckled his seat belt, crossed the street and walked to the front door.

No luck there, nor at the house to the right. Newcomers to the neighborhood. Didn't know Mrs. Robinette, sorry. At the house on the left, a woman in a floral housecoat suggested he talk with the old lady across the street. She gestured at the house Jack had parked in front of.

"She's older than God," the woman joked, then looked around to ensure no one else heard the blasphemy.

Jack thanked her and made his way to the front porch. A sad pink geranium struggled next to the door, in need of watering. Still wrapped in pink foil, it probably had been a gift. He knocked. A shadowy form passed by a window. He knocked again. Older people often didn't like opening the door to strangers. Sure that he was being watched and assessed, he fixed a mild expression on his face and knocked a third time. The door opened a crack and an ancient face glared at him.

"I'm not in the market," she snapped.

"Excuse me?"

"For aluminum sliding or carpet cleaning or whatever you're selling."

"No, ma'am. I'm not selling anything."

He heard her groan. "Not anything to do with Jehovah or Jesus either. I'm busy. Go away."

"I will, I promise. I just have a quick question. You've been in this neighborhood a long time. You know a lot of the people around here."

She cautiously grunted in reply.

"I just wonder if you knew the neighbors across the street. The Robinettes?"

"Knew them? They were like kin to me," then she caught herself and shut up. "Why exactly are you asking, young man?"

He cleared his throat. This was the moment. "I'm an old friend of their daughter's, Cassandra. I'm looking for her. Do you kn...."

Before he could finish the word, she barked out, "She's dead."

"Dead?" He couldn't seem to understand what she was saying. "When?"

"Decades ago. Some place overseas." A grim set to her mouth when she said this. "Broke her parents' hearts."

"She can't be dead." Jack said it to himself, but she took it as a challenge.

"And why not? People die all the time, young man."

Still, he didn't want to believe it. His question came out in a voice soft and low, full of yearning, "Can I visit her grave?"

The woman shook her head vigorously. "They had her buried there. I can't help you."

And she slammed the door shut.

For a long time, Jack couldn't move, frozen in place, staring sightlessly at the wilted pink geranium. She had died, after all. Cassie had died. This isn't how a quest is supposed to end, he thought vaguely as a piercing sense of loss began to penetrate his thick denials. He was destined to find her, wasn't he? Wasn't he?

His legs shook as he slowly descended the porch steps and staggered to the car. His hands shook as he unlocked and opened the door. His body shook as he deposited himself on the driver's seat. Then, despair engulfing him, he slumped over the steering wheel and sobbed.

HOURS MAY HAVE passed, years. He wasn't sure when he heard a sharp rap on the car's window. Slowly, he lifted his head. A wizened face – the elderly neighbor's – peered at him through the glass.

"You all right?" she shouted.

He found he couldn't speak but he nodded and waved a hand to signify that he was on his way.

"No, you aren't. You better get out of that hot car." When he didn't move, she pulled open the driver's side door, tugged at his arm, a dead weight. "Get on out. It's probably 130 degrees in there, sunny day like this. You could get a heat stroke."

He had no will or energy to object, so when she tugged again, he reluctantly swung his legs out and hoisted himself upright. Dizziness hit and he had to steady himself against the scorching car roof.

"You better come on inside for water," she advised sternly. Then she stopped a moment and studied his face. "You been crying, son?"

Wiping his eyes with a fist, he shook his head no. "Just sweat," he insisted. He was well trained to deny tears.

Then she grabbed his arm and hauled him up the steps and through the front door, into a tidy and frigid living room. She gestured at a worn leather recliner. "Sit down while I get you a glass of water." He fell heavily into the chair and closed his eyes. He was soaked in sweat, still too hot to think.

"You were in that closed car for seven full minutes," she shouted from the kitchen.

He wondered, was that all?

Water droplets beaded the glass as he took it from her and drank in one long gulp. Immediately, his dizziness receded, but the icy water sparked a headache behind the eyes. "Thank you. I didn't realize how hot it was."

"Yes, sir, heat can kill you in no time." She perched on the edge of the sofa. "Do you need more water? Or I have iced tea." She grabbed his empty glass and, before he could reply, decamped to the kitchen again, returning in a minute with two glasses of iced tea.

While he sipped the tea – sweet, not with lemon as he usually drank it – he looked at his unlikely host for the first time. Her eyes were inquisitive, but her mouth puckered, as if holding back an acerbic remark. Grey hair was pinned carelessly into bun, with eyeglasses balanced atop her head. She wore capris and an oversized man's shirt, both splattered with bright patches of paint. On her feet were a pair of worn black athletic shoes without socks. The shoes were speckled with paint as well, as was one cheek, he suddenly realized.

"You're a painter," Jack noted. He was trying to recall something that Cassie had told him once.

"And you're a detective," she said with mild sarcasm.

He started to remember. "Cassie told me once that you did watercolors."

"Did she? Well, I used to. Now I use acrylic."

Suddenly he knew her name. "You're Miss Millie!"

She stared hard at him a moment before she confirmed. "Indeed, I am. Miz Millicent Boudreaux to you." From her pronunciation, he wasn't sure if it was Mrs., Miss or Ms.

"Are these your paintings?" He stood carefully and walked toward several framed watercolors. The subject matter was exotic: river markets, temples, a huge reclining Buddha. "Cassie wrote that you painted scenes from the photographs and postcards she sent home. These are very good."

"Did she?" the woman repeated. Frowning slightly, she added, "So, tell me, young man. Just how did you know Cassie? I don't remember you being part of her college crowd."

Turning to look at her, Jack deliberated how to explain. "I wasn't. We met later, when she was on her way overseas. We got to talking and became friends. Corresponded for a while and then lost touch." The explanation sounded shallow even to his own ears.

The woman didn't respond at first. Finally, finishing her glass of tea, she stood up. "Come look at this," and she led Jack into a neat bedroom where several acrylics hung, and one watercolor. "From the last card she sent. Some gigantic mosque in Herat, Afghanistan. You might recognize it."

Jack's heart pounded as he moved close to the watercolor. "Beautiful," he said.

She scoffed. "I'm a glorified draftsman. But Ca...." She stopped herself.

Her words didn't register. Jack was absorbed; this was Herat, a piece in the puzzle. "Do you still have the postcard?" he asked, not expecting she did.

"That's what I want to show you." She disappeared and he heard rummaging from down the hallway, probably in her studio. He returned to the living room to wait. It wasn't long.

Handing him the paint-smudged postcard, she said, "Read it. Cassie mentions you, I believe." Millicent reclaimed her spot on the sofa and watched him, head cocked like a bird's.

Aching with curiosity, he only glanced at the card's caption and the date in her handwriting: *Aug. 30.* He eagerly read her note. So Cassie was learning a little Dari; interesting. And the message confirmed what he already knew: Marton and Danny were there but not Ralph. Disappointed, he saw no mention of himself.

"So, which one of these two gentlemen are you?"

"Marton or Danny? Neither. I'm so sorry. I should have introduced myself. My name's Jack Hunter. Please, call me Jack."

Millicent leaned away from him, forehead creased, eyebrows drawn down. "You can't be," She flatly announced.

"I am."

With vehemence, she was shaking her head no. "Absolutely not. That man is dead for a fact." Her guard up, she glared at Jack. "Tell me the truth. Who are you?!"

Quickly, Jack drew his driver's license from his wallet and handed it to her. "That's me," he insisted.

"These things can be forged," she said, settling her glasses on her nose.

"I could show you the letters she sent me. They're in the car." He stood, ready to retrieve them.

"They could be stolen," she replied, and he sat back down.

Frustrated, he wished he had his regular mobile phone, so he could get online and show her his university web page.

Then, in a flash, he understood that her suspicions were a wonderful sign. She would only think him dead if she had heard it from Cassie. That meant Cassie had gotten Helene's letter in Istanbul and, in all likelihood, made it back to Louisiana.

Jack tried to suppress the dangerous and seductive hope he was beginning to feel. To garner information, though, he had to proceed carefully; Millicent Boudreaux was a formidable guardian.

"I'm Jack Hunter, and I'm not dead." he repeated. "Let me explain what happened. My former girlfriend got jealous. She sent Cassie a letter saying that I was dead." Jack didn't know if Millicent was listening as she continued to examine his license. By now, she had brought out a magnifying glass. He kept talking. "And when I didn't hear back from her, I thought Cassie was breaking things off. I was an idiot."

"Your former girlfriend," Millicent said with sharp disdain, "was extremely mean. I hope you broke things off with *her*."

"No, actually. I married her." He fell back on the recliner. "I only recently found out about her lies. We're getting divorced."

"Married her! You *are* an idiot." She handed back the license, "And I suppose you *might* be Jack Hunter."

"I'll tell you whatever you want to know, answer any questions, to reassure you I'm not a bad guy. I just desperately need to know if Cassie is all right."

Millicent opened her mouth but closed it without saying a word. Then she opened it again. "All right then. Let's see what you know about Cassie, if you really were her friend. What's the name of the girl she stayed with in Bangkok?"

"Becky Dehart, a friend she met at Loyola. She married a man from the Mexican consulate in Bangkok. Her married name is Becky Gonzales." Jack had an idea. "You can call her, if you like. She'll confirm who I am."

"Do I look like a fool? Whoever you dial would confirm it, wouldn't they?" Jack lamely nodded and Millicent continued. "Did Cassie go to the wedding?"

"No, Becky never heard from her again after she and Ralph left Bangkok."

"That year she was traveling, where did she spend her birthday?"

Jack remembered the letter. "At the Oriental Hotel in Bangkok, with Becky and some others." He stood and walked to one of the watercolors in the living room. "This is it. She must have sent her parents a postcard."

Millicent stayed seated. "She sent that one to me. Okay, then. What was her college major?"

"Film studies. She wanted to make documentaries." Jack reclaimed his seat.

"Was Cassie an only child?"

He paused. "She had an older brother. He was killed when she was a kid. Car accident, I think."

"What was his name?"

That stumped him. Jack could not recall his name.

"When she was growing up, what was the name of her cat?"

"I don't know. She never talked about her cat." He felt miserable; he was failing the test.

"Cassie was pretty devout. I suppose she told you."

This one startled Jack. "Not when I met her. She talked about searching. She talked about distrusting religious institutions and leaders. She seemed to be struggling with faith, actually." He wondered if it was the right thing to say. Cassie may not have told family and close friends her true views. His interrogator paused thoughtfully. He thought he saw her nod; perhaps Cassie had told her.

Finally Millicent asked, "Why was she off traipsing around the world?"

Jack could almost hear Cassie's voice. "She'd wanted to travel since she was little. Since seeing photographs in *National Geographic*." He glanced again at the watercolors. "But it was more than just curiosity or adventure. There was a poem she liked, Robert Louis Stevenson. Something about feeling globe granite underfoot." That phrase in particular had stayed with him; it had reminded him of hiking part of the John Muir Trail when he himself was in college. "To experience the whole range and scope of life. She said that was why she traveled."

In a gentler voice now, Millicent said, "I gave her that poetry book for her twelfth birthday." She seemed briefly engaged in an internal argument, but Jack could see in her face that trust was winning over skepticism. Finally, she said kindly, "Okay, Mr. Hunter. Tell me about yourself."

He described his work at the university, his children, his decision to find Cassie after all these years. Then he recapped his findings to date: what he had learned from Becky, Ralph, Deb and Jahwed. What he knew of Cassie's time with Marton Zambo, and Zambo's new name. He produced the photos he had gotten from Jahwed and used them to illustrate his tale. Jack was tempted to edit his remarks, to exclude references to heroin and Danny's murder. He didn't want to upset her. But he sensed that Millicent would know instantly if he did. Keeping her trust was essential, and that meant telling the full truth. In any event, once he had finished, Millicent hadn't seemed surprised.

"And now you would like to know what happened to her." Millicent concluded.

"Yes, very much. I've realized something the past few months, in re-reading her letters, remembering our talks, meeting people who knew her. I've realized how much she meant to me, still means to me." He paused. "I've realized I've been in love with her from the start."

Millicent hadn't seemed surprised by this either. "Well, she told me once she loved you. It was a real shame you died when you did."

Jack looked down at his hands, her words stirring a complex brew of recrimination, sorrow and joy.

The old woman seemed caught in a similarly strange mood. "We were neighbors almost fifty years," she said. "Her mother was closer than a sister to me." She had to clear her throat before she could continue; Pernina's death was still a fresh grief. "And Cassie herself was special, but I guess you know that. When she came back home that time, she was in a terrible state. So skinny, no bigger than a minute. This horrible cigarette burn on her wrist, it almost went plum through her arm. And she was so very very sad. I've never seen anybody so sad, and I've been on this earth a long time. She'd just gotten that god-awful letter from your so-called girlfriend. She'd gone to Istanbul expecting to find you and instead there was that letter." She paused, lost in painful thought for the moment.

Jack burned with regret. Why hadn't he gone straightaway to Istanbul? Why had he waited for a specific date or place to meet? He could have wandered the streets until he found her.

Millicent took a deep breath. "She was bad off, but she was going to be okay. Her folks and I spent days with her, trying to cheer her up, setting up a slide show of her travel photos, making her favorite food to coach her to eat. It was just the three of us; she didn't want to see anybody else, not until she was better. We respected that."

Jack could no longer contain himself. "She came home. She's alive."

"I didn't say that, did I?" Millicent snapped. After a moment, she started her story again, "Anyway, things got really bad after that…" Suddenly, she stood. "I'm sorry, I can't go on just yet. I need a little time. Maybe I'll go and clean my brushes out. Everything's still a mess from when you showed up."

Distraught and confused by what he had heard so far, Jack stood with her. "I'll help. It's my fault things are a mess." He followed to what had originally been the master bedroom, a large room with north facing windows. Her studio. His eyes barely registered his surroundings, but he did as she directed. Together, they cleaned brushes, put away paints, stacked canvases, tossed old rags. The task took twenty minutes, but Millicent still wasn't ready to talk about Cassie. Instead, she suggested they have supper. Jack wasn't hungry, but when he saw on his watch that it was past five, he realized that Millicent might be.

"Let me take you out to dinner," he said. She frowned, so he added, "Or I can go and get us some take-out. What do you like to eat?"

"I have a better idea," she said and marched purposely toward the kitchen. "If you don't mind leftovers, I've got a big pot of jambalaya in the refrigerator. My art students had a party the other day and we all brought too much food."

"Sounds like fun," Jack said amiably. He liked the image of Millicent Boudreaux socializing at a young person's party. As he dished jambalaya on plates to be microwaved, he asked, "You still teach?"

"Of course! How else do you think I can afford art supplies?" She laughed, "And you know what they say: Young people keep you young. You must know that. You're a teacher yourself."

Dinner was a relief from the intensity of the afternoon. The jambalaya was well-seasoned and the conversation pleasant. They talked about everything except the topic that was tearing Jack up inside. He carried the empty plates to the kitchen and began to wash them.

"I can do that," Millicent said fussily, reaching vainly for the dish cloth. "In my house, guests don't do their own dishes."

Refusing to relinquish his position in front of the sink, Jack shrugged. "Then I suppose I'm not a guest. Not any longer." He gave her a sly smile. "I could be your apprentice."

"Ha! You don't know the first thing about art. But I'll tell you what. I'll make us a cup of coffee. And there's leftover bread pudding."

WITH A SECOND cup of chicory coffee, Jack and Millicent returned to the living room. She turned on a lamp and closed the drapes.

"That will give the neighbors something to talk about, me entertaining a young man with the curtains closed!" The idea seemed to delight her. Then she turned serious again. She sighed, "I need to start where I left off. Cassie at home, slowly mending."

This time, Jack said nothing to interrupt the story.

"She wanted to reach this fellow she had traveled with. I didn't know his name, but it must have been the one you mentioned. Danny. Anyway, she called his house in California and his parents told her about him being murdered. In the same town and on the same day she ran away from that Marton Zambo. Well, she went hysterical. Danny had been killed, you had been killed. She didn't have proof, she said, but she knew this Zambo fellow had somehow murdered you both."

"Wait. I was murdered?" This wasn't how Jack had imagined his death in Helene's letter. He had thought pneumonia or a car crash.

"Drive by shooting in your own neighborhood!"

A violent death. Jack was appalled.

Millicent continued. "When she was hiding in that hotel kitchen in Iran, that vile man tried to get her to come out by threatening her family and you by name. So then she got away and two people she cared about were immediately murdered. She'd expected him to hunt her down, but now he was hurting others. That was why she had to disappear."

Silence. A car drove by outside, its radio blasting the blues in the August evening. Silence again.

Millicent finally picked up the thread. "First thing, she begged us to tell everyone she was dead. She thought that would keep them safe, and her too. Then, as soon as she was feeling a little stronger, she had her mother drive her into Baton Rouge and she filed the paperwork to change her name. She wanted her parents to do it too, but her daddy wasn't about to let go of his Cajun heritage." She leaned toward Jack, conspiratorially, "Secretly, I think he wanted the man to come looking for her. I think he wanted to kill him for doing what he did." She stopped and took a sip of the now lukewarm coffee.

"Is she still alive?" Jack whispered.

This time, Millicent didn't rebuke him; she simply nodded.

Jack wanted to feel elated; Cassie had come home and planned her own disappearance. Instead, he felt sickened and disgusted with his own unwitting role in the tragedy. And it was a tragedy: Cassie had spent most of her life cut off from her oldest friends and much of her family. Living a falsehood; always in fear of discovery. What that must have cost her, isolated from her community and her past, terrified that somehow, someday, Marton Zambo would appear.

"It must have been heartbreaking for her and her parents," he said and Millicent nodded. "Rarely seeing them. Even having to go in disguise to their funerals."

"Oh, Lord, she didn't attend their funerals. And it was a good thing too!"

"What?"

"She could sneak in to see them in the nursing home, because there are so many other folks around. But only a dozen or so went to her mother's funeral; so many old friends have already passed, you know. Cassie would have stood out like a sore thumb. She really wanted to go, poor thing, got mad as a hornet with me when I stopped her. But it was good she didn't. A man was waiting there, at the cemetery, someone I'd never seen before."

"Her mother's doctor, maybe?" He thought Millicent might be overreacting.

"Nope. Pernina and I had the same doctor." She clutched his wrist and pushed her face close to his. "I'm telling you this man wasn't from around here. And listen to this: when he saw me looking at him, he came right up and asked about any kin coming to the funeral, so he could pay his respects. He lied and said he was a family friend from way back."

Jack caught his breath. "He knew Cassie was her daughter?! He tracked her down?!"

Millicent released his wrist. "No, I don't think so. I pointed out a few of the nieces and nephews attending, and told him that was it. He gave his condolences to them and left before Pernina was even in the ground. I think he was trawling. You know, going to things like Robinette funerals, seeing what fish showed up in the net."

"Red-headed man?" Jack could imagine an unctuous Clive Riley in a black suit.

Millicent shook her head. "Tall African American. Ramrod straight and good looking. I thought about asking if he'd pose for me when I first saw him."

Jack considered the description. "It might be a man who works for Marton Zane in Vancouver, Canada, name of Lawrence Williams."

Millicent grunted. "Yep, a foreign spy. I should have guessed it. He didn't even know how to pronounce Pernina's name. He called her Per-Neena," she scoffed. "Some family friend!"

Like the way that Jack had pronounced it in his head when he had first read the name, not like Becky Gonzales or Millicent did, Per-Nine-ah.

So, he thought, Zane had sent one of his henchmen to Cassie's mother's funeral. Maybe the man had gone to dozens of funerals around the country through the years, on the off chance that Cassie would attend. That meant Zane was unrelenting, still looking.

"I guess now you want to know her new name and how to reach her." Millicent leaned back on the sofa and waited. She trusted him now; she would tell him anything.

Jack sat silently and thought about it. He wanted so much to know. But now he fully understood the stakes, and he reluctantly shook his head no. "Honestly, you surprise me," Millicent said. "I thought you'd jump at the chance."

"Before I heard about Danny in Iran, I would have. Even driving here, I imagined seeing her again, telling her how I feel. But I keep thinking about what you said, how much she's given up to keep herself and others safe. In fact, I think…," he caught his breath and looked away. "I think it's too risky for me to know. I'd just want to see her. Without intending to, I'd lead Zane right to her door."

"But isn't that why you came here, to find her?"

"I guess it will have to be enough to know she's alive somewhere in the world."

Millicent made no reply. She pursed her lips, knitted her brows. From the coffee table, she picked up one of the photos he had brought, the one of Cassie on the hill above Kabul. She stared hard at the image.

"Did she ever marry? Have children?" Jack asked. He wanted to imagine a happy life.

She glanced up at him now and shook her head no, then returned to studying the photograph. "Her heart's in her work. She's very good, you know." In a moment, she mused, "And I don't think she ever felt safe enough."

"Safe enough?" He asked. To fall in love? To start a family? He wondered if it was because of Zane, or because of him. He waited but Millicent didn't elaborate. Her large living room clock loudly marked the passing minutes.

Eventually Jack accepted that there was nothing more to say. The sky was getting dark, he could see through the crack between the drapes. "I'd better be off. I can't thank you enough for talking with me. And for a great dinner." He stood to go. He had passed a motel on his drive in; he would stop there.

"Hold on a minute," Millicent said. "Please. I've been looking at this photo, at Cassie's wonderful smile. I have to tell you I haven't seen her smile like that in ages. Probably not since she came back home." She patted the sofa cushion for Jack to sit next to her and handed him the photograph to show him the radiant smile. "You know, your death almost destroyed her. Maybe your resurrection wouldn't be such a bad thing."

Incredulous, he stared at her. "What are you saying? Are you telling me to see her? Even after what I've told you?"

"I can't tell you to do anything. All I'm saying is that you may be Cassie's best chance of being happy again. I'm going to show you something and then you make up your own mind about what to do."

No, he didn't want to see anything. He knew himself; he knew he wouldn't be able to resist going to her. Yet he didn't stop Millicent. He felt himself tremble with anticipation and fear and love as she walked back to the studio.

In a few minutes, Millie emerged with an ordinary envelope. "She lives in Denver now, but has mail forwarded from Chicago." She extracted a folded page and handed it to him. "This arrived last Wednesday."

He unfolded the letter. For a minute, he could only stare at Cassie's handwriting; it hadn't changed in all these years. At the top was the date, early last week. He swallowed hard and began to read:

> *Dear Millicent:*
>
> *It's happening! The four-city exhibit in Central Europe that I told you about. I've just finalized the last details with the Museum of Photography in Berlin. The organizers are calling it Gray Ghosts: Women in War. It's not what I would have cho-*

sen. I think the word "ghosts" minimizes the women, downplays their agency & vitality. But the sponsors like the name so I agreed. We're including a few works by some of the early war-time women photojournalists: Françoise Demulder & Cathy Le Roy in Vietnam, Lee Miller in World War II. It's humbling to be in their company.

The show opens in Bratislava on August 16, at the Slovak Union of Visual Arts. I've known one of the Slovak photographers for more than a decade, since we worked together in Bosnia. He's helping me set it up. After that, the exhibit travels to Prague in early October, Berlin in January and February, and closes in Vienna next spring. The Grand Tour!

I'm excited but also nervous. I've never thought of my work as particularly artistic. I just snap pictures and hope for the best. (I know you're shaking your head right now.) If only you could be at the opening, it would be perfect. You were the one who first taught me composition, color and contrast. And the importance of ethics in the creative process. This honor re-ally belongs to you.

I'll write again from Bratislava. Meanwhile, take care of your health. High blood pressure is serious.

I miss you so much.

Kas

Kas. The same first name but different enough that it wouldn't automatically pop up on internet search engines. Jack could find her, if he was very careful, if he completely covered his tracks. He had a place and a date, only two weeks away. He lay the letter down, his heart pounding. War photography, not filmmaking. A high-risk profession but the choice made some sense; she loved travel and photography, and she was fearless. He looked up at Millicent.

"Thank you."

Without speaking, she handed him the envelope. He glanced at the return address, a Chicago post office box. And above that, a name; a name that stopped him cold. He read it a second time. The last name Kas had chosen was Hunter.

"Yes," Millicent said when she saw his stunned expression. "She took your name. I suppose it was her way of keeping you alive."

CHAPTER NINETEEN

August 11, 2007

Saturday

You look wonderful, younger than ever," Alexej said, his eyes flickering from the road to her face. Large and still muscular at forty, head shaved, Alex had an intimidating demeanor to those who didn't know him. But Kas saw only the gifted photographer and gentle intellectual.

She smiled at the compliment; she knew better. Through the years she had ignored doing many of the things that would have maintained a youthful appearance - the skin care, the hair coloring. But she didn't mind how she looked. Trekking beside refugees and squatting on dirt floors had kept her tan and agile. With water often too scarce for daily showers, she wore her hair in a boyish cut, the pale honey color shot through now with silver. She'd dispensed with eyeglasses too, because she kept breaking or losing them, so she had had laser eye surgery several years before. She didn't look bad for fifty-two, she thought, but she didn't look wonderful.

Still, it was a nice thing for Alex to say.

"Fatherhood suits you," she replied. "How old is your daughter now?"

"Andrea's six," he said proudly, "You'll see her when you come to dinner tonight." He added, "Martina is looking forward to meeting you at last." Martina was his wife.

"Me, too," she said. "I've brought her a gift." She showed him: French perfume from duty free.

He was impressed. "She'll like that. Much better than what I bring her."

"Laundry and lice," she laughed, an old joke about their typical souvenirs from work in the field. "I also have a Dr. Seuss book for Andrea," she added. "I hope she can read a little English."

Alexej grinned. "She's learning in school already. It's perfect." He looked over at her again. "It's good to have you here, Kas."

She agreed. It felt good to be here, almost like seeing family. She and Alex had gotten close covering the siege of Sarajevo in the early 1990s. An intense time: his first conflict, and her fourth. Since then, she had covered six more, but Alex had left the profession in late 2000, soon after Martina became pregnant. Kas considered that she might have made the same choice, if she'd ever had a child. But the question was moot; she hadn't met the right man. Or, rather, she hadn't even been looking. And a child without a life partner seemed singularly impractical, given her profession.

As the outskirts of Vienna flew past, she turned to look at Alex's profile. "Thanks for picking me up at the airport. I could have caught the train."

He gave a dismissive scowl. "How can you say that? You're my secret lucky charm. Of course, I would pick you up." He adroitly eased the car onto the main highway north, heading toward Bratislava, less than an hour away. "By the way, your crates arrived last week, safe and sound. The pieces you selected are very powerful."

"Terrific. Thanks."

Alex frowned slightly in thought. "Martina asked me an interesting question about you. She asked me why you do this, photographing war. She says with men it's easy to understand. We like the adrenalin and think we're invulnerable; we want to prove our virility. But a woman?"

"That's a pretty harsh judgment about men. Is that why you did it?"

"No, I just needed a job."

"Ha!" She grinned. She knew he had been as committed as she was, until the baby came. "Women and men aren't so very different, you know. Maybe I think I'm invulnerable, too," she joked.

"And maybe you are," he said, suddenly serious. "In Bosnia, I watched you. Even when you were focused on a shot, you still were aware of everything around you, like a sixth sense. Remember when you insisted we leave the wreckage of that school? We had been working there for hours and suddenly you said we had to leave. Immediately. I argued, but we did. And it was just in time."

Kas did remember. "I was lucky. We both were."

"There were other times too. It's as if you have a personal radar constantly scanning the perimeter. A very useful talent in a war zone. But it still doesn't answer why you do it."

Why, indeed. In the early years, when women war photographers were rare, she used to get asked that question a lot. So her answer now was sincere but well-rehearsed: "So much suffering in war is invisible, of families, of communities. It needs to be documented, honored, recompensed if possible, and, eventually, stopped." She paused when she caught sight of jagged stone ruins atop a lushly green hill. To her, the view wasn't serene and quaint; instead, she imagined the battle that had crumbled those walls. It was a reminder that even castles provided little security to those huddled within. Turning away, she said with more vehemence than she intended. "I hate the euphemism 'collateral damage', how we excuse our carnage against the innocent. I want my images to expose - no, to eviscerate that damn term."

Alex nodded; he felt it, too. And it was all true; the reason behind her work. Yet the full answer to the question of her motivation was more complex and selfish, and Kas didn't share it with anyone, even Alex. She only realized it herself after she had been covering combat for a decade.

What drove her was a deeply felt need to atone for running away, for surviving Marton Zambo. In saving herself by fleeing Mashhad, she had abandoned Jack and Danny to his rage. This wasn't specula- tion; she *knew* that somehow he had them killed. Afterward, guilt and shame had kept her silent, kept her from contacting their families or informing the police. She had felt complicit. She tried to justify her silence to herself: what evidence did she have? Who would believe her?

Now, decades later, she understood she put herself in harm's way out of some vague notion of serving the greater good: this had seemed the best way to make amends and restore her sense of dignity and worth.

It had basically worked. She had a more dispassionate view of the past now and a clearer understanding of the mechanics and mo- mentum of violence, of her own victimhood. And that made her more forgiving of the silly girl who had set out to travel the globe.

And, yet, she still wished she had acted differently, more honora- bly, starting in Kabul, starting with Ralph. She shifted uncomfortably in the car seat, recognizing a creeping, insistent remorse. The camel's nose under the tent, she thought wryly. She had to stop it. Remorse was an indulgence. She consciously shifted mental gears.

By now, they were on the outskirts of a city. "This is Bratislava?" she asked. The dense community of high rises reminded her of the outskirts of Seoul; hives for the city's productive bees.

"No, Bratislava is still ahead, across the Danube. See the castle?"

This one was intact, rising like a square white cake on the city's highest hill. No whimsical spires, no dragon lairs. The castle was substantial and imposing from miles away, suitable for the coronation of Habsburg kings. And, of course, the famous Habsburg Queen, Maria Theresa.

"What the hell...?" She pointed. The castle was threatened by a space ship?

Alex laughed. "It's a bar and restaurant, built at the top of Novy Most, the new bridge. It's called the UFO bar, of course. Across the bridge is Bratislava. You can start to see the Old Town. Right now we're driving through Petržalka."

The name disturbed a memory. "Petržalka," she repeated out loud, feeling the unusual sounds of the word, remembering where she had first felt those sounds in her mouth.

"You know the place?" Alex was surprised.

"Someone I met a long time ago came from there."

What was this? She ordinarily went months without thinking of Zambo, and now he had twice intruded on her thoughts. When she first arrived home, she had thought of him constantly, her pulse racing and hands shaking at the least noise. But she had seen a therapist for a few months and then landed a job and years passed. With enough time, even terror can lose its teeth, particularly since she had spent decades facing worse fears and documenting worse horrors than Marton Zambo's. It wasn't that she ever forgave or even understood him. She simply stopped bowing to his power. She was free. At most, he was a specter who lurked late at night when she had drunk too much.

Except this was the specter's hometown. Kas stared out at the refurbished apartment blocks and a posh riverside shopping mall. When agreeing to the exhibit, she had not envisioned Bratislava so close to Petržalka. Now she wondered if it would have made a difference, if she would have declined to come. No, she decided, she was still glad to be here. Not only was Alex a good friend, he was part of an innovative Central European photo cooperative. When the cooperative extended this opportunity to show her work, she instantly agreed. This exhibit would expose a broader audience to the message she wanted to convey about war.

As far as Zambo went, he was most likely dead; she hadn't found any mention of him in her casual searches over the years. Even if he was still alive, he was unlikely to have returned to Petržalka. She remembered his disdain for his father, his grief over the dead girl. This wasn't a place of happy memories for him.

Besides, she reminded herself, he had no power over her now.

For her mother and Millicent, though, Zambo had remained an active threat, a fat alligator on shore feigning sleep. Kas may have gotten past Zambo, but they hadn't. For their sake, she had kept a low profile during her visits, balking only once. It was over her mother's funeral. She was getting ready to go when Millicent stopped her and fiercely insisted that she stay away. They argued. In frustrated tears, Kas finally relented. Later, Millie concocted some tale about an agent of Zambo's lurking about the gravesite. Kas knew it was cognitive dissonance; Millie had to believe her paranoia was justified. Kas still mourned not going, but she couldn't stay angry at her old friend. With her parents both dead, she knew Millie saw herself as the last of Kas' guardians.

That's what made Millie's most recent letter so curious.

ACROSS THE DANUBE now, they pulled off the main highway that sliced through the Old Town, and turned right along the river, on a road named for Dostoyevsky. Alexej pointed out the Union of Slovak Arts, where a massive banner proclaimed that the show – her show – would open in less than a week. Kas was surprised at her delight.

"There isn't much left to do," Alex explained as he parked the car on the sidewalk in front. "You'll only have to approve the placement and lighting, edit the English language exhibit guide, and give media interviews."

"No photos of me, though," she said simply. An old habit of invisibility.

"Yes, I remember." He smiled indulgently. "Just of works from the exhibit."

As he opened the car's back door to retrieve her bag, Alex motioned with his chin across the street. "That's where you'll be staying. Convenient, isn't it? A great friend of the arts and her husband have loaned us the apartment for a few weeks. She doesn't speak English but her husband does; he's a retired school principal. I'm sure you'll have a chance to meet. They live in the next block."

Kas followed him across the street. Once he had unlocked an inconspicuous door, they passed through an entry hall to an elevator almost as old as Millicent. Alex manually closed its door behind them and the elevator jerked and clanged its way upward. When they emerged at last on the seventh floor, he closed the elevator door again, so it would be primed for its next passenger. They stood in a small dim hallway, with doors to two apartments barely visible. Alex unlocked the one on the right of the elevator and Kas went in.

She stopped, amazed at the contrast. The apartment was bright and airy, with a full bank of windows reflecting the late afternoon light. The living room's furniture was sleek and modern; bold abstract paintings hung on its white walls. As Kas started to enter, Alexej smiled and pointed at the white carpet, then at her sandals. Of course. She slipped them off and felt plush softness beneath bare feet. At the bank of windows, she gazed down at the Union of Slovak Arts, then at the Danube itself, a glinting belt of pewter. Ships passed in transit from Vienna to Budapest and beyond. She was mesmerized.

"What a perfect place," she murmured without turning around. "Thank you."

"Thank your hosts. They really are wonderful. But rest for now. You've had a long flight. I'll be back at seven to pick you up."

She hardly heard Alex, and then he was gone.

An hour later, she was unpacked and contemplating the bed. But she didn't feel sleepy. Instead, she gravitated to the window, opened the letter from Millicent and read again the last paragraph.

I am so proud of you! I really wish I could come to Bratislava but the doctor won't let me fly. I considered using my old broom stick, but the magic has worn off. So I'm sending a proxy, who is a new friend of mine and an old friend of yours. I know you'll be busy with the show, but please hear him out. He has an important message.

Forehead against the glass, she puzzled what Millicent could mean. Whom did she like enough, trust enough, to send in her stead? And what new friend of Millie's could also be an old friend of hers? Could it be Ralph, or an earlier boyfriend from Loyola? She didn't think so; Millie generally hadn't liked her boyfriends. Maybe Rene, the boy down the street? She and Rene used to build forts together in Millie's backyard.

And what could be the important message?

A knock interrupted her thoughts.

Kas opened the door to an older man in a pullover gray sweater and navy slacks.

He smiled. "Hello. I am Professor Viliam Kováč. I welcome you to Bratislava."

She realized immediately it was her host. "Thank you," she said eagerly. "Please come in, Professor Kovax."

He gently corrected her pronunciation and then added, "You call me Viliam, please." He stepped on to the tiled entrance.

She smiled. "Viliam, may I offer you coffee or tea?" Only when she spoke did she realize that she did not know if either was in the kitchen.

"No, no. But I thank you." He paused, frowning a little as he formed sentences. "Alexej say many good things about you. He was student to me many years ago. Also, my wife like your work very much. We are happy you come." He spoke carefully, as if rediscovering and dusting off a language long buried at Babel.

"I am delighted to be here," Kas answered truthfully. "You speak English well."

He shook his head. "Not so well. I learn long time ago. Sixty years, when I was young man at school."

Sixty years. That meant he was born perhaps eighty years ago, during the last days of the Austro-Hungarian Empire. After that was a brief romance with democracy, before the Nazis came and war, then the communists and Cold War. He had lived through tumultuous times.

He continued, "I am asking you to please come to dinner with my wife and me on Tuesday."

This was an unexpected treat. Kas smiled, "I would love to. Thank you for the invitation." It would be chance to thank his wife as well. And she was curious about her hosts, how they had survived the twentieth century.

He clapped his hands. "Excellent. Please come at seven." Handing her a note with an address carefully printed in English, he added, "Not so far away."

"I will be there at seven on Tuesday. You are very kind."

Once he'd left, Kas turned to the kitchen to check supplies. A package of coffee had been left for her, salami and a loaf of bread; in the refrigerator was butter, cream and a block of cheese marked Emmenthaler. Someone was taking care of her. As unaccustomed as she was to this, it felt nice.

344 | N. V. BAKER

KAS SPENT MONDAY and Tuesday at the gallery working with the staff. On Tuesday evening, she found the right address and knocked on the door, bearing gifts: a bag of chocolates and a highly recommended bottle of red wine, an Alibernet. It paired perfectly with the goulash Magdalena Kovacova had made.

Dinner conversation was lively, as Kas and Magdalena talked about art and photography by cobbling together a common tongue composed of bits of German and Spanish and French, with Viliam occasionally providing a necessary translation. Then, after dinner, the three of them sat in the living room, finishing dessert, while Viliam brought out a bottle of golden liquor, a slice of pear floating on the bottom. "Hruska," he explained as he poured each of them a small shot. Finally, with the liquor, he explained how he and Magdalena had met while he was principal of a gymnazium in Petržalka.

Once again, Zambo's memory pushed in. "I met a man once from Petržalka. He went to school there," Kas blurted out. Instantly, she regretted mentioning him. She had been swept up in the wine and warm feelings. Now she wondered, what if they knew him? What if they were friends? Almost as quickly, she scolded herself, what if they were? That didn't mean Viliam and Magdalena were part of some conspiracy to catch her. She would not distrust them; she would not become imprisoned by paranoia like Millicent.

Viliam shrugged. "I was only principal there until 1970. So he was before this? Or later?" he asked with mild curiosity.

Kas didn't see how she could avoid answering. "Before, maybe early 1968. He said he was good in math."

Suddenly Viliam seemed alert. He leaned close. "What was this man's name?"

Kas hesitated, then decided it was too late to prevaricate. "Marton Zambo."

Viliam fell back in his chair. "Marton Zámbó?! But I know this man! He went to my school." He paused, briefly lost in old memories "Very intelligent boy, gifted in mathematics. He won Prague competition that year. We were all very proud." He quickly translated their conversation for Magdalena. Admiration tinged his voice still.

Zambo was gifted; he had won. The news was somewhat of a surprise to Kas. She remembered Marton being aggrieved over the competition, over his life in general, over not receiving sufficient respect.

Viliam continued, "I cannot recall the father. He was alcoholic, I think. But the mother was important in the party. Marton had a place at Comenius University. I was surprised he left."

Another interesting detail, that Marton's mother was a party functionary and Marton had opportunities. Any vestige of pity Kas might have harbored toward him – as a poor discounted boy – disappeared. She was suddenly curious about what else he had fabricated about his past. "So he fled after Prague Spring, when the Soviets cracked down on the protestors?"

"No, no. Before Prague Spring. He was not part of Prague Spring." Here, Viliam stopped and spoke briefly again with his wife. "My wife went to school with his mother, so we know him as a child. How did you meet him? Is he well?"

"I don't know where he is now." Kas shivered at the surreal nature of the conversation. "I met him in 1978 when I was traveling in Central Asia. He had settled in Canada by then. I suppose he is still there."

The old man wandered again into his memories. "Marton Zámbó. He left when his girlfriend was killed."

"Killed? I knew she died; that's all he said." Kas was sliding into memories as well, disturbing ones. "He said her name was Katarina."

He frowned. "Katarina? I do not know. Well, it was long time ago. I remember she was murdered. A very sad story."

Their conversation veered now back to the exhibit, and the sad story was never told.

THE NEXT MORNING, Kas woke to the door's buzzer. She slipped on a robe and slippers, with a slight headache from the previous evening's wine. In the door stood the professor, carrying a bag of pastries and a file folder.

"Good morning!" he chirped.

"Good morning to you, too. Would you like a coffee?"

"Yes, please," he said, slipping off his shoes and following her into the narrow kitchen.

Kas set up the coffee maker as he sat at the kitchen table and arranged the pastries on a plate. The file folder lay next to him. She wondered what was in it, what he was doing here.

As she poured their cups of coffee, he told her. "I think about your Katarina last night. I don't sleep so well at my age. So I go to my basement, where we store old things. My wife say I should throw these old things away, but I cannot." He took a bite of pastry, then gently brushed crumbs from his mouth. "I found box of student records from gymnazium. And I have found the girl!"

With a triumphant flourish, Viliam drew from the folder a single page yellowed with age. He turned it toward Kas; it was a list of pupils. He pointed, "There. Katarina Petras."

The Katarina, Kas realized, Zambo's lost love.

"She was so young to die," Viliam continued.

"Young?"

He thought a moment, "She was fifteen. Most sad. The body … what is word for when body is examined?"

"The autopsy?"

"Yes. They discover she is pregnant."

Kas ached; too young to die and too young to be pregnant. Zambo would have been two years older, not yet an adult himself, but what was he doing having sex with a child? Kas considered: was this how he saw her in Afghanistan, when he compared her to Katarina?

Viliam leaned across the table toward her. "As soon as I read her name, I remember everything. The building superintendent crush her throat on roof of apartment building. This was soon after Marton returned so happy from winning math competition."

"The building superintendent?" Again, Kas was revising her suspicions about Zambo. Perhaps he was the victim he portrayed.

"Yes. He had key to roof, and his telephone number found in her pocket. He deny it, say he always love Katarina as a little girl."

"And he was convicted?"

"No, no. He hanged – hung? - himself in jail. I remember Marton took her death very hard. Police were sympathetic and not question him long."

Of course they would be, Kas thought, cynicism returning. A star student, the child of a politically connected mother, grieving for his girlfriend and their future child. She didn't need to revise her suspicions at all. The note with the phone number seemed circumstantial at best; further, she didn't doubt that Zambo could have planted it. And he certainly could have lifted the roof key from an unwitting superintendent.

Her imagination played out the scene on the roof: Marton confronting Katarina because he didn't want a child. Being a father would preclude college and the brilliant career he expected. Then Kas had a more disturbing thought, that Marton wanted a child but Katarina didn't. A brief scrap of memory broke through from the drive to Herat. Zambo had questioned her about having children, seemingly displeased she had an IUD. As she discovered soon enough, he assumed he had the right to control her. What if Katarina had felt trapped by him and wanted an abortion? Kas knew he might become enraged enough to kill her.

IT WAS THURSDAY afternoon and tomorrow the exhibit would open. Kas stretched; she had been hunched over the desk in a back office of the gallery too long, pen in hand, editing her remarks for the next day's opening reception. She could hear movement in the adjacent hall as Alex and two others finished hanging her work. On the floor next to her was a box of English language guides to the exhibit. Everything was almost ready.

Alexej abruptly appeared in the doorway. "Someone is here to see you." His voice carried meaning; she had told him a little about her ancient encounter with Marton Zambo, how she used to be so afraid. She had told him because some of the fear was creeping back, and she was trying hard to suppress it.

"Where?" she asked. "What does he look like?" Just in case. If he had pale blue eyes, Alex would remember. He had an excellent visual memory.

Alex shrugged. "American, a little shorter than me, dark hair and beard, some grey. He's in the lobby, outside of the gallery," and he gestured. "Do you want me to come with you?"

She knew her fear was irrational, so she shook her head no. It didn't sound like Zambo. "I'll be okay. But if I scream bloody murder …." She smiled a little when she said this.

He smiled too. "I'll come riding to the rescue on my white dragon."

Kas passed through the high-ceilinged exhibit space, well-lit from the partial glass roof on the structure's north side. A man in a leather jacket and jeans stood in the entry lobby, his back to her as he studied the poster advertising her show. It was probably the mystery man Millicent had mentioned, the one with the important message. As she neared, she could see his profile more clearly. He seemed vaguely familiar. Millie had said he was an old friend, but that didn't help. A fellow photographer? And then he turned.

"Hi, Cassie," he said.

And she stopped dead. She knew the face instantly. Except that it couldn't be his face. "Oh, God."

"Hardly," a self-deprecating joke. "It's me, Jack Hunter."

Who the hell was this? Had Marton found a look-alike? Was it a trick of her crazy wishful thinking? Could this be the man who had fooled Millicent, who was impossible to fool? A confused panic started filling her chest, closing her throat. Kas took a step back as the man took a step forward.

"No, you can't be." She turned, shaking, toward the outside door. She couldn't breathe; she had to get outside, out of this confined space.

"I am Jack." He insisted. "I'm not dead. I've been looking for…"

She didn't hear the rest. Without another word, Kas was out the door and down the flight of steps to the sidewalk. Without thinking, she turned right toward the old tram bridge over the Danube. She needed a moment – a year, a lifetime – to process this. She needed to be alone.

She heard steps behind her. Without thinking, she started to sprint.

His death had cost her so much. If it was Jack, where had he been? Why had he let her suffer so? If it was Jack, Zambo hadn't killed him; was Zambo even a threat? If it was Jack, everything she had given up – old friends, extended family, having children and a normal life – counted for nothing.

Halfway across the bridge, she could hear him gaining on her. She ran faster. And then she felt her knees buckle and her body sag. Grabbing the guardrail, she collapsed into a crouch on the empty walkway between the river banks. He approached, but she didn't have the energy or will to move.

He stopped next to her. "It is me, Cassie. I didn't die. Helene lied in that letter. I'm so sorry. I only found out …."

He reached out to touch her arm but she screamed, "Don't!" The myth shattered: she wasn't healed; she wasn't cool and brave.

She stared unseeing into the waters below, her thoughts caught in a whirlpool. Jack's death, then Danny's, were the reasons she had disappeared. No one else would die, she had promised herself. The old wound on her wrist was a constant reminder never to get close to another man. Another man could die because of Marton Zambo. Another man could be like Marton Zambo. Over and over, her thoughts swirled; the hole at the whirlpool's center was the unassailable fact that Jack Hunter was dead.

The man who might be Jack Hunter withdrew his hand and stood a pace apart from her. Watching her for a few minutes, then also staring into the river. Kas hoped and resented and feared who he was. She had grieved for so long. "Damn you," she whispered.

Without a word, he nodded. Silence wrapped around them. When he did speak, his voice was soft and sad. "I'm so sorry, Cassie. For giving you such a shock. I shouldn't have come here. I sent a letter to the Chicago P.O. box about two weeks ago, but I guess it arrived too late to be forwarded…." He paused.

Her heart rate was finally slowing, her capacity to think finally returning. "It's more than a shock. It's more complicated than that."

"I understand. Do you want me to leave?" Sincerely asked. A bicyclist passed behind him, then a couple with a toddler enjoying a summer walk on the bridge.

Kas looked up at him now, really looked at him. Slowly, unsteadily, she got to her feet. "Did Millie send you?" It was a foolish question; a lie was too easy. But she still had to ask.

He stroked his beard a moment before answering. "In a sense. I've been looking for you for months. I finally found Millicent. We talked for hours before she decided to show me your last letter. So I knew about the exhibit. By then I didn't want to come but she insisted." He took a deep breath and continued, "Truthfully, I wanted very much to come, but that was purely selfish."

"Back up. Why didn't you want to come?"

"Because of Marton Zane, I mean, Zambo. Because, with all my heart, I don't want him to find you."

Kas stood quietly a moment, leaning against the rail. Millicent must have told Jack about Zambo, must have convinced him that Zambo remained a threat. That must be the important message. Kas turned to Jack. "We need to talk."

But not here, not halfway to Petržalka. She led him off the bridge toward Bratislava, across the main road, down a side street for two blocks, then left at the blue church. He followed when she turned into a wine bar, past customers enjoying the pleasant air on the bar's small patio. Inside, the place was almost empty. They took the table in the back corner, surrounded by shelves populated with wine. Kas ordered a bottle of dark ruby Frankovka Modrá and two glasses.

She took a small sip; the taste of berries filled her mouth. "How did Millicent convince you that Zambo's still looking for me?"

"She didn't. I mean, she didn't need to. I met him in June. I agree with her that he's very dangerous, especially after what Jahwed told me in Mashhad."

This was totally unexpected. Kas stuttered, "You met Zambo and Jahwed?"

Sensing her shock, he started from the beginning. "I started looking for you back in March, after I rediscovered your letters. They gave me a clue on finding Becky Dehart. She's Becky Gonzales now. She led me to Ralph Johnson," Jack pronounced it the American way, "and he led me to Deb, Danny Mack's sister. She and I tracked down

Zambo. Then I went to Iran, Gonzales and here. You really covered your tracks well," an approving tone in his voice. "In the end, it was Millicent who .... "

"Wait, wait," Kas cried. She had been staring at him for some minutes. "You found Becky and Ralph and Danny's kid sister?" She had purposely not thought about them in decades. Now the idea that they were alive, working with Jack to find her, felt overwhelming. In fact, everything Jack said felt overwhelming.

"I know it's important not to give you away, but I'd like to let Becky know you're all right. And Jahwed. Maybe Ralph; your call."

Jumbled, chaotic thoughts; she had difficulty absorbing this. "Sure, okay. How about Deb?"

"Deb's here. She wants to meet you, to thank you for the note on Danny's letter. It kept her going through some rough times. By the way, her family had a memorial service for Danny just a few weeks ago. I wish we had known how to reach you for it."

"Why now? A memorial service after all these years?"

"Deb never believed he was killed. She spent her life trying to find him. But after I talked with Jahwed at the Hotel Khayyám and saw Danny's grave, I had to tell her that he really was dead."

Kas's mouth contorted. She could barely speak. In the surge of his words she felt herself dissolving into fresh grief. Danny Mack was one of so many people she had known and lost in this ridiculous life she had led. So many debts unpaid, mistakes made, love unexpressed. She couldn't help it; a sob suddenly caught in her throat and she buried her face in her hands.

Jack stopped and waited silently. When she lifted her head at last, he asked gently, "How have you been?"

A hysterical laugh escaped her: she couldn't help herself. The sheer absurdity of the question: "How have I been!?!" Thinking about it triggered more laughing, high pitched and humorless. The laughter hurt; she felt tears rimming her eyes and finally stopped to brush them away.

This time, Jack held his tongue and waited.

Minutes passed. When she found her voice again, Kas said simply, "Tell me what you've learned about Marton Zambo."

Jack nodded and spoke more deliberately. "I met him in June in Vancouver. He goes by Zane now, Marton Zane, a very rich Canadian businessman. He's obsessed with finding you. He even offered me money to report back. He has a team of investigators and thugs looking for you."

She shook her head to dislodge the disbelief. "The man at my mother's funeral?"

"Lawrence Williams, retired marine. I met him in Zane's office and recognized him from Millicent's description."

Kas felt nauseous. Millie was right, after all.

Jack cleared his throat. "I took precautions to make sure I wasn't followed here. Zane could probably discover I flew to Madrid but that's it. From there I've taken trains and buses and paid only in cash. Deb makes all the reservations in her name. I did the same thing when I went to Gonzales. That's because, when I was in Iran, I discovered that he was having me followed. Fortunately, I managed to lose the guy before I got to Mashhad."

She couldn't yet think about the implications of what Jack was saying. She could only observe, "And you found Jahwed."

"Yes. Your postcard led me to him. Nice man, concerned about you. He still runs the hotel. And it was good I went. We discovered that Marton Zambo arranged Danny's murder. We found the evidence you collected. Now the Iranian authorities have it too. They may prosecute."

"What evidence?"

From his jacket pocket, Jack brought out a stack of photographs. "These are yours. I hope it's all right, but I'd like to hang on to the negatives for a while, in case California decides to proceed against Zane also. They're in Deb's safe at her office."

As he fanned the photographs out in front of her, Kas sucked in her breath. She thought she had forgotten about these images, but a searing clarity brought back the moment she took each one. Her progeny, long abandoned. She tenderly touched each picture. When she reached the still life with the tea and the note, Jack interrupted.

"That one's especially important. Danny had that note on him when he died." He started to recite what he remembered of the Arabic but she held up her hand; she knew enough of the language now to read it for herself. As she read, her face registered the sickening realization of what the note meant. Finished, she slumped against her chair, too horrified to speak.

"And look," Jack unfolded the photocopy from the hotel guest book, "Check out Zambo's handwriting when he registered. It matches the note." His eyes blazed. "He also gave Danny a city map with the shrine circled, telling him it was the bus depot. Jahwed can testify to that." He pointed to another photograph, the one she had surreptitiously taken of Danny and Zambo in the Khayyám hotel room. "This one's important because it shows both of them in Mashhad. Zambo tried to tell me that neither of them went there."

"That's bullshit," she murmured.

"Exactly."

"You're building a case against him."

"Exactly."

An insight began to dawn on her. "And that's why Zambo wants me. Not some of obsessive romantic grudge. But because I was there, I know what he did. I'm too dangerous to stay alive."

"No, no, no," Jack quickly retreated. "Zambo doesn't know about these photos or the map or Jahwed or Deb or Danny's letter. I think, from his point of view, it is an obsessive romantic grudge." He remembered something. When he met her eyes, he continued. "I'm making a wild guess here, but is there some significance to a blue glass object? Zane had it on his desk and he seemed very protective of it. Wouldn't let me touch it."

"What?!"

Jack repeated his question.

Kas whispered, "He gave me a blue glass bird dish back in Herat. I left it behind."

"Well, he must have found it and kept it." Jack cleared his throat. "So, you see, it is an obsessive romantic grudge."

The news didn't reassure Kas. Romantic obsessions could be fatal. "He killed Katarina, you know, his first serious girlfriend. I'm sure of it. Strangled her when he was only seventeen." Learning of Zambo's role in Danny's death confirmed it for her.

"Katarina?"

"It's why he fled in 1968."

"Oh," Jack said. They sat silently for several moments, the red wine unattended in front of them.

Finally he reached out and took her hand. Kas did not pull away. "Hey," he said, "He doesn't know that we know what he did. And he doesn't know where you are. He's not as omniscient as he imagines. His arrogance blinds him."

"Don't underestimate him, Jack," Kas somberly warned. "He's calculating and charming. He can fool even decent people into helping him." She quietly pushed up her sleeve, showing Jack the burn scar. "He branded me. He thinks I belong to him."

Jack had heard about the burn from Millicent, but to see it, still evident after almost thirty years, sickened him. He knew she was right; Zane wouldn't give up. "You can't stay here," he said with sudden urgency. "If I found you, he could, too. Come with me. I have money and we can…"

Kas shook her head. "Assuming he finds me, I'm not running. Not ever again. I want my old life back. I want to see my oldest friends and family again. You've reminded me that he's stolen too much of my life already."

"Then let me stay with you."

"To protect me from his thugs? Thanks, but I don't think it's necessary. If Zambo wants to hurt me, he'll make sure I'm alone." She thought again of Katarina on the roof, of herself in the room in Mashhad. Cruelty, up close and personal, was Marton's style with women, essential to his sense of domination. Yet the prospect of confronting him again didn't terrify her as much as it once did. Resignation, anger, years in the battlefield: she was ready to face him if and when he ever showed up.

"But I love you," Jack exclaimed, the words pushing out of him. "I've always loved you. Please let me help."

"No, Jack, don't." Kas said sharply, holding up her hand. This was an emotional complication she couldn't take right now. "You can't love me. You don't even know me."

From his jacket he brought out the stack of blue aerogrammes and lay them on the table. "I think I do."

She recognized them at once. More long-lost children. Seeing them stung. "You loved the light-hearted girl in those letters. She's been dead a long time. There's too much darkness in me now."

"Not in your work. I see the same person there. The one who cares about people, who cares about beauty and justice and kindness."

"Then that's where all the light in me goes. I have nothing left over for love." She leaned away from him. "I'm genuinely sorry, Jack. I'm glad you found me. It's a real gift to see you alive, and a relief to hear about the others and that we might be able to hold Zambo accountable. But that's it." She stood to leave, then paused. "And for God's sake, if you ever do see Zambo again, don't tell him you love me. He'll only hurt you for it."

Jack pushed the stack of letters toward her. "Take them. They're yours. And read them. See yourself as you were then. Not very different from who you are now."

For a long minute, she simply stared at the stack on the table. She sensed deep inside she should leave them. What could they do but trigger anguish and self-doubt? She had long buried the past; a conscious act, carefully maintained. She wasn't about to exhume the body now. And yet.

She picked them up.

Her voice was rough with emotion when she said, "It's unfair, you know. You coming back after all this time. It's goddamn unfair." With that, she walked away.

WHEN HE AWOKE on Friday morning, Jack was determined to be hopeful. The night had been terrible, a black hole relieved by only a few hours of sleep. After the previous day's encounter with Kas, he had never felt so despondent, even after discovering Helene's infidelity. So much of his heart and soul had gone into finding her, declaring his love. Losing her again felt devastating.

But in the morning, as he drank coffee at a small café on the river, a natural optimism gradually reasserted itself, growing stronger when he took a brisk late morning hike up to the castle. He would see Kas at the gallery opening tonight. He was slated to go there with Deb, and they would join Kas and her crew for a late dinner. By then, Kas would have read her old letters and remembered how close they once had been. But even if she hadn't, Jack would use the opportunity to show that he cared deeply about her and her world. Not as a lover as he had fantasized; Kas had made that plain. But as a friend she could trust.

Deb was encouraging. When they had spoken first thing in the morning, he had mentioned his sleeplessness but downplayed his despair; he wasn't comfortable admitting that even to himself. But he had been candid about Kas's anger and reserve. Deb had advised that he give her time to get used to the idea that he was alive and real. Later in the day, Deb had called to report that her lunch with Kas had gone really well, that she and Kas had talked for hours. Jack envied their ease with each other.

Mid-afternoon, emotionally and physically exhausted from the previous twenty-four hours, Jack finally lay down for a nap and fell into a deep sleep.

"Damn it!" he shouted when he awoke and noticed the clock in his darkened room. He was late. The reception was just starting, but Jack had wanted to get there early to offer encouragement. He quickly dressed and hurried from the room. In the cramped elevator, his hand automatically patted his pockets for passport, wallet, keys and phone. "Damn it," he cursed again as he realized he had forgotten his phone. No matter; there wasn't time to go back, and he was sure he wouldn't need it.

The desk clerk smiled politely as he dropped off his oversized key. "Oh, something just came for you, sir," she said when she saw his room number. She handed over a small package. Curious, Jack took it and saw his name and room number neatly printed on the front. Who would have sent him a package? And a package of what? He was preparing to tear it open when he heard a movement behind him, then a voice.

"Why, hello, Jack."

That voice. That slight accent. His heart twisted.

CHAPTER TWENTY

August 17, 2007
Friday

L et's walk," Zane said, coming out of the lobby's shadows. Behind him, Jack recognized Williams and Brill, the bodyguards.

As he swiveled around to face Zane, Jack covertly slipped the package into his jacket pocket. All of the pain and grief and anger he had experienced in the past twenty-four hours crystallized in this moment, eclipsing his surprise. "Marton Zane, you sonofabitch."

"Come now, is that any way to greet friends so far from home?"

Jack eyed him coldly. "Stay away from Kas."

Zane ignored the demand. "We have things to discuss. We'll get coffee." The words were friendly enough but the tone was imperious.

"We have nothing to discuss. Leave now, before the police come looking for you." The police weren't, as far as he knew. But, after hearing about Katarina's death, he hoped the gambit would plant doubt in Zane's mind. With that, Jack pushed through the hotel's glass doors.

Outside, he joined the mass of tourists and residents strolling down the cobbled main street of the city's medieval quarter. Cars were banned here; instead, in the middle of the street were open air cafés, full now of boisterous crowds enjoying the summer twilight. Walking quickly, Jack turned right toward St. Michael's Gate and away from the river and Union of Slovak Arts. He adroitly wove his way through the throng of pedestrians but didn't run; he didn't want to attract attention. As he moved, he pondered how Zane had found him despite his elaborate travel precautions. The man's omniscience troubled him. But he didn't have to evade Zane for long; just long enough to warn Kas.

Jack's plan was rudimentary: to circle around through the warren of old streets and return to the hotel and his phone. Alternatively, he could duck into a store and ask to use their phone. That would be faster, he decided as he approached a chocolate shop, furtively glancing around to first ascertain Zane's whereabouts. He wasn't in sight and Jack hastened his steps.

But as he reached the shop doorway, Zane's henchmen materialized from the surrounding crowd and blocked him. He was bookended, one at either elbow. Jack weighed his odds of escape. He was in good shape; he could run fast and might be able to lose them in the crowd and maze of streets. But he knew he'd be tackled before he took two steps. Any alarmed passersby would be told that he was a purse snatcher or a drunken friend. And he didn't put it past Brill to give him a gratuitous kick in the groin.

He had to think of another way.

The men herded him down a less populated side street and through a restaurant entrance. Jack scanned the place; it was empty except for a couple at a table near the window. Then he spied Zane, sitting alone with his back against the far wall. Williams and Brill steered him to Zane's table, and then sat closer to the entrance, just out of hearing.

With an unblinking gaze, Zane watched as Jack stiffly sat down. "You insult me with your melodramatic escapades," he complained. "I expect basic courtesy. If I invite you to coffee, you come, do you understand?"

"So it's an order, not an invitation." Jack tersely replied.

"The difference in this case is meaningless. We have things ..."

Jack interrupted, "To discuss, yes, I get it. I don't have time for this." Jack stood. Instantly, so did the two bodyguards behind him.

"Sit down, Hunter."

Jack continued to stand. "Just to make myself clear: stay away from Kas," he repeated.

"Or what? You'll talk me to death?" Zane gave a sarcastic laugh. "I've met men like you before, ineffectual intellectuals dueling with words." Zane motioned for one of the bodyguards to come closer. "But as long as you're standing, raise your arms."

Sensing Brill behind him, Jack was incredulous. "You're going to search me?"

"A security precaution, that's all."

"Go to hell," he said and crossed his arms.

Zane sighed loudly. "Your petulance is beginning to irritate me. This is not a request. If you prefer, Mr. White and Mr. Black will escort you to the men's room and conduct a more thorough search."

He glared at Zane. "I'll yell to the waiter for help. He'll call the police."

"Will you stop talking about the police? You won't and he won't. And I'll tell you why. First, because my cousin owns this restaurant and the waiter knows me. And second, because you want to know what I'm going to do."

The last was true.

A minute ticked by as Jack considered his options, then slowly he extended his arms. Brill patted him down. The search was methodical and professional, his hands probing Jack's sides and back, around his waist, down each leg to his socks, and into his jacket pockets. He pulled out Jack's wallet and the package and tossed them on the table. Finally Brill gave a sign that the search was complete.

"Not even a phone," Zane mused. "You truly are a Luddite, Jack."

Jack sat, exhaling deeply in relief. Zane had shown no interest in the mysterious package. And Jack was glad that he had forgotten his phone; it contained contact numbers for Deb and Kas. He didn't think Zane knew yet about Danny's sister, and he needed to keep it that way.

Zane motioned to the waiter. "I believe I promised you a Viennese coffee."

DRESSED IN TAPERED black slacks and a loose blue silk tunic she had bought in India, Kas paced through the exhibit space. No one else was there. She was early, she knew. The doors wouldn't open for another thirty minutes, and her talk wasn't scheduled until an hour after that. But what if no one came? What if those who did detested her work?

Her eyes swept over the photographs. They were her favorites. Taken over a lifetime, they were on display together for the first time. She felt proud and anxious, a parent at a child's first recital. Would others understand what she was trying to convey? Would they see not just the horror, but the dignity and resilience of her subjects? Would they understand that these images are documentary evidence of war crimes? Or would they focus on the way she used light and color, only seeing artful interior decoration of a particularly macabre kind? It was so hard to objectively assess the impact of her work. She wished Millicent was coming; she trusted her acumen and honesty. Was this a role Millie intended Jack to play as her so-called proxy?

Jack. Thoughts of Jack had dogged her most of the day; almost subconsciously, like a low tune from a neighbor's radio. You can ignore it, but only to a point. Kas had tried but her thoughts wouldn't be silenced.

Alexej appeared from the back office, chatting with the two other co-organizers of the exhibit. They waved to her and Alex ambled over.

"Everything is set," he smiled. "It's a great show. We're all very excited."

Kas felt a rush of gratitude and relief. She thanked him again for making it possible. "Has anyone else arrived early? My friends Deb or Jack?" She hoped they were in the back office also.

"No, but I'll check the front steps, in case they're waiting."

She gave a small tight smile and shook her head. "I just did."

Alex appraised her; something in her voice must have alerted him. "You seem a little on edge, Kas. It's natural. But, really, there's nothing to worry about. Why not sit in the office for a few minutes, collect your thoughts? I'll let you know when I see them."

Kas drifted toward the darkened office and opted not to switch on the ceiling light. With only an ambient glow coming through the open doorway, she settled into the desk chair and took a deep breath.

What a day. Over a long lunch, she and Deb had talked about so much: Zane's brutality, Jack's discoveries about Danny's murder, the possibility of a prosecution someday. But they also spoke about growing up without the beloved older brother, which led them to reflect on family, anger, loneliness. They had laughed as well: each had stories to tell about Danny. Deb described how he had become a Hindu through a Hare Krishna friend, and how appalled their parents were when he chanted on the front lawn. Kas recounted his "happiest memory" of learning to surf, and his playful antics with children when they walked through Herat.

As she talked, Kas was surprised at how much she could suddenly remember from 1978, a year that she thought she had excised from her history. It was only last night - when she reluctantly began reading her letters to Jack - that fresh scraps of old memories began to reappear. Some of the memories were deeply disturbing; at one point in the evening, she even imagined hearing someone outside her apartment door. But most of them were happy memories; another surprise. The descriptions of that restaurant in Bangkok, the train ride in India, the walk through Kathmandu – how could she have forgotten so much? She was surprised as well at how free and open she had once been with Jack. She hadn't felt safe enough to be that way with anyone since.

Talking with Danny's sister about the past had been emotionally exhausting, yet Kas had felt energized as well. How comfortable she felt with her. Deb had observed that it was because they shared so much tragedy; a sisterhood of sorrow. But to Kas, it was more than that. She was experiencing something new: another woman's friendship. Long ago, when she went into hiding, she had purposely cut ties with old girlfriends, to keep both them and herself safe from Zambo. The friendships she made later were with the men she worked with, like Alex. And a few, although not Alex, had briefly become lovers. She had met other women, of course - photographers, editors, publishers – and liked and respected many of them. But she had not felt a deep connection – emotional as well as intellectual - until today, with Deb. Perhaps reading the old letters did that too, unearthed emotions as well as memories.

She roused herself when she heard voices in the gallery. The doors were opening; people were coming. As she entered the well-lit gallery space, she studied the scores of visitors for familiar faces. Martina had arrived and was talking with Alex, but there was no sign yet of Deb or Jack. Disappointed, Kas turned her gaze back to Alex. He was drawing his wife's attention to a photograph of gaunt teenaged faces she had taken in Sarajevo fifteen years before. The image triggered more memories: explosive sounds of sniper fire, dust, acrid smells, running for cover. She and Alex had reached safety that day, but the girl in the photograph had been killed, as well as another colleague. A wave of sadness washed over her. She was in the business of capturing heart-rending images, but that didn't mean she ever got hardened to them.

Suddenly Kas felt small arms encircling her legs and looked down to see their brown-haired daughter. She had to grin.

"Ahoj, Andrea," she greeted the six-year-old. "How are you?"

"Hello," the child said softly and shyly hid her face behind her hands. Then she dashed toward her parents and Alex scooped her into his arms. Kas was still watching them when she felt a tap on her shoulder. It was Deb. The women hugged and exchanged kisses on each cheek.

"I'm sorry I'm late. I've been outside waiting for Jack. Did he come in already? I might have missed him." Taller than Kas, she scanned the gathering crowd.

Kas shook her head. More people were arriving, but she would have noticed if Jack was among them. "Maybe he got held up."

"Maybe," Deb replied. "He's usually not late. I called him but no answer."

She sounded mildly concerned and Kas wondered if she should be worried too. Curious, she asked Deb what she thought of Jack.

The other woman smiled. "I like him. Why?" They drifted toward a table where wine was being served.

"Do you trust him?" To Kas, that was the key question, and quite distinct from liking.

Without hesitation, Deb said, "I trust him even more than I like him. And that's saying a lot." She frowned in thought as she picked up a glass of red wine. "Jack's real: unpretentious, honest." She took a sip of wine before adding, "Too bad he's not available."

Picking up her own glass, Kas wondered about Deb's meaning. "Not available?" she asked. "Do you mean emotionally? Legally? I thought he was divorced."

"Oh, I didn't mean Helene." Deb exclaimed and, in afterthought, observed, "What a bitch she was."

"Jack told you that?" Kas was disappointed; she believed people revealed much about themselves in how they described former lovers, and bitch was an ugly term.

"No, he's too nice. I guessed it from some of the things he said in passing. And, of course, the fact that she told you he was dead, and that she burned everything you sent after the postcard."

"She did?" Kas didn't know that part. So Jack hadn't gotten her letter from Tehran; that's why it wasn't in the stack he gave her.

"Didn't he tell you? The Mashhad postcard was the last thing he got. And he read it wrong. He thought you were calling everything off."

"Shit." Kas remembered re-reading the postcard last night. She had noted its awkward and oblique wording, had remembered her frightened rush in writing it. Only now, though, did she see how he might have misinterpreted the message. "I had no idea."

"Jack packed your letters away for almost thirty years. This spring, he discovered them again but so did Helene. She accused him of infidelity for keeping the letters against her explicit orders – she's the type to give explicit orders - and she punished him by taking a lover. End of marriage." Deb's approval of the divorce was clear when she added, "Lucky for Jack."

"Helene was jealous of a bunch of old letters? That's ridiculous."

Deb paused before responding. "Well, to be fair to Helene, I can kind of see her point. I'm not sure how I would react if my husband of – what? – twenty-eight years was still secretly enamored of a Great Lost Love."

"Me? I'm not anyone's great love, lost or otherwise."

"You are to Jack. You're the reason he's not available; that's what I meant. He deeply loves you."

Even before Deb said this, Kas sensed it was coming. The remark made her uncomfortable. She suspected Deb had been enlisted as Jack's ambassador, so she had to be clear. "Well, I'm not interested. I told him that already."

Deb drank more wine and then nodded slowly, "Okay. Good to know."

"Wait." Rare, unexpected and – in her mind – totally unwarranted, Kas felt a jab of jealousy. "Are you interested in Jack?"

Deb considered for a moment and then shrugged. "I haven't seriously thought about it, but why not? He's smart, he's nice, he's employed." She laughed when she said this. "And he's good looking. I guess I wouldn't throw him out of bed." She finished her wine.

Sex with Jack. The casual reference unsettled Kas precisely because she tried hard not to think of him that way. What feelings she had for him were strictly platonic, she told herself. "We're strictly platonic," she told Deb.

More people arrived and Deb glanced at her watch. It was eight. "Show time, amiga," she announced.

JACK STRAIGHTENED HIS shirt collar and coat sleeves, and said with irritation, "Hurry up and say what you have to say. I need to go. Friends are expecting me."

The waiter arrived with cream and sugar and two small trays: on each was a small cup of fragrant black coffee, a little glass of water, and a plate with two cookies wrapped in cellophane.

Zane stirred sugar and cream into his cup. "Don't worry about your friends. Mr. Red is at the gallery. He's looking out for Cassandra."

Mr. Red. Clive Riley. Jack had almost forgotten about him. So Riley was monitoring Kas and reporting back. Would Deb recognize him from Jack's description and alert Kas? Would they get out of the gallery before he could grab them? Jack stared into his black coffee and tried to convince himself that they already had slipped his surveillance, as Jack had done in Tehran.

Zane tasted his coffee, nodding to himself in approval. Then he broke into Jack's reverie. "To be frank, I was surprised to learn you were here." Zane paused to light a cigarette.

"I thought you had me followed, like you did in Tehran." He had taken it for granted.

Zane exhaled and then casually said, "Ah, yes. Tehran. What took you there, by the way? I doubt it was an interest in cigarette trade deals."

So this was the reason behind Zane's insistence on talking. Jack considered how to answer. "You told me that's where she was headed when she left Herat. I thought I could pick up some clues."

"And did you?"

"No," Jack lied. "Records at the American embassy were destroyed the next year, when it was seized."

"You might have discovered something outside of the city." Zane nonchalantly studied the tip of his cigarette.

Jack shook his head. "I didn't know where else to go. And the Iranians don't like fishing expeditions."

Zane nodded, seemingly satisfied. "I admit I had you followed in Iran, but only out of curiosity. But no, I didn't have you followed this time." He took a long drag on the cigarette and exhaled slowly. "I didn't need to. You told me in Vancouver all I needed to know to find Cassie."

Jack scowled. "What the hell did I tell you in Vancouver?" He racked his brain; he could come up with nothing.

Zane gave an enigmatic smile. "Your name."

With a sinking feeling, Jack understood. Years ago, Zane had probably figured out that Kas had changed her surname - as he himself had done - but he would not have known where to start looking. Not until the arrival of Dr. Hunter, Cassie's professor friend. Jack berated himself for contacting Zane at all.

"You've known since June, then. What stopped you from getting in touch with her earlier?"

"Well, I stopped by her apartment last night but decided not to disturb her so late. As for earlier, let's just say I wasn't interested in touring western Iraq. Even for Cassie."

Western Iraq; Jack winced. He hadn't realized Kas had been there this summer, one of the most dangerous places on the planet. Meanwhile, he had been sitting in air conditioning, sifting through files. Of course he should have known; that was her job.

"I tried to find her home in the States, but she seems to be invisible." Zane paused. "Which makes sense, given vengeful warlords out there who don't appreciate her work. And which raises the question of how you managed to find Cassie."

So Zane didn't know about Millicent or the others. Jack felt mildly heartened. " The Internet. Lucky guess," he answered.

"Just as I thought," Zane said, considering Jack. "Although it took you long enough to catch that your own name was the key." Zane gave an appreciative chuckle at Jack's expense. "Well, it doesn't matter. Now that you've found her, you must realize your mistake."

Puzzled, Jack frowned, shook his head.

"Come now, Jack. You saw her yesterday, how upset she was. She certainly wasn't happy to see you, not according to Mr. Black."

Jack hadn't expected this and shot back defensively, "But only because I'd surprised her." For some reason, he added, "We're old friends."

"Old friends," Zane scoffed. "Of course you are. The prodigal friend. She probably wondered where you've been all these years while she was trapped in war zones. You in your smug little life hardly giving her a thought for decades. One day, on a whim, you decide to look her up and can't find her. So it became a game for you, didn't it? And you like to win games." He leaned forward, his gaze so intensely focused on Jack that it felt physical. "So tell me then. If you're such good friends, why did she run away?"

How could he explain? Why should he even try? Jack let several seconds pass before stating, "She didn't run away. She stopped and we talked."

"More talk." Zane gestured dismissively with his cigarette. "She doesn't want you, and you're too fixated on winning the game to see it."

Tiny kernels of truth in Zane's remarks choked Jack. Sullen, he was about to argue when he suddenly caught sight of the cigarette's glowing red tip and his mind went blank. All he could see was the image of the puckered scar on Kas's wrist. That thought led inexorably to Danny, beaten to death as Kas was being burned. In an instant, on a visceral level, Jack now understood how truly dangerous Zane was. Not a rival, not an opponent, but a lethal adversary unconstrained by social mores and skilled at manipulation. Zane was provoking him for a reason; he wanted Jack angry and off balance. Jack made an educated guess why, that Zane wanted him to storm out and go home. A second thought: that Zane was still probing about Iran, that he suspected Jack of hiding something.

Jack was determined to stay calm and analytical, ignoring the barbs. He decided to shift the focus to Zane's plans for Kas, if he had come to Bratislava as her erstwhile lover or her executioner. Taking a deep breath, Jack observed, "You're playing the same game, hunting Kas down. What do you want with her?"

"To protect her." Zane said it loudly and clearly. Across the room, the waiter looked up from a glass he was drying.

The answer startled Jack. "From what?"

"From you, of course."

"I'm not a threat. You are. You're obsessed with her."

"Who's obsessed? Let's review the facts." Zane continued in a loud voice. "You left your wife, your job and your children to travel around the world searching for a woman you hadn't seen in three decades. All because she was once your pen pal." He spoke the last two words derisively. Zane leaned toward Jack but didn't lower his voice. "She's told you she's not interested, and yet you persist. Go home. Let her be."

Again, there was a disconcerting element of truth in Zane's remarks, but now Jack refused to let himself be shaken. He went on the offensive. "Kas is hiding from you."

"Or from you. Did you ever consider that?"

"So she changed her last name to mine? I don't think so. I accept that she doesn't love me, that we're only friends. But that's not enough for you, is it? You need to possess her."

Jack must have hit home this time, because Zane instantly shot back, "You understand nothing about Cassie; nothing about real love and commitment. You North Americans think love is either banal sentimentality or the rutting of animals."

"She stopped yesterday so I could catch up; your man over there will tell you." Jack gestured slightly toward Williams. "But she's run from you for decades and she'll never stop."

Zane hissed, "She and I are connected on a very deep level."

"You knew each other for a little over a week." Jack observed mockingly. "Great love affair that was."

Zane fumed, his face and fists so tight that Jack braced himself for a blow. But then Zane checked himself, leaning back in his chair, closing his eyes and slowing his breath. Minutes passed. Jack was fascinated to witness the transformation. Zane's body remained immobile, but the molecules of his face appeared to rearrange themselves into a mask of composure. When Zane spoke again, his voice was controlled. "The connection between us has never broken." With a casual backhand movement, he added, "We'll be lovers our entire lives. Nothing can change that."

That's when Jack knew with certitude that fantasy had brought Zane here. Not murderous intent. Yet he, like Kas, realized that obsessive fantasy could also be deadly. Jack recalibrated his responses, changed his tactics. He wondered if reason would work with Zane. "You say you share a great love with Kas. But you've loved a lot of other women. You married three of them. You fathered children. That seems like love to me."

"Bourgeois," Zane replied dismissively. "Engels was right. Marriage is legal prostitution, sex in exchange for wealth. It exists solely to serve state and economic interests." He spoke as if reading an academic treatise. "That applies to virtually every marriage, including mine. Particularly mine." A brief pause ensued, then, in a somber reflective tone, he added, "Marriage with Cassie would have been different. Because Cassie is different. Even you can appreciate that."

Strangely, his last remarks moved Jack. Stillness enveloped the two men for a few moments, before Jack could articulate his next question. He needed to know Zane's mind. "How? How is she different for you?"

Zane took a long time answering. "When I was young, I lost a girl I loved very much. Cassie understood. She ... made the world right again."

"You need her." It was an observation that Jack hadn't intended to say out loud.

Zane gave a slight nod. "I didn't think so, not at first. But the world is such a sordid place." Looking away, staring into some middle ground, he added, "There's purity in her, and strength."

Purity and strength. That's what Zane thought he needed from Kas. Jack saw the same qualities in her yet he hadn't found the words and Zane had. Then he corrected himself: Kas was so much more than those mere two words. Zane failed to grasp her complexity; to Zane, she was an ideal, like the goddess Athena, the virgin warrior. Hell, Jack thought, even Athena was more complex than that.

"She can't save you," Jack said. "No one can. That's not how it works. Other people can give love and support, but the rest is up to you." It was a lesson he had only learned recently, when he accepted that he could never make the world – or himself - perfect enough for Helene.

"In a way, I pity you, Jack. Despite all your academic degrees, there's so much you don't understand." Zane finished his coffee and sat upright, signaling the end of the conversation. He glanced at his watch, gestured toward Williams. "I have to go. Stay here with Mr. Black until I call." His voice was firm and directive again. "And then go back to the hotel and pack your bags and fly home. Leave Cassie alone, Jack. I warn you." He stood.

In protest, Jack stood as well but he didn't have a chance to speak before Zane leaned in close and whispered in his ear, "You love your children, Max and Sandy, don't you?" Then Zane straightened and tossed a thousand-crown banknote on the table, about forty dollars. "Sit, Jack. Finish your coffee."

With that, he strode out of the restaurant, burly Todd Brill at his heels.

The vulnerable Dr. Jekyll had disappeared, Jack realized. Mr. Hyde was back in command. He felt ill.

Williams settled across from him and motioned to the waiter.

KAS WAS RELIEVED; her speech was over. She was relieved but she wasn't pleased. Much of the talk had sounded trite in her ears. Furthermore, she had stumbled over some of her points and forgotten to pay tribute to the many photojournalists who had died on the job.

This was her first public address and she'd botched it.

The crowd responded warmly though, and pushed forward to congratulate her and compliment her work as she walked from the lectern. They wanted to ask about her aesthetic sense, her technique, and her work experiences. Disheartened, she realized there was little interest in the women in the photographs: who they were, what had happened to them. But then she saw Deb, across the room, clapping and smiling, and Alexej, next to Deb, giving a thumbs up. Kas scanned the room but still no sign of Jack. She told herself that it didn't matter.

Suddenly pushing through the throng was Magdalena, in a brilliantly colored flowing jacket, with Viliam like a gray boat in her wake. Both were warm smiles, kisses, congratulations. They spoke for a few moments before Viliam took her hand and stared into her eyes.

"We have lovely surprise for you." He said softly. "I think you will be very pleased, no? It is the old friend we spoke of."

With this, he stepped aside. Behind him stood a handsome older man, uncommonly thin and expensively dressed, with the palest blue eyes imaginable. For a moment, Kas couldn't breathe.

"It is Marton Zámbó," Viliam told her, as if she might not recognize him. "My pupil from so long ago." Then, to the man, he said, "Perhaps you remember Miss Kas Hunter, our guest. An amazing coincidence you both come to Bratislava at same time."

"Amazing, indeed," the man said and then gently took her shoulders and kissed each cheek. A subtle scent of expensive men's cologne. "It is wonderful to see you again, Cassie."

Kas flinched when he touched her but was too stunned to pull back. "Marton" was all she managed to say. She didn't bother correcting him on her name.

"And what an exhibit. I read about your work, but to see it in person is a rare privilege. And to see you again, rare indeed."

Magdalena affectionately patted her arm as the elderly couple slipped away. They were discreet; they would give Kas and Marton space for their happy reunion. Kas badly wanted to take Magdalena's arm and slip away too, but her knees were locked in place, her eyes locked on Zane's.

Once alone with her, Zane studied her face, "You're beautiful still. I'm glad. Older, of course. I didn't know what to expect. I couldn't find any photographs of you anywhere."

She was only gradually finding her voice. "No, I don't like photos of myself." She hesitated; his intense scrutiny made her uncomfortable. "Why are you here, Marton? Are you visiting family?"

Zane shook his head. "Of course not, Cassie. I came for you."

The sentence she had long dreaded. It wasn't as if his finding her was totally unexpected. She and Jack had just talked about the possibility. Yet now, seeing him, the resolve she had felt the day before was gone, and she found herself seized by the same terror that had propelled her out of the Hotel Khayyám and into a life of flight. Almost immediately, though, her rational mind reasserted its control. She ordered herself not to succumb to fear. Even assuming he wanted to, he couldn't hurt her here, not in front of everyone.

Zane seemed to be waiting for her to say something, so she coolly observed, "It's been a long time. I'm surprised you remember me at all." She looked away, avoiding those eyes. Her gaze settled on one of the most exquisite, deceptive and disturbing images in the exhibit: beneath a turquoise sky, a field of flowers grew in a wild profusion of color. Only on closer inspection was the subject clear: they were not flowers at all but a jumbled mass of corpses in brightly colored clothes, most of them women. Kas had taken the photo in the Democratic Republic of Congo.

"Of course I remember you. And you remember me. I'm not surprised. We meant a lot to each other." Then, following her gaze, he abruptly changed the subject. "What does surprise me, though, is your work. I expected something less ... gruesome. What drives you to want to photograph such things?" He pointed toward the image. "What were you thinking when you took that one, for example?

Confused and mildly irritated, she faced him. "What do you mean?"

Studying the photograph, he frowned in thought. "What were you feeling at the moment you made this? Sad? Outraged? Revolted? Aroused?" His voice had a penetrating edge.

Kas hadn't expected a psychological analysis of her motives. In fact, she felt there was something voyeuristic, indecent, about his question. Her eyes returned to the image. Terrible memories arose: stench of rotting flesh, drone of black flies on her skin and theirs, stultifying damp heat, even under the shade of the tree where she stood to take the photograph. To breathe, she'd had to tie a kerchief over her nose and mouth. She remembered wiping tears away with her dirty sleeve before she could put the camera to her eye and peer through the viewfinder. An old-fashioned camera, not digital. The viewfinder had distanced her from the horror, at least for the minute it took to frame and focus. So what did she experience the moment the shutter clicked? Kas felt a flush of shame as she realized Zane's guess was close. In the face of such horror, she had felt excited. The image was so compelling and beautiful.

"I didn't feel anything, Marton. I felt numb."

He nodded but took a moment to respond. "I've seen terrible things in my life, too. We have a lot in common."

He knows I'm lying, she thought. Feeling exposed, she turned her body away.

With a graceful step, he moved in front of her. "We need to talk, Cassie, somewhere quiet."

That was the last thing she wanted. "I can't. It's my show. I have to stay."

He surveyed the room. "No, you don't. You've given your speech. They applauded. Now they're drinking wine and gossiping about their lives. They won't miss you."

"My friends will."

"Do you mean Jack?" Before she could respond he added, "He can't be here. He sends his regrets."

The news alarmed her. She didn't ask Zane how he had found Jack. She knew the answer already. Zane must have had Jack followed, and that's how he had found her, too. Now Zane was holding Jack against his will, Kas was sure of it. "Where's Jack? Is he all right?" she demanded, dread tight in her chest.

"I assume he is," Zane said simply. "He was leaving for the airport when I saw him. He did seem upset for some reason. He said he's going home; he missed his children." With a hint of concern, Zane added, "Didn't he tell you?"

Kas wondered if she could believe him. Jack was leaving? It seemed so sudden. Yet it was possible; she remembered Jack's sadness when she'd left him at the wine shop. But they had made plans to get together this evening. Or, rather, Deb had made the plans, which meant Deb didn't know either. Was he that unhappy? Kas felt dispirited knowing she wouldn't see him tonight; worse to think she might never see him again.

"Come with me, Cassie," Zane gently insisted. "You talked with him. Now talk with me."

Kas labored to clear her head of thoughts of Jack; she had to stay focused on Marton Zane and what he was saying. "No, not possible," she said curtly. It was more than fear that fueled her resistance; her anger was returning, over all of the years that she had wasted being afraid.

"I have something very important to tell you, something I know you'll want to hear."

"There's nothing you can say that I want to hear," she asserted. But her resolve was weakening. She had started to consider the implication of avoiding him. He could easily confront her later, when she was completely alone. Across the room, Kas caught a glimpse of Viliam and Magdalena chatting with Alex. Seeing them reminded her of Katarina, made her think she should talk with Zane after all, to try to elicit some clues about the girl's murder. An investigation into her death might help Kas atone for Danny's.

"I have waited so long to see you," he said. His voice was warm, even gentle, with no hint of retribution over her leaving him or alarm that she knew too much about his past.

All right," she conceded slowly and warily, "for a few minutes. The back office will work. It's quiet."

"Not here. I know a better place."

Zane moved to touch her arm but she swiftly pulled away. She was adamant. "We talk here, Marton. I won't leave."

His smile was kind. "Cassie, it's only a conversation. What are you worried about?" He paused briefly and then, in a solicitous tone, acknowledged, "Ah, I understand. I frightened you the last time. I was hot headed when I was young, but I've changed. I really have."

Zane's appeal hung in the air between them, seeming so sensible and sincere.

She didn't think he had changed, but she knew she had. Her fear was dissipating as her anger grew. Other than get a few answers, she wanted to be rid of him forever. Kas had an idea. "If I agree to meet with you – if – you have to promise that you'll leave me alone from now on. That's the deal." Finally being free of him.

Zane regarded her with a serious expression. "I hope to change your mind. However, once we've talked, if you tell me you never want to see me again, then you will never see me again. I promise you that."

Her old life back. She nodded. "We can talk for an hour. And in public, here, in town."

"An hour is fine." His broad smile was dazzling. "I know a perfect place, a quiet bar but public. My car is just outside."

"Well, then," Kas said abruptly. "Let's go. I need to be back here before ten." She had plans for a late supper in old town with Deb, Alex and the other organizers. Jack, she remembered sadly, would miss it. "Wait a moment. My handbag is in the office. I'll be right back."

"There's no need. We'll only be gone an hour," he said reassuringly. "My treat. Just like the time we went for kebabs in Kabul, isn't it?"

I was wary of you then as well, Kas thought. My mistake came later, when I convinced myself I was wrong about you. "One hour," she reiterated. "In town."

In the crowd clustered between the wine bar and the exit, Kas spied Deb in earnest conversation with a nice-looking man with red hair. She considered approaching Deb, telling her about Jack's departure and her meeting Zane. But at that moment, Deb laughed at something the redhead said; Kas noticed that they were holding hands. Oh, hell, Kas thought, Deb deserved to have a good time without thinking about Marton Zane. There would be time later to tell her about it.

Close behind her, Kas felt Zane's breath on her ear as he whispered, "Do you remember that American song, Cassie?" He sang softly, "*Fly me to the moon and let me play among the stars.*" He gave a low chuckle. "That's what we're going to do. We're going to fly to the moon and stars tonight." His elation was almost boyish.

Kas recognized the love song and moved quickly to disabuse him of romantic fantasies. "It's only a conversation, Marton. That's all."

He didn't speak, just continued humming the tune as he guided her to the door. At that moment, Kas glanced back at Deb and saw her friend observing her with a quizzical expression. As she watched,

Deb's red-headed friend left Deb's side and moved toward her. Another man, taller and more muscular than the redhead, also drew closer. Involuntarily, Kas stepped backward, through the gallery doors. As she tried to make sense of what she had seen, Zane took her arm and led her down the steps into the cool evening air. He guided her into the backseat of a highly polished black sedan and slid in next to her.

Only then did Kas realize that the men had been approaching Zane, not her. They must be working for him, she concluded. But she still couldn't grasp why one of them was talking with Deb. Had Deb been Zane's indemnity in case she hadn't agreed to come? Did Zane know she was Danny's sister? Something about the whole scenario felt wrong.

Suddenly, Kas knew she had to get out. She scooted across the seat to the other side and reached toward the car handle, but the door abruptly swung open and the redheaded man quickly climbed in. Trapped now between him and Zane, Kas wondered in panic: *What have I done?*

An enraged shout broke into her thoughts and she craned her neck to peer through the back window. There was Deb – like one of the avenging Furies of Greek mythology - tearing out of the gallery and down its steps at full speed, shrieking invectives at Zane. Kas's view of the sidewalk was suddenly blocked by the wide back of the muscular man. The next thing Kas could see was Deb crumpling to the ground.

"No!" Kas screamed.

Deb's assailant, massaging his fist, climbed into the front passenger seat, and the car sped away.

CHAPTER TWENTY-ONE

August 17, 2007
Friday

J ack was distraught. He loved Kas and he had to warn her. Yet he needed to warn his children first. But Marton was so close to Kas; maybe he should warn her first. He took a deep breath to force himself into clarity. He'd get his phone, then he would go to the gallery. For both of those things to happen, he had to persuade his guard to let him go.

Mentally, he reviewed what he knew about the man across from him, from the dossier Deb's private investigator had compiled weeks before.

"You're Lawrence Williams, aren't you?"

The big man scowled. "How do you know my name?"

"You were a Master Sergeant in the marines, right? I've seen your military record. Impressive."

Williams just lifted a curious eyebrow.

"Wounded in the Persian Gulf war. Saved two other wounded marines. Decorated; a genuine war hero. Do you mind if I ask you a few questions, Sergeant?"

"Knock yourself out," Williams said, stirring sugar into his coffee.

Jack studied his face, "How long have you been working for Marton Zane?"

He shrugged slightly. "A little over four years."

"That long? Well, I'm surprised. You're working for a real monster, Sergeant Williams. Don't you see that? He's not one of the good guys."

Williams gave a disparaging grunt. "What I see is a great man. Always thinking, always working, loyal to the people who are loyal to him." He paused a moment in thought. "Sure, he can be tough when he has to be. He's a very successful businessman, after all. But he's generous, and good to his people."

"Charity balls with Hollywood celebrities and beautiful women," Jack wryly observed, remembering the newspaper clippings.

Williams shook his head vigorously. "No, real people." He glared at Jack. "My father, for instance. He needed heart surgery soon after I started to work for Mr. Zane. But he didn't have insurance or qualify yet for Medicare. Mr. Zane found out and paid all the medical bills, got him the best care in the world. My father is alive today because of Mr. Zane. To me and my family, he'll always be one of the good guys."

Jack hadn't expected Zane to be so adept at instilling allegiance. "Your father was lucky then. It shows that Zane values you. But I'm telling you he can easily turn violent if someone gets in his way."

"I've never seen it." Williams crossed his arms. "What are you up to, Hunter? What is this, extortion? Is that why you're here? You don't think he's paying you enough?"

Incensed, Jack protested, "I'm not working for that bastard and he's not paying me."

A small smile played on Williams' lips. "I can tell when I've hit a nerve, man. I saw him pay you; I was there. So this is all about money."

The check, Jack realized. Back in Vancouver, Williams had seen Zane write that hundred-thousand-dollar check. "Let me show you something." Jack opened his wallet and, from a deep credit card slot, extricated a tightly folded piece of paper. Opening it up, he lay the creased check on the table between them. "It's yours if you let me go."

Williams didn't smile, didn't shake his head. He gave Jack a stony look. "If you know so much about me, you know I don't take bribes."

Jack nodded. "Apologies," he said. He picked up the check and tore it into tiny pieces, leaving a tidy pile of paper next to his unopened package of cookies.

Williams looked aghast. "Are you nuts?! That's a lot of money!"

"It's blood money." He tried to explain, "Zane paid me to spy on her, the woman you saw me with yesterday. And I won't do it."

"No, he paid you to leave her alone," Williams insisted.

Jack countered, "He wants me to do his dirty work, like you and Todd Brill and Clive Riley."

"We don't do dirty work." Williams was offended.

"Well, Brill beats people up, and Riley snoops on them and rifles through their confidential files. I have first-hand experience with both fine gentlemen. And you stalk women at art galleries and funerals."

Williams bristled. "I'm a professional bodyguard. I protect Mr. Zane and, when he requests it, his friends. Like I said, I don't do dirty work."

Jack considered for a minute. "Okay, I get it. You think you were protecting the woman you followed yesterday. But who are you protecting now? Why aren't you with him, if you're his bodyguard? Why has he left you behind to babysit me?" Jack leaned forward, "I think

Zane doesn't want you to see what he's going to do. He knows you wouldn't stand for it."

Williams didn't answer. He stared at Jack for several minutes before he finally said, "All I know is that you're a crazy motherfucker. You aren't after the money, so maybe you're after the woman. That's what the others think. Riley says there's shit about you all over the internet. Whatever your agenda is, we're not going to let you hurt her."

Jack shot back, "It's your boss who's the psychopath, not me." He was so irritated that he didn't register the reference to the internet. "Zane has hurt her in the past and he'll do it again, if I don't stop him."

Williams was unmoved. "It's called projection, what you're doing. Projecting your actions and beliefs on to someone else."

"That's ridiculous," Jack countered. "What did Zane tell you about me anyway?"

"He didn't have to tell me anything. I can see for myself. Just do what he says. Leave her alone."

Jack was galled: Zane had successfully characterized him as the threat. While he weighed how to convince Williams otherwise, he noticed that the unopened package still lay on the table. Williams saw him look.

"Go ahead and open it," Williams said, adding sarcastically, "I won't steal anything."

Jack wished he hadn't drawn attention to the package. He didn't know what Deb might have sent. "I'll open it later."

Before Jack could react, Williams took the package and read the return address. "It's from a pharmacy. Are you sick?"

Jack grabbed the package and read the address, the lekáreň near his hotel. Curious, he ripped the top of the package open. A bottle of pills. He looked for a note but there was none. Then he read the label out loud: "Aripiprazole." He had heard of it: two semesters ago, a graduate student on it had told him that one side effect was drowsiness, affecting the student's ability to stay awake in class. Perhaps Deb ordered them because of Jack's sleeplessness last night. But it was only one night, and Deb wouldn't have sent something without asking him first, something that probably required a prescription.

"Aripiprazole is an anti-psychotic," Williams said. "Now things are starting to make sense."

An anti-psychotic? Jack was certain that Deb hadn't sent the pills. "They aren't mine," he responded, pushing them across the table.

Williams pushed them back. "It's your name, brother. You probably forgot you ordered them."

"I didn't order them," Jack insisted angrily. "I don't need anti-psychotics."

Williams gave him a hard look. He clearly didn't believe Jack. "My advice? Get back on your meds. You'll feel better. And you'll realize then that you have no business being here." His voice was firm but gentle. He had evidently dealt with a recalcitrant patient before.

"Zane ordered them," Jack blurted out, "To convince you that I'm unstable and dangerous. Believe me, I'm not." He stopped when he saw the pitying look on Williams's face. Jack understood: the more he argued that he wasn't psychotic, the more Williams would believe he was. He stared at the bottle for a moment, then pocketed it. "I assure you I'm not psychotic, Sergeant. But, to satisfy you, I'll take the pills with me for now, because I want you to listen closely. Kas Hunter – Cassie Robinette – is in serious danger. You say you're interested in her welfare. If, for any reason, I'm not around, you have to protect her from Zane."

Williams only briefly considered Jack's request. "She's not in danger, not from Mr. Zane. He loves her and for all I know she loves him. Let them work it out. It's no concern of yours." His attention shifted to the front of the restaurant where a boisterous group of German tourists were entering. Almost to himself, he added, "He's known her for years, that's what he told me once. She was his first girl-friend."

"The hell she was," Jack retorted. "He strangled his first girl-friend, here, in an apartment across the river. A pregnant teenager."

Williams shook his head. "You're talking paranoid bullshit again and I'm not going to listen."

"Ask him why he left the country in 1968. Ask him why he changed his name from Zambo. And ask him what happened to his first bodyguard, a kid named Danny Mack. Back in 1978 in Afghani-stan, Zane hired him to produce heroin. Kas was there; ask her. When Danny tried to warn her about him, Zane had Danny killed. I've got evidence ..."

Williams lost his temper. "I'm telling you to shut the fuck up."

"This is the man you work for. He founded his empire on heroin. He killed his first girlfriend and his first bodyguard. He terrorized Kas so badly after one week that she fled, changed her name and went into hiding for the rest of her life. She didn't even go to her mother's fu-neral." Jack paused to take a breath. "But you know that. You were there."

Williams had stopped responding. He wouldn't even look at Jack. Immobile and rigid, he was a stone warrior at a palace gate. But Jack could see how tightly his jaws clenched, how the veins in his neck stood out.

Jack lowered his voice, trying to convey the loss he had sensed in Kas when she had talked about her mother's funeral. "It was about three years ago in Gonzales, Louisiana. People there remember you. And because you went as Zane's spy, Kas couldn't go. Not even to bury her mother."

"I went to pay respects," Williams replied slowly, in an equally quiet but adamant voice. "Mr. Zane wanted to honor Mrs. Robinette. All I did was to ask about her closest family members to give them his condolences directly. As it happens, no one close was still alive so I left. Mr. Zane has a special relationship with the Robinettes. I've paid respects at two other funerals for family members."

"Doesn't that strike you as odd that he would send his body-guard?"

Williams' mobile phone then rang and he stood to answer it, keeping an eye on Jack. The conversation was short.

"I'm leaving now. And you do as Mr. Zane said. Get on a plane and go home. Leave the woman alone. He's serious and so am I." And with that, Lawrence Williams turned and left.

"LET ME OUT!" Kas demanded. She tried to scramble over the man with red hair to reach the door. It was locked. She frantically tried to push the button to open the window. It was locked as well. The man – not roughly - pushed her off his lap and back into the mid-dle.

"Apologize to the lady," Zane charged the man in front who had punched Deb.

"Sorry, ma'am, I didn't mean to hit your friend," he mumbled, barely turning his head in her direction. The apology was perfunctory, insincere.

"Cassie," Zane said soothingly, "listen to me. That never should have happened. Mr. White overreacted to what he thought was a threat to me. It won't happen again."

"She's hurt!" Kas raged. "She needs to go to a hospital! Turn the car around right now!"

"That won't be necessary," and Zane extracted his phone. Kas heard him issuing instructions to someone for an ambulance to arrive at the gallery. He turned back to her. "Medical professionals are on their way there now. We'll just be underfoot if we return."

The black sedan stayed on course.

Kas was deeply shaken. Once again she had stupidly believed him. He hadn't changed.

Staring straight ahead, jaw set, she came to a decision. She would never live in fear of him again. If he reneged on his promise to let her go, if he got abusive, she wouldn't run and hide this time. She would fight back. Her experiences had changed her, given her means to deal with someone violent.

Sitting close to Zane, she suddenly felt serene and deadly.

IN LESS THAN a second after Williams' departure, Jack scrambled to his feet and dashed out the door. He stood still for a moment to get his bearings, then headed left. His instincts were right; he quickly found his way to Michaelska Street and from there to his hotel. Once in his room, he dumped the pills in the trash and retrieved his phone. Running down the hotel's steps minutes later, he dialed Sandy. She didn't answer, nor did Max. Neither Kas nor Deb responded. For a terrible minute, he imagined he was too late. He began to run toward the gallery. Then his phone vibrated, and he hurriedly held it to his ear.

"Hi Dad. I saw you called. What's up?' It was his daughter.

"Sandy!" Jack yelled breathlessly. "Are you okay?!"

"Of course I'm okay. Why? You sound strange."

He slowed his pace and tried to moderate the fear in his voice. "I'm fine. Still in Bratislava. Things are getting tricky here though."

"Tricky? What's the matter?"

"Remember that guy I told you about? Marton Zane? He's here. I just want to make sure he can't find you or Max."

"Why would he try to find us?"

"I don't think there's anything to worry about," he lied. "But humor me, okay? Just stay away from anyone you don't know. At least for a few days."

"Sure, no problem. I'm at my girlfriend's lake cabin this week-end." Sandy paused, "Tell me what this is all about. You're scaring me, Dad."

"I can't. I have to call Max."

"I'll call Max; I'll tell him. But I'm worried about you. What the hell is going on?"

"I'll call later to let you know. I promise. Right now, I gotta run."

"Dad!"

"I love you so much, Sandy. Max too," and he signed off.

He quickened his pace again, weaving through the dark streets toward the river. He kept trying to reach either Deb or Kas. All he had was an earlier voice mail from Deb wondering where he was. He tried calling her hotel room, Kas's apartment. Still no answers.

Suddenly his cell phone vibrated again. It was Deb.

With no preliminaries, she cried, "I didn't recognize him at first! I reacted too slowly. She's gone, Jack!"

She was talking so quickly that Jack had a hard time following. "Wait, what's happened!?" He was hoping he had misheard.

Deb – stoic even at her brother's memorial service - was almost hysterical. "I was not even five feet away, and Kas walked out with him! I tried to follow but…." Her voice broke in a sob.

Zane had Kas. Jack stopped in his tracks. He felt a wrench in his gut. *Think clearly,* he lectured himself. *You're no use if you don't think clearly.* To himself as much as to Deb, he said, "Let's take it one step at a time. So she's with Zane."

He could hear Deb breathing deeply to calm herself, to focus on the facts. "Yes, and two other men." She swallowed. "They left the gallery in a black car about fifteen minutes ago. Well, it looked like it was a black car."

A fifteen-minute head start, Jack thought. He was on the edge of the old town now, at a busy intersection. He examined every dark car that passed, imagining he saw Kas. Haunting the perimeter of his mind was the thought that he should have been there; he could have stopped them. Jack shook his head. Self-recrimination was useless. And it sounded from Deb as if Kas had left willingly. He needed more information. "Do you know where they've gone?" He started to move again as he talked, at a slower pace now.

"No idea. I'm so sorry, Jack. Do you think he'll hurt her?" Deb seemed on the verge of tears again.

He caught his breath at the question, but answered reflexively, "No. Kas is smart; she'll play it cool until she can escape. And anyway we'll find her." He heard another uncharacteristic sob and suddenly realized something. "Deb, are you okay?"

A momentary pause before she answered, "No. Not really."

"You're hurt?" He imagined a fall down the brick gallery steps.

"The big guy punched me in the stomach. But I'll live."

"Brill hit you?!" Jack was dumbstruck. He felt a galling rage rising in his throat, thickening his tongue.

"Alex found me lying in the street. We're heading to the police station now. A friend of his is a detective." Saying these words seemed to calm her. They calmed Jack a little as well. Finally some positive news, he thought. A friend who is a detective.

"Together, we'll find her," he reassured Deb. *We've got to*, he said to himself.

By now he had reached the river and wondered which direction to turn: left to the gallery, right to the castle, across the river, or somewhere behind him, in the city of half a million. He tried to put himself in Zane's mind to imagine where he might have taken Kas but Jack only saw a blank wall.

Deb broke into his thoughts. "I did hear Zane sing part of an old pop tune when they were leaving. I think it was *Fly me to the moon*. It seemed strange, out of place. Could that mean something?"

Jack knew the song; he had heard Diana Krall's version on the flight over. The lyrics came back to him unbidden: *Let me play among the stars; let me see what spring is like on Jupiter and Mars...*

And then he saw it. "I think I know where she is!" he declared and broke into a hard run. High above the New Bridge, hovering over the Danube, was a space ship, the UFO bar.

"WE'RE ALMOST THERE," Zane said and briefly brushed her knee. "Someplace special. Tremendous views above the Danube."

"You love heights," she noted flatly. "Like the High Tatras."

"You remember!" He sounded pleased.

Kas turned her head toward him. In the shadowed interior of the car, he couldn't see her face nor she his. Even so, she imagined she was staring him down. "I remember a lot about you, actually."

The car stopped. Kas was momentarily disoriented; they had driven across and under a bridge. Now the driver opened the door for her and Zane. The other two men left the car on the opposite side and edged next to Kas. As the car pulled away, the four of them walked to an elevator. A sign announced the UFO bar and restaurant. Kas looked up to see that the elevator ended in a saucer-shaped building suspended above the bridge. A public place; at least Zane had kept that part of his word. A cool breeze from the river caused Kas to shiver in her thin silk tunic.

"You're cold," Zane observed as they waited for the elevator. He removed his jacket and draped it across her shoulders.

Kas recoiled from the warmth of the jacket, the warmth from his body. "I'm fine." She shrugged the jacket off and handed it back to Zane.

"Are you hungry? We'll order dinner."

"No," she replied. "No, thanks." She wondered what fantasy he was playing at, imagining this was an amorous rendezvous. Was he delusional enough to think that she loved him? The idea triggered another involuntary shiver.

The elevator arrived and Zane held the doors as she entered. He stood beside her, with his two men in front, staring ahead. No one spoke on the short ride up.

The doors opened into a small vestibule; beyond it was a large room where low lights reflected warm tones of yellow and pink. A few patrons sat on stools along the curved bar; others occupied low sofas and chairs. Contemporary music played softly in the background. Full length windows wrapped around the room, displaying striking views of Bratislava, Petržalka and the dark glossy Danube below.

When Kas paused to scan the room for possible points of exit, Zane thought she was admiring the view. "It's even more stunning on the roof," he said. "Three hundred and sixty-degree views."

The man with the red hair stayed in the vestibule, near the elevator and stairwell; the man who had assaulted Deb – Zane called him Mr. White - followed them into the bar. Zane guided Kas away from the other patrons, toward a low divan overlooking Petržalka. A waiter promptly approached.

"It is good to see you again, sir." The waiter spoke in English, sounding both deferential and sincere. "Would you care for a club soda and lime as usual, sir? And for the lady?"

"She'll have a gin martini, two olives."

"Very good, sir."

Zane looked at Kas. "You see, I remember a lot about you as well."

"No martini," she bluntly told the waiter. "I'll have hot tea, čaj." The word in Slovak sounded similar to chai. She added, "Earl Grey. Ďakujem."

The waiter slightly inclined his head, "You are welcome, madam." Then he waited for Zane to clarify which drink to bring her. Finally, hearing nothing, he disappeared.

Ignoring the waiter's confusion. Zane smiled at Kas. "Another reminder of our first days together, when you were always thanking waiters."

She remembered it too, his defense of elitism at the Kabul Intercontinental. "And you didn't approve."

He gave a slight shrug. "I may have underestimated the value of social graces when I was younger. Now, I realize you were very astute."

Civility reduced to a tactic, Kas thought as she shifted her gaze to the view out of the window. "This is where you grew up, isn't it?" If she could get Zane to reminisce, he might open up about Katarina.

"It looked very different then," he answered, keeping his eyes fixed on Kas.

"And where your girlfriend died. What was her name again? You told me once."

"It doesn't matter. Ancient history."

"I remember. Katarina. She was your neighbor. Really young, too. I think you said she was only fifteen."

Zane paused, an edge in his voice. "I don't believe I ever said."

He was right, she realized. She had learned Katarina's age from Viliam. Kas backtracked. "My mistake. I guess I just imagined that. But what a tragedy for you. What happened to her? Was she ill?"

"As I said, ancient history. Let's talk about something else. Let's talk about us."

She had to push past his reluctance. "1968, wasn't it? You were just a boy yourself." With sympathetic warmth in her voice, she said, "You told me you had been to a math competition in Prague. You had won, I remember. Is that when it happened? Or were you able to be by her side when she…"

"Shut up, Cassie," he ordered. I don't want to talk about that b…" Zane caught himself mid-word. The waiter arrived with a soda and lime, martini, and cup of scalding hot tea.

Her heart pounding, Kas positioned the tea in front of her and ignored the martini. As if waiting for the tea to cool, she placed her hands – gripped in tight fists – in her lap and replayed his ugly reaction in her mind. Confirmation enough for her but not direct evidence for a court. To calm herself down, Kas imagined throwing the hot liquid into Zane's face.

The interruption enabled Zane to regain his composure. He pretended to finish the sentence, "… beautiful girl." He cleared his throat. "It's a painful memory and I don't want to talk about it."

The fear Kas had felt when she saw him at the gallery was long gone. Now, with intense dislike, she remarked, "You told me once you loved her."

He didn't catch the antipathy in her voice. "I did," he replied. "I loved her very much." Then Zane moved next to Kas on the low couch. "But let's not talk about sad memories. I know you're haunted by them, too; I've seen it in your photographs. Let's remember the happy times we had together."

She leaned away from him. "It's been almost thirty years, Marton. As you said, ancient history."

"Not for us. We transcend time. See this?" And from his coat pocket he produced a blue glass object and set it on the table next to her tea.

He was right; time did fall away. Kas felt her throat closing as unpleasant memories rushed in. "The bird cage water dish," she said in a monotone, wishing she had broken the damn piece back in Mashhad.

"You forgot it. I've been saving it for you." He picked up the piece of Herati glass and turned it around in the bar's pink and yellow light. "I searched but couldn't find the silver belt, which is when I knew you took it with you. When I knew you loved me. I still like to imagine you wearing it." His voice was husky when he asked, "Do you remember that night when I gave it to you?"

Shame. That was what she remembered of that night. Her recollections of the past were completely different than his, and she didn't know how long she could pretend otherwise. What would he do if she left now, before the hour was up? Stealing a quick glance at the muscular bodyguard called Mr. White, she wondered if he would try to stop her.

Zane followed her eye movements and again misread her thoughts. Believing that modesty kept her from answering, he motioned slightly to the man who then retreated several steps, out of hearing range.

Kas watched and understood Zane's nonverbal message. "Discreet," she said, picking up her cup of tea to hide her agitation. "You like that in a bodyguard."

"I do value discretion, yes."

"Danny wasn't discreet," Kas said. She saw Zane's jaw muscle spasm as he checked another surge of irritation.

"Danny was a fool. Getting himself killed like that. Typical Danny." He shifted in his seat, briefly pushed his hand against his stomach.

It was an odd move, Kas thought. Maybe he had an ulcer, maybe the flu. She didn't care. "Danny was a young, dumb kid," she said. "Like me."

"Not like you, Cassie, never like you." Zane gently took her chin in his hand and studied her face. "I've missed you so much. The Herati glass has sat on my office desk for more than twenty years, reminding me every day that I should never have let you go."

Kas pulled back. "You didn't let me go, Marton. I ran away. There's a difference."

A slight nod to signify that he had thought of this, too. "I wasn't good enough to you then. But I can be now. I have the resources to give you anything you want." He leaned closer to her. "For most women, its clothes, jewelry, mansions, status." He paused. "Those are yours for the asking. But you won't ask because you don't bother with trifles. You're not like any woman I've ever known."

There was nothing she could say in reply.

"I can help, Cassie. I have vast wealth. We can use that money to help people, refugees, anyone you like. That's what I want to tell you." He took her hand. "Think of the good we can do, together."

She stared at him: they could funnel millions of dollars to mitigate the worst humanitarian crises in the world. For a nanosecond she was tempted. But gifts from Zane came with high costs. Almost instantly she recalled the note and city map he had given Danny, gifts that had gotten him killed. She recalled too the painful souvenir Zane had given her. Wordlessly, she lifted the end of one blue silk sleeve and exposed the white pucker on the light tan flesh of her inner wrist.

With a sharp intake of breath, Zane tenderly took her arm and studied the scar. He traced it with his fingertip. "You made me so crazy," he murmured. "I never meant to hurt you."

Not an explanation, not an apology. Kas noted that he kept the blame on her.

"This is my answer, Marton. This is why I have to refuse your offer. You hurt people, not help them. That's what you do." There was so much more she could have added.

His continued fascination with the old burn unnerved her. She reclaimed her arm and pulled down her sleeve. She decided it was time to go. "Thanks for the tea. You've said what you wanted to say. Now I have to get back to the gallery." She stood. "You stay and relax. I'll catch a cab." He didn't move. With some amazement, she thought he was letting her go.

But then he frowned. "Not yet," he demurred, "It hasn't been an hour yet. Sit down."

"You said what you wanted to say to me," she repeated. "I listened." She felt herself getting angrier. "We had a deal, Marton. You promised to leave me alone if I did that."

"That's not quite accurate," he corrected her.

She looked directly into those unearthly eyes so he would not mistake her meaning. "You're right. You said you'd give me my life back if I told you that I didn't want to see you again. And I don't."

"No," he said carefully. "I promised nothing about having your life back. I said you would never see me again." He took a tiny sip of soda and lime, only enough to wet his lip. His hand shook as he set the glass down again. "I always keep my promises. That is clearly more than I can say for you."

She frowned. "I never made you any promises."

"You're wrong again, Cassie. You made so many. You promised to come to Geneva, to help my business, to stay with me. And not just with words. You promised with your eyes, your voice, your body." He stood and leaned over her. "You betrayed me once and I forgave you. And now you betray me again, after I offer you everything I have. Everything."

His voice was a low and soft, and it terrified her. But it also infuriated her and she didn't back down. "You're the one who's wrong, Marton. I promised you nothing. You imagined it. Nothing special happened between us the night of the silver belt, or any of the other nights. Only sex." She said the last two words firmly, definitively. "And I didn't take that damn silver belt with me, either. I gave it to someone to help me escape."

Instantly his tone changed, to a hateful hiss. "My mistake was to trust you, to think all this time that you were different. But you're not. You're just a cunt, like the rest. No, not even that. You're nothing."

Kas saw those blue eyes flick to movement behind her. She had only turned halfway to see when she felt the blow on the back of her head. No chance to step away, no chance to cry for help. Her body fell forward, collapsing face first on the divan.

To REACH THE UFO bar, Jack ran along the wide pedestrian walkway beneath the New Bridge. He was more than half way across when, in the distance, he could see its elevator. Lawrence Williams stood guard; Jack's hunch had been right. Before Williams spied him, he stopped and sent Deb a cryptic text: *UFO bar.* Then he threw the phone into the river, the contact numbers forever out of Zane's reach. Because he knew that, before the night was over, he would confront Zane again.

As he approached, Williams was turning a young couple away, telling them the bar was reserved for a private party that evening. When Williams saw him, he frowned in dismay. "What the fuck are you doing here? You're supposed to be on your way to Vienna."

"I can't leave. I need to go up there."

"Hell, no."

"You know I'm not dangerous."

"No, I don't."

Jack pleaded, "I've got to stop him."

"You've got to go. Now."

"Listen to me," Jack implored. "Kas is in danger. I know this man. I know what he's capable of."

Williams turned his back, shutting him out.

"He's using you, Sergeant. First you play babysitter and now you're a door man. Why do you think that is, when you should be with your boss upstairs?"

Just then, a few people frantically pushed out of the stairwell and ran, followed closely by others, some tripping on the bottom steps in their rush to get out. Several were shouting and gesticulating, others sobbing. Two dozen or more emerged, well dressed international travelers and affluent Slovaks. Three wait-staff, several kitchen staff and the cook came out, then the manager, ashen and silent, making sure everyone else was safely out.

Jack strained to understand what people were saying, but even those who spoke English were incomprehensible. Their fear was palpable. At last he caught the gist of the uproar: terrorists had taken the bar; they were holding hostages, an older man and his wife. Reportedly, at least one terrorist spoke English; he sounded American. Someone said their phones had been seized before they were allowed to leave, to keep them from calling for help right away. Someone else said there might be a bomb. In shock, they crowded together just beyond the elevator, then jostled one another as they started down the pedestrian walkway, most of them moving toward the closer town of Petržalka for their cars and taxis.

Kas wasn't among the fleeing customers. Desperate now, Jack cornered an elegant older woman with an American accent. "What happened?! There are hostages?!"

"Yes, two of them. A man and a woman. The woman's hurt, I think. One of the terrorists hit her. Do you have a phone?!" She clutched his hand.

Shaking his head no, Jack asked, "She's hurt? Badly?"

"I don't know. She wasn't moving when we left. Her husband was holding her." Sensing that Jack knew them, she tried to sound reassuring, "It could be for ransom, not terrorism. One waiter said the man's a Canadian billionaire, in which case they'll be released, won't they? I didn't peg him as Canadian. He spoke Slovak so fluently."

Jack's heart was sinking. "What did he say, this hostage? Do you know?"

The American tried to explain politely but quickly; she was clearly anxious to leave and join her companions on their hurried trek to safety. "One of the terrorists screamed at us in English to get out, and some of the Slovaks didn't understand. The hostage translated it for them. He also told us about the bomb. He said he and his wife were being held hostage but we…" Her voice broke. "But we had to get to safety. He asked that we remember them in our prayers." She pulled at Jack's arm. "You can't help your friends. You have to get away from here. The whole place could blow." Eyes wide, she glanced up once and then rushed off.

"Thanks! And get help!" Jack shouted. The woman waved back.

The last of the UFO patrons had gone. Abruptly, a surreal silence enveloped Jack and Williams. The bodyguard remained impassive; he hadn't moved from his post.

Jack watched Williams closely before observing, "You're awfully calm, Sergeant. Not worried about terrorists killing your boss?" It was a rhetorical question. Both men knew there was no terrorist threat.

Williams shrugged. "Mr. Zane told me this might happen. He wanted everyone out, and it's not up to me to second guess his methods. All I know is that a terrorist threat guarantees the police are here in a hurry. In case you try anything." His mobile rang. He moved a few paces from Jack and spoke quietly into the phone. When he finished, he returned to the elevator door.

Jack was primed for an argument. "But that doesn't make sense. I'm not even up there. How can I try anything?"

Williams ignored the question. "You should have gone home. Now Mr. Zane is angry. He wants me to bring you up."

Just then the elevator doors opened and Clive Riley stepped out. Studiously avoiding looking at Jack, Riley nodded quickly at Williams, then took his place as guard. Williams pointed Jack toward the elevator.

As they ascended, Jack saw the pieces fall into place. "It's a set-up," he said. "Kas will be killed. Zane will be 'rescued.' And Brill will be shot on sight by the police. The big, bad terrorist. It's not far-fetched; Brill was the leader of a skin head group when Zane recruited him. Did you know that? Lots of virulent anti-Semitic rants on his web page. I'm sure Riley can plant more incriminating evidence." Jack thought a moment. "And me? What part do I play? An unlucky bar patron shot by Brill? Or maybe I'm cast as another terrorist, killed in the course of Zane's heroics. He'd like that." He leveled a hard look at Williams. "And you're here to back up the boss, make it all seem credible. That's your role in the farce: The Man of Integrity."

Williams looked genuinely puzzled by his outburst. "You really are a paranoid psychotic." Then the elevator doors opened.

Jack gave a gruff laugh, "Naturally you're in the dark, Sergeant. You have to be. It adds a crucial element of believability."

"Ridiculous." Williams was irritated. As he shoved Jack from the elevator, he grunted, "Nobody's getting killed. I'll make sure of that."

"You'd better," Jack warned brusquely, steeling himself against the awful possibility that Kas was dead already. He swore to himself that, if she was, he would get Zane. He wouldn't let her death be chalked up as a phony terrorism statistic.

Now in the vestibule, Jack noted from the corner of his eye that Brill was halfway up the stairwell leading to the roof. He was hauling a large duffle. A flash of alarm seized him before Jack realized that the bag wasn't bulky enough to be carrying her body.

A second later, entering the bar, Jack's hope was confirmed. There she was, slumped on a divan near a low table which held three empty martini glasses and fragments of blue glass. Her eyes were closed but he thought he saw an eyelid flutter.

"Kas!" Jack shouted. Before he took two steps toward her, Williams grabbed his arm, almost jerking him off his feet.

"I told you, Hunter. I won't let you touch a hair on her head."

Zane approached. "It's all right, Mr. Black. Mr. Hunter is here to apologize to Miss Robinette for stalking her and then he will leave. Forever. I can handle him." Nestled comfortably in his hand was a .38

Special. With his free hand, Zane pointed to the exit. "The police should be here soon. Mr. Red has the elevator, you take the stairs. Notify me the moment they arrive." When Williams still did not release Jack's arm, Zane repeated, "The stairs. Now."

With a last warning look at Jack, Williams walked to the stairway and disappeared down it.

"Well, well, well," Zane said to Jack, not at all displeased. "I thought I might be seeing you again." Then he addressed Kas's limp form. "Now that Professor Hunter has deigned to join us, we can go to the roof to enjoy that view I told you about." He pulled her to her feet and pushed her toward Jack.

Jack caught her; she was barely conscious.

"Kas," he said softly. "Are you with me, Kas? Come on, wake up." He felt her muscles begin to stiffen as she gradually revived. Then he noticed a small trickle of blood from one ear. As he suspected and feared, she wasn't drunk, despite the strong smell of alcohol on her clothes. "You hurt her," he accused Zane.

Not bothering to reply, Zane motioned with the gun toward the ascending stairwell.

Kas heard him and looked up, still dazed, eyes not fully open. "Jack? Jack, you're back!"

"Yes, I'm here, Kas. We have to walk now. Can you do that?" He held her tightly to keep her from stumbling. "One step at a time. That's good." Her legs awkwardly took over the task of walking. He was relieved; they stood a better chance if they could both run. In the vestibule, Jack inched them closer to the elevator, a few steps ahead of Zane. Then he furtively pushed the down button. Its light did not come on.

"Foolish move, Jack," Zane said coming up behind them. He pushed the revolver against the small of Jack's back. "Try it again," he challenged.

By now, full consciousness had returned to Kas. Jack felt her stiffen as she looked into his face and whispered in dismay, "I'm so sorry I brought you here."

"The roof, if you please," Zane hissed.

They started to climb the stairs. "Where else would I be?" He said it lightly, but his arm tightened around her waist.

"Keep walking," Zane ordered, prodding Jack with the revolver, foreclosing any chance of escape down the stairs.

They took each step carefully, Kas exaggerating her dizziness to slow their pace. Trying to buy time to think, to plan, to act. Eventually, they reached the roof. Zane appeared agitated at the delay, and impatiently pushed them away as Brill approached him. In low voices, they conferred while Jack and Kas, still holding each other, took in the spectacular scene.

Without a moon, the constellations stood in stark relief against the black sky, some stars bright enough to cast their light on the river below. In one direction stood the frosted square cake of Bratislava castle, brightly lit and imposing. In the other was the town of Petržalka, ablaze with shopping centers, apartment buildings and highways. From here, everything seemed so festive, a party in progress. Except at the top of the roof itself, which was cloaked in shadow.

As Jack's eyes adjusted to the darkness, he could discern a solid white wall, waist high, encircling the roof. A higher wall would block the view, of course, but to keep inebriated visitors from stumbling off, a six-foot tall chain link fence ran the circumference of a catwalk constructed three feet below the roof itself. A three-foot fall from the roof to the catwalk would hurt but not prove fatal. Jack let go of Kas to look for the passageway from the roof to the catwalk, with some idea of forcing Zane and Brill down there. He found it, a gate in the white wall already standing open. Directly beyond it, secured with a thick chain and massive padlock, was an unobtrusive utility gate in the chain link fence, providing access for service personnel to clean the acres of windows and repair power lines snaking up the side of the building. Workers had to be careful, though. Beyond the utility gate was only the sky.

"Cops just arrived." Williams' voice broke from the top of the stairwell. Only his head and shoulders were visible. "Got the call from Mr. Red. The elevator's out for some reason, so they have to come up the stairs. Could be a few minutes," he reported.

"We'll be careful until they get here." Zane looked pointedly at Jack, indicating to Williams that Jack was not yet a danger.

"Need me to stay?" Williams asked.

"No, I need you downstairs at the bar. When the police get there, direct them up here. And make sure that Mr. Red stays at his post."

The police had arrived; Jack was ecstatic. "Wait!" he yelled at Williams. "Get Kas out of here!" But Williams had already vanished down the stairwell. That instant, Brill punched Jack hard in the belly and he collapsed to his knees. Bent over in pain, he cursed himself for being too slow in reacting to Williams. He was dimly aware that Kas was calling his name, asking him if he was all right. He stumbled to his feet.

By the time he had regained his footing, Kas was intently watching Brill at the utility gate as he positioned a hefty bolt cutter over the thick chain. Jack recognized the empty nylon duffel bag at Brill's feet. Cutting the chain wasn't easy. Even as big as he was, Brill grunted with effort before finally cutting through it. He tossed the bolt cutter to the roof and unfastened the chain. The gate to nothingness swung free.

That's when Jack realized that a different storyline was in play, Zane's Plan B. The ruse of a terrorist attack, Plan A, wasn't needed. Zane didn't have to lose Brill after all; reliable thugs were probably hard to find. Nor did Zane need to risk that Brill – if he survived the night - would talk once he faced terrorism charges. As far as any testimony from the fleeing clientele was concerned, Jack could almost hear Zane explaining that they had misunderstood; that it wasn't a terrorist but a psychotic killer who had threatened them. And the psychotic killer was Jack.

So his arrival on the scene had been planned for, even hoped for. It made Plan B possible. With the gate to the sky open, little effort would be necessary to push Kas and Jack into the void. Zane had already written a plausible script for criminal investigators to follow: the antipsychotic medication in Jack's hotel room, Jack's single-minded effort to track Kas down, the testimony of witnesses – Williams among them - that Kas had rejected him. If needed, Riley could plant evidence online; perhaps he already had. All in all, Jack conceded, ample substantiation for a homicide/suicide.

Zane's fiction would fall apart once investigators took the time to examine Jack's real life. With Deb's persistence, they might even suspect Zane and his men. But those facts were irrelevant to the plan's success. Jack and Kas would be dead and Zane beyond reach in Canada behind a firewall of money and attorneys.

KAS WAS THINKING along the same lines. "You're such a goddamn coward, Zambo. You weasel your way out of all blame for your crimes. Frame others, that's your *modus operandi*. With Katarina, Danny, probably others."

"You're hallucinating, likely menopausal," Zane said implacably, checking his gun.

Kas was fierce. "Your thug here will push us off the roof and make it look like Jack killed me and then himself. And you think of yourself as a big man, the hero of a grand epic." She added scornfully, "You're no hero. You don't have the nerve to do your own killing. Except when it comes to little girls. Why is that? Did strangling Katarina sexually excite you?"

"She was a whore," Zane snapped suddenly. Kas's accusations had started to roil his placid demeanor, like rocks thrown into a lake.

"She was fifteen and pregnant, by you. Which makes it statutory rape, Zambo."

"I never raped anyone," he said savagely.

Kas remembered how with her he had studiously avoided any appearance of sexual coercion. It was part of his self-image, she reasoned, that women wanted him and he never had to force himself. So with vicious pleasure she repeated, "It was rape, though." She was figuring something out about him: charges of sexual predation disturbed him more than accusations of murder did. "Pedophile," she sneered.

"Shut the fuck up," he warned, waving the gun at her.

Good, Kas thought. Cursing was also uncharacteristic; a loss of control.

Kas looked hard at Zane. "Having sex with a child is one thing, but killing her? Why? Because she didn't want your baby? Because she couldn't stand the idea that it was yours?"

Her jabs worked. His breathing rapid and shallow, his expression wild, he brought his face close to hers and hissed, "Because she made me do it!"

JACK READ THE opening. While Zane brandished the gun and Brill stared in fascination, he grabbed the handles of the bolt cutter and swung the sharp end of the heavy tool at Brill's head. Brill somehow sensed it coming and adroitly sidestepped the blow. Jack swung a second time and a third, both at Brill's torso, keeping Brill from tackling him. The bolt cutter weighed a lot but Jack's summer training helped; even so, he felt fatigue creeping up his arms and into his shoulders. He knew he couldn't keep this up indefinitely. But he didn't need to; the police should arrive any moment. He swung again, this time getting very close to connecting with Brill's skull.

Kas gave a strangled whelp. Jack looked up to see her body arched back against Zane's, his left arm around her throat. Against her temple, his right hand held the short-barreled revolver.

"Game over," Zane announced. "Drop it."

Jack clutched the tool more tightly. "You won't shoot her," he declared. "Bullet wounds would contradict your murder-suicide fable." He hoped desperately that he was right. He hoped desperately that the police were only seconds away.

Eerily calm now, Zane said, "Don't concern yourself. I don't expect the authorities to find your bodies, at least not before the fish have a chance to enjoy them. And if your bodies are found, the gun in your pocket will explain all. Personally, I'd prefer Cassie to be alive for her flight. But if I have to shoot her, I will. I might even shoot her in the abdomen," and he moved the barrel to her belly. "I've been told it's a painful way to die." Jack could see Kas struggling against the chokehold.

Carefully laying down the bolt cutter, Jack seethed, "You'll get caught, Zane."

He shrugged. "Perhaps. But I don't think so. I think you're just killing time. So let's end this little drama." With his gun hand, he signaled for Brill to seize Jack and then he added, "By the way, thank you for your fingerprints. I really couldn't fake that piece of evidence."

Jack looked in horror at his hands, then at Brill's. The young thug was wearing surgical gloves. Only Jack's prints would be on the bolt cutter.

Zane was almost laughing.

But as Jack watched in fascination, Kas tucked down her chin, stepped forward and kicked back hard against Zane's shin. Almost simultaneously, she grabbed the thumb of his gun hand, pulling the wrist joint, twisting it outward and down. Jack could hear Zane grunt. Off balance and in pain, he lost his grip on her throat and on the revolver. In one fluid movement, Kas seized the gun, ducked her head beneath his arm and pivoted out of reach. By the time Jack's brain registered what had happened, she was pointing the handgun at Zane's heart.

A practiced maneuver, Jack realized with a start. She had done this before.

Kas was panting with exertion but her voice was steady. "Get over there," she ordered Zane, motioning with the barrel toward Brill. Zane took a few slow steps in that direction. "Let's go, Jack." Jack was already moving toward her, close enough now to see how the gun in her hand trembled slightly. He wondered if she was fighting the urge to shoot Zane. It would be justifiable homicide, in Jack's opinion, but he was glad for her sake when she didn't.

But before Jack could reach her, Brill lunged from behind and grabbed him as a shield.

"Stop it!" Kas shrieked. "Let him go!" She glared at Brill but aimed at Zane.

Zane's hands flew up in surrender. "Cassie, you can't shoot me. I'm unarmed." He moved a step closer to her. "I'm no threat to you or Jack. Hit Brill. He's your enemy, not me."

A moment's indecision, shifting the aim from one man to the other. "Let him go," she commanded the dark form restraining Jack. But she couldn't get a clear shot and swung the aim toward Zane again.

His hands remained high but his stance was poised, like a feral cat's. "There are 206 bones in the body, Cassie. Did you know that?"

The comment made no sense to Kas, but she knew Zane was plotting something. "Shut up. And go over there with your guy."

Zane didn't budge. "A lot can break from a fall of this height. The collar bone, for example." He lightly touched his.

While Kas was frowning at Zane, Brill caught the cue, pulled his fist up and back, and landed a ferocious blow on Jack's right clavicle. Jack yelled in surprised agony.

Kas jerked the revolver toward them, searching in vain for the slightest opening to shoot. Even in the dim starlight, she could see how the right side of Jack's body sagged despite Brill's tight grasp. All she could think of was the 205 bones remaining.

By now, Zane had stealthily moved behind her. She sensed his presence and spun around. Zane - close and ready - grabbed her wrist and twisted. A shot went off, meaningless, into the air. The gun was back in his hands. He shoved her down and stood over her. Even in the half light, she could see his grin.

"Let's change the story." He aimed at her left eye, then her right, then her stomach again. "Jack shoots you and then, in remorse, throws himself off the roof. Mr. White and I can testify that we tried to stop him but..." Zane shrugged in mock sorrow. "Tragedies happen every day."

Suddenly, out of the stairwell, Lawrence Williams lunged.

Williams shoved Zane to the ground and the revolver flew. Then he stormed Brill, who stood immobile, too astonished to react. Williams grabbed the arm that pinned Jack and fractured the wrist. Now it was Brill who howled. Then he broke his other wrist.

Jack fell free. On his knees, he scrambled one-armed toward the discarded bolt cutter.

Williams wheeled on Zane. The sweat on Williams' face glistened in the lights from Petržalka, heightening the harshness of his expression.

Zane had recovered from the blow and the shock, and now crouched in the shadows searching for the gun. He saw it, inches in front of the passage to the catwalk. In the same instant, Kas saw it too. Both dashed toward the weapon but Zane was closer. As he bent to retrieve it, though, Williams dove on his back and both men landed heavily on the roof.

The revolver lay unclaimed. Kas tried to get near, but the two men grappled and rolled and blocked her way.

In size and training, Williams had the wrestling advantage. Several times, he came close to pinning Zane down but he couldn't hold him. Zane, though thin, was pure adrenalin and muscle, and his torso twisted like an eel's. Then he kneed Williams' groin, and suddenly Zane was back on his feet, grimacing and bent over but heading straight for the handgun. He snatched it up and pointed it at Kas, the worst traitor.

With painful effort, Jack hurled the bolt cutter at Zane. Heavy and oddly shaped, it made a slow and clumsy projectile, and Zane veered out of its path. It fell harmlessly and loudly a foot to the left of Zane. Yet it diverted him long enough for Williams to charge. Roaring with fury, he slammed his head into Zane's abdomen. The gun went flying again and Zane reeled backward.

Kas ran to Jack's side and they watched spellbound as Zane toppled. At any moment they expected to see him catch himself, but he kept tilting back, feet almost off the ground. He tumbled backward off the steps to the catwalk and, a second later, through the utility gate. He grabbed at the chain link fence. He missed.

Without uttering a word, Marton Zane flew into the night sky, arms outstretched, reaching toward the gate and life and Cassie Robinette. He caught her eye. For the briefest moment, he seemed to her to be suspended in starlight, a moment of terrible magical power. Then he was gone.

No one could speak.

CHAPTER TWENTY-TWO

August 17, 2007
Friday

"I didn't mean to kill him," Williams said. He was squatting on the roof, hands hanging limp between his knees.

Kas could hear the anguish in his voice. She didn't know Williams, other than the fact that he had worked with Zane and, in the end, had come to their rescue. But she knew from his voice that he wasn't someone who relished taking another life.

"It was an accident," Jack tried to reassure him. "We all saw it." He added, "And thank you, Sergeant. You stopped him. You saved our lives."

Brill grunted, cradling his weirdly bent wrists, one in the other. "Maybe I didn't see it that way."

Kas stared at him. Delusional, she thought; he imagined he could call the shots now that Zane was gone, as if he had leverage. Disgusted, she turned away, unable to think of anything civil to say.

But Jack did. Looking hard at Brill, he replied, "Fine. The other scenario is this: you're a terrorist. Zane already told that to the people in the bar. We'll confirm it."

Brill frowned a moment. "No, wait," he muttered. He wasn't smart, but he's wasn't stupid either. "Maybe I didn't get such a clear look after all."

Williams remained anguished. "I wanted that bastard prosecuted. I wanted him in prison, not dead."

Jack sympathized. "He saved your father's life," he said simply. But he sensed there was more to it. For Jack, at least, arrest, prosecution and conviction provided the classic morality play necessary to the order of things. Only in that way could chaotic violence be made more comprehensible, manageable.

Kas quietly observed. "It was suicide."

All three men stared at her, mouths open.

"How can you...?" Jack started.

It was so obvious to her. "He could have braced himself when you charged, but he didn't. And when you hit, he let himself fall backward."

This time it was Williams who objected. "We all saw him. He tried to save himself and couldn't. Up to the end, he was trying to save himself."

"No, he wasn't. Not seriously." She thought it curious that the others didn't see this.

"Why do you think so, Kas?" Jack probed. He wasn't convinced; she could hear it in his voice. But he was open to a new interpretation of events.

"Didn't you hear him?"

"He didn't say anything," Williams broke in. "It happened too fast."

"No, I mean before then, when he was reaching for the gun, then pointing it at me. He was humming. I know the tune. It was the suicide song."

"That means shit," Brill asserted aggressively. "He'd never kill himself."

Kas waved her hand dismissively. To the others she said, "He'd failed and he knew it. He was out of time. The police were arriving. Everyone was against him."

"Not me," Brill interjected, a poisonous glare at Williams.

This time she ignored him completely. "In his mind, he had no choice." He might even have seen his death as tragically romantic, she thought. And a reproach to her; once again, the message: *See what you made me do?*

They didn't have time to argue. Kas was right on one count, at least. Within seconds, the police did arrive. Officers in SWAT gear poured from the stairwell and surrounded them with weapons drawn. The police didn't know good guys from bad guys. They were all bad guys.

IN THE WAKE of the SWAT team came a homicide detective with Alexej; Deb was just steps behind.

"Deb!" Kas and Jack said at once.

The detective spoke with quiet urgency to the officer in charge, then he turned toward Kas. Jack could overhear a few murmured questions, essentially the same question in different words: had Zane said anything to her about the death of Katarina Petras? Jack couldn't hear Kas's response, but he saw the detective nod and jot a few notes. Then the detective gave Kas a business card and said he'd conduct a formal interview later at the station.

While Kas and the detective were talking, Deb ran to Jack. "You're alive! You're both alive!"

He and Kas were alive; the nightmare was over. Elation cutting through his pain and confusion, Jack almost laughed, "Damn straight!"

Deb squinted her eyes against the glare of the police flashlights. "Where's Zane?"

He looked at the gate in the chain-link fence, still hanging open. "Dead." An easy answer yet not an easy answer.

She opened her mouth, but before she could say anything, an officer on the SWAT team pulled her away.

Williams, Brill, Jack and Kas were separated and, after preliminary questioning on the roof, Williams was taken directly to the police station. The other three, under police escort, first received medical care. Jack and Brill had their broken bones set, and Kas had a CT scan to check for brain injury from Brill's blow. When she and a police officer later passed Deb in the hospital corridor, waiting for a CT scan of her abdomen, the women exchanged looks but no words. Kas realized then that there had been no ambulance to attend to Deb earlier; it had been another of Zane's many lies.

By dawn, Deb and Alexej were separately giving statements about what they knew; later in the morning and throughout the day, others did as well. Among them were Viliam and Magdalena, distraught and overwhelmed, confirming that Marton Zane had been Marton Zámbó, that at his request they had reunited him with Kas Hunter.

By the time the police had finished questioning Jack, it was mid-morning and he was beyond exhaustion. Yet the events of the previous night kept him keyed up, on edge. Now, leaving the building, he shifted his arm in the sling, trying to find a more comfortable position. Searing pain shot through his shoulder. He fretted about how he was going to get back to the hotel; he knew his judgment was clouded. He had never felt older.

Then he spied Deb outside the station next to a taxi. She saw him and waved. With childlike relief, he hurried over. Without thinking, they moved to hug each other, then both involuntarily winced.

"Sorry, I forgot." he said. "Are you all right?"

"Bruised and sore but nothing serious. No yoga poses for a while. How about you? How's the collar bone?"

Jack gestured "so-so" with his undamaged arm. "I'm lucky. It's a clean break. The doctor said I shouldn't need the sling more than a few weeks." He studied her. Deb looked as drained as he felt. "Did you get any sleep?"

"Not really. I got back here about an hour ago to wait for you guys. Alex was still here," she explained, opening the door of the taxi.

Jack looked back at the station. "Aren't we going to wait for Kas?"

"She came out about half an hour ago. Alex took her to his place. With the head injury, she shouldn't be alone for a while." Reading Jack's expression, Deb quickly added, "Don't worry, Jack. She has a concussion. It may take a few days or weeks, but she should be fine. That's what she told me."

He nodded, restrained in his relief, wondering if Kas had given the full story. He also felt unaccountably low at having missed her. He reproached himself for being selfish; friends were looking out for her.

"First thing this morning, I alerted the American embassy to arrange for counsel," Deb said briskly as the cab drove them back to Jack's hotel. "Brill's defense attorney got here just before you came out. I expect someone will be here soon to see Sergeant Williams. The authorities have twenty-four hours to charge him or let him go. He'll probably get an interpreter as well."

"Good, good." Even in his fuzzy state, Jack registered that Deb had done some homework. He knew a fair amount of comparative law, but the Slovak legal system was new to him. "Any word on Clive Riley?"

She shook her head no. "My theory is that he melted away in the crowd as soon as the police arrived. He's long gone."

They were riding through downtown when Deb said, "I talked with your kids last night. I thought they needed to know you were all right. I didn't want them to worry when they see the headlines."

He groaned; he hadn't thought of the anxiety his family must be feeling not hearing from him since his cryptic warning about Zane. "Damn, I didn't call. I threw my phone off the bridge, right after I sent you the text." In retrospect, he regretted it. At the time, it seemed a reasonable precaution, but now the gesture seemed unnecessary and melodramatic.

"You can use mine. Better yet, use my laptop. That way you can Skype."

Deeply fatigued, Jack leaned against the taxi seat and, for an instant, closed his eyes. "Thanks for taking care of things. Deb." He opened his eyes and looked directly at her. "Honestly, I don't know what I'd do without you."

"I owe you, Jack. You got that motherfucker. I'll never be able to thank you enough."

MAX ANSWERED RIGHT away and they talked for half an hour. But Sandy wasn't responding on Skype. Finally she accepted the connection.

Her first words were, "Thanks for finally getting in touch."

Sarcasm? Resentment? Jack hadn't heard that tone in her voice for years. He didn't need to ask her mood; her face communicated fury.

"You have every right to be angry, Sandy. I am profoundly sorry to have endangered you and Max," he said.

She shook her head. "I am angry, but that's not why. You almost died. You could have been killed." Sandy stopped and took several deep breaths. A few moments passed before she could continue. "I've never been so scared in my life. Not knowing. You should have told me."

"Told you what, sweetheart? I didn't plan this."

She brushed off his comment. "You've changed, Dad."

"I'm sorry," he said again. That's what he feared; no longer the reliable father, the rock.

She turned her head away from the screen, looked into the distance. "I never ever imagined that my father would fight off killers on a roof in some foreign capital."

Jack replied, "I know I took risks I shouldn't have. But I had to act quickly ..."

"Risks? You've never intentionally taken a big risk in your life. You don't even like to switch coffee brands. Or at least you didn't."

"I was stodgy. That's what your mother always said." He thought back to his collection of kitsch from around the world; gifts or purchases from garage sales and junk shops, souvenirs of other people's adventures. Never his own. Helene had ridiculed him for it.

His remark stopped Sandy. In a softer tone, she continued, "No, not stodgy. That's not what I mean. You're always open to new ideas. You take intellectual risks." She paused briefly again, and the edge returned to her voice. "But this action hero adventure shit? I didn't expect it of you."

"Honey, it's not like I had a choice. He was going to kill Cassie. And he would have, if Williams hadn't stopped him. He's the real action hero."

He could see her shaking her head. "And you're the one who persuaded Williams to act. Deb told me she overheard him tell that to the police. He said he should have listened to you. That it was his fault things got violent in the end."

It wasn't his fault. Williams have saved their lives. But now wasn't the time to argue; Jack saw Sandy wipe her eyes. Tears? To his knowledge, she hadn't cried since third grade. He ached to hold her. "I wish ...."

"Dad," Sandy interrupted and cleared her throat, "What I'm trying to say is this. That I'm mad as hell, yeah. But I'm also incredibly proud."

THE DAY PASSED, and the next. Forensic evidence from the scene was gathered and processed, rooms were searched, mobile phone records accessed. In Zane's hotel room, nothing useful showed up. He was – had been – a careful and meticulous man.

The hunt for Clive Riley continued. Late Saturday afternoon, a man answering his description was located on the train to Berlin. When Riley was brought into custody, he proclaimed his innocence and refused to answer questions. But his fingerprints made clear that he had dismantled the elevator, slowing down the police. The pharmacy clerk identified him as the man posing as Jack Hunter who had left a prescription for Aripiprazole. And several of the people who had fled the bar placed him with Brill and Zane. Riley was arrested.

Gradually, investigators gleaned a rough understanding of what had transpired. The accounts given by Williams, Kas and Jack were confirmed. Brill was held on charges of assault, kidnapping, attempted murder and threatening the public. Williams was charged with manslaughter, not homicide; his attorney was cautiously optimistic that the charges would be further reduced.

On Sunday, Jack managed to Skype with Frank Constant, recounting the incident in case the White House or diplomatic channels could help Williams.

Frank already knew a good deal, although some of his information was inaccurate, speculative or wildly improbable. The strange death of billionaire Marton Zane triggered intense international interest. Yet few involved in the investigation would comment to the news media on or off the record. Kas categorically refused. Jack eventually assented to an interview with *The Guardian,* but he kept his remarks as non-sensational as possible. He didn't want to complicate Williams's defense or the prosecution of Brill or Riley. Or – for that matter – further compromise Kas's cherished privacy, although keeping her out of the story was impossible. At least he was able to short-circuit a rumor that she and Zane had been long time secret lovers.

That falsehood - Jack thought angrily – might have made Zane's actions almost comprehensible to some people.

Meanwhile, the authorities methodically searched the river for Zane's body. Because he had been a Canadian citizen, the Canadian chargé d'affaires was staying abreast of the search and the investigation into his death. So was the Vienna-based embassy of the Islamic Republic of Iran, a fact that surprised Slovak law enforcement and the Canadians, but not Jack.

ON WEDNESDAY, KAS stood at the window of the apartment on Dostojevskyho, cradling a cup of now-tepid tea and staring sightlessly across the river. This morning, she had gotten a call that Zane's body had been found in the river, on its way to Budapest. Just like him to leave the scene of the crime, she thought the moment she heard the news. When she was told that an autopsy had been performed, she was glad; it would at least confirm their accounts that Zane hadn't been shot. But the autopsy also found something no one had expected: Marton Zane had stage IV pancreatic cancer.

The diagnosis made sense, in retrospect. It explained how thin he had become, his evident abdominal pain, her ability to overpower him and briefly reclaim the gun. No wonder he hadn't tried to save himself; he didn't have long to live.

She knew she should feel relief. All week, she had harbored a nagging apprehension that Zambo - as she still thought of him - wasn't really dead and could reappear at any moment. She knew the fear was unreasonable, but that's often how fear worked. Instead of relief, however, she felt lost. With Jack's resurrection and Zambo's death, two of the organizing principles of her adult life were gone: grief and fear. How should she structure her life now?

Well, things were wrapping up in Bratislava, she thought. For now, her part in the investigation was over; she would return for the judicial proceedings, if necessary. Deb had left already; her law office called with pressing business. Jack's flight home was this evening. In a few hours, they would say goodbye. That prospect did bring relief; she desperately wanted to be left alone.

As for her own future, Kas considered her choices. Her small Denver apartment was little more than a place to sleep in between assignments. She could stay in Bratislava until the exhibit was ready to travel to Prague in early October; that was Alexej's advice, echoed by Viliam and Magdalena who offered the apartment rent free. They still felt badly about bringing Zambo to her exhibit, even though she repeatedly reassured them that he would have found her regardless. Their invitation was tempting; she liked Bratislava and could explore Central Europe.

There were other options as well. On Tuesday, she'd received an intriguing email from a contact in Manila, an offer to escort her to the island of Jolo to photograph the impact of the Abu Sayyaf insurgency. Months earlier, she had searched unsuccessfully for a low-profile way to get there; now she had it.

Or she could just disappear completely. With years of savings and her small inheritance, Kas had enough funds to quit the heartbreaking work of chronicling the human costs of war. She could spend the rest of her life in a casita in a quiet fishing village in Baja California. It was an idea she had harbored for some time, a necessary fantasy on especially difficult days.

Then last night, Jack proposed another alternative. They had been dining alone after saying goodbye to Deb, when Jack suggested she return to Louisiana, to revisit Gonzales and her old haunts in the French Quarter. Kas knew she had changed too much. "I can't go back. I don't belong there anymore," she told Jack. His response was gently chiding, "You would make a lot of people happy, if you did."

His comment irritated her. Everything these days irritated her.

Their dinner had been stilted, full of formal courtesies and awkward pauses. It was the first time they had been alone since that day before Zane appeared. Jack had since tried to contact her, but Kas demurred. Of everyone in this drama, he was the hardest person to be with. She couldn't explain it to him; she couldn't explain it to herself. He had been kind and attentive, and hadn't repeated his uncomfortable declaration of love, loaded as it would be with expectations she couldn't meet.

Kas took the teacup back to the kitchen and sat at the small table, trying to disentangle her complex feelings. Some of it was guilt and anger at herself. She had impulsively changed her last name to his, which not only led Zane straight to her; it put Jack in Zane's sights. She had foolishly left the gallery with Zane, forgetting that Jack would likely follow. In fact, her stupidity had put Jack, a virtual stranger, in extreme jeopardy.

She felt envy, too. So many people loved Jack. Deb probably did. And Deb had told her about his children, his friends Ben and Lana and the one in the White House, university colleagues, students, all the people who had been checking in on him since the news broke. But it wasn't the love she envied as much as what that love represented: rootedness, connection. Kas felt the opposite, disconnected from the communal web. Broken.

"Oh, get a grip," she scolded herself in a low voice, annoyed at her self-pity and perplexed why she still felt so emotionally raw. Zane was out of her life forever. She should be celebrating. "It's the concussion," she said aloud. Moodiness and irritability were to be expected, along with the headaches.

She snorted, "Good god. And now I'm talking to myself."

JACK ARRIVED THIRTY minutes early in Bratislava's medieval main square, the Hlavné námestie. Time enough, he hoped, to think about what he would say to Kas. He had no illusion that she loved him. But he couldn't accept her self-denigration, her assertion that she was too damaged to return to ordinary life.

He observed the passing crowds: backpackers balancing kebabs and bottles of Kafola soda; children running around the Renaissance fountain; diners tasting pastries at the outdoor cafés. Above it all stood the pale-yellow tower of the old city's Town Hall. He took a deep breath and settled on a bench where a life-sized statue of a Napoleonic soldier leaned. The old town was full of whimsical statues: a photographer, a worker in a manhole, a man tipping his hat, an alchemist. Jack crossed his arms and stretched out his legs. Minutes ticked by as he thought about the previous days, wishing he was an alchemist too, with the secret to healing things with Kas.

And then he saw her. Standing in the shadow of a building, as still as a statue, observing him. Startled, he straightened up, gave a small wave. She walked toward him, her expression grave, her shoulders tight and high in a defensive posture.

"Hello, there," he said as she approached, moving over to make room for her on the bench.

"You're here early," Kas replied as she sat, her oversized canvas purse like a paperweight on her lap.

"You, too. I could have met you at your place instead."

"No, this is fine." She glanced around the square, then at the hovering bronze soldier. "Who's your pal?"

"You never know when you need backup," Jack quipped, then winced to himself. It wasn't a good joke; it reminded him of that night at the UFO bar.

They sat in silence for a few seconds before she said, "I'm sorry for everything that happened. I'm really sorry you were hurt." She looked at his sling.

He was quick to respond. "I'll be okay. Really." He glanced at the fountain. "Anyway, it's my fault, not yours. I led him here."

"Wrong. I did that. Adopting your name."

"Which he only figured out because I contacted him." Jack paused, swallowed hard. "And I'm glad you did, by the way. Adopt my name."

Kas shifted on the bench to look directly at him. "I have to ask you something. Was it worth it? Your search?" Before he could answer, she added, "The way I am now? Definitely not the girl in the letters."

He thought about her courage and vulnerability, her curiosity and grace. "You're still the woman in the letters. So, yes, finding you again has been worth whatever cost you think I've paid." Then he thought about how different he had become since the start of the search. "It's also worth it because of what I've learned from you."

Kas looked skeptical. "From me? Such as?"

"I've learned to push myself out of my comfort zone, to fight for the things I love and value. You've shaken me out of a very comfortable complacency."

"God, I hope not. That was one of the things I liked about you from the start; your steadiness, your composure. What you call complacency." With a small frown, she added, "Don't groan, Jack. It's a rare thing, being someone others can count on."

Church bells briefly interrupted them. Five o'clock, Jack thought, counting the peals. The bus for the airport left at six-thirty. When silence resumed, he looked intently at Kas. "What are your plans now?"

She turned away, studied the children splashing at the fountain. "Still deciding."

He leaned toward her. "Come with me, then. As a friend," he urged. "I can help, Kas. You said it yourself, you can count on me."

Her back stiffened. "You don't understand." Tears began to rim her eyes. "I'm disintegrating, splintering apart. I don't know how else to describe it. Zane's death doesn't change that." Abruptly, she stopped and looked away.

He moved to touch her shoulder, to soothe her, but she involuntarily flinched. He pulled back, hurt and confused.

Suddenly she stood, ran a finger under her moist eyes, shifted the weight of her purse on her shoulder. "Safe travels, Jack. Thank you for everything. With luck, we'll meet again someday." There was no kiss, no hug, no touch; Kas simply turned and walked away.

Standing too, he called after her, "Wait. Please. Don't go yet. There's still time before I have to leave. Let's get coffee. Let's talk."

She was smiling sadly when she turned to face him. "You're wonderful. I know you'll find love someday. Goodbye, Jack Hunter."

He couldn't reply. Dumfounded, aching, he could only watch as she disappeared into the crowd.

That's it, he thought. *It's over; the quest is complete. I found her.* He chided himself for expecting more.

Finally, turning in the opposite direction, he walked slowly through the city's medieval heart, absorbing the sensations around him. The laughter, the arguments. The scent of grilled chicken. Rock music from the open door of a Hungarian café. A boy pushing past his legs. He stopped to gaze at the vibrant chaos swirling around him. Everything was so alive.

And so was she. He nodded to himself. That's all that really matters, he thought. And it's enough.

October 5, 2007
Friday

The autumn morning air felt fresh and cool on Kas's arms. She considered going inside for one of Millicent's thick cotton sweaters, but knew the day would soon warm. And she didn't want to miss this time in the back yard. Bird Time.

The first one she saw, always in attendance somewhere in the vicinity, was a crow, stately thief of other birds' eggs. Then a hummingbird whisked by on its way to the feeder, ruby-throated. Yes, that was its name, she realized, pleased she remembered. Concentrating now, she caught sight of the yellow chest of a meadowlark on a fence-post near the pines, heard its high and piercing tune, echoed somewhere by its companion. Then came a different sound, a little trill; was that a wren? Because it bordered on pine woods, Millie's backyard was full of birds. Kas used to know most of their names, spending hours beneath the dogwood tree in the middle of the lawn. The tree evoked memories too, of playing with Rene and Johnny Jones beneath its pink blooms in spring, its red leaves in autumn. Rene was in construction and had moved to Tampa, according to Millie. Johnny was long gone, killed in one of the last battles of the Vietnam War. Kas had forgotten that too, until just now.

Memory was peculiar. For years, she'd successfully kept it caged. Reading Jack's letters back in August had opened the lock, but the full range of her recollections was emerging only now.

Memory was important. It was the thread she was using to stitch her separate selves back together. Before coming here, she had pictured the process of integrating her two lives as surgical, reattaching a severed hand one muscle, one vein, one strip of sinew at a time. But the image was too bloody for Millie's backyard, so now she imagined that she, like Peter Pan, was sewing her shadow back on. Or perhaps she was the shadow reattaching her former self.

Reconnection took time and an emotional toll. A phone call to a college friend, lunch with cousins, drinks with former co-workers in New Orleans, emails to others who had thought her long dead. Yesterday was difficult; her best friend from high school couldn't forgive her for the decades of deception. But most people were understanding, once they had heard the reason for her disappearance. Even Ralph, when she'd called. A few old friends, like Becky Gonzales, cried with relief and joy. That was worse than angry recrimination; it made her hate herself for the pain she'd caused.

But gradually she was feeling whole again, less disconnected from others, her history, herself. Tomorrow, she would write to Jahwed; she had finally found a Persian translator. Someday, she hoped to find Saaleh or his sister.

Being here helped. This place spanned both of her identities. During her invisible years, she had never stayed more than an hour or two, except that one time, the night before her mother's funeral. Now she had been here two weeks and had no inclination to leave. Eventually, she knew she would have to. She couldn't impose indefinitely on Millie's hospitality.

That raised the question of what she should do with her life. Kas had decided on the flight back to the States that she couldn't take any more battlefield assignments. Previously, she'd convinced herself that her photos were a call to action. Who could look at them and not demand an end to killings, torture, rape? Yet that hadn't happened; she'd been naïve to think her images would help even a single person.

Maybe if she trained her camera closer to home, on local injustices. Social media could help mobilize political change. Of course so many talented photographers were doing that already. And some of the most powerful indictments came from ordinary cell phones. Still, it was something to think about, some way to find meaning.

The screen door banged shut, startling Kas and the birds. Millie was carrying a tray with two tall glasses of sweet iced tea. Kas scrambled to her feet to help. Millie shrugged her off.

"What? Do you think I'm old or something?" demanded the eighty-two year old. She laid the tray on a table between two rocking chairs on the back porch.

"Thanks," Kas smiled as she sat again and lifted the frosted glass to her lips. Her phone rang. It was the third time this morning. As she had before, she glanced at the number and returned the phone to her pocket.

"Why don't you answer that dang thing?" Millie asked.

"Because I know who's calling," she said.

"Well, who is it then?"

"A ghost, Millie. Just a ghost." More accurately, the ghost's agent. On voicemail the day before, an associate at some Canadian law firm had asked Kas to get in touch at her earliest convenience; one of the partners, Mr. Marras, needed to speak with her on an urgent matter regarding Marton Zane.

"Ghosts call you often?"

"This one does."

"Well, if you want it to rest in peace, you'll have to listen to what it has to say."

"I can guess what it has to say, some manipulative bullshit." Even dead, Zane was trying to intrude on her life, and she resented it.

"Don't speak in riddles. Do you mean Zambo? There's nothing in the world he can do to you now." When Kas merely shrugged, Millie gave her a sharp look. "Whoever's calling you won't stop. You might as well call back."

Millie was right. To exorcise a malevolent spirit, she had to confront it. Sighing audibly for Millie's benefit, she dialed the number and asked to speak to Mr. Marras.

"I appreciate you returning my call, Mrs. Hunter," said a male voice formally.

"Ms. Hunter, please."

"Of course, my apologies. Our condolences on the loss of our mutual friend, Marton Zane."

Didn't this man know that Zane had tried to kill her? Surely he had followed the news accounts of Zane's death. He must have persuaded himself that the news accounts were false.

Marras continued as if her silence was part of her grief. "I apologize for our delay in contacting you. You've been difficult to reach."

"Yes, I'm sorry to interrupt, but I'm very busy. What is this in regard to?"

"Why, the will, of course." A brief pause and then the polished voice continued. "We assumed that you knew that Mr. Zane changed his will two months before his death to make you his sole heir. I regret to inform you that we do not expect the will to be uncontested. His estranged wife and dependent son have already hired an attorney to argue moral obligation. In addition, his adult children and previous wives have indicated an intent to challenge the will. So please be cognizant of the fact that it is likely you will receive less than the entire estate."

Kas had stopped rocking. "I don't want to receive any of the estate," she stated firmly.

"You may, of course, refuse. But I strongly advise you to speak with counsel before making a final decision. There's a substantial sum of money involved, possibly more than a billion dollars U.S. Mr. Zane wanted you to have it."

"Whatever for?" she blurted out.

"His wish was that you establish a philanthropic foundation in his name."

Astounded at Zane's spite and arrogance, Kas couldn't speak.

"Our law firm is committed to ensuring that his wishes are met, so we are, of course, handling the legal challenges. Mr. Zane was not only a longtime client, he was also a friend." Marras cleared his throat. "I'll contact you again once we have a clearer picture of how the provincial court will rule on the legal issues I've mentioned." He politely bid her good day.

Kas had to fight the impulse to throw the phone across the yard.

Wealthy industrialists and tycoons historically had established philanthropic foundations to create new legacies, to erase the sometimes unsavory deeds of their earlier careers. So, Kas thought furiously, Marton Zane wanted her to help him join the ranks of Andrew Carnegie, J. Paul Getty, and Henry Ford. She recalled his assertion not long after they had met, when he vehemently denied wanting money to buy things. No, he demanded respect. And, giving a billion dollars away to good causes would guarantee respect, even admiration.

Millicent was watching her expectantly, so Kas bluntly explained, "He left me money for a foundation. A lot of it."

"A million?!"

"A billion."

"Good Lord."

Shaking her head, Kas moaned, "I can't take it, Millie. How can I?" She refused to whitewash his sordid history. She refused to redeem him, because that's what this amounted to. Suddenly, she started to cry.

Millie, alarmed, stood and put her arm around her shoulders, patted her back. "There, honey lamb, it's all right."

But it wasn't all right. Anguish roiled her the moment she thought of the word *redeem*. The man who had tried to kill her and Jack, who had murdered Katarina and Danny and did countless other evil acts in his pursuit of wealth and acclaim, was also the lonely boy with a scar and sad song, the white-haired man dogged by death and a burning need for redemption. Redemption through her, which she could not – and never would – give.

"YOU'VE GOT TO take that money." Millie declared during dinner, pointing at Kas with a forkful of potato salad. The evening was humid, and she had to speak loudly over the rotating fan in the corner of the kitchen. "Think of the good you could do with it."

Listlessly staring at a bite of Andouille sausage, Kas didn't reply. Other than describing the attorney's phone call, she had barely spoken all afternoon. She had tried to think things through, but her brain kept cycling across the same confused terrain.

Millie had left her alone, but now she was ready to talk, even if Kas wasn't. "Good Heavens, Cassandra, you look like your cat just died. I don't understand your reaction."

Kas said softly, "I'm not going to do anything to honor that awful man."

Leaning back from the table, Millie considered her. "I see. You're torn up because you want to take the money but you feel you can't. But I say you can. Nobody cares a fig what a foundation is called as long as it benefits people. *What's in a name?* Romeo was right. Or was it Juliet? Anyway, names mean nothing. You can call it the Southern Louisiana Marton Zane Greater Gumbo Giveaway. Who cares?"

Unwillingly, Kas laughed, then observed, "Well, I care." She raised her eyes to Millie's. "He was a monster." Even if a vulnerable and sick one, she thought to herself.

Millie cocked her head to the side. "See what Jack says. I'll bet you the dirty dishes he'll agree with me."

"He won't. He tore up a one hundred-thousand-dollar check that Zane gave him. He'll understand why I can't accept the money."

"Posh, a hundred thousand dollars. Peanuts." Millie squinted at Kas and said in her most no-nonsense tone, "A billion is a whole different ballgame." She crossed her arms.

Avoiding the look, Kas carried their plates to the counter and scraped them clean. She ran hot water in the sink, squirted in dish soap, then washed and rinsed the dishes, stacking them on the drain rack. All the while, she was thinking about Jack. They had stayed somewhat in touch through emails and texts: perfunctory checks that each was well and updates about Deb, Millie, Lawrence Williams, her photo exhibit. But they hadn't talked since Bratislava. She really didn't know why. Maybe she would call him, get his advice, hear his voice. She dried her hands and picked up the phone.

"YOU SEEM TO be doing so much better," Lana said. "I'm really glad." Beside her on the sofa, Ben nodded.

They'd had lasagna – Jack had finally learned to make it - and were relaxing in his living room with bowls of ice cream.

"I am, thanks to you two." Jack's gratitude was genuine. Ever since his old friends had picked him up at the airport, they had looked after him. Meals, movies, long conversations about everything imaginable, games of pool and pickle ball.

Lana continued, "We were worried, you know. When you first got back, you seemed so ... not sad exactly... downcast? Well, that's understandable, after almost being killed by that madman." She lightly rested her hand on Jack's arm. "But in the last few weeks, you seem to have made peace with the world. You seem – I don't know -- happier, calmer."

"Like a Buddhist," Ben quipped, finishing his dessert. "Except at pickle ball."

Jack grinned. They were right; he did feel at peace. It was a novel sensation. With Helene, he'd often been boisterous in company, almost manic, a diversionary tactic to deflect attention from her prickliness and perfectionism. The search for Cassie had triggered a different type of mania in him, alternating between hope and desperation. Jubilant once he'd found her, melancholy when he'd come home alone. But time healed. Or at least was helping him accept the things he couldn't change.

All things considered, Jack was content. His children were doing well. Sandy had found love with someone who was kind and smart; they were talking about a civil union ceremony in the spring. Jack agreed to help, hiding his ire that they couldn't be legally married as they wished. As for Max, he and his longtime girlfriend were starting graduate studies in computer science in the fall. Even Helene seemed fine; Max had told him she had a new love interest, another CDC scientist. She had left Frank Constant, or vice versa; Jack found that he didn't really care.

This urge to be coupled. Oddly, he no longer felt the imperative. In fact, he found he rather liked solitude. There were fewer demands on his time and attention, on his emotional life.

Since returning from Europe, though, he did feel a growing discontent with his work. Teaching was satisfying, and he felt closer to his colleagues than ever. But, perhaps due to his close call with death, he found himself questioning the value of his research. His books and articles, editorials and public talks all seemed to have had very little impact on either domestic or international affairs. He had spoken about it with Ben, who had assured him that every serious scholar experiences doubt like that. Jack wasn't convinced.

This was on his mind when, a few minutes after Ben and Lana left for the evening, he checked his mobile phone for messages. During their visit, the ringer had been off.

He blinked. Kas had called that evening. Twice. She had finally sent a text: *Call me pls.* Jack was troubled. Kas sent emails but never called. Something must be wrong, he thought, hands shaking as he held the phone to his ear.

"Hi, Jack. Thanks for getting back to me. I know it's late, but I need your advice on something."

Her voice sounded clear and strong. He had missed hearing it. "Are you and Millicent all right?"

"Yes. No. It's that bastard Marton Zane," Kas said crossly.

Jack was puzzled. "What did he do?" What could he do, being dead?

"He left me money in his will, to set up a foundation. I can't do it, Jack. Millie thinks I should. What do you think?"

"A will can't make you do anything," he replied, trying to understand Kas's concern.

"Sorry. Let me explain. His will is leaving me a billion dollars to set up a philanthropic foundation in his name."

Jack whistled at the amount. "In his name," he repeated.

"That's the deal."

Jack was silent for a few moments, absorbing the news, considering the ramifications. "I see your dilemma," he finally said.

"I can't be a party to the lie that Marton Zane was a decent human being. But it's a billion dollars. Think of the people that could help."

"Thousands. Hundreds of thousands even. Millie's right. You've got to accept it."

"But, Jack, you tore up his check."

"Because he wanted me to spy on you. This is different."

"No, it's not. He wants me to canonize him. A great benefactor of humanity, that's how future generations will think of him."

"Call it the Asshole Marton Zane Foundation. That'll memorialize him for posterity."

"You're as bad as Millie."

Jack was silent for a moment and then asked her, "What does the will actually say? Do you have to set up a foundation with the money? Do you have to name it after him?"

"I think so." Kas paused. "I don't know. The lawyer said it was Zane's wish."

"*If wishes were horses…*"

"Yes, I know. *Beggars would ride.* But Zane was no beggar. Even dead, it seems he can have whatever he wants."

"Not you. He couldn't have you," Jack said. "It just seems like something he'd do, give you money without strings, believing he knew you better than anyone else in the world. Believing you shared a transcendental love and you'd honor his wishes," he mused.

"Then he didn't know me at all."

Jack chuckled. "So do the opposite. Buy an island and a Lear jet and whatever else the top one percent wants. That'll prove him wrong."

Kas initially thought he was serious. Aghast, she said, "I would never do that, Jack."

"Exactly. And I suspect he knew that about you. Ask the attorney if there are any conditions on receiving the money. If there are, we'll brainstorm about how to get around them. If there aren't, you have carte blanche. You can set up your own international foundation, named whatever you damn well please."

Silence. Jack wondered if she had hung up on him. Finally, she said, "In which case, I'll name it for Danny and Katarina. I've been thinking about them a lot lately. I'll call it the Mack and Petras Foundation. What do you think?"

"MAP," Jack replied. "I like it."

THE FOLLOWING MONDAY, Kas found it was only Zane's wish; no legal conditions were attached in the will. She immediately called Jack. Over the next two months, they talked several more times about the MAP Foundation. It would focus on fighting violence against women and children, Kas insisted, whether the perpetrators are governments, non-governmental organizations, neighbors or families. That meant grants would be made to local groups and small associations, which in turn meant the foundation would need people on the ground in difficult and even dangerous places, people who could discover what was needed and then help communities apply for aid.

Jack was struck by how much her passion and energy reminded him of her younger self. That was the real legacy of the bequest, he realized. Zane's death wasn't sufficient to restore her spirit, but this was.

Now at the Louis Armstrong International Airport, he hoisted the strap of his overnight bag on to his shoulder. He hadn't brought more luggage; he didn't expect to stay long. Kas had asked him to come to New Orleans to help her draft a mission statement and governing document, material she needed to start the application process with the IRS. He had initially demurred. The end of the semester was approaching and he had lots of grading to do. He also knew she was working with two professional consultants and doubted that she needed him. But when she persisted, he finally agreed. So here he was.

And there she was, just beyond the security gate, dressed in jeans and a black turtleneck sweater, a rain jacket over her arm. She was so familiar, yet different too. He noted the changes in her relaxed posture, easy movements.

Smiling broadly, Kas approached and kissed him on both cheeks. "You made it!"

"How are you? You look great." Jack couldn't take his eyes off her face. Before she could notice, though, he forced himself to turn his attention to the terminal. This is where it started, he thought, where we met almost thirty years ago. His mind slipped into the old fantasy of what might have happened if he had taken the next flight to Bangkok. He wondered if she ever thought about it. Too late now, he chided himself; get over it.

Kas looped her arm through his, seemingly unaware. They started to walk. "Thanks for coming on such short notice. I feel badly pulling you away from your students."

An inappropriate thrill at her touch. Jack had not expected such a strong reaction to seeing her in person, and he fought to keep his voice casual. "I'm glad to help. I have a terrific grad assistant. She's handling my classes for a few days."

"Only a few days? I thought you could stay longer."

For several moments, he didn't reply. "Next week are final exams."

"Of course! Early December, I forgot. But then you'll come back, won't you?"

"Well, it depends ..." He let the sentence hang. He changed the subject. "Do you know yet what you'll receive from the estate? After the legal challenges and charges and everything?"

"Oh, didn't I tell you? It looks like we'll get close to two billion dollars." She said the amount slowly, triumphantly. "This is really happening, Jack. Pretty amazing." She grinned at him. "Or, as Danny would have said, pretty *fucking* amazing." Kas laughed and, still holding his arm, guided him to her car.

They got in and she drove, soon merging onto the highway. A light rain started to fall and the pavement glistened. To avoid staring at her profile, Jack studied the drops hitting the windshield.

She spoke excitedly, words tumbling out. "We'll need an experienced executive director, someone who shares our vision and believes in collaboration. I can't stand hierarchy, as you may recall. Maybe this week you and I can try drafting a job description. I've got some samples from that consultant I mentioned. I've also retained an attorney and accounting firm. There'll be staff, of course, but board members will be actively involved in the site visits to prospective recipients. It won't be one of those rubber-stamp boards that meets just once a month. I hope you don't mind that I'm assuming you'll be on it with me? Deb's agreed too; isn't that great? She's moving here the first of the year. We need to find a few other like-minded souls. By the way, we should see if Lawrence Williams is interested in a staff position in security after he's released. What do you think? Oh, and I finished reading your book on human rights in the age of terror. It's so relevant!"

Listening to her, Jack fell in love all over again, and it saddened him. She was friendly and warm but gave no indication that her feelings toward him had changed. He felt acutely, keenly aware of the loss and couldn't imagine how he could work with her on a close and regular basis without going mad.

They turned down Canal Street, heading toward the river. Still not noticing his reticence, Kas continued. "I made a reservation for you at the Grenoble House in the Quarter. It's not far from my place. Do you want to check in now or go to the office first?"

"I shouldn't have come." He disliked the abruptness of his tone, but he couldn't wait any longer.

"What?"

"It's my fault. I was fine working with you by email and phone. But coming here… it's a big mistake."

Her voice was strained as she pleaded, "We're almost there, Jack. Just wait. We'll get to the office and we can talk."

She parked at the first open spot and got out. Jack leaned across the seat back and pulled up his bag.

Once he joined her on the sidewalk, Kas said, "You can leave that in the car. I'll drop you by the hotel after I show you the office. You can go home tomorrow if you like. But today ..."

Jack took her hand and interrupted. "I'm heading back now, Kas. I'm sorry. I can't do this. We can still work long distance. It's the face-to-face I find I can't handle."

"You can't leave now. I need you."

"You don't need me. You've got everything under control. You can do this," he said encouragingly. "You've got the resources to make it happen, and the people. Deb's on the board, Alex, the others. And you can call me any time. You'll do great things, Kas." He signaled a passing taxi.

"Are you angry at me? I understand if you are. I was so selfish and sad in Bratislava. I didn't know what to do. But I'm better now."

"I know you are. And I'm not angry. It's not your fault. It's mine. I can't not love you. I've tried, God knows. What I just discovered is that I can't pretend that I don't. You'll be uncomfortable working with me and I'll be miserable. It really is best for both of us that I go." He kissed her lightly on the forehead and climbed into the cab. It eased away from the curb.

He sensed she was standing there, wondering what the hell was going on. Jack had a powerful urge to turn around to see her once more, but he knew he would go back if he did. He didn't let himself look. His heart was breaking.

"PLEASE DON'T GO," she begged as the cab pulled away. But it was too late. The taxi was already part of the rush hour traffic. Frantic, Kas ran back to her car and started the engine.

She replayed his comments in her head but still could make little sense of them. How could he think she'd feel uncomfortable around him? All right, in Bratislava she had been skittish, but he was blowing that out of proportion. She never asked him to hide his feelings. She cared for him as well. And with the foundation, they'd be partners. Wasn't that enough?

The rain was falling more heavily now, her car's wipers in a rhythmic hypnotizing sweep across the windshield and back. With one hand, Kas dialed her mobile phone; the call went to his voice mail. He had probably forgotten to turn on his phone after the flight, she realized. She stared moodily at the passing blur of cars, headlights reflecting back through a gray mist. A surreal scape, as if no world existed beyond.

Kas marshaled her arguments for why he had to stay. First, his knowledge and reasoning skills were essential to the foundation's work. She'd read a lot more of his research than she'd told him about, and all of it confirmed her belief that he would be a powerful advocate. His ideas excited and inspired her, helped her understand and articulate her own inchoate thinking. In fact, the foundation's work was a natural progression of his scholarly interests, a way for his ideas to have a concrete impact on the world. That was a second point she would make. Further, they shared key values and vision, they spoke with one voice on critical issues. More than anyone else on the board, even Deb, Kas felt she knew Jack. Finally, the foundation needed Jack's personal qualities. His insight and intellectual honesty were tempered with patience and respect for others. The board needed that; even more, the foundation's on-site investigations needed that. Jack invited trust; he intuitively knew how to draw people out. Kas herself was evidence.

"Dammit," she smacked the steering wheel. "We're friends, aren't we?" Why couldn't he help her out of friendship?

She would convince him. She had to. The trick was finding him. What if he already had a return ticket? If he did, he might be going through security right now. She'd need a boarding pass to follow him. Well, she'd get a ticket too, on the same flight if possible.

Poor visibility and rain slowed the traffic. Kas had to concentrate to negotiate one impasse and then was briefly delayed by another. Finally freed of the tangle of cars, she sped toward the airport, puddles in the road spraying fountains behind her tires.

She arrived at last. In case she had to catch a flight, she didn't want to leave the car at the curb. The short-term parking lot was further away than she remembered; she sprinted through the downpour to get to the terminal.

Once inside, she scanned the vast entrance hall for any sign of him, then walked quickly toward the ticket counters, aware of the squeak of her damp running shoes on the polished floor. The place was packed. Most travelers were checking in at the airline kiosks, but not Jack. Where the hell was he? Her heart was racing, panic closing off her throat.

Finally she saw him, standing at the end of a line for a ticket agent. He stepped listlessly forward. As she neared, she thought the rain droplets looked like beads of glass on his hair and the shoulders of his leather jacket. His eyes were down, and he didn't notice when she got into line behind him. She touched his arm but he simply shifted. That moment, she knew the real reason she couldn't let him go. She just didn't know how to tell him.

She touched him again and said his name. He gave a half turn and saw her.

"Kas?" he said, turning fully to face her. "Why are you here?"

She tried to sound light. "Hey, maybe I'll come with you. You asked me to in Bratislava, remember? I should have said yes."

He shook his head. "You did the smart thing. You knew what you needed: time and space to heal. And you have." He cleared his throat. "I'll call when I'm home. We can still work on the mission statement together."

"Stay with me, Jack."

"I'm so sorry. I can't, as much as I want to. Please try to understand."

Kas felt herself verbally stumble, uncertain how to express herself. "I want to show you something." She opened her purse and dug through it, pulled out a worn green leather passport wallet. In it, instead of a passport, was a crumpled photograph of a grinning young man with a dog. "I've carried this just about everywhere. It's my talisman."

It was his photograph, with Sherlock, from 1978.

Jack frowned at the image, not angrily but mystified. She watched his eyes shift from it to her face. He's waiting for some explanation, she realized. She had to be explicit, yet saying the words was difficult.

"My heart's been closed such a long time. It's not easy prying it open." She remembered struggling with an oyster shell on the Gulf Coast when she was a girl. She shook her head to refocus. "The point is, I can't say goodbye to you again. I love you, Jack Hunter. I want to share my life with you." She was surprised at how easily the words came out once the shell popped open. "I love you so much," she repeated. She hadn't spoken those words since Ralph, and hadn't known then what love meant. Now she did, now she felt the full power of those words.

As she spoke, she saw Jack's expression soften, the tension around his eyes and mouth relax. He took her hand and gently led her away from the line. His hand was warm and trembling slightly. Or was that her own? Kas didn't breathe.

Dropping his bag at their feet, Jack held her face in both hands and then kissed her the way he had in the airport in San Francisco. This time, she kissed back, with the intensity of three decades of love and longing.

When they finally stepped apart, his entire face was smiling. Kas was flushed and breathless.

"Do you like oysters?" she suddenly asked. "For some reason, I'm in the mood for oysters."

Jack laughed. "You never cease to amaze me, Kassie. Oysters! That sounds fantastic." He picked up his bag and put his arm around her shoulders. "Lead on, partner."

So she did.

Acknowledgements

I n late April 1978, I said goodbye to family and boarded a plane for Bangkok, Thailand, to begin an overland journey around the world. I carried along a notebook and an Olympus OM-1 camera with several rolls of slide film. During that thirteen-month journey, I wrote almost five hundred pages of notes, took more than six hundred slides, and sent dozens of letters. That cache sparked this novel. My first thanks must go to those who helped me or shared their stories, notably in Bangkok, Srinigar, Kabul, Mashhad, Istanbul, West Berlin and Paris. I feel especially grateful to my late father and mother for encouraging me to go, and my late mother for joining me on the final leg of the journey.

In addition to this experience, I drew on these valuable sources: Ann Dupree, Louis Dupree and A.A. Motamedi, *A Guide to the Kabul Museum, the National Museum of Afghanistan* (Kabul: Afghan Tourist Organization, 1968); Nancy Hatch Dupree, *A Historical Guide to Afghanistan* (Kabul: Afghan Tourist Organization, 1971); and the news archives of *The New York Times.*

The manuscript benefited enormously from the constructive criticism, editing, encouragement and camaraderie offered by colleagues in the Canterbury Group: Susan Lapid, Yosef Lapid and Peter Goodman. Other insightful early readers were Dael Goodman, Robert McNamara, Manal Hamzeh al Smadi, Donna Tate, Elizabeth Czerniak and Robert Czerniak. Helping with specific points in the story were Donna Tate, who lived in Isfahan, Iran, in the late 1970s, and Natalie

Harmening, who demonstrated how to disarm someone holding a gun to my head. Sincere appreciation to each of them for helping me make this a better book. Any inaccuracies and flaws, however, are entirely my own.

Thanks are also due to the friends my husband and I made in Bratislava in 2011 and 2013, who introduced us to a fascinating city and region. We were able to learn about Slovak history and current affairs, teach Slovak students, explore the High Tatras and enjoy delicious regional wines and cuisine. This experience was possible through the Fulbright Scholar Program.

My deepest gratitude goes to Peter Gregware. With me throughout this writing journey, he is my first reader, logic checker, patient listener, travel companion, house mixologist, hiking buddy and cherished partner in life.

Photo by author
Pear vendors, Kabul, August 1978

About the Author

Photo by Sterling Trantham
sterlingtranthamphotography.com

N. V. Baker writes literary suspense and mysteries set against an international backdrop. A former journalist and political science professor, she has authored two novels and three books of non-fiction, two in the field of presidential/legal studies. She and her partner, Peter, live in the high desert in New Mexico.

Visit her on Facebook and at www.nvbaker.com.

THE BOY IN THE SUITCASE

A lonely woman in transit. A bullied boy with a secret. Will friendship be enough to save them?

On the cusp of 40, long-time Goth Lena takes a Baltic Sea cruise hoping to meet someone who likes her for who she is. An 11-year-old boy considering suicide wasn't who she had in mind.

Both lonely outsiders, they find their friendship growing after Lena talks Carter from the ledge, and he shares his deepest secret. Yet that evening, in her unsuccessful pursuit of an attractive fellow passenger, Lena almost forgets her young friend.

Until he turns up missing.

Ship security labels it a suicide, and the grieving parents agree. Lena isn't convinced. But if the boy didn't jump, where is he? Her dread mounting, she realizes she alone must solve the mystery and find the child. With time running out and self-doubt creeping in, Lena must discover the truth before the ship reaches its final destination....

Book One in *The Concealing Sea* mystery series.

Praise for **The Boy in the Suitcase**

"A haunting and beautifully written tale [that] kept me happily engaged and reading until I reluctantly turned over the last page."

- Readers' Favorite

"A fast-paced crime thriller with a ticking clock [and] rife with tough themes.... Highly recommended."

- Manhattan Book Review

Made in the USA
Columbia, SC
14 May 2019